Once a reporter for Independent Television News, Gerald Seymour has lived in the West Country for the last fourteen years. His best-selling novels include, among others, *Harry's Game*, *The Glory Boys*, *Red Fox*, *Field of Blood*, *The Journeyman Tailor*, *The Heart of Danger*, *Killing Ground*, *The Waiting Time* and, most recently, *A Line in the Sand*. His latest novel, *Holding the Zero*, is now available from Bantam Press.

D0796926

RED FOX

Gerald Seymour

CORGI BOOKS

RED FOX
A CORGI BOOK : 0 552 14727 3

Originally published in Great Britain by Collins

PRINTING HISTORY
Collins edition published 1979
Fontana edition published 1980
Corgi edition published 2000

Set in 10/12pt Palatino by Kestrel Data, Exeter, Devon.

Corgi Books are published by Transworld Publishers,
61–63 Uxbridge Road, London W5 5SA,
a division of The Random House Group Ltd,
in Australia by Random House Australia (Pty) Ltd,
20 Alfred Street, Milsons Point, Sydney, NSW 2061, Australia,
in New Zealand by Random House New Zealand Ltd,
18 Poland Road, Glenfield, Auckland 10, New Zealand
and in South Africa by Random House (Pty) Ltd,
Endulini, 5a Jubilee Road, Parktown 2193, South Africa.

Reproduced, printed and bound in Great Britain by
Cox & Wyman Ltd, Reading, Berks.

To Gillian and Nicholas and James

Chapter One

An hour now they had been in position. The car was nestled off the road under a blanket of high mushroomed pine branches. It was back from the main route and on a parking space that later would be used by those who came to play tennis on the courts behind. The place was quiet and unobserved as they wanted it.

Not that the car was here by chance, nothing in these matters was casual and unplanned and spontaneous. For a clear fortnight the men had toured this discreet web of sidestreets, watching and eyeing and considering the location that would afford them the greatest advantage, accepting and rejecting the alternatives and the options, weighing the chances of attack and escape. They had not chosen this place till all were satisfied, and then they had reported back and another had come on the morning of the previous day and had heard from them their description of what would happen and nodded his head, slapping them lightly on the shoulders to affirm his agreement and accolade.

So the ambush was set, the trap was sprung, the wires taut, and the men could scrutinize their wristwatches, bright with chrome and status, and wonder whether the prey would be punctual or tardy.

In front of their car the road ran down a gentle hill towards the main six-lane route into and from the city, which it joined at an intersection two hundred and fifty yards from them. Under the pines the road was shadowed and grey, the potholes and rainwater tracks in dark relief. There was no chance that when he came in his car he would be speeding. He'd be doing thirty kilometres at most, because he would be safeguarding the expensive framework of his Mercedes, creeping between the ruts, avoiding the hazards, and as unaware and unsuspicious as they all were.

The car in which the men sat had been stolen three weeks earlier from outside a hotel in the centre of Anzio away to the south of Rome. By the time the loss had been reported, written in the ledger book by the polizia, the Alfetta had already been fitted with new number plates, likewise stolen, but from a car owned in Arezzo to the north. The number plates had originally belonged to a Mirafiori Fiat. The calculation was that the marriage of the stolen car and the stolen number plates would be too complex for any casual check by the Polizia Stradale. The paperwork of insurance and tax had been matched to the vehicle's new identity by men who specialized in such work.

Three men were in the car, all sharing the lank, coarse hair and mahogany-sheened faces of the deep south, of the toe of Italy. Men of Calabria, of the rugged and daunting Aspromonte mountains. This was their game, their playtime. Their experience qualified them for such occasions. Men who travelled from the lofty villages down to the big city to effect the grab and then fled back to the safety of their families, their community, where they lived uncharted and unknown to the police computers. The smell in the car was of the crudely packed MS cigarettes that they smoked incessantly, drawn to their mouths by roughened fingers that carried the blister scars of work in the fields, and mingling with the tobacco was the night-old stench of the Perroni beer they had consumed the evening before. Men close to middle age. The one who sat in front of the steering-wheel had the proud hair on his forehead receding in spite of the many and varied ways he combed it, and the one who sat beside him carried traces of grey at his temples highlighted by the grease he anointed himself with, and the lone one in the back wore a wide belly strapped beneath his leather belt.

There was little talk in the car as the minute hands of the watches moved on towards seven-thirty. They had nothing to communicate, conversation was futile, and wasted breath. The man in the back drew from a grip bag that rested on the floor between his legs the stocking masks that they would wear, purchased the previous afternoon in the Standa supermarket and pierced with a knife for eye and mouth vents. Without a word, he passed two forward to his companions, then dived again into the bag. A snub-barrelled Beretta pistol for the driver, who probably had no need for a gun at all as his work was to drive. For himself and the front passenger there were squat submachine-guns made angular as he fitted the magazine sticks. The quiet in the car was fractured by the heavy metallic clacking of the weapons being armed. Last to be taken from the bag was the hammer, a shiny varnished handle of new wood weighted with its grey-painted iron head.

They had a man to lift this time. A man of their own age, their own fitness, their own skill. It would be harder than the last one, because that had been a child. Just a child toddling to kindergarten in Aventino with the Eritrean maid. She'd screamed at the sight of them, the black whore, and collapsed in a dead faint on the pavement and the dog shit by the time they'd reached the child, and the brat hadn't struggled, had almost run with them to the car. The car had been stationary no more than fifteen seconds before they were moving again with the kid on the floor and out of sight and only the noise of the keening wail of the maid to let anyone know that anything had happened. Two hundred and fifty million they'd paid out, the parents. Good as gold, placid as sheep, shut the door on the investigations of the polizia and the carabinieri, co-operated as they'd been told to, sold the shares, went and tapped the grandfather up in Genova just as it had been planned they would. Nice and clean and organized. Good quick payout, used 50,000-lire notes, and not a uniform in sight. Just the way it should always be. But how this one would react, there was no way of knowing, whether he'd fight, whether he'd struggle, whether he'd be a fool . . . The man in the back fingered the hammer-head, stroking its smoothness with his fingers. And in all their minds was the thought of the welcome the big men would provide if there was failure, if the car came back empty, if the cash investment were not repaid . . . no room for failure, no possibility . . . the big bastard would skin them. From behind his ample bottom, muffled by his trousers, came the screech of static noise, and then the call sign. He wriggled round, heaved his bulk so that it no longer suffocated the transmitter/receiver radio, pulled the device clear and to his face. They hadn't used the system before, but this was advancement, this was progress.

'Yes. Yes.'

'Number Two?'

'Yes.'

There had been a code, an agreed one, but the suddenness of the transmission had seemed to surprise him and he was aware of the frustration of the men in front at his fumbling. They'd practised the link often enough in the last week, assured themselves that the receiver would pick up from behind the first block a hundred metres up the hill. He saw the anger on the driver's face.

'Yes, this is Number One.'

'He is coming . . . it is the Mercedes and he is alone. Only the one.'

For each man in the car the distorted and distant voice brought a syringe of excitement. Each felt the tension rise and writhe through his intestines, felt the snap of stiffness come to the legs, clasped at the security of the guns. Never able to escape it, however many times they were involved, never a familiarity with the moment when the bridge was crossed and spanned, when the only road was forward. He'd skin them if they failed, the big man would.

'Did you hear me, Number One? Did you receive?'

'We hear you, Number Two.' Spoken with the grey lips against the built-in microphone.

Big and large and fat and juicy, that was what the big man called it, the capo. A foreigner, and with a renowned company behind him, a multi-national, and they'd pay up well, pay past and pay deep. A billion lire in this one, that for minimum . . . could be two billion. Spiral of noughts filling the minds. What was two billion to a multi-national? Nothing. A million and a half dollars, nothing.

The man in the back switched off the radio, its work completed.

Burdening silence filled the car again. All ears strained for the drive of the heavy Mercedes engine. And when it came there was the whine of the low gear, the careful negotiation of the pitfalls of the road. Creeping forward, cutting distance. The growing thunder of the wasp wings as the insect closes on the web the spider has set.

The driver, Vanni, half turned, winked and grimaced, muttered something inaudible and indistinct, gave Mario in the front, Claudio in the back, the curl of a smile.

'Come on.' Nerves building in the back.

'Time to go get the package.' Vanni raised his voice. 'Time to go pluck the rooster.'

He thrust the gear lever forward, eased his foot on to the accelerator, nudged the car out into the narrowness of the road as all three peered left and upwards to the bend.

A black monster of a machine. The Mercedes, sleek and washed. A machine that justified its existence only on the autostrada but which was now confined and crippled on the broken surfaces. Clawing towards them.

Ear-splitting in the confines of the car, Claudio shouted.

'Go, Vanni. Go.'

The Alfetta surged forward. Swinging right with the tyres protesting across the loose roadside gravel. The wrench of the brakes took Mario and Claudio unawares, punching them in their seats. Thirty metres in front of the Mercedes, the Alfetta bucked to a stop across the road, blocking it, closing it. The drumroll of action as the passengers dragged the stockings over their heads, reducing their features to nondescript contours. This was a moment for Vanni to savour – the visible anger of the driver as he closed in on them. He knew the man's background, knew he had been nineteen months in the country, and saw framed in his overhead mirror the caricature of the Italian gesture of annoyance. The flick of the wrist, the point of the fingers, as if this were a sufficient protest, as if this were a common drivers' altercation.

Vanni heard the door beside him and the one behind crash open. As he spun in his seat to see the scene better there was the impact of splintering glass, vicious and vulgar. He saw Claudio, hammer in one hand, machine-pistol in the other, at the driver's door, and Mario beside him and wrenching it open. A moment of pathetic struggle and Mario had the collar of his jacket and was pulling him irresistibly clear. Making it hard for himself, wriggling, the stupid bastard, but then the men usually did. Vanni felt a shiver in his seat, involuntary and unwelcome, as he saw a car turn on the bend of the hill, begin its descent. Unseen by Mario and Claudio, both wrestling with the idiot and on the point of victory. He reached for the pistol from his lap, heart pumping, the cry of warning gorging his throat.

Just a woman. Just a signora from the hill in her little car, hair neatly coiffed, who would be on her way to the Condotti for early morning shopping before the sun was up. He eased his fingers from the gun and back to their places on the gear stick and the wheel. She'd sit there till it was over. A woman wouldn't hurt them. Hear nothing, see nothing, know nothing.

The man still struggled as if the shrill of the brakes behind him had provided the faint hope of salvation, and then Mario's fist caught him flush on the jutting chin, and the light, the resistance, died.

All finished.

The man spreadeagled over the back seat and floor of the Alfetta, Mario and Claudio towering over him, and there was a shout for Vanni to be on his way. Critical to get clear before the polizia blocked the roads, stifled their escape. First fifteen minutes critical and vital. Vanni wrenched at the wheel, muscles rising in his forearms as he spun left at the junction, flicked his fingers to the traffic horn, dared another to cut him out, and won through with his bravado. From the back came first a grovelling whimper and then nothing but the movement of his friends and the breathing of their prey as the stench of the chloroform drifted forward.

The crisis for Vanni would soon be over. Clear of the immediate scene, the principal hazards would disperse. A few hundred metres on the narrow Tor di Quinto, then faster for two kilometres on the two-lane Foro Olympico, before he slowed at the lights at the Salaria junction and then left on the main road leading to the north and the autostrada away from the city. He could have driven it with his eyes covered. There was no necessity now for speed, no need for haste, just steady distance. He must not attract attention, nor invite notice, and there was no reason why he should if he did not fall into the panic pit. He felt Claudio's fingers tighten on the collar of his shirt and press against the flesh of his shoulder; ignoring him, he kept his attention for the road as he pulled out behind a lorry, passed it, slotted back into the slower lane.

Claudio could not sense his mood. He was a big man, heavy in weight and grip and with a dulled speed of thought unable to judge the moment when he should speak, when he should bide his time. Past the lorry safe, and clear and cruising. Claudio did not look down at the prone body, easy in its sleep, the head resting on his lap, the torso and legs on the carpet floor enmeshed between Mario's shins.

'Brave boy, Vanni. You took us clear and did it well. How long till the garage?'

He should have known the answer himself; they had made the journey four times in the previous week; they knew to within three minutes the time it would take to cover the distance. But Claudio wanted to talk, always wanted to talk, a man to whom silence was a punishment. He could be removed from his cigarettes, his beer and his women, but he would die if he were left to the cruelty of his own company. Vanni appreciated the loneliness of a man who must be spoken to and talked with at all times.

'Four or five minutes. Past the BMW depot and the Bank sports place . . . just past there.'

'He fought us, you know. When we had to take him from the car.'

'You took him well, Claudio. You gave him no chance.'

'If he had gone on then I would have hit him with the hammer.'

'You don't know the sap in your arm,' Vanni chuckled. 'They'd pay little for a corpse.'

'How long did you say to the garage?'

'Three more minutes, a little less than when you last asked. Idiot of Calabria, are you frightened of losing us? You would like to come with us on the train this afternoon? Poor Claudio, you must endure a night of the boredom and the tedium of Rome. You must be patient, as the capo said. A bad night for the whores, eh Claudio?'

'We could all have travelled together.'

'Not what the capo said. Travel separately, break the group. Give Claudio his night between the thighs. Don't you go hurting those girls, big boy.' Vanni laughed softly; it was part of the game, the prowess of Claudio the lover. If a girl spoke to the buffoon he'd fall on his arse in fright.

'I would like to be back in Palmi,' Claudio said simply.

'Calabria can wait for you just one day more. Calabria will survive without you.'

'It's a bastard strain – on your own.'

'You will find someone to talk to, you'll find some fat cow who thinks you're a great man. But don't go flashing her, not your money anyway, not five million.' And the laughter faded. 'That's how they get you, Claudio, how the polizia take you, when you have the money running free in your palm.'

'Perhaps Claudio should put his money in the bank,' murmured Mario.

'And have some criminal bastard walk in with a shooter and take it? Never! Don't do that, Claudio.'

They laughed together, heaving their bodies in the seats. Exaggerated, childish humour because through that came a relaxation from the tension that had taken three weeks to build since the outline of the plan was first put to them.

Beyond the Rieti turn-off they went right and drove on a rough track skirting a recently completed four-floor block of flats and towards the garages that lay to the rear, partly shielded from the upper windows by a line of vigorous conifers. There was a van waiting there, old and with its paintwork scratched from frequent scarrings and the rust showing at the mudguards and road dirt coating the small window set in the rear doors. Two men lounged, elbows on the bonnet, waiting for the arrival of the Alfetta. Vanni did not hear what was said as Mario and Claudio carried the crumpled, drugged form of their prisoner from the back seat to the opened rear doors of the van. It would be of little interest, the passing of a moment between men hitherto unknown to each other who would not meet again. When the doors were closed an envelope passed between fingers, and Claudio slapped the men on their backs and kissed their cheeks, and his face was wreathed in happiness, and Mario handed the grip bag to new owners.

Mario led the way back to the car, then paused by the open door to watch the men fasten the back of

17

their van with a padlock and drive away. There was a certain wistfulness on his features as if he regretted that his own part in the matter was now completed. When Claudio joined him, he looked away from the retreating vehicle, and slid back into his seat. Then the vultures were at the envelope, ripping at it, tearing it apart till the bundles in the pretty coloured plastic bands were falling on their knees. One hundred notes for each. Some hardly used in transactions, others elderly and spoiled from passage of time and frequency of handling. Silence reigned while each counted his bounty, flicking the tops of the notes to a rhythm of counting.

Vanni loaded his money into the folds of his wallet, pulled a small key from his pocket, climbed from the car and walked to one of the garage doors. He unlocked it, then returned to the car and motioned for Mario and Claudio to leave. He drove the car into the garage, satisfied himself that the doors prevented a casual glance from the building seeing his work, and spent five slow minutes wiping clean the plastic and wood surfaces of the interior with his handkerchief, and then, when he was satisfied, the outer doors. When he was finished he came out into the warmth and slammed the garage doors shut. The garage had been rented by telephone, a letter with a bogus address containing cash had provided the deposit and confirmation. He threw the key far on to the flat roof, where it clattered momentarily. The rent had six weeks to run, time enough for the Alfetta to rest there, and by the time an irate landlord prised open the doors all other traces of the group would have been covered.

Together the three men walked out past the flats

and to the main road and then along the pavement to the green-painted bus stop sign. It was the safest way into the city and ultimately to the railway station.

On that morning, in a flat across two Roman hills, the first of the occupants to wake was the boy Giancarlo.

Lithe on his bare feet, he padded across the carpet of the living-room, sleep still heavy and confusing to his eyes, blurring the shapes and images of the furnishings. He avoided the low tables and velvet-seated chairs, stumbling on a light flex as he pulled a shirt over his young, undeveloped shoulders. He had shaken Franca gently and with the care and wonderment and awe of a boy who wakes for the first time in a woman's bed and is frightened that the tumult and emotion of the night will be relegated by dawn to a fantasy and dream. He had scratched his fingers across her collar-bone and pulled quietly at the lobe of her ear, and whispered her name, and that it was time. He had looked down on her face, gazed intoxicated on the shoulder skin and the contour of the drawn-up sheet, and left her.

A small flat they lived in. The one living-room. The bathroom that was a box which crammed in a toilet, a bidet and a shower unit. The kitchen with a sink buried under abandoned plates and a cooker that had not seen a damp cloth round the burners for more than a week. The bedroom where Enrico still slept noisily and where there was the unused bed that till last night had been Giancarlo's. And there was Franca's room with the single narrow divan, her clothes draped as haphazard carpeting across the woodblock floor. A small hallway and a door with three locks and a spyhole, and a metal bar with chain that enabled the door to be opened an inch for additional checking of a visitor. It was a good flat for their needs.

The requirements of Franca Tantardini, Enrico Panicucci and Giancarlo Battestini were not great, not complex. It was determined that they should live among the borghese, in a middle-class area, where there was wealth, prosperity, where lives were shuttered, self-reliant affairs and closed to the inquisitive. Vigna Clara hill suited them well, left them secure and unnoticed in the heart of enemy territory. They were anonymous in a land of Ferraris and Mercedes and Jaguars, among the servants and the spoiled children and the long holidays through the summer, and the formidable foreign bank accounts. There was a basement garage and a lift that could carry them out of sight to their own door in the attic of the building, affording them the possibility of cloaking their movements, coming and going without observation. Not that they went out much; they did not roam the streets because that was dangerous and put them at risk. Better that they should spend their hours cooped between the walls, profiting from seclusion, reducing the threat of casual recognition by the polizia. Expensive, of course, to live there. Four hundred and seventy-five thousand a month they paid, but there was money in the movement. Enough money was available to meet the basic precautions of survival, and they settled in cash on the first day of the month and did not ask for the contract to be registered and witnessed and the sum to figure on their landlord's tax return. There was no difficulty finding premises that were private and discreet.

Giancarlo was a boy with two terms of psychology study at the University of Rome behind him, and nine more months in the Regina Coeli gaol locked in a damp cell low down by the Tiber river. Still a boy, little more than a child, but bedded now, bedded by a woman in every way his senior. She was eight years older than he was, so that he had seen in the first creeping light of the bedroom the needle lines at her neck and mouth and the faint trembling of the weight at her buttocks as she had turned in her sleep, resting on his arm, uncovered and uncaring till he had pulled the sheet about her. Eight years of seniority in the movement, and that he knew of too, because her picture was in the mind of every car load of the Squadra Mobile, and her name was on the lips of the capo of the Squadra Anti-Terrorismo when he called his conferences at the Viminale. Eight years of importance to the movement; that too Giancarlo knew of, because the assignment of Enrico and himself was to guard and protect her, to maintain her freedom.

The bright, expansive heat drove through the slatted shutters, bathing the furniture in zebra shades of colour, illuminating the filled ashtrays and the empty supermarket wine bottles and the uncleared plates with the pasta sauce still clinging to them, and the spreadeagled newspapers. The light flickered on the glass of the pictures with which the room was hung, expensive and modern and rectangular in their motifs, not of their choosing but provided with the premises, and which hurt their sensitivities as they whiled away the cramped hours waiting for instructions and orders of reconnaissance and planning and ultimately of attack. All of it, all of the surroundings grated on the boy, disturbed him, nurturing his distrust for the flat in which they lived. They should not have been in a place like this, not with the plumage and trappings of the enemy, and the comforts and ornaments of those they fought against. But Giancarlo was nineteen years old and new to the movement, and he was quick to learn to keep his silence at the contradictions.

He heard the noise of her feet tripping to the bedroom door, swung round and in haste dragged his shirt tails into the waist of his trousers and fastened the top button and heaved at the zip. She stood in the open doorway and there was the look of a cat about her mouth and her slow, distant smile. A towel was draped uselessly around her waist, and above its line were the drooping bronzed breasts where Giancarlo's curls had rested; they hung heavily because she forswore the use of a brassiere under her daily uniform of a straining blouse. Wonderful to the boy, a dream image. His hands were still on the zip-fastener.

'Put it away, little boy, before you run dry.' She rippled with her laughter.

Giancarlo blushed. Tore his eyes from her to the silent, unmoving door to Enrico's room.

'Don't be jealous, little fox.' She read him, and there was the trace of mocking, the suspicion of scorn. 'Enrico won't take my little fox away, Enrico won't supplant him.'

She came across the room to Giancarlo, straight and direct, and circled her arms around his neck and nuzzled at his ear, pecked and bit at it, and he stayed motionless because he thought that if he moved the towel would fall, and it was morning and the room was bright.

'Now we've made a man of you, Giancarlo, don't behave like a man. Don't be tedious and possessive and middle-aged . . . not after just once.'

He kissed her almost curtly on the forehead where it rested against his mouth, and she giggled.

'I worship you, Franca.'

She laughed again. 'Then make some coffee, and heat the bread if it's stale, and get that pig Enrico out of his bed, and don't go boasting to him. Those can be the first labours of your worship.'

She disentangled herself, and he felt a trembling in his legs and the tightness in his arms, and close to his nostrils was the damp, lived-with scent of her hair. He watched her glide to the bathroom, flouncing and swinging her hips, her hair rippling on her shoulder muscles. An officer of the Nuclei Armati Proletaria, organizer and undisputed leader of a cell, a symbol of resistance, her liberty was a hammered nail in the cross of the State. She gave him a little wave with a small and delicate fist as the towel fell from her waist, and there was the flash of whitened skin and the moment of darkened hair and the tinkle of her laugh before the door closed on her. A sweet and gentle little fist that he had known for its softness and persuasion, divorced from the clamped grip of a week ago as it held the Beretta P38 and pumped the shells into the legs of the falling, screaming personnel officer outside the factory gate.

Giancarlo hammered at Enrico's door. He battered on through the stream of obscenities and protest till he heard the muffled voice cleared of sleep and the tread lumbering for the door.

Enrico's face appeared, the leer spreading. 'Keep you warm, boy, did she? Ready to go back to your Mama now? Going to sleep all afternoon . . .'

Giancarlo dragged the door closed, flushed and hurried for the kitchen to fill the kettle, rinse the mugs, and test with his hands the state of the two-day-old bread.

He went next to Franca's bedroom, walking with care to avoid stepping on her clothes, staring at the indented mattress and the stripped sheets. He slid to his knees and dragged from the hiding-place under the bed the cheap plastic suitcase that always rested there, unfastened the straps and pulled the lid back. This was the arsenal of the covo – three machine-guns of Czech manufacture, two pistols, magazines, loose cartridges, batteries, wires of red and blue flex, the little plastic bag which held the detonators. He moved aside the metal-cased box with its dials and telescopic aerial that was marketed openly for radio-controlled aeroplanes and boats and which they utilized for the triggering of remote explosions. Buried at the bottom was his own P38. The rallying cry of the young people of anger and dispute – P trent' otto – available, reliable, the symbol of the fight with the spreading tentacles of fascism. P38, I love you. The token of manhood, of the coming of age. P38, we fight together. And when Franca ordered him he would be ready. He squinted his eyes down the gunsight. P38, my friend. Enrico could get his own, bastard. He fastened the straps again and pushed the bag away under the bed, brushing his hand against her pants, clenching them in his

24

fingers, carrying them to his lips. A whole day to wait before he would be back there, lying like a dog on his back in surrender, feeling the pressures on his body.

Time to get the rosetti out of the oven and find the instant coffee.

She was standing at the doorway.

'Impatient, little fox?'

'I had been at the case,' Giancarlo floundered. 'If we are to be at the Post when it opens . . .'

Her smile faded. 'Right. We should not be late there. Enrico is ready?'

'He will not be long. We have time for coffee.'

It was an abomination, an ordeal, to drink the manufactured 'instant brand' but the bars where they could drink the real, the special, the habitual, were too dangerous. She used to joke that the absence of bar coffee in the mornings was the ultimate sacrifice of her life.

'Get him moving. He has enough time to sleep in the rest of the day, all the hours of the day.' The kindness, the motherliness, had fled from her, the authority had taken over, the softness and the warmth and the smell washed away with the shower water.

They must go to the Post to pay the quarterly telephone bill. Bills should always be paid promptly, she said. If there are delays there is suspicion, and checks are made and investigations are instituted. If they went early, were there when the Post opened, then they would head the queue at the Conti Correnti counter where the bills must be met in cash, and they would hang around for the least time, minimize the vulnerability. There was no need for her to go with Enrico and Giancarlo but the flat bred its own culture of claustrophobia, wearing and nagging at her patience.

'Hurry him up,' she snapped, wriggling the jeans up the length of her thighs.

Stretching herself in the bed, arching her body under the silk of the pink nightgown, irritation and annoyance surfacing on her cream-whitened face, Violet Harrison attempted to identify the source of the noise. She had wanted to sleep another hour at least, a minimum of another hour. She rolled over in the double bed seeking to press her face into the depth of the pillows, looking for an escape from the penetration of the sound that enveloped and cascaded round the room. Geoffrey had gone out quietly enough, put his shoes on in the hall, hadn't disturbed her. She had barely felt the snap of his quick kiss on her cheek before he left for the office, and the sprinkling of toast crumbs from his mouth.

She did not have to wake yet, not till Maria came and cleared the kitchen and washed up the plates from last night, and the lazy cow didn't appear before nine. God, it was hot! Not eight o'clock and already there was a sweat on her forehead and at her neck and under her arms. Bloody Geoffrey, too mean to fit air-conditioning in the flat. She'd asked for it enough times, and he'd hedged and delayed and said the summer was too short and prattled about the expense and how long would they be there anyway. He didn't spend his day in a Turkish bath, he didn't have to walk around with a stain in the armpit and an itch in his pants. Air-conditioning at the office, but not at home. No, that wasn't necessary. Bloody Geoffrey . . .

And the noise was still there.

. . . She'd go to the beach that morning. At least there was a wind at the beach. Not much of it, precious little. But some sort of cool from off the sea, and the boy might be there. He'd said he would be. Cheeky little devil, little blighter. Old enough to be his . . . Enough problems without the clichés, Violet. All sinews and flat stomach and those ridiculous little curly hairs on his shins and thighs, chattering his compliments, encroaching on her towel. Enough to get his face slapped on an English summer beach. And going off and buying ice-cream, three bloody flavours, my dear, and licking his own in that way. Dirty little boy. But she was a big girl now. Big enough, Violet Harrison, to take care of herself, and have a dash of amusement too. Needed something to liven things, stuck in this bloody flat. Geoffrey out all day and coming home and moaning how tired he was and what a boring day he'd had, and the Italians didn't know the way to run an office, and why hadn't she learned to cook pasta the way it was in the ristorante at lunchtime, and couldn't she use less electricity and save a bit on the petrol for her car. Why shouldn't she have a little taste of the fun, a little nibble?

Still that bloody noise down in the road. Couldn't erase it, not without getting out of bed and closing the window.

It took her a full minute to identify the source of the intrusion that had broken her rest. Sirens baying out their immediacy.

In response to a woman's emergency call the first police cars were arriving at the scene of the kidnapping of Geoffrey Harrison.

Chapter Two

The cars were Enrico's responsibility.

This week it was a Fiat 128, the fortnight before a 500 that was hardly large enough for the three of them, before that a Mirafiori, before that an Alfasud. Enrico's speciality. He would drift away from the flat, be gone three or four hours, and then open the front door smiling away his success and urging Franca to come to the basement garage to inspect his handiwork. Usually it was night when he made the switches, with no preference between the city centre and the distant southern suburbs. Good and clean and quick, and Franca would nod in appreciation and squeeze his arm and even the gorilla, even Enrico, would weaken and allow a trace of pleasure.

He was well satisfied with the 128, lucky to have found a car with a painstaking owner and an overhauled engine. Fast in acceleration, lively to the touch of his feet at the controls. Coming down off Vigna Clara, heading for the Corso Francia, they seemed like three affluent young people, the right image, the right camouflage, blending into their surroundings. And if Giancarlo sitting hunched in the back was unshaven, poorly dressed, it was not conspicuous because few of the sons of the borghese who had their flats on the hill would have bothered with a razor in high summer; and if Franca sitting in the front passenger seat had her hair tied with a creased scarf, neither was that of importance because the daughters of the rich did not require their finery so early in the morning. Enrico drove fast and with ease and confidence, understanding the mechanism of the car, rejoicing in the freedom of escape from the confines of the flat. Too fast for Franca. She slapped her hand on his wrist, shouted for him to be more careful as he overtook on the inside, weaved among the traffic, hooted his way past the more sedate drivers.

'Don't be a fool, Enrico. If we touch something . . .'

'We never have, we won't now.'

Enrico's familiar uncurbed response to correction. As always, Giancarlo was perplexed that he treated Franca with such small deference. Wouldn't grovel, wouldn't dip his head in apology. Always ready with a rejoinder. Brooding and generally uncommunicative, as if breeding a private, secret hatred that he would not share. His moments of humanity and humour were rare, fleeting, paced out. Giancarlo wondered what Enrico had thought of the unmade bed, his absence in the night hours, wondered if it stirred the pulse, kicked at the indifference that Enrico presented to all around him. He doubted if it would. Self-sufficient, self-reliant, an emotional eunuch with his shoulders rounded over the wheel. Three weeks Giancarlo had been at the covo, three weeks as guard at the safe house of the prize of the movement, but Enrico had been with her many months. There must be a trust and understanding between him and Franca, a tolerance between her and this strange padding animal who left her side only when she slept. It was beyond Giancarlo to unravel it; this was a relationship too complex, too eccentric for his comprehension.

The three young people in a car that carried a licence plate and a valid tax disc on the windscreen merged without effort into the soft, flatulent society with which they were at war. Two days earlier Franca had exclaimed with triumph, shouted for Giancarlo and Enrico to come to the side of her chair and read to them a statistic from the newspaper. In Italy, she had declaimed, the increase of political violence on the previous year's figures was greater than in any country in the world.

'Even Argentina we lead, even the people of the Monteneros. So we're wounding the pigs, hurting them. And this year we wound them more, we hurt them harder.'

She had played her part in the compilation of those figures, had not been backward in advancing herself and had earned the accolade bestowed on her by the magazines and tabloids of 'Public Enemy Number One (Women)', and shrieked with laughter when she read it the first time.

'Chauvinist bastards. Typical of them that whatever I do I cannot be labelled as the greatest threat, because I am a woman. They would choke rather than admit that a woman can do them the greatest damage. My title has to be embroidered with a category.'

Eight times in the past twelve months she had led the strike squads, the action commandos. Target ambushes. Bullets blasted into the lower limbs because the sentence of maiming was thought more psychologically devastating than death. Eight times, and still no sign that many beyond the hierarchy of the colossus knew of her existence, or cared. Eight times, and still no indication that the uprising of the proletariat forces was imminent. It was as if she was teased, mocked to do her worst, undo herself in the very audacity she was taunted towards. When she thought like that, in the late evening when the flat was subdued, when Enrico was sleeping, then she came for the boys who were Enrico's constant but changing companions. That was when she demanded the pawing, clumsy association with the juvenile, that her mood might be broken, her despair smashed under the weight of a young body.

These were hard and dangerous times for the movement. The odour of risk was in the air, constant after the kidnapping and execution of Aldo Moro, the mobilization of the forces of the State, the harrying of the groups. The gesture on the grand scale by the Brigatisti had been the taking of Moro and the People's Court to try him and pass sentence. But there were many who disputed that this was the way to fight, who counselled caution, argued against the massive strike and favoured instead the process of wearing erosion. More men were rallied against them now, there was more awareness, more sophistication. It was a time for the groups to burrow deeper, and when they surfaced on the street it was in the knowledge that the risks were greater, the possibility of failure increased.

Swerving across the traffic lanes, Enrico brought the car to rest spanning the gutter, half on the pavement, half in the road. Franca wore a watch on her wrist, but still asked with a flow of irritation in her voice:

'How long till it opens?'

Enrico, accustomed to her, did not reply.

'Two minutes, perhaps three, if they begin on time,' Giancarlo said.

'Well, we can't sit here all morning. Let's get there.'

She slipped the door open, swung her feet out and stretched on the pavement, leaving the boy to fiddle at getting her seat forward so that he could follow her. As she started to walk away Enrico went hurrying after her because his place was at her side and she should not walk without him. To Giancarlo, her stride was light and perfect, shivering in the taut and faded jeans. And she should walk well, thought the boy, because she does not carry the cold clear shape of the P38 against her flesh buried beneath a shirt and trouser belt. Not that Giancarlo would have been without his gun. It was more than a tube of chewing gum, more than a packet of Marlboro. It was something he could no longer live without, something that had become an extension of his personality. It owned a divinity to Giancarlo, the P38 with its simple mechanism, its gas routes and magazines, its hair-trigger, its power.

'No need for us all to be in there,' Franca said when Giancarlo was at her side, Enrico on the other flank, and they were close to the Post doorway. 'Get yourself across the road to the papers. And get plenty if we're to be stuck in the flat for the rest of the day.'

He didn't wish to leave her side, but it was an instruction, a dismissal.

Giancarlo turned away. He faced the wide and scurrying lanes of early morning traffic, looked for the opening that would enable him to reach the raised centre bank of the Corso Francia. There was a newspaper stall on the far side nearly opposite the Post. There was no hurry for him because however early you came to the Post there was always a man there before you; the pathetic fools who were paid to take the bills and the money for gas and telephone and electricity because it was beneath the dignity of the borghese to stand and wait in a line. He saw the opening, a slowing in the traffic and launched himself through the welter of bonnets and bumpers and spirited horns and spinning wheels. A hesitation in the centre. Another delay before the passage was clear and he was off again, skipping, young-footed, across the remaining roadway to the stand with its gaudy decoration of magazine covers and paperbacks. He had not looked back at Franca and did not see the slowly cruising car of the Squadra Mobile far out in the traffic flow of the road behind him. Giancarlo was unaware of the moment of surging danger, the startled gape of recognition on the face of the vice brigadiere as he riveted on the features of the woman, half in profile at the entrance to the Post and waiting for the lifting of the steel shutter. Giancarlo did not know as he took his place in the queue to be served that the policeman had savagely urged his driver to maintain speed, create no warning, as he rifled through the folder of photographs kept permanently in the glove box of the car.

The boy was still shuffling forward as the first radio message was beamed to the Questura in central Rome.

Giancarlo stood, hands in pockets, mind on a woman as the radio transmissions hit the air. While cars were scrambling, accelerating, guns being armed and cocked, Giancarlo searched his memories, finding again the breasts and thighs of Franca.

He did not protest as the woman in the cream coat pushed past him without ceremony, passing up the opportunity to sneer and laugh so that she should be discomfited. He knew the newspapers he should buy. *L'Unità* of the PCI, the communists; *La Stampa* of Turin, the paper of Fiat and Agnelli; *Repubblica* of the Socialists; *Popolo* of the right, *Il Messaggero* of the left. Necessary always, Franca said, to have *Il Messaggero* so that they could browse through the 'Cronaca di Roma' section and read of the successes of their colleagues in different and separated cells, learn where the Molotovs had landed in the night, what enemy had been hit, what friend taken. Five papers, a thousand lire. Giancarlo scratched in the hip pocket of his trousers for the dribble of coins and the crumpled notes he would need, counting out the money, standing his ground against the pushing of the man behind him. He would ask Franca to replace it, it was she who kept the cell's money, in the small wall safe in her room with the combination lock and the documents for identity changes, and the files on targets of future attacks. She should replace the money – a thousand lire, three bottles of beer if he went to the bar in the evening. It was all right for him to go out after dark, it was only Franca who should not. But he would not be drinking beer that evening, he would be sitting on the rug at the feet of the woman and close to her, rubbing his shoulder against her knee, resting his elbow on her thigh, waiting for the indications of her tiredness, her willingness for bed. He had been to the bar the night before, after their meal, and come back to find her drooped in the chair and Enrico sprawled and sleeping opposite her on the sofa with his feet on the cushions. She had said nothing, just taken his hand and turned off the lights and led him like a lamb to her room, and still she had not spoken as her hands slipped down the length of his shirt to his waist.

The agony of waiting for her would be unendurable.

Giancarlo paid his money, stepped back from the counter with the folded newspapers and scanned the front page of *Il Messaggero*. Carillo of Spain and Berlinguer of Italy were meeting in Rome, a Eurocommunist summit, middle-class, middle-aged, a betrayal of the true proletariat. A former Minister of Shipping was accused of having his hand in the till, what you'd expect from the bastard Democrazia Cristiana. The steering committee of the Socialists was sitting down with the DC, games being played, circles of words. A banker arrested for tax evasion. All the sickness, all the foetid corruption was here, all the cancer of the world they struggled to usurp. And then he found the headlines that would bring the smile and the cold mirth to Franca; the successes and the triumphs. One of their own, Antonio de Laurentis of Napoli, missing inside the maximum security gaol on Favignana island, described as 'most dangerous', a leader of the NAP, inside the prison and they'd lost him. An executive of Fiat shot in the legs in Turin, the thirty-seventh that year to have the people's sentence inflicted and the year not eight months old.

He tucked the papers under his arm and looked out across the road to the Post. Franca would be furious, icy, if he kept her waiting. It was heavily parked now around their 128. Two yellow Alfettas there and a grey Alfasud, close to their own car. He wondered whether they'd be able to get out. God, she'd be angry if they were boxed. Over the top of the traffic, solid and unpassable to him, Giancarlo saw Enrico emerge from the doorway, cautious and wary. Two paces behind him, Franca, cool, commanding. His woman. Christ, she walked well, with the loping stride, never an eye left nor right.

And the blur of movement. Shatteringly fast. Too quick for the boy to retain. Franca and Enrico were five, six metres from the entrance to the Post. The doors of the three intruding cars bulged and split open. Men running, shouting. The moment of clarity for Giancarlo, he saw the guns in their hands. The two at the front sprinted forward, then dived for the crouch with the automatics held straight arm to the front. Enrico twisted his arm back for the hanging flap of the shirt tail and the concealed Beretta.

Across the traffic and tarmac void Giancarlo heard the shriek of the doomed Enrico. The cry for the woman to run. The scream of the stag that will stand against the dogs to give time for the hind to hasten to the thickets. But her eyes were faster than his, her mind quicker and better able to assess the realities of the moment. As his gun came up to face the aggressors she made the quicksilver decision of survival. The boy saw her head duck and disappear behind the roofs of the passing cars, and then there was the vision of her, prone on the stomach, hands on her head.

Enrico would not see her, would believe in his last sand-running moments that his sacrifice had achieved its purpose. Even as he fired, he was cut down by the swarm of bullets aimed at him in a thunderclap of gunfire, and lay writhing on the pavement as if trying to shake away a great agony, rolling and rolling from his back to his belly. The men ran forward, still suspicious that their enemy might bite, might hurt. There was a trail of blood from Enrico's mouth, another two from his chest that meandered together and then separated, and more crimson paths etching from his shattered legs. But his life lingered and a hand scrabbled at the dirt for the gun that had been dropped, that had fallen beyond reach. The men who towered above him wore jeans and casual slacks and sweatshirts, and some were unshaven or bearded or carried their hair long on their shoulders. Nothing to tell them from Enrico and Giancarlo. These were the men of the Squadra Anti-Terrorismo, undercover, dedicated, as hard and ruthless as those they opposed. A single shot destroyed the frenzy of Enrico's groping hands.

An execution bullet. Just as it had been said it was when the carabinieri dropped La Muscio on the church steps near the Colosseo. Bastards, bastard pigs.

A man beside Giancarlo crossed himself in haste, a private gesture in the glare of a public moment. Down the road a woman bent in sickness. A priest in a long cassock abandoned his car in the road and ran forward. Two of the men covered the figure of Franca, their guns roaming close to her head.

A terrible pain coursed through the boy as his hands stayed clamped on the folded newspapers and

37

would not waver towards the gun buried in the flesh of his buttock. He watched, part of the gathering crowd, terrified of risking the intervention that Enrico had affected. He willed himself to run forward and shoot because that was the job the movement had chosen for him, protector and bodyguard of Franca Tantardini. But if he did his blood would run in the deep gutter, company for Enrico's. There was no thrust in his legs, no jolt in his arms; he was a part of those who stayed and waited for the show to end.

They pulled the woman, unresisting and limp, to her feet and dragged her to a car. Two had their hands on her upper arms, another walked in front with his fist caught in the long blond strands of her hair. There was a kick that missed at her shins. He could see that her eyes were open but bewildered, unrecognizing as she went to the opened car door.

Would she have seen the boy she had opened herself to a short night before?

Would she have seen him?

He wanted to wave, give a sign, shout out that he had not abandoned her. How to show that, Giancarlo? Enrico dead, and Giancarlo alive and breathing, because he had stepped back, had dissociated. How to show it, Giancarlo? The car revved its engine and its horn was raucous as it pulled out into the open road, another Alfetta close in escort behind. The cars swung across the central reservation, lurching and shaken, and completed their turn in front of where Giancarlo stood. The crowd around him pressed forward to see better the face of the woman, and the boy was among them. And then they were gone and one of the men held a machine-gun at the car window. A fanfare of sirens, an explosion of engine power. For a few moments only he was able to follow the passage of the cars in the growing traffic before they were lost to him, and the sight of Enrico was taken from him by a moving bus.

Deep in a gathering shame at the scope of his failure, Giancarlo began slowly to walk away along the pavement. Twice he bumped into men who hurried towards him, fearful that they had missed the excitement and that there was nothing remaining for them to see. Giancarlo was careful not to run, just walked away, not thinking where he should go, where he should hide. Too logical, such thoughts for his fractured mind to cope with. He saw only the stunned deep golden eyes of Franca, who was handcuffed and for whom a boy had not stepped forward.

She had called him her little fox and scratched with her nails at his body, had kissed him far down on the flatness of his stomach, had governed and tutored him, and he drifted from the place, feet leaden, unseeing with the moisture in his eyelids.

The British Embassy in Rome occupies a prime site set back from high railings and lawns and a stone-skirted artificial lake at 80a Via XX Settembre. The building itself, unlikely and original, supported by pillars of grey cement and with narrow arrow-slit windows, was conceived by a noted English architect after the previous occupant of the grounds had been destroyed by the gelignite of Jewish terrorists . . . or guerrillas . . . or freedom fighters, a stop-over in their search for a homeland. The architect had fashioned his designs at a time when the representatives of the

Queen in this city were numerous and influential. Expense and expediency had whittled down the staff list. Many diplomats now doubled on two separate jobs.

The First Secretary, who handled matters of political importance in Italian affairs, had also taken under his umbrella the area of liaison with the Questura and the Viminale. Politics and security, the aesthetic and the earthy, strange bed partners. That Michael Charlesworth's two previous foreign postings had been in Vientiane and Reykjavik was a source of astonishment neither to himself nor his colleagues. He was expected to master the local intricacies of a situation inside three years, and this accomplished, he could correctly anticipate that he would be sent to a country about which he had only the most superficial knowledge. After Iceland and the tangled arguments of the Cod War, with the island's fishing interests ranged against the need of his countrymen to eat northern water fish from old newspapers, Roman politics and police had a certain charm. He was not dissatisfied.

Charlesworth had demanded and won a rise in rent allowance from his Ambassador and had been able to set up home with his wife in a high-roofed flat within earshot, but not sight, of the Piazza del Popolo in the centro storico. The garaging of a car there was next to impossible and while his wife's veteran 500 was parked beneath the condescending eyes of the Vigili Urbani in the piazza, he himself cycled to work on the machine he had first used twenty years earlier as a Cambridge undergraduate. The sight of the dark-stripe-suited Englishman pedalling hard along the Corso d'Italia and the Via

Piave with collapsible umbrella and attaché case clamped to the carrier over the rear wheel was a pleasing sight to Italian motorists, who from respect for his efforts afforded him unusual circumspection. Once the slopes of the Borghese Gardens had been surmounted, the bicycle provided Charlesworth with fast and intrepid transport, and often he was the first of the senior diplomatic staff to reach his desk.

A salute from the gatekeeper, the parking and padlocking of the machine, the shaking free of trouser turn-ups from the clips, a wave to security in the ground-floor hall, a gallop up two flights of stairs, and he was striding along the back second-floor corridor. Fully three doors away he heard the telephone ringing from his office. Fast with the key into the lock, swinging the door open to confront the noise, abandoning the briefcase and umbrella to the floor, he lunged for the receiver.

'*Pronto.*' Panting a little, not the way he liked to be.

'*Signor Charlesworth*?'

'Yes.'

'*La Questura. Dottore Giuseppe Carboni . . . momento.*'

Delay. First a crossed line. Apology, rampant clicking and interruption before Charlesworth heard the Questura switchboard announce with pride to Carboni that the task was accomplished, the connection successful. They were not friends, the policeman and Michael Charlesworth, but known to each other, acquainted. Carboni would know that Charlesworth was happier in English, that language courses were not always victorious. With a faint American accent Carboni spoke.

'Charlesworth, that is you?'

'Yes.' Caution. No man is happy talking to the police, least of all to foreign police at fourteen minutes past eight in the morning.

'I have bad news for you, my friend. Bad news to give you for which I am sorry. You have a businessman in the city, a resident, a man called Harrison. He is the financial controller of ICH in EUR, International Chemical Holdings. They are at Viale Pasteur in EUR, many of the multinationals favour that area . . .' What's the silly blighter done, thought Charlesworth, resigned. Socked a copper? Drunk himself stupid? No, couldn't be that, not if Carboni was calling, not if it was at that level. '. . . I regret very much, Charlesworth, to have to tell you that Geoffrey Harrison was kidnapped this morning. Armed men, forced from his car near his home.'

'Christ,' muttered Charlesworth, low but audible.

'I understand your feelings. He is the first of the foreign residents, the first of the foreign commercials to be affected by this plague.'

'I know.'

'We are doing everything we can. There are road blocks . . .' The distant voice tailed and died, as if Carboni knew the futility of boasting to this man. He came again. 'But you know, Charlesworth, these people are very organized, very sophisticated. It is unlikely, and you will understand me, it is unlikely that what we can do will be sufficient.'

'I know,' said Charlesworth. An honest man he was talking to, and what to say that wouldn't be churlish. 'I am confident you will exercise all your agencies in this matter, completely confident.'

'You can help me, Charlesworth. I have called you early, it is not half an hour since the attack, and we have not yet been to the family. We have not spoken to his wife. Perhaps she does not speak Italian, perhaps she speaks only English, we thought it better if someone from the Embassy should be with her first, to give her the news.'

The dose prescribed for diplomats seeking nightmares was purveying ill-tidings to their own nationals far from home. A stinking, lousy job and indefinite involvement. 'That was very considerate of you.'

'It is better also that you have a doctor go to her this morning. In many cases we find that necessary in the first hours. It is a shock . . . you will understand.'

'Yes.'

'I do not want to lecture you at this stage, because soon you will be busy, and I am busy myself in this matter, but you should make a contact with Harrison's employer. It is a London-based company, I believe. If they have taken the employee of a multinational they will be asking for more than poor Harrison's bank balance can provide. They will believe they are ransoming the company. It could be expensive, Charlesworth.'

'You would like me to alert the company to this situation?' Charlesworth scribbled hard on his memo pad.

'They must make their attitude clear, and quickly. When the contact is made they must know what attitude they will take.'

'What a way to start the bloody day. Well, they'll ask me this, and it may colour their judgement: you would presume that this is the work of a professional, an experienced gang?'

43

There was a faint laugh, quavering over the telephone line before Carboni replied. 'How can I say, Charlesworth? You read our newspapers, you watch the Telegiornale in the evening. You know what we are up against. You know how many times the gangs are successful, how many times we beat them. We do not hide the figures, you know that too. If you look at the results you will see that a few of the gangs are amateur – you English, always you want to reduce everything to sport – and we catch those ones. Does that give us a winning score? I would like to say so, but I cannot. It is very hard to beat the professionals. And you should tell Harrison's firm when you speak with them that the greater the police efforts to release him, the greater the risk to his life. They should not forget that.'

Charlesworth sucked at his pencil top. 'You would expect the company to pay what they are asked to?'

'We should talk of that later. Perhaps it is premature at this moment.' A gentle correction, made with kindness, but a correction nevertheless. Not manners to talk of the will and the beneficiaries while the corpse is still warm. 'But I do not think that we would expect the family or the company of a foreigner to adopt a differing procedure to that taken by our own families when they are faced with identical problems.'

The invitation to pay. It wouldn't be made clearer than that. The invitation not to be stubborn and principled. Pragmatism winning through, and a bloody awful scene for a policeman to have to get his nose into.

'There may be some difficulty. We don't do it like that in England.'

'But you are not in England, Charlesworth.' The taint of impatience from Carboni. 'And in England you have not always been successful. I remember two cases, two ransom demands unmet, two victims found, two deaths. It is not a straightforward area of decision, and not one which we can debate. Later perhaps, but now I think there are other things that you wish to do.'

'I appreciate greatly what you have done, Dottore.'

'It is nothing.' Carboni rang off.

Five minutes later Charlesworth was in the ground-floor hall of the Embassy waiting for the arrival of the Ambassador, still shrill in his ears the piercing protests of the woman he had telephoned.

Who was going to pay?

Didn't they know they hadn't any money?

Nothing in the bank, just a few savings.

Who was going to take responsibility?

Not a conversation that Charlesworth had relished and his calming noises had been shouted out till he'd said he had to go because he must see the Ambassador. No more blustering after that; just a deep sobbing, a pain echoing down the wire to him, as if some dam of control and inhibition had been broken.

Where was he, the poor sod? What were they doing to him? Must be a terrible loneliness. Mind-bending, horrific. And damn-all for comfort. Didn't even know that idiots like Michael Charlesworth and Giuseppe Carboni were flapping their wings and running in circles. Better he didn't know it; it might make him turn over and give up. And what chance the Ambassador being in before nine? What bloody chance?

They'd tied him expertly as they would have done a lively bullock going to slaughter. Not a casual job, not just a length of rope round his legs.

Geoffrey Harrison had lain perhaps twenty minutes on the coarse sacking on the van floor before he had tried to move his ankles and wrists. The effects of the chloroform were dissipating, the shock of capture and the numbness of disorientation sliding. The nobbled bones on the inside of his ankles wrapped in cord caught hard against each other, digging at the flesh. The metal handcuffs on his wrists, set too tight for him, pressed on the veins and arteries. Tape, adhesive and broad, was across his mouth, forcing him to breathe through his nose, reducing any sounds he could make to a jumbled, incomprehensible moan. One man had trussed him swiftly before the chloroform had gone to be replaced by the desperate passiveness of terror in an alien surrounding. And they'd hooded him, reducing his horizons to the limited things he could touch and smell. The hood was cool and damp as if it had spent the night in the grass, been subject to the light dew and retrieved before the coming of the drying warmth of the early sun. Because of the handcuffs behind his back he lay on his right side where the undulations of the road surface caused his shoulder to impact through the sacking against the ribbed metal floor.

They seemed to move at a constant speed as if far from the reach of traffic lights and road junctions, and many times Harrison heard the whine of overtaking engines, and occasionally the van shuddered as if under strain and pulled out to the left. Just once they stopped, for a short time, and he heard voices, a rapid exchange, before the van was moving again, riding through its gears, getting under way and back to the undisturbed progress. He thought about and conjured a route along the Raccordo Annulare with its festoons of white and pink oleander between the central crash barrier, and imagined the halt must have been at the toll gate for entry to an autostrada. Could be north on the Florence road, or west for L'Aquila and the Adriatic coast, or south for Naples. Could be any bloody direction, any road the animals wanted to use. He'd thought he'd been clever and superior in his intellect to make the calculations, and then came the wave of antipathy, carried on the wing. What did it matter which direction they took? It was a futile and petty exercise, because the control of his destiny was removed, turning him into a bloody vegetable. Anger surfaced for the first time, and spent itself straining against the ankle cords, striving to bite with his teeth against the tape across his mouth. It created a force and a power that struggled even as the tears rose and welled. In one convulsion, one final effort to win even the minimum of freedom for any of his limbs, he arched his back, forced his muscles.

Couldn't shift. Couldn't move. Couldn't change anything.

Pack it in, Geoffrey, you're being bloody pathetic.

Once more?

Forget it. They don't come with machine-guns and chloroform and then find, surprise, surprise, that they don't know how to tie knots.

Chapter Three

The immediate sense of survival was uppermost now in the mind of Giancarlo.

It was the instinct of the stoat or the weasel that has lost its mate and must abandon its den, move on, but has no notion of where to go, only that it must creep stealthily away from the scene of its enemies' vengeance. He wanted to run, to outstrip the pedestrians who cluttered and barred the pavements, but his training won out. He did not hurry. He strolled, because he must blend, must forsake the identity bestowed on him by the P38.

The noise and confusion and shouting of the beginning of a new day swamped him. The hooting of impatient motorists. The crashing intrusion of the alimentari shutters rising in their doorways and windows to display the cheese and hams and tins and bottles. The arguments that spilled from the bars. Confident, secure sounds, belonging and with a right to be there, swarming around Giancarlo. The boy tried to shut inside himself his concentration and avoid the cancer of these people that swept and surged past him. He belonged to no part of them.

Since the NAP had drifted into existence in the

early nineteen-seventies, coalesced from a meeting of minds and aspirations to an organization, it had derived its principal security from the cell system. Nothing new, nothing revolutionary in that; laid down by Mao and Ho and Guevara. Standard in the theoretical treatises. Separated in their cells the members had no need for the identity of other names, for the location of other safe houses. It was essential procedure, and when one was taken, then the wound to the movement could be swiftly cauterized. Franca was their cell leader. She alone knew the hidden places where ammunition and materials were stored, the telephone numbers of the policy committee, and the lists of addresses. She had not shared with Enrico, much less with the boy, the probationer, because neither required such information.

He could not go back to his previous flat where he had lived with a girl and two boys as that had been closed and abandoned. He could not tour the cars and streets of Pietralata behind the Tiburtina station and ask for them by name; he wouldn't know where to begin, and who to ask. It made him shudder as he walked, the depths of the isolation in which the movement had so successfully cloaked him.

Where among the streaming, scrambling crowds that passed on either side of him did he find the nod and handshake of recognition? It was frightening to the boy because without Franca he was truly alone. Storm clouds rising, sails full, rudder flapping, and the rocks high and sharp and waiting.

Giancarlo Battestini, nineteen years old.

Short and without weight, a physical nonentity. A

body that looked perpetually starved, a face that seemed forever hungry, a boy that a woman would want to take in and fatten because she would fear that unless she hurried he might wither and fade. Dark hair above the growth of his cheeks that was curled and untidy. A sallow, wan complexion as if the sun had not sought him out, had avoided the lustreless skin. Acne spots at his chin and the sides of his mouth that were red and angry against the surrounding flesh and to which his fingers moved with embarrassed frequency. The pale and puckered line across the bridge of his nose that deviated on across the upper cheekbone under his right eye was his major distinguishing mark. He had the polizia of the Primo Celere to thank for the scar, the baton charge across the Ponte Garibaldi when the boy had slipped in headlong flight and turned his ankle. He had been a student then, enrolled two terms at the University of Rome, choosing the study of psychology for no better reason than that the course was a long one and his father could pay for four years of education. And what else was there to do?

The University with its bulging inefficiency had seemed to Giancarlo a paradise of liberation. Lectures too clogged to attend unless you took a seat or standing place a full hour before the professor came. Tutorials that were late or cancelled. Exams that were postponed. A hostel within walking distance in the Viale Regina Elena where the talk was long and bold and brave.

Heady battles they had fought around the University that winter. The Autonomia in the van, they had driven the polizia back from the front façade of arches and across the street to their trucks. They had expelled by force Luciano Lama, the big union man of the PCI, who had come to talk to them on moderation and conformity and responsibility; thrown him out, the turncoat communist in his suit and polished shoes. Six hundred formed the core of the Autonomia, the separatists, and Giancarlo had first hung round their fringe, then attended their meetings and finally sidled towards the leaders and stammered his pledge of support. Warm acceptance had followed. A paradise indeed to the boy from the seaside at Pescara where his father owned a shop and carried a stock of fine cotton dresses and blouses and skirts in summer, and wool and leather and suede in winter.

Hit and run. Strike and retreat. The tactical battles of the Autonomia were in the name of repression in Argentina, the deaths in Stamheim of comrades Baader and Raspe and Enselin, the changing of the curriculum. No long searches for cause and justification. Hurt the polizia and the carabinieri, the forces of the new fascism. Goad them into retaliatory dashes from the wide streets that were safe to the narrow maze of centro storico where the Molotovs and the P38s could score and wound. Formidable the polizia looked, with their white bullet-proof tunics lolling to their knees and their stovepipe face masks behind which they felt a false invulnerability. But they could not run in their new and expensive equipment, could only fire the gas and beat the clubs on the plastic shields. They were loath to follow the kids, the Pied Pipers, when the range of the pistols and the petrol diminished.

A scarf tight across his face for protection both from press photographs and the gas, Giancarlo had never before experienced such orgasmic, pained excitement as when he had sprinted forward on the bridge and launched the bottle with its litre of petrol and smouldering rag at the Primo Celere huddled behind their armoured jeep. A shriek of noise had erupted as the bottle splintered. The flames scattered. There was a roar of approval from behind as the boy stood his ground in defiance while the gas shells flourished about him. Then the retaliation. Twenty of them running, and Giancarlo had turned for his escape. The desperate, terrifying moment when the ground was rising, space under his feet, control lost, and in his ears the drumming of the boots that were in pursuit. His hands covering his head were pulled away as they put the baton in, and there was blood cool across his face and sweet in his mouth, and blows to the leg, kicks to the belly. Voices from the south, from the peasant south, from the servants of the Democrazia Cristiana, from the workers who had been bought and were too stupid to know it.

Two months in the Regina Coeli gaol awaiting his court appearance.

Seven months' imprisonment for throwing the Molotov to be served in the Queen of Heaven.

A whore of a place, that gaol. Intolerable heat and stench through that first summer when he had bunked in a cell with two others. Devoid of draught and privacy, assimilated into a world of homosexuality, thieving, deprivation. Food inedible, boredom impossible, company illiterate. Hatred and loathing bit deep in the boy when he was the guest of the Queen of Heaven. Hatred and loathing of those who had put him there, of the polizia who had clubbed him and spat in his face in the truck

53

and laughed in their dialect at the little, humbled *intellettuale*.

Giancarlo sought his counterstrike and found the potential for revenge in the top-floor cells of the 'B' Wing where the men of the Nuclei Armati Proletaria were incarcerated, some on remand, some sentenced. They could read in the boy's eyes and in the twist of his lower lip that here was a progeny that could be useful and exploited. He learned in those heated, sweating cells the theory and the practice, the expertise and the strategy of urban guerrilla conflict. A new recruit, a new volunteer. The men gave him diagrams to memorize of the mechanism of weapons, lectured him in the study of concealment and ambush, droned at him of the politics of their struggle, hectored him with the case histories of corruption and malpractice in government and capitalist business. These men would not see the fruits of their work but took comfort that they had found one so malleable, so supple to their will. They were pleased with what they saw. Word of his friendship spread along the landings of his own wing. The homosexuals did not sidle close and flash their hands at his genitals, the thieves left undisturbed the bag under his bunk where he kept his few personal possessions, the Agenti did not bully.

In the months in gaol he passed from the student of casual and fashionable protest to the political militant.

His parents never visited him in the Queen of Heaven. He had not seen them since they had stood at the back of the court, half masked from his sight by the guard's shoulders. Anger on his father's face, tears making the mascara run on his mother's cheeks. His father wore a Sunday suit, his mother dressed in a black coat as if that would impress the magistrate. The chains on his wrists had been long and loose, and they gave him the opportunity to raise his right arm, clenched fist, the salute of the left, the gesture of the fighter. Screw them. Give them something to think on when they took the autostrada back across the mountains to Pescara. And his picture would be in the Adriatic paper and would be seen by the ladies who came to buy from the shop and they would whisper and titter behind their hands. In all his time in the gaol he received only one letter, written in the spider hand of his brother Fabrizio, a graduate lawyer and five years his elder. There was a room for him at home, Mama still kept his bedroom as it had been before he had gone to Rome. Papa would find work for him. There could be a new start, he would be forgiven. Methodically Giancarlo had torn the single sheet of notepaper into many pieces that flaked to the cell floor.

When the time came for Giancarlo's release he was clear on the instructions that had been given him from the men in 'B' Wing. He had walked out through the steel gates and on to the Lungotevere and not looked back at the crumbling plaster of the high ochre-stained walls. The car was waiting as he had been told it would be and a girl had moved across the back seat to make room for him. First names they called themselves by, and they took him for a coffee and poured a measure of Scotch whisky into the foaming milk of the cappuccino and brought him cigarettes that were imported and expensive.

Half a year now of being hunted, half a year of

running and caution and care, and he had wondered what was the life expectancy of freedom, thought of how long his wings would stay unclipped by cell bars and locked doors.

Once he had been in the same flat as the one they called the Chief, had seen his profile through an opened door, bushy-bearded, short, vital in the eyes and mouth – the Chief who stayed now on the island prison of Asinara and who they said had been betrayed.

Once he had strayed into the bedroom of a covo carrying the cigarettes he had been sent to buy, looking for the man who had despatched him, and recognized the sleeping form of the one they said was expert with explosives. He too, they said, had been betrayed to a life sentence on the island.

Once he had been taken to stand for a moment on the steps of a church where Antonio La Muscio and Mia Vianale had sat and eaten plums on a summer evening, and he now in his grave with half a carabinieri magazine to put him there, and the fruit unfinished, and La Vianale rotting in the gaol at Messina.

Hard and dangerous times, only recently made safer by the skill and calm of Franca.

But as the net grew closer, shrinking around the group, Franca had disowned the safety of inactivity.

'Two hundred and fifty political prisoners of the left in the gaols, and they believe we are close to the moment of our destruction, that is what they say on the RAI, that is what they say at the DC congress. So we must fight, demonstrate beyond their concealment that we are not crushed, not neutered.'

Franca did not talk in the slogans of the kids of his

first covo. She had no use for the parrot words of 'enemies of the proletariat', the 'forces of repression', 'capitalist exploitation'. It confused the boy because they had become a part of his life, a habit of his tongue, cemented to his vocabulary. Franca vented her anger without words, displayed her dedication with the squeezed, arctic index finger of her right hand. Three bedridden victims in the Policlinico, another in a private room of the nursing home on the Trionfale, they were her vengeance – men who might never walk again with freedom, would not run with their children, and one among them who would not sleep with and satisfy his wife.

Inevitable that it must end. The risks were too great, the pace too heady, the struggle unequal.

Giancarlo crossed a road, not looking for the cars, nor for the green-lit 'Avanti' sign, not hearing the shriek of the brakes, ignorant of the bellowed insult. Perhaps he would have brought her flowers that evening. Perhaps he would have gone to the piazza and bought from the gypsy woman some violets, or a sprig of pansies. Nothing gaudy, nothing that would win a sneer from her. Simple flowers from the fields to make her smile and her face soften, to erase the harshness of her mouth that he had first seen as she walked from the shooting of the personnel officer.

But flowers would not help her now, not from the boy who had declined to step forward, who had walked away.

There was a hunger already in his stomach and little chance to appease it. His wallet still lay in the flat on the small table beside his unused bed. There was some loose change in his hip pocket and the mini-assegni notes that were worth not more than a hundred and a hundred and fifty lire apiece. In all he had enough for a bowl of pasta or a sandwich, and a coffee or a beer, and after that – nothing. He must keep two hundred lire for an afternoon paper when they came on the news stands – *Paese Sera* or *Momento Sera*. Meanwhile his wallet was in the flat. His wallet that he touched and handled through the day, held with his finger-tips, the contour whorls that were only his own and that the police finger-print dust would find and feed to the files. They had taken his fingerprints months back in the police station after his arrest.

They will have your name by the afternoon, Giancarlo, and your photograph. All they want about you they will have.

Time to begin to think again, to throw off the weight of depression and self-examination. Stupid bastard, take a hold. Behave like a man of the NAP. Save yourself and survive.

Where to start?

The University.

In the vacation, in the summer? When there is no-one there?

Where else? Where else do you go to, Giancarlo? Home to Mama, to tell her it was all a mistake, that you met bad people . . . ?

Perhaps there would be someone at the University.

The University offered him the best chance of a bed with no questions asked among the students of the Autonomia whom he had known many months before. He had not been there since his release and he would have to exercise the utmost care as he approached the faculties. The campus was heavy with informers and policemen who carried books and mingled. But if he could find the right boys, then they would hide him, and they would respect him because he had graduated from the sit-ins and the lock-ins and the Molotovs to the real war of the fully fledged, of the men. They would look after him at the University.

A long walk it would be, across the wide Ponte Flaminio, through the Parioli, along the tree-lined ribbon of the Viale Regina Margherita. With the decision taken and his mind clearing he quickened his step. It was a risk to go that far and his name and description and his clothing would soon be radioed to the polizia who cruised and watched over the city, but there were no alternatives.

Because he worked directly to the Minister of the Interior, Francesco Vellosi's office was on the second floor of the lowering grey stonework of the Viminale. His subordinates were found either a kilometre away at the Questura, or far to the west in the Criminalpol building at EUR. But the capo of the Squadra Anti-Terrorismo was required to be close to the seat of power, just down the corridor from it, which served to emphasize the recognition of the threat to the country posed by the rash of urban guerrilla groups. A fine room he occupied, reached through high double doors of polished wood, with an ornate ceiling from which hung electric bulbs set in a shivering chandelier of light, oil paintings on the walls, a wide desk with an inlaid leather top, easy chairs for the visitors, a coffee table for magazines and ashtrays, and a signed photograph of the President between the tall twin windows. Francesco Vellosi, thirty years in the police, detested the room, and would have given much to have exchanged the brilliance of the surroundings for a shirt-sleeves working area. The room got the sun in the afternoons but on this July morning the brightness had not yet reached it.

The radio telephone in his armour-plated car had warned Vellosi when mid-way between his bachelor flat and place of work that his men had met with a major and significant success that morning, and waiting for him when he bustled into the office had been the initial incident report and photostats of the files held on Franca Tantardini and Enrico Panicucci.

Vellosi gutted the paperwork with enthusiasm. A bad winter and spring they had had, built on the depressive foundation of the loss the previous year of Aldo Moro. There had been arrests, some significant, some worthless, but the plague of bombings and shootings had kept up its headlong pace, prompting the disquiet of the Deputies in the Chamber of the Democrazia Cristiana, the ridicule of the newspapers, and the perpetual demand of his Minister for solutions. Always they came to Vellosi, hurrying in pursuit of the news of a fresh outrage. He was long tired of trying to find the politician or the senior civil servant who would take responsibility for what he called the necessary methods, the hard and ruthless crackdown that he believed essential; he was still looking for his man.

Here at last was good news, and he would issue his own order that the photographers should have a good look at the Tantardini woman. The national habit of self-denigration went too deep, and it was good when the opportunity presented itself to boast a little and swagger with success.

A tall, heavily built boar of a man, the roughness of his figure softened by the cut of his jacket, the elegance of his silk tie, Vellosi shouted acknowledgement across the room of the light tap at his door. The men who entered the presence were from a different caste. Two in tattered suede boots. Two in canvas training shoes. Faded jeans. A variety of T-shirt colours. An absence of razors. Hard men whose faces seemed relaxed while the eyes were ever alert and alive and bright. Vellosi's lions, the men who fought the war far below the surface of the city's life. The sewer rats, because that was where they had to exist if they were to find the rodent pests.

The four eased a careful way across the thick carpet, and when he gestured to them, sat with care on the deep, comfortable chairs. They were the officers of the squad that had taken the woman, destroyed the animal Panicucci, and they had come to receive their plaudits, tell at first hand of the exploit, and bring a little solace to the days of Vellosi in the Viminale.

He wriggled with pleasure in his seat as the work of the morning was recounted. Nothing omitted, nothing spared, so that he could savour and live in his mind the moment when Panicucci and the woman had emerged from the Post. As it should be, and he'd wheel them in to shake the hand of the Minister and blunt the back-stab knives that were always honing for him. He limited himself to the briefest of interruptions, preferring to let the steady flow of the story bathe him in the triumph of his squad.

The telephone broke into the recital.

Vellosi's face showed his annoyance at the interference – the annoyance of a man who hopes to make it and is on the couch with his girl when the doorbell sounds. He waved his hand to halt the flow; he would return to it as soon as the business of the call was despatched. It was the Questura.

Had Vellosi's men been certain when they took the woman that there was not another boy with her? Had they missed one?

The covo had been found, the address taken from the telephone slip just paid by the Tantardini woman. The polizia had visited the flat and found there the clothes of another boy, far too small to be those of Panicucci. There was a woman on the ground floor of the block, sick, and from the moment she was dressed in the morning she would sit and watch from her window the passing street; when the ragazzi drove their car from the garage there were always three, and there were three that morning. Fingerprinting had begun, there was another set and fresh, not to be confused with Tantardini's and Panicucci's. The polizia had been careful to check with the woman at the window the time of the departure of the car from the block and compare it with the timing of the incident at the Post. It was their opinion that there had been no time for a substantial deviation to drop off a second male.

A cold sponge was squeezed over Vellosi.

'Have you a description of this second man?'

'The woman says he is not a man, just a boy really. There are many identity cards in the flat, one of the photographs may be genuine, but we are working on a photo-fit now. Your own people are there now, no doubt they will brief you. We think the boy is eighteen, perhaps nineteen. We thought you would like to know.'

'You are very kind,' Vellosi said quietly, then hammered the telephone down.

He ran his eyes over the men in front of him, brought them sitting upright and awkward on the edge of their seats.

'We missed one.' Spoken with coldness, the pleasure eroded from the session.

'There was no-one else at the Post. The car had no driver waiting in it, and only the two came out. They were well clear of the doorway when we moved.' The defensive, bridling argument came from a man who an hour earlier had faced the barrel of a Beretta, who had out-thought, out-manoeuvred his opponent and fired for his own survival.

'Three came from the flat. The car went straight to the Post.'

The inquisition was resented. 'He was not there when we came. And after the shooting some of our people watched the crowd, as is standard. Nobody ran from the scene.'

Vellosi shrugged, resigned. Like eels, these people. Always one of them wriggled away, slipped through the finest meshes. Always one of a group escaped, so that you could never cut off the head and know that the body was beyond another spawning. 'He is very young, this one that we have lost.'

Three of the men stayed silent, peeved that the moment of accolade had turned to recrimination. The fourth spoke up, undaunted by his superior's grimness. 'If it is a boy, then it will have been her runner, there to fetch and carry for her, and to serve

63

in the whore's bed. Always she has one like that. Panicucci she did not use, only the young ones she liked. It is well known in the NAP.'

'If you are right, it is not a great loss.'

'It is an irritation, nothing more. The fat cat we have, the gorilla we have killed; that the flea is out is only a nuisance.'

It was not yet ten o'clock and there were smiles as Vellosi produced the bottle from the lower drawer of his desk, and then reached again for the small cut-glass tumblers. It was too early for champagne but Scotch was right. The brat had broken the pattern of perfection, like a summer picnic when it rains and the tablecloth must be scooped up, but the best of the day had gone before.

Only a nuisance, only an irritation, the missing of the boy.

He knew they had been travelling many hours because the van floor on which he lay was warmed by the outside sun even through the layer of sacking. The air around Geoffrey Harrison was thick, tasting of petrol fumes, pricking against his skin as if all the cool and freshness of the morning's start had been expelled, thrust out. It was painfully hot, and under the weight of the hood over his head he had sometimes begun to pant for air, with accompanying hallucinations that his lungs might not cope, that he might suffocate in the dark around him. Occasionally he heard two slight voices in conversation but the words, even had he been able to understand them, were muffled by the engine noise. Two different tones, that was all he could distinguish. And they talked infrequently, the two men riding in the seats

64

in front. There were long periods of quiet between them and then a brief flurry of chatter as if something they passed took their fancy, attracted their eyes.

The motion of the van was constant, its progress uneventful, releasing him to his thoughts. It was as if he were a package of freight being transported to a far destination by two men who had neither interest nor concern in him and thought only of their delivery time.

In the *Daily News* and the *Daily American* and the Italian papers that he struggled with in the office Harrison had read many times of the techniques practised by the flourishing Italian kidnap gangs. In the bar of the Olgiata Golf Club, little America, little Mid-West, where there were Tom Collins and Bourbon mixes, he had joined the drift of conversation when the foreigners had talked of the Italian disease. Different setting, different values; easy then to relate all sickness to the bloody inefficiency of Italians, and what else could you expect when you were half way to the Middle East. Well down the road to Damascus here, right? Wasn't it a scandal, the transatlantic executives would say, that a fellow could get picked off the street and have to cough up a million dollars, however many noughts that was in lire, to get himself back to his wife and kids? And wasn't it about time that something was done about it? Couldn't happen at home, of course – not in London, not in Los Angeles . . . not in Birmingham, not in Boston. And there'd always be one there, elbow at the bar and face pulled with authority, to drop his voice beneath the reach of the Italian members, and lean forward and whisper, 'Wouldn't happen if old Musso was running the place. And it's what they need again. A damn great shock up the ass, and someone like Musso to give it to them. Not exactly Musso, because he was an idiot, but someone with a damn great stick.' Simple answers, more drinks, and none of them had an idea. He wondered whether they'd remember him: young Harrison, quite a junior fellow, didn't make it up this way that often, always hanging on the edge of a chat, and a wife with bright lipstick. Just a drinking member.

Perhaps you're lucky, Geoffrey, perhaps you're lucky you didn't struggle. You put up a bit of a show, but not much. Just enough for vague self-respect. Remember the picture in the paper of the man from Milan, the man who'd fought back and mixed it. Stone dead in a box, with the wife in black and the kids holding her hands walking behind. At least you're bloody alive. Because they don't muck about, these people; they're not governed by Queensberry or any other set of rules. Hard, vicious bastards. Remember the black-and-white images on the television in the living-room; the body of little Christina, eighteen years old, being dragged out of the rubbish tip and the ransom had been paid. Remember the race-course king; he made the front pages, trussed like a chicken and a hood on him, just like you are now except that he had a hunk of cement to weight him down in the lake near Como. Remember the boy in the village in Calabria with his ear sliced away to encourage his father to dig deeper into the family savings . . .

Horrible bastards.

Not like anything those stupid sods in the bar would know about when they came off their nine holes. All a bit of a joke over a pre-lunch gin, a bit of a chuckle. Something local that didn't affect foreigners. They should have seen them for themselves, those bloody faces under the stockings, the way the guns came, and the hammer. That would have splashed the tonic round a bit, would have stifled all the rectitude, the platitudes. They'd never bloody laugh again, those sods in the bar, not if they saw that crowd coming at them. Remember the Telegiornale, Geoffrey, what happens to the Italian families. Drawn curtains, shuttered windows, people hurrying by on the pavement below, not wishing to look in as if that would somehow involve them with a family that flew the yellow flag of quarantine. The face of a child or a mother in the doorway who looked for support and sympathy and found none; the humble car of the priest pulling up on the pavement and scattering the waiting photographers. Geoffrey knew the pictures, knew the way the story was chronicled on the first day and never mentioned again afterwards until the moment of conclusion. Stale in twenty-four hours.

Pray God there isn't some pompous fool in there.

What do you mean?

Well, some stupid ass with a good lunch inside him and letters after his name who wants to talk about the principle of paying.

What do you mean?

Well, if some ape says it's not right to pay, that you have to stand up to these people, that if you give way now what do you do next time.

They wouldn't say that, would they, not really say that?

They're not where you are, Geoffrey. They're in a

Chapter Four

His Excellency the Ambassador of Her Britannic Majesty, who had known the tap of her sword on his right shoulder and had kissed her hand and valued his audience, was a man who admired discipline of action, and protocol of approach. He had not disguised his distaste at what he regarded as the breathy intervention of young Charlesworth when he was only one foot out of his official burnished transport. He had been short with his First Secretary, had permitted only the briefest of résumés and failed to raise his eyebrows in either shock or astonishment. And as he had marched away, smiling at the doorman, with Charlesworth snapping like a lap dog at his heels, he had suggested that something on paper by lunchtime would satisfy his requirements for information.

As he strode down the drive to the security lodge, Charlesworth cursed himself for his flustered account, for his failure to interest his superior, regretting that he had allowed himself to be put down as a bubbling child is by an overburdened parent. He recalled that the Ambassador was hosting a luncheon-party that day; the newly appointed

Foreign Minister would be at his right hand, the guest of honour. Present would be the senior members of the diplomatic corps, a smattering of ranking civil servants, the best bone china and the silverware out from the cupboard. The Ambassador had his priorities, Charlesworth growled to himself. The soup shouldn't be too salted, the plates must be warm, the wine chilled, the conversation clever. He had too much on his mind to worry about the fears of a hysterical woman, and a man trussed and perhaps half dead who was experiencing the greatest degree of terror he had known in his life. He'd be far too busy for such sordidness, and a piece of paper with some aptly chosen words presented before the sherry flowed would be sufficient.

Charlesworth dived out into the road beyond the regimented railings of the Embassy, scanning the traffic that burst through the arches of the ancient reddened brick city wall. Getting a taxi would need the luck of old Jupiter. But luck was with him, the yellow Fiat snaking to the pavement, and he waved frantically and hurried towards its stopping point. He saw the face in the back, equal shades of mauve and pink. 'Buster' Henderson; Military Cross in Korea God knows how many years ago and for doing something nobody sane would have dreamed of; military attaché; half-colonel; always took a cab in, and one home in the afternoon. Charlesworth didn't know how he could afford it, not that and the gin as well.

'In a hurry, young man?' Charlesworth detested the way the older staff regarded him as a juvenile. 'Flap on, is there? Eyeties declared war on us . . . ?' A boom of laughter. Must have been the life and soul of some gory cavalry mess east of the Rhine.

'One of our people has been kidnapped this morning.'

'One of the Embassy chaps?' Henderson was waiting for the change from his 10,000-lire note.

'No, it's not the end of the world, not one of ours. It's a businessman, a fellow who works out here. I've to get up to his wife.'

'Poor bastard,' said Henderson quietly. His wallet was open, the notes being carefully put away in order of value, damn-all of a tip. 'Poor devil, rather him . . .'

'Could be rather a shambles for us. It's the first time a foreigner has been lifted. Well, only the Getty boy, and that was different, I suppose.'

Henderson held the door open for Charlesworth. 'You'll be handling our end, eh? Well, if you get a bit overwhelmed, give us a shout. Damn-all I have to worry about at the moment, diary's empty as a larder these next three days. Don't hang about if you want a hand, if you want to talk it over.'

'Thank you . . . thank you very much. It's most kind . . . Buster.'

Charlesworth had never called him that before, never really had a conversation with the army officer on any more substantive subject than whether it would rain on QBP day, whether they'd have to retire to the marquee for the annual Queen's Birthday Party celebrations. Silly little thing, the offer of help, but he was grateful, grateful because he was stepping on stones that he did not know.

'Poor devil, rather him . . .' Charlesworth heard half-colonel 'Buster' Henderson mutter again as he closed the taxi-door on himself.

*   *   *

He walked in what shade he could find, seeking out the places where the sun was denied sight of the pavements by the towering blocks of flats flanking the Regina Margherita. Unable now to control the speed of his legs as they pumped a way along the uneven flagstones, hurrying when he knew he should be calm, because the coolness he had first sought to impose on himself was disappearing, slipping from his grasp. Giancarlo was feeling the stress and lead weight of the fugitive.

Not that the shade offered him solace. The stinking, brutalizing heat of the morning penetrated the air, broke open his white skin and thrust out the carousing sweat rivers that saturated his few clothes, soaking and irritating him. No wind down at street level. Just the furnace and the car exhausts, nothing to bluster across his face and limbs. He tramped on for the sanctuary of the University, where a face might be familiar, where the environs would be known, where there would be an end to the perpetual swinging of his head for a first glimpse of the coasting police cars. It was a new experience for Giancarlo. Never before had he known the feeling of being hunted, of being loose and adrift from the companionship of the group, of being cast outside the protective womb of the NAP.

When Giancarlo had walked at the side of Franca Tantardini, the NAP had seemed to him a great and powerful organization. Limitless authority and potential gushed when he had been close to her, and the words of victory and success and triumph had cascaded from her tongue. Now the sheen of safety was stripped from him and Enrico was dead, washing his face in his own blood, and Franca taken. He fled towards the reassurance of the nursery, the safety of the crèche, to the University.

Tired legs, sore feet, a heaving chest, the classic symptoms of flight. He turned left towards the Piazza Giorgio Fabrizio, then right into the Viale del Policlinico. He stumbled from tiredness as he passed the huge, drawn-out complex of the hospital. The signs of PRONTO SOCCORSO that guided the racing, siren-loud ambulances to where they should bring their emergencies were on his right. Where they brought Franca's victims. Where they deposited the men with the gunshot wounds for the first immediate life-saving operation to counter the work of the P38. The boy saw the men who waited in their short white coats and the nurses in their belted dresses who lounged under the trees alert for the screaming of the ambulance approach that would send them scurrying in preparation to Casualty Reception.

Going past the Policlinico, Giancarlo knew with the sureness of the first lightning flash in a storm why they would hate him, track him, spend a lifetime edging towards his back. No forgiveness, no charity, not while men lay in pain on the metal bedframes of the Policlinico, and shouted in the night for their wives. A great army they would bring against him, and a mind with a limitless and unbroken memory.

A boy who was as nothing. Devoid of possessions, importance, status. Armed with a P38 and a magazine of eight shells.

Devoid of plan and programme and blueprint.

Armed with a detestation of cruel force against the system that rallied now to crush him.

73

Bereft of friendship and accomplices and the strength of a leader to guide.

Armed with the love of a girl who had taken him into herself. Armed with the love of Franca Tantardini. For she must have loved him, she must have wanted him, Giancarlo Battestini, or he would not have known her bed and her warmth and her murmurs and her fingers. If it took a week or a month or a year, he would take her from them. Repossess her freedom, the freedom of the bird to escape the cage. Because she had loved him.

Dwarfing the boy were the great white stone walls and archway of the University. Designed for immortality, designed to stand for a thousand years as proof to a grateful worker class of the power wielded by the black shirt and the leather boot. Giancarlo took in the daubed slogans of the paint spray aerosols, bright colours of graffiti that disfigured the impression of omnipotence, but only as high as a student's arm could rise. Above the reach of the protester was the clean-cut stone of the rejected regime. The slogans of the Autonomia were here at shoulder height. The painted outline of the closed fist with the first and second fingers extended – the P trent'otto. Here were daubed the cries of hate against the Ministers of government, the parties of democracy, the polizia, the carabinieri, the borghese. He had arrived at the place where succour might be found.

Stretching away in front of him was the wide avenue between the Science and Medical Faculties and the Administration buildings. Many doors were closed, many windows shuttered, because the academic year and examinations had terminated six weeks earlier. But there would be some students here, those who had taken a cause and rejected the cloying parental hand over the family holiday, they would have stayed. Giancarlo broke into a run. He lifted the weariness from his legs, lengthened his stride, till he was sprinting down the gentle hill.

The taxi, its driver displaying caution rare in his vocation, nudged up the hill at a crawl and rounded the three police cars straddled in front of the Mercedes. Charlesworth saw the driver's side window breached and shattered, frozen glass glittering in the gravel surface of the road.

The polizia, in blue and mauve trousers with the thin maroon cord astride their thighs and open blue shirts and caps pushed back on their foreheads, were working round the smitten vehicle. They dabbed on fingerprint dust and a tin was beside them in which plaster glistened wetly and which would be used if the impression of a tyre grip needed recording. It was too warm for the polizia to move with energy and their inertia was augmented by the very familiarity of the scene. There was nothing new, the scene of crime procedures for a kidnap. As the taxi circumvented the blockage, Charlesworth saw two men in civilian suits, and they were the only ones that mattered. Only two. Not the young boys in their crumpled uniforms recruited from the Mezzo Giorno who knew less of crime than a Neapolitan pickpocket or a Milanese burglar and wore the uniform because it was the only escape from the region of unemployment. Just two, the trained ones who took the privilege of wearing their own clothes, enough to make him heave and throw up. Dear old Carboni, with his courtesy and his compromise, who had promised nothing, he knew the limitations of his force. And why should they bust a gut – because the man who'd been lifted had a blue passport with a lion rampant and English scroll inside the front flap? Carboni had marked Charlesworth's card, said there should be a payout, that they should get the misery over, forget the games. So what's in it for a policeman, standing on his big flat feet, when more money will be paid than he'll see in a lifetime, and it won't be missed, won't be noticed, and his own chief says that's the way to do business?

He paid the driver, stepped out of the taxi and looked around him.

A wide street on a sloping hill. Flats which owned areas of neat lawn in front and flower-bushes that had been tended and cropped and watered that morning by the porters. Blocks of five floors with deep terraces and canvas awnings and jungles of foliage. The ladies' cars parked bumper to bumper; the little runabout city motors. Dust floated softly down onto Charlesworth's jacket and the maid in the starched apron stared him out as she shook her mop. Not much poverty here, not much malaise from the economic crisis, not up here on the hill. And there was the reaction to the affluence for him to see, provided by those who crept up the slope under cover of night: paint-sprayed swastikas, the daubed MORTE AL FASCISTI that could never be scrubbed from the marble veneer surfaces.

Didn't do badly for their people, the old multinationals. If International Chemical Holdings had put their man in here, then they were solvent, they had no liquidity problems. And the bastards would have known that, or Geoffrey Harrison would be sitting at his desk right now, clobbering his secretary for the lateness of the post, straightening his tie for his next appointment. Money here, and plenty of it, and these people knew where to sniff the air for it, where to strike, where the dividend was assured.

Charlesworth walked into the hallway of the block, paused at the porter's nook where a man with a saddened and troubled face sat, mentioned the name and was told which floor. A slow lift creaked and swayed upwards. Two policemen lolled against the wall beside the door of the flat. They straightened when they saw the diplomat, not dramatically but enough to swing the holstered pistols that hung from waistbelts. Charlesworth said nothing, merely nodded, and pressed the bell.

Soft, slippered feet shuffled to the door. An age passed while four sets of locks were unfastened. The door opened an inch and a half, as far as a chain would allow. Like a bloody fortress, he thought. But they all lived like that on the hill and damn-all good it did them when the vultures began to circle. It was dark inside and he could see nothing through the gap.

'Who is it?' A small voice, invisible and inanimate.

'It's Charlesworth, Michael Charlesworth. From the Embassy.'

A pause, and then the door was closed. He heard the button on the end of the chain being withdrawn from its socket. The door opened again, not extravagantly, but sufficient to admit him.

'I'm Violet Harrison. Thank you for coming.'

He turned, almost startled, two steps inside the hall, as if he had not expected the voice to materialize from behind – a quick movement that betrayed his unease. She came out of the shadows and her hand took his elbow and manoeuvred him towards the living-room where the blinds were drawn and the low table lights lit. He followed meekly behind the tented swirl of her trailing cotton dressing-gown with the big flowers embroidered across the shapes of her back and her buttocks and legs. He stole a glance at the silhouette against a light and dug his nails into the palm of a hand. You'd have thought she'd have dressed by now, on a morning like this, with a bloody deluge of visitors about to come tripping in. You'd have thought the woman would put some clothes on.

He saw her the first time when she reached her chair and angled her face at him. She might not have dressed but she'd made her face, had worked at it long enough to give the tears scope to smudge and spoil her efforts. She would have been crying from the time he telephoned. The eyelids were puffy and bulging, red above the dark broad painted eye shadow. A small tight-turned nose that had taken the sun and the freckles offset her cheeks that were smooth and bronzed. Attractive but not remarkable. Well shaped but not beautiful. His eyes flickered over her, unwilling but compelled, and she gazed back at him, no hint of embarrassment. Charlesworth looked away, the blush rising in him. Been caught like a schoolboy hadn't he? Been seen peering in the Soho bookshop windows during school holidays. Been noticed ogling a woman who wore a sheer nightdress and a light cotton wrap.

'I'm very sorry for what has happened, Mrs Harrison,' he said.

'Would you like some coffee . . . there's only instant.'

'You're very kind, but no. Thank you.'

'There's tea, I can make a cup.' A small, far voice.

'No, thanks. Thank you again, but I won't. Would you like me to put the kettle on for you? Can I make you some tea?'

'I don't want any tea. Would you like a cigarette?' Still staring at his eyes, raking and examining them.

'It's very nice of you, but I don't. I don't smoke.' He felt he should apologize because he didn't want Nescafé, didn't want teabags, didn't want a cigarette.

She sat down in an armchair, flanked by the tables that carried last night's glasses and last night's coffee cups, with a flurry of shin and knee glimpsing out. He followed into a chair across the central rug, felt himself going down, slipping away, falling into far-settling cushions, the sort that you drown in and then forever feel ill at ease with because you're too low and can't dominate the conversation, and your nose is half way to the carpet. She was still looking into him, boring and penetrating.

'Mrs Harrison, first I should tell you who I am. I have responsibility for political affairs at the Embassy, but I also double on matters affecting the police, relations between the British community in Rome and the Italian police. Those, that is, that aren't covered by the Consular Department . . .' Come on, Charlesworth, you're not doing your own testimonial; not applying for a job either. '. . . So I was called this morning by a fellow called Carboni, he's one of the bigger men at the Questura. There wasn't very much known then, it was just a few minutes after your husband had been seized. Dr Carboni gave me a solemn assurance that everything possible was being done to secure your husband's early release.'

'And that's bugger all,' she said slowly and with deliberation.

Charlesworth rocked back, rode it, but the blow had done damage, confused and deflected what was building in his mind. 'I can only repeat . . .' He hesitated. They didn't use that sort of language, the Embassy secretaries and his wife's friends. First Secretary at the British Embassy he was, and she should be listening to him, and grateful that he'd taken the time to come out and see her. 'What Dr Carboni said was that everything would be done . . .'

'And what's everything? Half of nothing, if that much.'

Charlesworth bridled. 'It's not a very sensible attitude to take in the circumstances, Mrs Harrison. You'd be better . . .'

'I've had my cry, Mr Charlesworth. I got that over before you came. It won't happen again. You know you don't have to come here with platitudes and a bottle of Librium. I'm pleased you came, grateful to you, but I don't need a shoulder to weep on, and I want to know what's going to happen. What's going to happen, not what a crummy Italian policeman says he's doing. And I want to know who's going to pay.'

Bit early, wasn't it? Knots hardly settled on the old man's wrists and she was chattering about money. God Almighty. 'I can advise you on procedures,' Charlesworth ploughed on, coldness undisguised, 'I can tell you what has happened in the past, to Italians. I can suggest what I think that you should do, and I can indicate the areas where I think the Embassy can be of service.'

'That's what I want to hear.'

'When they write about kidnapping in the Italian papers they call it a successful growth industry. That's a fair enough description. Since 1970 there have been more than three hundred cases. What you'd expect, of course, but the people responsible vary enormously. There are the big gangs, big organizations, well led, well funded, well briefed, probably originating from the real south, probably with what we'd call the Mafia at their roots. I never quite know what's meant by the Mafia, it's an overused word, something simplistic to cover whatever you want it to. In my book the Mafia means skill and ruthlessness and power and patience. If your husband has been taken by these people, then there will be an initial contact followed by a drawn-out haggle over money, and it will end with a business transaction. Very clinical and quite slow because they will want to know that their tracks are well covered.'

'And if it's such a group how will they treat my husband?'

A long time coming, that question, thought Charlesworth. 'Probably quite well. They'd keep him fed and dry and marginally comfortable, enough to sustain his health . . . in a basement, perhaps a farmhouse . . .'

'That's as long as they think we're going to pay?'

'Yes.'

'And if they aren't sure we're going to pay?'

Charlesworth looked hard at her, slipped behind the swollen eyes, delved beyond the mascara. He wondered how his own wife would react in these circumstances, loved her and knew for all that she'd be a disaster. Helpless as a bloody ship on the rocks and thrashing around for someone to blame. She was different, this woman. Different because she didn't wear her concern and her care on her shoulders. Hadn't even put her knickers on for the great day. Didn't sound as if it meant a damn to her beyond the inconvenience.

'Then they'll kill him.'

She didn't react beyond a flutter of the eyebrows, a slight and fractional quiver at the mouth, but nothing that he would have noticed if he hadn't been watching her, absorbing her face.

'And if we go to the police and throw it all into their lap, give it to your Mr Carboni, what then?'

'If they see through an indiscretion or a clumsiness that we have offered full co-operation with the police, and if they feel that endangers their security, then too they will kill him.' He turned the knife because the realization of how much he disliked the woman, how alien she was to his background, seeped through him. 'I put it to you, Mrs Harrison, that the people who have your husband will not hesitate to murder him if that serves their purpose better than keeping him alive.'

He paused, allowed the message to sink and spread, find its own water level. He found his advantage growing. The signs of fear were shown by the slight pant in her chest, the motion of the fingers.

'And even if we pay, if the company pays, we still have no guarantee . . .'

He anticipated her. 'There are never guarantees in these matters.' That was about as strongly as he had the stomach to put it. He couldn't bring himself to tell her of Luisa di Capua whose husband had been dead two months before the body was found, and who had received the last ransom note the day before the discovery. 'No guarantees, we would just have to hope.'

He won a shrill, short laugh from her.

'How much will they ask, Mr Charlesworth? How much is my Geoffrey worth on the Italian market?'

'They'll ask for more than they'll be happy to end up with. Starters would probably be around five million dollars, and they'll settle for perhaps two. Not less than one million.'

'Which I don't have.' She was faster now, and louder and the control was fracturing. 'I don't have it, do you understand that? Geoffrey doesn't, his parents don't. We don't own that sort of money.'

'It's not really your husband that's being ransomed, it's his company. The group will expect the company to pay.'

'And they're tight bastards,' she spat across at him. 'Tight and mean and penny-pinching.'

He remembered the exterior of the block, allowed himself to glance across the interior fittings of the flat.

'I'm sure they will look favourably when they have had the situation explained to them. I had intended to speak to them after I had seen you. I thought that might be valuable to them.'

'So what happens now? What do I do?'

The questions rolled from her, as if Charlesworth were some all-knowing guru on the subject of kidnap reaction. 'We have to await the first contact, probably by telephone. Then it can take quite a time for them to decide what arrangements they want to make for payment.'

'So what do I do, sit by the bloody telephone all day? And I don't even speak the bloody language, just what I need round the shops in the morning. I don't speak their bloody language. I won't know what they're bloody well saying.' Shouting for the first time, dipping into hysteria. Charlesworth fidgeted in the deep chair, willed the session to end.

'We can have it said in the papers that your husband's office is standing by to receive a message.'

'But they're all bloody Italians . . . what the hell do they know about it?'

'A damn sight more than we do, because they live with it every day of the year. Because every one of your husband's senior colleagues knows this can happen to him any time, and a fair few of them will ring their wives each morning as soon as they've sat down at their desks, just so that the woman will know they've made it safely. They know more about this than you or I do, or your husband's company in London. If your husband is to come out of this alive you'll need the help of all his friends in that office. All of those "bloody Italians", you'll need all of their help.'

He was out of the chair, backside clear of the cushions, fingers gripping for leverage into the upholstered arm rests. Poor old show, Charlesworth. A stupid, ignorant cow she may be, but not your job to pass judgement. Lost your rag and you shouldn't have done. He sagged back, ashamed that he had battered the remnants of the calm, destroyed

84

the very thing that he had come to maintain. The colour had fled from her face, which had taken a pallid glow in the shock of his counter-attack. Not a whimper from her, not a choke. Only the eyes to give the message, those of someone who has just stepped from a car accident in which driver or passenger has died and who knows dimly of catastrophe but does not have the power to identify and evaluate the debris.

'Mrs Harrison, you mustn't think yourself alone. Many people will now be working for your husband's release. You must believe in that.'

He stood up, shuffled a little, edged towards the door.

She looked up at him from her chair, cheeks very pale below the saucer eyes, knees apart and the gown gaping. 'I hate this bloody place,' she said. 'I've hated it from the day we arrived. I've hated every hour of it. He'd told me we wouldn't have to stay here, not more than another year, he'd promised me we'd go home. And now you want to go, Mr Charlesworth, well, don't hang about because of me. Thank you again for coming, thank you for your advice, thank you for your help, and thanks to bloody everybody.'

'I'll get a doctor to come round. He'll have something for you. It's a very great shock, what has happened.'

'Don't bother, don't inconvenience anyone.'

'I'll send a doctor round.'

'Don't bother, I'll be a good girl. I'll sit beside the telephone and wait.'

'Haven't you got a friend who could come and stay with you?'

The old laugh back again, high and clean and tinkling. 'Friends in this bloody hole? You're joking, of course.'

Charlesworth hurried to the door, mumbled over his shoulder, 'I'll be in touch and don't hesitate to call me at the Embassy, the number's in the book.'

Trying to master the different locks delayed his flight sufficiently for him to hear her call from the remoteness of the living-room. 'You'll come again, Mr Charlesworth? You'll come again and see me?'

He pulled the door brutally shut behind him, erasing from his ears the trickle of her laughter.

Some five minutes the colonnello spent attempting to marshal the moving waves of photographers and reporters into a straight line. He threatened, pleaded, negotiated the issue of how many paces the prisoner should walk in front of the lenses and microphones before he was finally satisfied with his arrangements in the square internal courtyard of the Questura.

'And remember, no interviews. Interviews are absolutely forbidden.'

He shouted the last exhortation for discipline before the wave of his arm to the polizia who stood shaded in a distant doorway.

When she emerged Franca Tantardini held her head high, jutted her chin, thrust her eyes unwaveringly into the sun. The chains at her wrists dangled against her knees as she walked. Her jeans and blouse were smeared with the street dirt of the pavement outside the Post. To her right the polizia linked arms to hold back the press of cameramen. An officer gripped tightly at each of her elbows; they were not the men who had taken her, not the men who had killed Enrico Panicucci, because those were anonymous and undercover and would not be photographed. These were men in uniform, spruced, with combed and greased hair and polished shoes, who preened themselves and swelled with importance. She ignored the babble of shouted questions and walked on until she was level with the place where the crowd was densest, the pushing at the police shoulders most acute, the cameras closest. A glance she spared for the scrummaging, then ripped her right arm clear of her escort's hold, swung it aloft into the air, clenched her fist in salute, seemed to hover a smile at the chatter of the camera shutters. The policeman regained his hold, dragged her arm down, she was pulled through a doorway, lost from sight. Show completed. Police taking their kudos, cameramen their pictures. Satisfaction of all parties. A triumphal procession of victor and vanquished, and smoothly done.

From an upper window, unnoticed by the journalists, Francesco Vellosi had watched the courtyard parade. At his side stood an Under-Secretary of the Interior Ministry.

'Still defiant, la leonessa. Magnificent even in defeat,' the Under-Secretary murmured.

'A year in Messina, perhaps two, then she'll be tamed,' responded Vellosi.

'Magnificent, quite magnificent. Such hate, such pride.'

'We should have shot her on the street.' There was a cold and bitter snarl on Vellosi's lips.

The computer trace on the third set of fingerprints found by police in the covo was fast and efficient.

But then the equipment was German, modern and expensive, the sort of item on which the government, harassed and defensive, was prepared to lavish its money in the fight against the urban activist. The print-out on the teleprinter was clear and concise.

CRIMINALPOL EUR ROMA
XXXXXXX 25 7 80 XXXXX REF: A419/B78
BATTESTINI GIANCARLO MARCO BORN 12 3 60
82C VIA PESARO PESCARA
RIOTOUS ASSEMBLY SENTENCED 7 MONTHS 11 5 79
PHOTOGRAPHED FINGERPRINTED 9 3 79

More information would follow later, but a name and a picture would be waiting on Francesco Vellosi's desk when he returned from the Questura. Another identity, another set of features, another case history to settle on the top of his mountain of files of wanted persons.

He thought of Violet, poor old Violet. She'd know by now, she'd have heard and the police would be swarming round the flat and she'd be shouting at them and crying, and unless someone came who spoke English she wouldn't have a clue what they were talking about. Poor old Violet, who'd wrung it out of him that they wouldn't stay past next summer – two and a half years she'd have existed then, and she'd said that was her limit, that was enough. She should have adjusted, shouldn't she? Should have compromised, made something of it.

Of course it was different to England, but people go abroad and people cope. She should have been able to find some friends to coffee-morning with, go walk-about the ruins with. Didn't seem to make the effort, though, did she? And didn't seem interested, not in anything, not in his job, not in his business colleagues, not in the few foreigners who lived within walking distance of the flat. She'd never accepted living in a flat and not having neighbours she could lean over a fence and gossip with, never accepted that people who spoke a different language were still human beings and intelligent and kindly and funny, and that if they weren't British it didn't mean they wiped their backsides with their hands.

Bloody ridiculous it was, old Violet locked up in her castle on the hill and not letting the drawbridge down. Tried hard enough, hadn't he? Yes, Geoffrey. Well, what the hell else could be done? Couldn't throw her out of the front door with a street map and shout down the terraces that she mustn't be back before six. He remembered when her parents had come to visit from Stoke-on-Trent. Never been out of England before. Didn't know whether they should put their teeth in the water at night. Didn't hold with all the wine at meals. Didn't master the coils of spaghetti falling off their forks when he took them all out to dinner. Set them back, the pair of them, that visit, they'd argued about it endlessly after the old people had gone; he telling her she should make more effort and not live like a bloody mole and what an advantage and opportunity she had; she telling him she hated it, wanted out and to England. He telling her to get interested in the city, get off her bottom and visit the Vatican and the Foro Italico; she telling him she was buggered if she'd be ordered to tramp round museums. Poor old Violet. Must have been out of her mind with boredom. And she didn't even hit the bottle, because he looked each night when he came home, checked the gin level and the Martini Bianco level and the Tio Pepe level. She didn't even drink the time away.

Only thing she seemed to like was getting down to the beach and that was bloody ridiculous too. There was a nice quiet pool just down the road for her to use, and some very decent families using it. But she preferred the beach and a hell of a drive down to Ostia and all the filth and the oil to sit on, pressed in close by those Italians burning themselves nigger brown. A total bloody mystery. Getting the sand in her hair, not speaking to anyone. Poor old Violet, poor bored old Violet. Hadn't thought about her for a long time, had he? Not like this, not examining her day. Well, he didn't have time, did he? Someone had to put the clothes on her back, the food in her fridge. A damn good job he had in Rome. Better prospects, better pay than he could have hoped for in London. He wished she'd see that. Working damned hard he was, and he could do without the abuse when he flopped home in the evenings.

They were slow rambling thoughts, indulgent and close, lulling him from the crisis, until there was another change in the engine pitch and he felt the movement of the gears, the slowing of the engine, the application of brakes. The van bumped crazily on rough ground. A dead stop. Voices that were clearer with the motor cut. The complacency vanished, the trembling began again, because this was frightening to the man who was bound and gagged and hooded and who had no horizons of sight. A way of existence that had become settled, achieved tranquillity, was ruptured.

The van had left the autostrada half way between Cassino and Capua, bypassed the small town of Vairano Scalo, avoiding the single wide street and central piazza. They had turned east on a winding open hill road that would eventually reach the village of Pietramelara, the home of just over a thousand people with shuttered minds and uninquisitive tongues who would not question the presence of a strange vehicle with distant number plates that might rest for half an hour among the trees and off the road short of their community.

Harrison felt himself bracing his muscles as if trying to push his way further back into the interior of the van, crawl on his buttocks away from the rear door. He heard the slamming at the front and the gouging scratch of feet on the ground that walked along the length of the side walls and then the noise of a lock being turned and a handle being tugged. When the door opened there was a slight smudge of light filtering through the weave of the hood and the floor of the van bucked under a new weight. He felt the shape, alien and revolting to him, brush against his knees and thighs, and then there were hands at the hood, scrabbling close to his chin, at the back of his neck, as the cloth was drawn back across his face. He wanted to scream, wanted to vomit, to expel the fear. Taut, tensed, terrorized. The smell of garlic was close to his nose, and the odour of a farm.

The light, brilliant, blinding, flooded over him, hurting so that he screwed up his face and tried to twist away. But he was not just turning from the intrusive sun, but also from the man who was bent double under the low roof and now loomed above him. Boots close to his head, hard, roughened, un-polished, cracked with wear. Trousers that were old and patched and shapeless, grease-stained. A shirt of red check material, sleeves turned high on muscled forearms. And dominating, compelling his eyes, was the hood, black cloth with eye slits and the crudely cut hole that simulated the position of the mouth. Nowhere for Harrison to writhe to. Nowhere for him to find refuge. The hands, coarse and blistered, thrust to the tapes across his mouth. One savage pull ripped them clear and left the skin as a vast, single abrasion. He coughed hard, spluttered with his face smarting, eyes heavy with tears at the sharpness of the pain.

No word from the man above who screwed up and tossed away the jumble of adhesive tape. There was another silhouetted against the light of the door-way, and Harrison saw him pass forward a roll of bread that bulged with lettuce and tomato and ham.

Big and fat and filling it would have been if he were hungry. The bread was placed against his mouth. He bit and swallowed. Bit again, swallowed again. Around him an awareness of the surroundings grew. The tastes were of the far countryside, distant and removed from the city that was his home. The air was closed to urban sounds, open only to the calls of the birds that were free and roaming at their will. Harrison ate half the roll, could stomach no more and shook his head, and the man threw it casually behind him, successful in his aim avoiding his friend. They let him swig from a bottle of water; aqua minerale, lively with gas and bubbles from the movement of the van. One drink and then the bottle was withdrawn. He lay numbly still, unresisting, as his face was again taped. Instinctively he pleaded with his eyes because they were the only vehicle of argument left to him, but the hood was returned to its place. Back in his realm of darkness, his stomach ground on the food it had taken down, his bowels were loose and confused by the content of what he had eaten. He heard the back door close, the lock being fastened, the men walking back to the front of the van. The engine started.

No threat, no kindness. No cruelty, no comfort.

Men without any minuscule, foetal sensitivity. Vicious bastards, without emotion, without charity. To take a blindfold off a man who was terrorized, holding his muscles to keep his pants clean; to rip the gag from his mouth and offer him nothing, nothing in communication, nothing as one human being to another. The one who had fed him had worn on the third finger of his left hand, the hand that held the bread, the wide gold band of a wedding-ring.

He had a wife whom he would hold close to him and sweat and grunt his passion against, and children who would call to him and laugh. The bastard, the fucking bastard, who could extinguish compassion, drown it, say not a word, give not a sign to a fellow creature who was in pain and suffering and alone.

So help me God, if ever I have the chance I'll kill that bastard. Beat his head with a stone, smash and pound and break it. While he pleads, while he cries, while the blood spatters. So help me God, I want to kill him, I want to hear him scream.

You've never hit anyone in your life, Geoffrey, you wouldn't know how.

The van moved off.

They drove slowly into the village of Pietramelara. The driver found what he was looking for without difficulty. A bar with the circular sign of a tele-phone dial that heralded the presence of a coin-box machine. He left his passenger in the seat, nodded respectfully to the village priest hurrying home for his lunch, accepted the smile of greeting. Conversa-tion in the bar was not interrupted. The driver pulled from his pocket a clutch of gettoni, the tokens necessary for the call. He took from the breast pocket of his shirt a packet of cigarettes, and deciphered the number written on the inside of the cardboard lining. Six gettoni he required for Rome. He remembered the zero six prefix, then carefully repeated the seven-figure number from the packet. When the answer came he spoke quickly, gave only his first name and that of the village and his estimation that the journey would be completed in eight hours.

Had there been difficulties?

There had been none.

The call was terminated by the other party. The driver did not know to whom he was speaking. He walked back to the van anxious to be on his way. He faced a long drive, far into the very toes of the Italian boot, into the mountain country of Calabria. And tonight he would sleep in his own cottage, sleep against the cool stomach of his woman.

The driver's contact would permit the organization in the group that had kidnapped Geoffrey Harrison to make their first contact with the Englishman's home. They now knew that their merchandise was far beyond the reach of rescue by the polizia, that the cordons and road blocks were way outstripped.

Claudio stood with his hands in his pockets among the little groups of waving Romans. A varied sadness painted all those who watched the train, the anaconda, snake away from the long platform of the Termini, bending at the first far curve, engine already lost. Mario and Vanni gone, settled into their seats in the grey carriage that carried the sign of Reggio Calabria, nine hundred kilometres to the south. Their going left Claudio without a companion, condemned to wait away the night, contain his resentment that he was not with his friends. Time to be killed and frittered as a man does when he is in a strange city that has no heart, no belonging for him.

Once he waved, simply and without demonstration, lifting his arm and waggling his fingers at the train as it diminished and blended with the softness of the heat haze that distorted and tricked.

As Mario and Vanni walked along the platform he had been tempted to follow and join them, but fear of the men of the organization was enough to cast the apple from big Claudio's mouth. Some before had discarded the instructions of the organization, trifled with their orders. All had been awarded a fine funeral, two or more priests to celebrate the Mass, many boys to sing in the choir, enough flowers to cover all the stones in the cemetery, enough tears to make a dead man believe he was mourned. Claudio had stayed behind and waved; he would catch tomorrow's train.

He swung his eyes away from the converging, empty tracks and headed for the bar and the first of a new session of Perroni beers that would help him watch the hour and minute hands of his watch.

Later he would find a room near the station.

Sometimes hurrying, sometimes slowly when the lethargy bred from failure was on him, Giancarlo searched among the familiar places, the rooms and corridors where he expected to find his friends. He had gone to the Faculty of Letters where the walls were bright in a Technicolor of protest paint and wandered the high plaster-coated corridors, past the stripped notice-boards, past the locked lecture theatres, into the quiet of the library. To some who were relaxed and lounging in chairs he had spoken. Not with confidence but sidling towards them. He had mentioned a name and seen a head shaken; moved on, another name, shoulders shrugged in response. On from the Faculty of Letters to the Faculty of Social Sciences and further echoing and deserted corridors that rang with his thin-soled shoes and in which reverberated the laughter of those who belonged and knew their place.

97

Hopeless for him to ask the question directly.

Where are the people of the Autonomia? Where can I find any member of the Autonomia? It was not information that would be given to a stranger, not in a casual conversation. He plodded on, wet and constricted in his clothes, dampened and caught in his unhappiness. On from the Faculty of Social Sciences, heading for the Faculty of Physics. Two hours Giancarlo paced the University complex. There was no-one he knew among the students who sat and talked in the sunshine, or walked with their bundles of books, or crouched over the printed words of their study texts. No-one who could send him with a smile and a gabble of directions to where he might discover the people of the Autonomia.

Still careful, still watchful, he hesitated by the great opened doors of the Faculty of Physics, pausing in the shadow short of the sun-bright steps that led down into the central yard of the University, traversed with his eyes, as a fox will when it sniffs the early air before leaving its den. Giancarlo quivered, stiffened, focused on the grey gunmetal Alfasud parked back and out of the light, far into the shade of the trees. The car was distinctive because of its radio aerial, high and set above the right rear wheel, and because of the three men sprawled in the seats. Bearded two of them, clean-shaven the third, but all of them too old to be students. He watched the car for many minutes, hidden by shadow as it was, observing the men fidget and shift in response to the comfort of their seats, assimilating their mood, their state of preparedness. There was nothing exceptional about the police being there, he told himself, the place crawled with the pigs and their informers, and there was no urgency about these men as they watched the young people move across their vision. Dumb bastards, because even if they had his name and his picture they telegraphed their presence by their age, by their location.

Had they his name yet?

Not so quickly, surely, not within a few hours. Confidence and depression, ebullience and fear, competed in the boy's mind as he scurried for a side entrance and cover among the parked buses at the Tiburtina termini. Rampant in his imagination was the sight of the three men low in the seats of their car. The one with his newspaper, the one with his arm trailing through the open window with the dangled cigarette, the one with the barely opened eyes. They had made him run, hastened the end of his fruitless, wasted search, and that was how it would always be, till the gutter time, till the shooting time, till he no longer needed to scan the cars and the faces for the polizia.

Pig bastards. There would be a moment when he stood his ground. A moment when they would know of him. When, Giancarlo? The moment when he would take Franca Tantardini from them. By yourself, Giancarlo? There was a pain at the boy's eyes, and agony behind the lids, because this was a public place among the buses and the people who waited and they must not see him weep.

He climbed on to a bus. Chose it not for its route but because it was one that did not have a conductor to collect money and hand out tickets, and relied instead on a machine and the honesty of passengers.

Heart pumping, blood coursing fast, the little boy who had lost his protection and was running.

*   *   *

The girl in faded jeans and a flowing, wrist-buttoned blouse came quickly to the top of the high steps at the entrance to the Faculty of Social Sciences. She paused there, raking the open ground in front of her, then jogged down the steps and across the car park towards the grey Alfasud. It was not remarkable that she could identify the unmarked police car, any student could have done that. As she approached the car she saw the interest of the occupants quicken, the cigarette stubbed, the newspaper dropped, the backs straightened. At the driver's open window she hesitated as the men's eyes soaked into her, for this was a public place for an informant to work.

'You are looking for a boy?'

The cool smile from the front passenger in response, the lighting of another cigarette.

'Dark curly hair – jeans and a shirt – not tall, thin.'

The man in the back seat flipped casually at a notepad in which were scribbled words.

'A boy like that came into the library, it was just a few minutes ago. He was nervous, you could see that, in his voice, in his hands . . .'

The notebook was passed to the front, examined with a secrecy as if the knowledge written there were to be denied to the girl.

'. . . he asked a friend if two boys were in the University. The boys are both of the Autonomia, both were arrested after the last fight, more than three months ago.'

She was answered. The front passenger drew his Beretta pistol from the glove drawer and armed it, the man in the back groped to the floor for a short-barrelled machine-gun. The driver snapped a question: 'Where did he go?'

'I don't know. There is the students' lounge, he went in that direction . . .'

The girl had to step back as the car doors whipped open. Hand-guns pocketed, the machine-gun closed to view under a light jacket, the three policemen ran for the Faculty entrance.

They searched methodically for an hour in the public places of the University, while more men of the anti-terrorist squad arrived to augment their efforts. There were curses of frustration at the failure of the hunt, but satisfaction could be drawn from the knowledge that the identification if it were genuine showed that the kid was short of a covo. It would not be long before the boy was taken, not if he were scouting the University for friends more than twelve weeks in the cells.

That night the University and its hostels would be watched. Men would be detailed to stand in their silence in the shadows and doorways. Pray God, the bastard returns.

By telephone the message from Pietramelara was relayed to the capo. That the initial moments of the kidnapping of the Englishman had met with success he knew from the radio beside his desk. The communiqué bearing the fruits of his enterprise had been broadcast with commendable speed by the RAI networks.

How they help us, he thought, how they facilitate our business. And now the cargo was moving beyond the scope of the road checks. Soon he would authorize the initial approaches to the family and the company, and set in motion the financial procedures in the matter laid down by his specialist accountant. A fat, choice haul, and the lifting sharp and surgical.

It was not for a man of the prominence of the capo to consider and burden himself with the machinery of the extortion of ransom; a team he paid did that; he paid them well so that tracks should be smothered and hidden. He let himself out of his office, locked his door from a wide ring of keys and crossed the pavement to his car. For the long journey to the south and the hill village where his wife and children lived, he used the Dino Ferrari that would eat into the kilometres to the Golfo di Policastro, where he would break the journey back to his family. Beside the sea, in the sprouting coastal resorts, his business was fuelled by the new and flourishing source of revenue. He cut a good figure as he climbed athletically into the low-slung sports car. To the superficial watcher there was nothing in his bearing or his dress to link him with profitable crime, painstakingly organized, ruthlessly executed. He would be at the resort area by early evening, in time to take a functionary of the regional planning office to dinner, and when the man was drunk and grateful for the attention the capo would leave him and motor on to his villa in the Aspromonte.

He drove aggressively from the kerbside, attracting notice. To those who saw him go there was a feeling that this was a man on whom the sun shone.

Violet Harrison had no clear intention of going to the beach at Ostia that afternoon. Nothing definite in her mind, no commitment to escape from the funereal movements of her maid, but there had to be an alternative to sitting and smoking and drinking coffee and straining for the telephone's first ecstatic ring. She had taken the three newest bikinis from the drawer of the chest in her bedroom, one in yellow, one in black, the third in pink with white dots, and laid them with a neatness that was not usually hers out on the bedspread, and looked at their flimsy defiance.

'Bit on the small side, isn't it?' Geoffrey had laughed. 'Bit of a risk running round in that in these parts.' That was last week and he'd slapped her bottom, kissed her on the cheek and never mentioned it again. But written all over his bloody face, What's an Old Girl like you wanting a Teenager's fripperies for? He'd settled in his chair with a drink in his hand and a folder of accounts on his lap. 'Bit on the small side . . .' and he'd held her most recent purchase, pink with white dots, between his fingers, dangling. She'd found it in the boutique window down past the market, wanted it, urged herself to buy it. She'd ignored the superciliousness of the stare of the shop girl, tall and manicured and straight-backed; haughty bitch who said with her eyes what her husband had spoken five hours later.

Violet Harrison had only worn the pink and white bikini once. Just the one time, the day before, while she lay on the beach at Ostia and listened to the virulent run of conversation around her. Couldn't understand a word they said, to her it was a medley of silly chatter and giggling and exuberance. But it made a state of independence for her, a secret hideout. Among the people and litter from the ice-cream wrappers and the beer bottles and Pepsi cartons, it was her place, unknown to the cool and moneyed world of the inhabitants of Collina Fleming. Marvellous she felt there, bloody marvellous, and the sun burned into her skin, and the sand flicked across her face and went unnoticed. The nearest thing to happiness and guiltless pleasure. And then the silly kid had started talking to her. All part of the game, wasn't it? All part of the scenario of escape and freedom. A silly little kid trying to pick up an English matron, old enough to be . . . his aunt anyway. Trying to pick her off as if she were an au-pair on an afternoon out. And he'd said he'd be there that afternoon.

It's not my bloody fault, Geoffrey.

What am I supposed to do? Dress in black tights and put Polaroid specs on so that people can't see that I haven't cried for four hours? Put flowers round the living-room and wear soft shoes so I'll make no noise when I pace up and down, and keep the bloody place looking like a laying-out parlour?

What do you want me to do? Sit here all day, sit here and weep, and ask Mummy to come out and hold my hand and make mugs of tea? I don't mean that, Geoffrey, not like that. I don't mean you any harm. I can't just sit here, you understand that, I can't just eke it all out. I'm not strong enough, that's what I mean . . . I'm not a public person's wife.

But I'm not going to go, anyway. I mean it, I'm not going to the beach. I'm going to stay here and wait for the telephone, that's what I have to do, isn't it? I have to suffer with you because you're out there, somewhere. Are you frightened, Geoffrey? . . . A man came to see me, some idiot from the Embassy, and he said they wouldn't hurt you. Well, he didn't quite say that, but they won't actually hurt you if everything goes well, if nothing is wrong. That's what he said.

She grabbed the bikini from the bedcover, the little cotton triangles, the linking cords, the fastening straps. Crushed them in her fist and hurled the pieces towards the corner that housed the neat formation of Geoffrey's shoes.

She started to run from the bedroom, drawn always faster by the piercing, siren call of the telephone. Crashing through doors, slipping on the smooth floor surface. The caller was patient, allowed the bell to ring out its summons, let the persistence of the noise swamp the flat, cutting the walls, floating to the crannies.

Again the air-conditioning was not working.

Michael Charlesworth sat in his office, jacket draped over his chair, tie loosened, top three shirt buttons undone. No surprise, the air-conditioning, had to be phlegmatic about it. What chance of finding a maintenance man who wouldn't carve half the wall off pulling at the pipes, and who wasn't like the rest of the city, prostrate with the heat or on holiday?

Sweat coated the paper in front of him, running the ink where he'd written with his ballpoint, and beside his elbow the telephone was still wet from his palm print. A great quiet in a building usually leaking with noise; the Ambassador and his guests at lunch, attachés and First and Second Secretaries disappeared to the shaded restaurants near the Porta Pia and the Via Nomentana. The typists had covered their machines, the clerks locked their filing cabinets. Charlesworth scribbled on fiercely.

He had started with a list of his immediates. A call to Carboni at the Questura, to ensure the message was discreetly fed to the afternoon newspapers that Harrison's office was standing ready to receive contact. He had barely put the phone down when Violet Harrison rang; she had seemed detached, distant. Enough for him to wonder if a doctor had called with sedatives. She had spoken of a message and a man who talked only in Italian and she had shouted and he had shouted, each obliterating the words of the other. There was a great calmness about her, as if a narcotic were at work, and a politeness as she had told Charlesworth that she was going out for a few hours.

'I can't just sit here,' she'd said, matter of fact, untroubled by crisis. 'I can't just hang about. I think you understand.'

He had tried to reach the Ambassador, sent a spiritless message through to the Personal Secretary, and received the reply he anticipated.

'If nothing has changed the Old Man would be happy to see you about five. He wouldn't want to be disturbed before that. At least, not unless it's a case of life and death, you know.'

A nice girl, the Personal Secretary, long and leggy and combed and sweet, projecting out of cotton print dresses, but fierce and loyal in her protectiveness. And what was a case of life and death? A guy on his back, crapping himself and bound so that he lay in his filth, and savage bastards round him who'd kill if it was to their advantage. Life and death? Not in the Old Man's terms, not enough reason to spoil a good lunch. And there wasn't anything new, not if he were honest about it. Just that a woman was having a plucky try and likely to succeed at a nice and public nervous breakdown, not a special woman who knew an MP back home with clout, or who'd figure on the Embassy scones-and-tea invitation list. But Michael Charlesworth hadn't provided the granite pillar for Violet Harrison to support herself against, nor the shoulder, nor the handkerchief. A dreadful woman, awful manners, disastrous sense of occasion, but worthy of some small charity – yes, Michael Charlesworth? His teeth played on his lower lip as he heaved in his chair and grabbed again for the telephone.

'It's ten minutes since I asked for that London call, sweetheart. Ten minutes, and that's too long.' He called her Miss Foreman normally.

'I can't help it, Mr Charlesworth. The operator on International won't answer. You know how it is.' The syrup voice of a lady who knitted and took holidays in Welsh hotels off-season, and thought of Italians as dirty, and wished she was twenty years younger, not too old to be loved.

'Can't you just dial it for me, darling . . . ?'

'You know that's not allowed, Mr Charlesworth.'

'You can dial it for me.' Wearying of the game.

'You'll have to sign for it. One of the girls will have to come up to Second when she's free and get your signature . . .'

'Just get me the call.' Charlesworth's temper fraying, ragged.

'As soon as we've looked out a priority form and a girl's available I'll send her up.'

'Get me that bloody call, get it now. Dial it. A man's bloody life may depend . . .'

'You don't have to swear, there's no need for offensiveness.'

'Just get me the call, darling. I'll sign the Priority later, but it's important that I speak to London and that cretins like you don't waste any more of my time.'

The earpiece exploded in the sounds of switch-board mechanics. Plugs extracted, plugs inserted. Numbers dialled and whirring on their arcs. The ringing tone. He'd never spoken to Miss Gladys Foreman MBE like that. Doubted if anyone ever had, not in three decades anyway. Like urinating right across the lounge carpet at a stand-up buffet at the Residence.

Two rings and the plastic, automated voice of a faraway girl.

'International Chemical Holdings. Can I help you, please?'

'It's the British Embassy in Rome. Michael Charlesworth speaking. I need to talk with the Managing Director.'

Delays, re-routings, a false start and the call retrieved. Charlesworth sat at his desk, soaking up the sunlight, telling a secretary that he was damned if he was going to précis his message and that he wanted her master, and she should pull her bloody finger out and get off the line. Yes, he could wait a moment, he could wait all day, why not? Different whether the other blighter could, whether Geoffrey Harrison could.

'Adams speaking. What can I do for you, Mr Charlesworth?' Sir David Adams, captain of industry, clipped voice, a brusqueness that demanded information and warned against wasted time.

'It's good of you to speak to me. I have to tell you that your representative in Rome, Mr Geoffrey

Harrison, was kidnapped this morning on his way to your office.' Charlesworth paused, cleared his throat, a guttural clatter, then launched into the few available facts, recounted his conversations with the Questura. Not a great deal to say, and the inadequacy hurt.

'I've read in the newspapers of these happenings, but I confess I was under the impression this was an Italian problem, a domestic one.' A sharp voice distorted to a high pitch by the static of the communication.

'Your man is the first of the foreign business community.'

'And it could be expensive?'

'Very expensive, Sir David.' Lurched to the heart of the issue, hadn't he? Charlesworth contained himself from laughing. Get the priorities right, lad. Get the balance sheets organized and the rest follows.

'To get him back, what sort of figure might we be talking about?'

'The asking price might be anything up to four or five million dollars.' That'll set him swinging in his black leather chair, that'll start him gawping out over the City skyline. 'There might be a possibility of negotiation, but it won't be easy for a company like yours to plead poverty.'

'And if we don't pay?'

'Then you are in for a long widow's pension. Mrs Harrison is a young woman.'

'Well, that's a Board decision. And in the meantime, what action should we take?'

'The only thing you have to do is to get that decision taken, and fast. It could go very hard for Mr Harrison if the group that hold him thought you were prevaricating. As you probably realize, in this country there is a tradition of paying up, they would not respond well to the breaking of that custom.'

Don't ever say I didn't root for you, Geoffrey Harrison. Don't ever say I didn't go in there with two feet kicking. A silence on the line, the big man chewing on it, deliberating. A slow smile winning across Michael Charlesworth's face.

When Sir David Adams spoke again, the chisel had blunted in his voice. 'It's a great deal of money, Mr Charlesworth. My Board would have to be very certain that it's totally necessary to pay the sort of sum you mention. They won't like it. And there's a question of principle too; there's a tradition in this country that we don't crumble to blackmail.'

'Then you would have to make the decision that on a point of principle you were prepared to sacrifice the life of Mr Harrison. Of course, it might not come to that, but the possibility, perhaps the probability, exists.'

'You are very frank, Mr Charlesworth.' There was the trace of disapproval in the scraped gravel tones. 'If we suppose, and only suppose, that we were to pay a very considerable sum, then who would control the arrangements?'

'It would be best done by your office in Rome. The Embassy couldn't get involved.'

Charlesworth heard the low laugh in response. Ten minutes they'd been talking, ten minutes in querying the profit and loss columns, and whether a ransom should be paid. Principle or expediency. A martyr for the greater good of the majority or a shame-laden deal for the return of one man. Perhaps, Charlesworth thought, he'd minimized the issues at

110

stake. Perhaps a line had to be drawn. No deals, no bargains, no compromise, there would be many willing to shout that clarion call. If you gave in once, if you slipped one time into the shadows with a suitcase of used banknotes and a string of Zürich bank account numbers, then how many other poor bastards were going to follow the road of Geoffrey Harrison? Not his business, though, not his concern, because as he'd said most clearly, the Embassy couldn't be involved, would stand detached within its glass walls and watch and murmur occasional interest. That was why Sir David Adams, Managing Director of International Chemical Holdings in the City of London, could laugh lightly at him, without humour, without rancour, at the moment of dismissal.

'You've been very kind, Mr Charlesworth. I'll get one of my people on the plane this evening. I'd like him to be in touch with you.'

The call was terminated.

Michael Charlesworth flopped back into the small comforts offered by the plastic padding of his chair. A time for reflection. He must call Miss Foreman, he must apologize, and there would be some flowers for her basement bunker tomorrow in the morning. And then the bell again, the bloody telephone.

The Questura had been informed from the offices of ICH in Viale Pasteur that a demand of two million dollars for the return of Geoffrey Harrison had been received. There should be no contact with the police, further details of arrangement for payment would follow through intermediaries. Dottore Carboni was not in his office at present but he had requested that the information be passed to Signor

111

Charlesworth. There were mutual thanks and politeness.

Two million dollars. More than a million in sterling at whatever the fluctuating rate. Four million Swiss francs. Cascades of figures. And less than he'd thought it would be, as if those who had taken Harrison had settled for a bargain basement price and would not haggle and barter, but expect settlement without delay.

Michael Charlesworth changed his mind. He would apologize in person to Gladys Foreman. He fastened his shirt buttons, straightened his tie, slipped on his jacket and walked slowly out of his office. He wondered what the man looked like, Geoffrey Harrison, how his voice sounded, whether he'd be good company for dinner, if he told a good joke. He felt himself inextricably involved with a man he did not know, could not picture and might never meet unless a company on the other side of the continent jettisoned an issue of principle and made available more money than he could decently imagine.

Chapter Six

The Termini was a good place for Giancarlo to come to.

A great extended white stone frontage before which the buses parked, the taxis queued, the traders hawked gaudy toys and shiny shoes and polished belts, and where thousands streamed each morning and afternoon on their way to and from the business of the city. Shops and bars and restaurants and even a subterranean aquarium catered for those who had time to pass. Vast, sprawling, a dinosaur dedicated to the days before the private car and the growth of the autostrada. Businessmen were there, neat and watching the departure board for the evening expresses for Torino and Milano and Napoli. Families of impatient mothers and fretful children waited for connections to the resorts of Rimini and Ricci and the towns south of Bari. Soldiers and sailors and airmen looked for the trains that would carry them to far distant barracks or back to their homes, the routine of conscription broken for a few short days. Gypsy girls in ankle-length wraparound skirts and painful faces of destitution held out paper cups for money. Noise and movement and blurred features, and the mingling of accents of Lombardia, Piemonte, Umbria and Lazio and Toscana.

Tired, famished, with a throat desert dried, he stalked slowly and still with care and watchfulness on to the main concourse. It was a good place for Giancarlo because there were many here. Too many people, too many scuffling feet for the polizia to notice one small boy. The training of the NAP was well etched in the youth so that the places of concealment were second nature as he sought camouflage to his presence. With his weariness had come no sense of defeat, no will to cringe and concede, only a confusion as to how he might best strike back at those who had taken Franca Tantardini. A white scabbed face, bristle on his cheeks, hair hanging, eyes sunken. Past the stalls for the children's toys, past the stands of newspapers and magazines and books, oblivious of the broadcast news of platform changes and delays, he walked the wide length of the concourse.

The second time he passed the big bar, the one that faced the platforms, he saw the man and stirred the response of recognition.

It took Giancarlo many more dragging steps as he racked his memory to identify the fatted face, threatening body, dropped shoulders of the man who leaned on his elbows with a glass in his hand and gazed out of the bar. The boy had to examine a host of recent experiences, sift through them and reject the failures before there was satisfaction and confirmation.

The one they called *gigante* – the huge one, that was the man in the bar. He saw him on the iron steps that led between the landings, his great strides that echoed down the yawning corridors, men stepping back from his path and skirting his strength. All had conceded precedence to the gigante, all except the NAP men on 'B' Wing. Claudio – he could even place his name. Not his other name, only the first one, the given one. Claudio – treated with respect in the Regina Coeli because his fist was the width of a pizza portion and his temper short and his sensitivity slight. To the boy he seemed gross in his stomach, looked to have taken his food, and from the tilt of the glass his beer was not the early one of the day.

Giancarlo turned on his heel, retraced his way till he came and stood at the doorway of the bar that was open to lure the faint breeze into the heated interior. Stood stationary waiting for the head to rise and the gaze to fasten. The boy stood statue still until the sleep-lost, narrow eyes of the big man rolled across the doorway and past him, and then swept backwards as if awakened. Giancarlo smiled and slipped forward.

'Ciao, Claudio,' the boy said quietly, close to him.

The big man stiffened, the prodded bullock, as if recognition ruffled and unsettled him.

'It's a long time, Claudio, but I think you remember me.'

He read the uncertainty in the other's face, watched the war going on between the frown lines of his shallow forehead, the fight to put a name and a place to the boy who had accosted him. Giancarlo prompted.

'At the Queen of Heaven, Claudio. Do you not remember me, do you not remember my friends? My friends were in the political wing, and I was under their protection.'

'I've not seen you before.' Something in the denial that was weak and furtive, and the big man looked round, peering about him.

'But I know your name. And I could tell you the number on the cell door, perhaps even I could tell you the names of those that slept there with you.' A half smile played on Giancarlo's lips, and an ebb tide of relaxation was running in him. It was the first time in the day, through the long hours since the Post, that he felt an intuition of advantage. 'If we had coffee and we talked then you might remember more of me and of my friends. My friends were in the political wing, they were people of influence in the Queen of Heaven, they still hold that influence.' His voice died away, the message of menace inherent in the boast of his pedigree.

Claudio laughed with a ripple of nervousness and looked past the boy as if to be certain that he was alone, that a trap was not set for him. He walked away without explanation to the girl at the cash desk, shouldered his way past others. Giancarlo saw a thickened wad of notes emerge from the hip pocket, saw the hands that trembled and scuffed at the notes before the 1,000-lire note was produced. Money, endless rolls of it, enough to quicken the attention of the boy. As a pilot fish clings to a shark that he may feed from the droppings at its jaws, so Giancarlo stayed close to the reluctant Claudio.

'You will have a beer with me,' said Claudio when he was back from the bar.

Slowly and stilted, the man and the boy circled each other in sporadic conversation over the first beer. Claudio seeking to determine what the other wanted of him, Giancarlo working at the crannies of information and looking for advantage and the area of profit. A second beer, and a third, and Claudio's head was rolling from the intake, his words sluggish and with a creeping edge of confidence leading him forward. By the fourth bottle of tight, gassed Perroni, Claudio's arm was across Giancarlo's bent shoulder, and together they scanned the front page of the afternoon paper. A pudgy, scarred finger, grime to the quick of the nail, stabbed at the report on the front page of the kidnapping of a British business-man as he had left his home that morning.

When Giancarlo looked sharply into the big man's face there was a dissolve of giggles.

The boy struggled to stay alert, to hose out the beer that flowed in him, seeking the information that might lead to power over his drinking companion. Claudio was from the south, Giancarlo's memory told him, the fact confirmed by the thickened accent of Calabria, and he was waiting for a train from Rome and there was the music of his laughter and his attention to a kidnapping. Here was a source of money, a source of protection, because the big man was running too, was also a fugitive and had betrayed himself.

'But we are not the most important news today,' muttered Claudio with a tinge of disappointment, an actor denied limelight. 'Because they have taken one of yours. They have taken a whore of the NAP. They took her this morning and that is what excites the polizia.' Giancarlo kept his peace, and the finger was moving again, dabbing down and smudging with dirt the picture of Franca Tantardini. 'A leader of the NAP they call her, and the one that guarded her dead. Silly bitch, to have been out in the open.

Silly cow. Did you know her, boy? She looks worth knowing.'

'I had met her.' Giancarlo kept the casualness in his words. 'But there are many like her and she will be avenged. They will not hold her in prison, her friends will release her. They cannot hold our people.' In the picture Franca's head was high and her blouse tight, and the camera had caught the sting of the nipple and the clasp of the manacles at her wrists.

'That's shit, boy. When they have her, they hold her. Good-looking bitch,' mouthed Claudio. And then it was as if a clarity had come to him and the beer vapour was dispersed and the interest crawled like a spider's path across his face. 'That is why you are running. Why you are here without food, without money, sponging from an old peasant. It is because they have taken her.'

Giancarlo looked back at him, unwavering, deep into the bloodstreams of his eyes. 'It is why I seek the help of a friend.'

'You were with the girl?'

'I need the help of a friend.'

'Because they have taken her you have no place?'

'I have no place to go.'

'In a city, in Rome, you have nowhere to cover yourself?'

'I am alone,' said Giancarlo.

'But there are friends, there are others.'

'We do not have that structure. We have the cell grouping. We are separated because that is the rule of the NAP.'

Around their ears the noise and chaos of the bar was rampant. Arms pressing against them, orders shouted to the white-shirted men behind the bar. Humour, rancour, impatience buffeting at their ears. But they had created their island, were immune to disturbance.

'Perhaps you should go home.' Something softer from the big man. 'You should go back to your family. Bury yourself away, let the thing pass.'

'I am hunted. I was with her when she was taken, and the other who was with her was killed by the pigs. They are searching for me.' The supremacy over Claudio was lost, frittered away. Giancarlo was searching for comfort, and turning for it to a hardened, brute-fashioned animal. 'I have walked all day. I have nowhere to go.'

'I remember you, boy, because you were the one that went always to their cells. You had their protection.' The arm was tight on Giancarlo's shoulders and the breath of garlic bread and sausage and beer was close to his nostrils. 'So you became a man in the movement, something of substance, and now you turn to a Calabrian idiot for help, a man from the farms, one you would have dismissed as an ignorant and stupid pig.'

'I would not dismiss you as an ignorant and stupid one. You have money in your pocket. You are not the victim of exploitation and oppression.'

'You have eyes then, my little lost one.' Something cold and bovine in Claudio's face. 'You watch a man when he has too much beer.'

Giancarlo smiled with richness and warmth and cracked the frozen stare. More beers, and Claudio spoke of a hotel room, but of a meal first. Playing the grand host, he would be provider, he said, for a few hours of shelter and safety. Giancarlo wondered why, laid the reasoning of the other man at the bottles of beer he had drunk, and acquiesced.

The Mafia and its tentacles were hated and despised by the politicized groups such as the NAP. To the organizations of the extreme left, organized crime represented the total and complete control of the working classes, its survival dependent on fear and repression inflicted on the lesser and weaker, and its helpers were the senior and corrupt officials in administration. In the revolutionary war of Giancarlo, high on the list of enemies would be the gangs that operated for money and chattels. Venality was despicable. So Claudio was Giancarlo's opponent, but the boy would be patient because he had need of the other man and because he would use him for his purposes. If Claudio had been sober, if his limited wits had been alerted, he would not have countenanced the liaison, but he was well oiled now and had lost his native and naive cunning for self-preservation.

In the boy's mind was the first budding of a plan. Something that needed to be cultivated and pruned if it were to show a bloom. A way to win back from the bastards his Franca. A desperate, deep yearning for her, for her body and the cavities and the bright laugh and the brazen love. He wanted it so that his shape quivered and glowed and his belly ached. Franca, Franca, a muted shout. And they went into the humid night air.

The political activist and the kidnap gorilla, arms unequally around each other, bloated by beer, headed together from the Termini in search of a plate of spaghetti.

*   *   *

Caught now in a static turmoil of traffic on the Raccordo Annulare, both lanes blocked, the possibility of advancement denied, Violet Harrison cursed and shouted her abuse at the unhearing, uncaring audience. One hundred metres she had crawled in the last eight minutes. On the back seat of the car was the plastic bag with the towel thrown angrily inside so that on her return it would be creased and untidy, and beneath it the pink polka dot bikini, buried and unworn.

She had willed herself to stand her ground in the flat, to sit beside the telephone because that was the proper and right thing for her to do, the proper and right place for her to be. But the desire for self-preservation had won the field. She had turned her back, abandoned the apartment, driven to the beach.

A ludicrous sight she must have seemed, that much she knew. A woman, a foreigner, pacing the length of the sand, her feet slipping and stumbling in its insecurity. Scanning with her eyes peering at the boys with the golden torsos and bare legs and muscled shoulders. Seeking to keep an assignation, and showing to all who cared to watch, the torment and humiliation of not finding him whom she had chosen to meet. A grown woman with a fertile womb, and thighs that were thickening, and a waist no longer slender, and a throat that showed the time ravages, and she had succumbed and come back to the beach to talk to a boy whose name she did not know. Salted, angry tears ran without hindrance on her cheeks by the time she had climbed back into the car and surged away in the glowering dusk.

Perhaps if she had come at the time she was always at the beach, perhaps he would have been there. Bloody boy, as if he had no knowledge of what she had sacrificed to come to find him. He couldn't have known the pain he inflicted or he would have been there. Bloody child.

I'm sorry, Geoffrey. As God is my witness, I can't help myself. I even ironed the bikini.

Michael Charlesworth cycled home without enthusiasm, taking no pleasure from the ease with which he skirted the piled, slow-moving cars and ignored the impatient defiles. Normally he revelled in the freedom of the bicycle, but not this evening.

His meeting with the Ambassador had been predictable. The aftermath of the lunch and flowing hospitality had left His Excellency with scant reserves of attention for matters outside the strict protocol of functions exercised by the Embassy.

'In a criminal kidnapping there can be no area of responsibility for us,' the Ambassador had remarked, his cigar tapering between his fingers. 'It's a matter for this poor devil's company. It's their decision whether to pay, and how to conduct their negotiations. Personally I don't think they've any option in the matter, local conditions being what they are. The company can afford it, and let's hope they get it over as quickly as is decently possible. And don't forget the legal problems. If they're not discreet they can run into all sorts of internal problems with the law here. It's not that I'm unsympathetic, just that it's a fraught area, and not one for us. So I see no need for our feet to go in any deeper, and we should let the matter rest in the hands of those directly involved.'

So the bowl of water had been brought to the throne and the hands had been rinsed. Charlesworth returned to analysis of the newly announced power structure in the Central Committee of the PCI. The Old Man was right, of course; he invariably was. Paying out ransom money could be assessed as aiding and abetting a felony; thin ice for diplomatic boots to step on. But the ice wasn't thick under Geoffrey Harrison, and he was without his woollies and a life-jacket. Poor bastard. Geoffrey Harrison could scratch Michael Charlesworth off his list of angels.

He flung out his left arm, failed to turn his head, swerved across two traffic lanes, ignored the hurt scream of tyres and brakes. Their country, so do it their way. Local conditions, he thought. Local conditions, the catchphrase of the day.

Through the afternoon and early evening Francesco Vellosi had wrestled with the temptation, until at the time he would normally have left the Viminale for his home he had finally asked his private secretary to warn the Questura that he was coming to their offices and that he wanted to sit in on the interrogation of Franca Tantardini. There was no place on such an occasion for a man in his position, nothing that he could usefully learn by being present that could not as satisfactorily be taken from the transcripts that would await him in the morning. But the admiration of the Under-Secretary, the reverence in which the civil servant had clothed the distant chained figure as she had been paraded for the photographers, had haunted and disturbed him through the day. Most of those taken were humbled figures by the time their photographs had been executed in the basement cells, bravery leaking, the struggle and fervour of the revolution drained. It was the same with both factions, with the red fascists and the black fascists, the maniacs of the extreme left and the extreme right. But to Vellosi this girl had been particular, unique. Haughty and proud, as if beaten in only a skirmish, not a battle. As an experienced and dedicated policeman who had learned his trade in the hard schools of Milano and Reggio, his favour was sought after, his presence was the delight of a dinner-party hostess. He was a man regarded with envy by his colleagues because of his competence and single-minded determination. Yet the sight of the woman in the warm Questura yard had unsettled Vellosi. Two years they had hunted her, countless man-hours had been expended in the following of scrappy particles of information, the watching of buildings, the frustration and the disappointment. Two years of the treadmill, and now that they had her there was an absence of the satisfaction that the capture should have brought.

In the back of his car, mindful of the escort vehicle behind him without which it was deemed unsafe for him to travel, Vellosi pondered the equation he had set himself. What made the Tantardini woman turn aside from the world that the majority were grateful to accept? Where did the web of conformity break? Where did the grotesque mutation spawn? There were more than five hundred of them, red and black, in the gaols. Mostly minnows, mostly idiots, mostly the cruel oddities of life who saw in violence and maiming the only outlet they might capture in their desire to be heard of, shouted about.

But not this woman. Too intelligent, too trained, too vicious to be classified with the herd. From a good family in Bergamo. From a convent school. From money and opportunity . . . The real and worthy opponent, the one that taxed and exhausted Francesco Vellosi. A woman who could make a man bend and crawl and suffer. She could grind me, this one, he thought, could squeeze and suck me dry between her legs, between her brain. And there was little to confront her with, nothing to frighten her with, no instrument with which to break her.

'Mauro, I've said it before today and I say it again. We should have shot the bitch on the pavement.' He spoke quietly to his driver, the trusted dustbin for his musings. 'More people have been killed or crippled in the name of Renato Curcio than ever were attacked while he was at liberty. More of these bastard kids are motivated by the name of La Vianale than ever were before we took her. We shall build another rallying-point when we lock up Franca Tantardini. We can put her down in Messina, throw the key away and it will change nothing. If we segregate her from other prisoners then it's called inhuman treatment, mental torture. If we put her with the pack it's too easy for her, she'll be over the wall. Each month she's in Messina the Radicali will be yelling her name in the Camera. All ways we approach it, we lose. Eh, Mauro?'

It was not the driver's place to reply. He nodded agreement. His attention was on the road, always watchful for a car closing too fast on the open side, looking to his mirror that the escort should not have become separated.

'They have called for a demonstration tonight,' Vellosi continued his monologue. 'The students, the unemployed, the men of the Democrazia Proletaria, the children of the Autonomia. A medley of the discontented. The Questura has banned it, no march, no meeting is permitted, but the rats will be out once they have the night to hide them. The murder of Enrico Panicucci is the rallying cry. They will break some limbs and smash some shops and burn some cars and scream about the violence of the State. And Tantardini's name will be heard in the centro storico and the ones that shout it would not have heard of her before this morning's radio. Mauro, I feel I should weep for Italy.'

The driver, sensing the discourse was exhausted, again nodded, decisively and with agreement. Perhaps if the Dottore had a wife and children then he would be changed, not bleed himself so copiously. But Vellosi was alone, and his home was his office and his furniture was his filing cabinet, and his family were the young men he sent on to the streets at darkness to fight his war. The cars swept into the back entrance of the Questura, recognized and saluted by the officer on the barrier.

Francesco Vellosi was not a man to be kept waiting. A greeting party of three inclined their heads as he emerged from his car. If the Dottore would follow them they would lead to the interrogation room. Tantardini was eating in the cell block. She had been questioned once; a shrug of the shoulders and a grimace to demonstrate how much had been learned. The session was about to be resumed. Vellosi followed his guides through pale lit corridors, down steps, past guards. Down into the bowels of the building. There were more handshakes at the entrance to the designated room and then Vellosi's escort abandoned him. He was left with his own people, the ones prepared to dirty their hands, while those who had brought him this far could retreat from the subterranean world of violence and counter-violence and breathe again the real air that was not conducted by ageing generators and fans. There were two men in the room, both known to Vellosi because they were his appointees; hard men, and efficient and devoid of soul. Skilful in interrogation, impatient of prevarication, these were their credentials. And what other criteria could be used in recruitment? What other men could be found to muddy their fingers in defence of a gross and obese society? The excitement was running for Vellosi because these were his colleagues, and in their company he was content and at ease.

He gestured his readiness and sat himself on a bare wooden chair in the shadow of the door where he would face the interrogators. The prisoner would not see him as the lights shone in her eyes, where she would be confronted by her questioners; her back would be to him. Vellosi heard the far distant, the approaching tramp of weighted shoes, and he found himself arched and taut as the woman, eclipsing the lights, was brought through the door. She blazoned her indifference, casually flopped down in a chair in front of the lone table. This was the enemy, the opponent of menace and hazard, and all he could see were the angular shoulder-blades of a good-looking woman with her hair circled by a cheap cotton scarf. Dirty jeans and unwashed blouse, no lipstick and a sneer to substantiate the threat. Where were her tanks, and her ADCs? Where was her army and her regiments and platoons? Where was her serial number and her rank? Dead still Vellosi stayed, because that way she had no reason to turn and face him. That way he was the voyeur, the intruder at a private party.

One interrogator lounged across the table from her. The second man was further back behind him with the file and the notepad on his knees. There was no paper laid out on the table because the man who would ask questions and seek to find flaws in her defiance must demonstrate his knowledge, must have no need for typed reports, must dominate if he were to succeed.

'You have had your food, Tantardini?' He spoke conversationally, without rancour.

Vellosi heard her snort, the derision that communicated tension.

'You have no complaints about the food?'

No response.

'And you have not been hurt, you have not been tortured?'

Vellosi saw her shrug. Non-committal, as if the question were unimportant. But then the woman had no audience; she would be a changed person in the cockpit of the public courtroom.

'We have not treated you in any way that violates the constitution? We have behaved, Tantardini, is that right?' He mocked her gently, feeling his way forward, amused.

Again the shrug.

'And that is not as you would have expected? Am I correct? That is not what the communiqués will state, am I correct?'

No response.

'But then we play by different rules from yours.'

She drove back at him, seeking to destroy the

smugness and complacency that he had fashioned on his face. 'If you do not hurt me it is because you are afraid. There is no compassion in lackeys like yourself. There is no kindness among you pigs. Fear governs you. Fear of the reach of our arm. The society that you are servile to cannot protect you. If you lay a hand on me, a finger, a nail, then we will strike you down. That is why you give me food. That is why you do not touch me.'

'We are afraid of no-one, Tantardini. Least of all the little ones, like yourself. Perhaps we are cautious of the strength of the Brigate Rosse, cautious only, perhaps we treat them with care. But the NAP does not match the Brigate Rosse, the NAP is trivial and without muscle.'

'You hunt us hard. If we have no muscle you spend much time on us.'

The interrogator smiled, still sparring, still dancing far apart, as if unwilling yet to clash with the gloves. Then he leaned forward and the grin was erased.

'In twenty-five years' time, Tantardini, how old will you be?'

Vellosi could see the outline of the woman's neck, could see the smooth bright skin of youth.

'You have the files, you have the information,' she replied.

'You will be old, Tantardini. Old and withered and barren. In twenty-five years there will be new generations. Young men and women will grow and take their places in society and they will never have heard of La Tantardini. You will be a dinosaur to them. An ancient creature, verging on extinction.'

Perhaps he has hurt her, perhaps that is the way to her. Vellosi sat very still, breathing quietly, satisfied she was unaware of his presence. There was no response from her.

'That is the future, that is what you have to consider, Tantardini. Twenty-five years to brood on your revolution.' The interrogator droned on. 'You'll be a senile hag, a dowager of anarchy, when you are released. A tedious symbol of a phase in our history, courted by a few sociologists, dug out for documentaries by the RAI. And all will marvel at your stupidity. That is the future, Tantardini.'

'Will you say that when the bullets strike your legs?' she hissed, the cobra at bay. 'When the comrades are at you, when there are no chains at their wrists? Will you make speeches to me then?'

'There will be no bullets. Because you and your kind will be buried behind the walls of Messina and Asinara and Favignana. Removed from the reach of ordinary and decent people . . .'

'You will die in your own blood. It will not be in the legs, it will be to kill.' She shouted now, her voice dinning across the room. Vellosi saw the veins leaping at her neck, straining down into the collar of her blouse. Fierce and untamed, the magnificent savage. La leonessa, as the civil servant had christened her.

'La Vianale cursed her judge, but I think he is well and with his family tonight, and it is now two years that her threat has been empty and hollow.' The interrogator spoke quietly.

'Be careful, my friend. Do not look for paper victories, for victories that you can boast of. We have an army of strength. We will follow you, we will find you.'

'And where will you find your army? Where

130

will you recruit your children, from which kindergarten?'

'You will find the answer. You will find it one morning as you kiss your wife. As you walk back from school from setting the children down. You will see the power of the proletarian masses.'

'That's shit, Tantardini. Proletarian masses, it means nothing. Revolutionary warfare, nothing. Struggle of the workers, nothing. It's gibberish, boring and rejected gibberish.'

'You will see.' Her voice was a whisper and there was a cold in the room that clutched at the man who wrote the notes behind the interrogator and which made him thankful that he was far from the front line, a non-combatant, obscure and unrecognized.

'It's shit, Tantardini, because you have no army. You go to war with sick children. What have you to throw against me? Giancarlo Battestini, is that the hero who will strike—'

The pain fled her face. She shrieked with laughter, pealed it round the faces of the watching men. 'Giancarlo? Is that what you think we are made of? Little Giancarlo?'

'We have his name, we have his fingerprints, his photograph. Where will he go, Tantardini?'

'What do you want with him, little Giancarlo? His capture won't win you a war.'

Angered for the first time, resenting the dismissal of a situation he had worked towards with care and precision, the interrogator slammed his fist to the table. 'We want the boy. Tantardini, Panicucci, Battestini, we want the package.'

She jeered back at him. 'He is nothing, not to us, not to you. A little bed-wetter, looking for a mother. A thrower of Molotovs. Good for demonstrations.'

'Good enough for your bed,' he chanced.

'Even you might be good enough for my bed. Even you, little pig, if there was darkness, if you washed your mouth.'

'He was with you at the shooting of Cesare Fulni, at the factory.'

'Sitting in the car, watching, messing his pants, masturbating most likely.' She laughed again, as if in enjoyment.

Vellosi smiled, deep and safe in his privacy. She was a worthy enemy. Unique, styled, irreplaceable as an opponent.

'Where will he go?' The interrogator was flustered and unsettled.

'If you want Giancarlo go and stand outside his mother's door, wait till it is cold, wait till he is hungry.'

The interrogator shook his shoulders, closed his eyes, seemed to mutter an obscenity. His fingers were clamped together, knuckles showing white. 'Twenty-five years, Franca. For a man or a woman it is a lifetime. You know you can help us, and we can help you.'

'You begin to bore me.'

Vellosi saw the hate summoned to the man's narrowed lips.

'I will come one day each year and stand over the exercise yard and I will watch you, and then you will tell me whether I bore you.'

'I will look for you. And on the day that you have broken the rendezvous then I will laugh. You will hear me, pig, however deep you are buried, however far is your grave. You will hear me. You do not frighten me because already you are running.'

'You stupid little whore.'

She waved her hand carelessly at him. 'I am tired. You do not interest me and I would like to go now. I would like to go back to my room.'

She stood up, proud and erect, and seemed to Vellosi to mesmerize her questioner because he came round the table and opened the door for her. She was gone without a backward glance, leaving the room abandoned and without a presence.

The interrogator looked sheepishly at his chief. 'The boy, sweet little Giancarlo, she would have eaten him, bitten him down to the bone.'

'A very serious lady,' replied Francesco Vellosi with as composed a face as he could muster. 'She will have given her little bed-wetter and Molotov-thrower a night he will not quickly forget.'

Chapter Seven

For four undemanding years Archie Carpenter had been on the sprawling staff list of International Chemical Holdings. Four years in which his life revolved around negotiated office hours, a stipulated lunch break, five weeks' annual holiday, and days off for working public holidays. A 'soft old number, Archie', his one-time friends in the Special Branch of the Metropolitan Police called it when the old ties proved too strong and he hunted them out in the pub behind the Yard for a grouse and a gossip. He had settled for a predictable backwater in an unremarkable current. So, it had been a traumatic evening. First, he had been summoned to the Managing Director's suite of offices. He'd stood with puzzlement on his face through a briefing on the kidnapping of Geoffrey Harrison and its company implications. The Personnel Director had handed him an open-dated return ticket to Rome on the way out. In a fluster he'd been ushered to the front entrance where a company car waited to speed him to Heathrow. Last on to the plane.

But he wasn't in Rome. Hadn't arrived at his destination. Archie Carpenter was in front of the departure board at Linate, Milan's international air-port. Strike in Rome, he'd been told. Cockpit crew, and he was lucky to have reached this far. There might be a flight later and he must wait as everybody else was waiting. He'd asked repeatedly whether he would have a ticket for the first flight to leave for Fiumicino. He was smiled at and had learned in twenty minutes that the shaken shoulder of a man in uniform meant everything or nothing, the inter-pretation was free. All done up for the party, and nowhere to go. He paced, cursing, through the ant-scurrying crowds of fellow travellers, always returning to the crush around the board. Four years ago he wouldn't have been flapping, would have made his assessment and either sat back and let the tide take him or jumped off his backside and done something about it, like a self-drive hire car, or a taxi down to the Central Station and an express to the capital. But the improvisation was on the way out, the mechanics of initiative were rusty, and so he tramped the concourse and breathed his abuse.

A Detective Chief Inspector in Special Branch had been Archie Carpenter's lofty ranking in the Metro-politan Police when he had moved over into 'industry', as his wife liked to spell it out to the neighbours. All the big firms in the City had been frantic for security-trained personnel to advise them on protection from the rash of Provisional IRA bomb-ings in London. Frightened half to death they'd been at the prospect of letter bombs in the mailbags, of explosive devices in the corridors and the under-ground car park, looking for chaps with a confident jargon who seemed to know what they were at. ICH, a multinational colossus, officers and factories half way round the world, had one small plant outside Ballymena, County Antrim in Northern Ireland. The Board of Directors had determined that this put the vast conglomerate at risk and was sufficient reason to lure Archie Carpenter from sixteen hours a day five days a week of plodding with the Branch. They had popped him into a nice, clean, air-conditioned office with a secretary to write his letters, a pension when he was senile and nine thousand a year for his bank account. It had seemed like one long holiday. No more surveillance on winter evenings, no more meetings of the political loonies to drift into, no more Irish pubs to swill Guinness in, no more tetchy Arabs to stand alongside with a Smith and Wesson rammed in his belt. It had taken him a month to seal Chemical House, to put a system into operation that reduced the always faint threat to a minimum, and after that it had been more than comfortable, with little to worry him beyond the occasional pilfering from the typists' lockers, and the one great drama of the loss of a set of board-room minutes. He didn't complain, didn't want it to change.

He wasn't a small man. Had a good set of shoulders on him, and a stomach to go with it from four years of canteen lunches. But they availed him nothing when the herd of would-be passengers responded to the loudspeaker announcement and surged for the nominated check-in counter. Slight little girls bouncing him aside, chaps with concave chests pushing him half off his feet. Never seen anything like it.

'Wait a minute. Excuse me, won't you. You don't have to push like that, you know.' Helped him not at all.

Archie Carpenter's anger rose, the tired flush driving up his cheeks, and he thrust with the best of them and was almost ashamed at his progress. The gaps opened for his sharp, driving kneecaps and the heave of his elbows, and there were pained stares. Bit heavy, perhaps, but I didn't start it, darling, did I? So don't curl your bloody lip and flick your fingers. A little victory it had been, and one worth winning if there wasn't anything else about to compete for.

Ticket and boarding card in his hand, step a little lighter, Archie Carpenter headed for the security gates dividing the concourse from the departure lounges. His face twisted in distaste at the sight of the polizia, slacks that looked as if they'd been sat in for a week, dowdy pointed shoes, and those bloody great machine-pistols. What were they going to do with them? In a crowded space like an airport lounge, what was going to happen if they let one of those things off? Be a massacre, a Bloody Sunday, a St Valentine's Day job. Needed marksmen, didn't they? Chaps who'd be selective, not wallpaper merchants. First impressions, Archie, and they're the worst. Fair enough, sunshine, but if that's the mob that has to bust out Harrison, then draw the curtain and forget it. He'd carried a gun a dozen times in eight years with the Branch, always under a jacket, and it hurt him, professionally, to see these kids with their hardware lolling against their chests.

With no moon and a heavy darkness round them, the Alitalia DC9 lifted off. Hours late they'd be into Rome, and then all the joke of the money change queue and finding whether he'd been met and if the hotel had a booking. Stop bloody moaning, Archie. Off on your holidays, aren't you? Remember what the wife said. Her mum had brought back from Viareggio some nice leather purses, be good for Christmas presents for the family, mustn't forget to bring something like that. I'm not going for my health, for a saunter round, darling. But you'll have some time off. Not for a shopping spree. Well, what are you going for? Haven't time to tell you now, darling, but it's all a bit messy and the plane's leaving five minutes ago. And he hadn't any clean underwear. He'd rung off, gently put down the telephone in the Chemical House hallway. Would have shaken the poor old sweetheart. Weren't many fellows in Churchill Avenue, Motspur Park who charged off abroad without so much as a toothbrush to hold on to.

All a bit messy, Archie Carpenter.

No drinks on the flight. Cockpit crew strike ended. Cabin crew strike continuing.

The Managing Director had been explicit enough. They'd pay up and pay quickly. Head Office didn't want it lingering. The locals would set it up and he was there to oversee the arrangements and report back. Going to cause a bit of pain, paying out that sort of cash. Surprised him really, that they'd made up their minds so fast and hadn't thought of brazening it out.

Fifty minutes of sitting cramped in his seat and nothing to read but Personnel's photostat file on Geoffrey Harrison with a six-digit number stamped on the outside. In the file was a blown-up passport photograph of the man, dated eighteen months earlier. He looked to be a reasonable enough chap, pleasant nondescript sort of face, the sort people always had problems describing afterwards. But then, Archie Carpenter thought, that's what he probably is, pleasant and nondescript. Why should he be anything else?

They had stripped the hood from him before he was brought from the van, affording a vast relief at the freedom from the musk of the material that had strained and scratched at his throat. The plaster too had been pulled away from his mouth, just as they had done hours earlier when they had fed him. The tape around his legs had been loosened and the blood flowed, quick and tingling, to his feet.

All that Geoffrey Harrison had seen of his new prison had been from the beam of the torch that one of the masked men had carried as they pushed him along a way between small stones and across sun-dried earth, until they had come after a few metres to the shadowed outline of a farmer's shed. The beam had played vaguely on a small sturdy building, where the mortar was crumbling from between the rough-hewn stones and replaced by dangling grass weed. Windowless and with twin doors at each end and a shallow sloping corrugated tin roof. They had hurried him through the door and the light had discovered a ladder set against piled hay bales. No words from his captors, only the instruction of the jabbed fist that he should climb, and immediately he started to move there was the weight and shudder of another man on the rungs below him, steadying and supporting because his hands were still fastened at his back.

Between the roof and the upper level of the hay bed was a space some four feet in height. The man in the darkness behind shoved Harrison forward with a lurch and he crawled ahead along the noisy shifting floor of bales. Then there was a hand at his shoulder to halt him. His wrist was taken in a vice grip. One ring of the handcuffs was unlocked. He looked upwards as the man worked in haste by torchlight. His hand that was still held was jerked high and the ratchet action of the handcuff closed on a steel chain that hung from a beam to which the roofing iron was nailed. A chain of the width and strength to subdue a farmyard Alsatian dog.

Geoffrey Harrison had been brought to the safe house. He had been hidden in a distant barn long disused for anything except the storage of winter fodder for cattle. The barn lay a hundred metres off a dirt track that in turn was a tributary of the high-banked tarmac road a kilometre away that linked the town of Palmi with the village of Castellace in the pimpled foothills of the Aspromonte. Through the day and the greater part of the night the van had travelled more than nine hundred kilometres.

To the north-east of the barn was the village of San Martino, to the south-east the village of Castellace. To the north-west were Melicucca and San Procopio, to the south-west the community of Cosoleto. From the rooftop of the barn it would have been possible to identify the separated lights of the villages, bandaged tightly by the darkness, lonely and glowing places of habitation. This was the country of lightly rolling rockstrewn hills decorated with the cover of olive groves, the territory of shepherds who minded small sheep flocks and herds of goats and who carried shotguns and shunned the company of strangers. These were the wild hill lands of Calabria

140

that claimed a fierce independence, the highest crime rate per capita in the Republic, the lowest incidence of arrest. A primitive, feudal, battened-down society.

The low voices of two men were Harrison's company as he lay on the bales, the talk of men who are well known to each other and who speak merely because they have time on their hands and long hours to pass.

As a formality he ran his left hand over the hand-cuff, then tested with his fingers the route of the chain over the bar, and groped without hope at the padlock that held it there. No possibility of movement, no prospect of loosening either his wrist or the chain attachment. But it had been a cursory examination, that of a man numbed with exhaustion who had burned deep into the core of his emotion.

On the warm softness of the hay he was soon asleep, curled on his side with his knees pressed up against his chest. His mind closed to all around him, permitting neither dream nor nightmare, he found a peace, stirring hardly at all, his breathing calm and regular.

The clashes spread far through the centro storico of the capital city. Under cover of darkness the gangs of young people, small and co-ordinated, smashed a trail of broken shop windows and burned-out cars. The night air echoed with the crack of Molotovs on the cobbles, the howl of police sirens and the reports of carabinieri rifles that threw gas shells into the narrow streets. A night full of the noise of street battle and the cries of 'Death to the fascists', 'Death to the assassins of Panicucci' and 'Freedom for Tantardini'.

Twenty-nine arrests, five polizia injured, eleven shops damaged and eighteen cars. And the name of Franca Tantardini had been heard and would be seen when morning came to the city written large on the walls in dripping paint.

His guests gone, the dinner table of the executive suite in ICH House cleared, Sir David Adams retreated to his office. In midweek he frequently worked late, his justification for prohibiting business interference during weekends at his country retreat. The principal officers of the company had learned to expect his staccato tones on the telephone at any hour before he cleared his desk and walked across to his Barbican flat for the trifle of sleep that he needed.

His target this evening was his Personnel Director, who took the call on a bedside extension line. The conversation was typically to the point.

'The man we sent to Rome, he got away all right?'

'Yes, Sir David. I checked with Alitalia, he was diverted to Milan, but he managed an onward to Rome.'

'Have you called Harrison's wife?'

'Couldn't get through. I tried before I left the office, but this fellow Carpenter will do that.'

'He'll be in touch with her?'

'First thing in the morning.'

'How's Harrison going to stand up to all this? The man from the Embassy who called me was pretty blunt in his scenario.'

'I've been through Harrison's file, Sir David.

Doesn't tell us much. He's a damn good record with the company . . . well, that's obvious for him to have had the posting. He's a figures man . . .'

'I know all that. What's he going to be like under this sort of pressure, how's he going to take it?'

'He's fine under business pressure . . .'

The Personnel Director heard a sigh of annoyance whistle at his ear.

'Is he an outdoor type, does he have any outdoor hobbies listed on his file?'

'Not really, Sir David. He listed "reading" . . .'

There was a snort on the line. 'You know what that means. That he comes home, switches on television, drinks three gins and gets to his bed and his sleep. A man who offers reading as a hobby is a recreational eunuch in my book.'

'What are you implying?'

'That the poor blighter is totally unfitted for the hoop he's going to be put through. I'll see you in the morning.' Sir David Adams rang off.

In a restaurant in the northern outskirts of Rome, secure and far from the running street fight, Guiseppe Carboni shuffled his ample wife around the cleared dance floor. The tables and chairs had been pushed back against the walls to make space for the entertainment. A gypsy fiddler, a young man with a bright accordion and his father with a guitar, provided the music for the assortment of guests. It was a gathering of friends, an annual occasion and one valued by Carboni. The kidnapping of Geoffrey Harrison provided no reason for him to stay away from the evening of fancy dress enjoyment.

He had come dressed as a ghost, his wife and her

143

sewing-machine concocting from an old white sheet and a pillow-slip with eye slits the costume that had caused loud acclamation on his entry. She was robed in the costume of a Sardinian peasant girl. They had eaten well and drunk deep of the Friuli wine and the night would serve as a brief escape from the dreary piling of reports on his desk at the Questura. And there was advantage for Carboni in such company. An Under-Secretary of the Ministry of the Interior, in a mouse's habit with tail hanging from his rump, was dancing close to his shoulder. Across the floor a deputy of the Democrazia Cristiana, and one spoken of as ambitious and well-connected, clutched at the hips of a girl both blonde and beautiful and attired solely in a toga created from the Stars and Stripes. Good company for Carboni to be keeping; and what good would be achieved sitting in his flat with an ear cocked for the telephone? It was too early in the Harrison matter for intervention. Always it was easier to work when the money had been paid, when there were not tearful wives and stone-faced legal men complaining in high places that the life of their dear one and their client was being endangered by police investigation.

He bobbed his head at the Under-Secretary, smirked beneath his pillowcase at the deputy, and propelled his wife forward. There were few enough of these evenings when he was safe from disturbance and aggravation. He bowed to the man in property who wore the fading theatrical uniform of a Napoleonic dragoon and who was said to be a holiday companion at the villa of the President of the Council of Ministers. Diamonds catching brightly in the guttering candlelight, the crisp cackle of laughter,

144

the sweet ring of the violin chords. Movement and life and pleasure, and the white-coated waiters weaved among the guests dispensing brandy tumblers and glasses of sambucca and amaro. The man in property was beside him, more smiles and a hand released from his wife's waist so that Carboni could greet the interloper.

'Please forgive me, Signora Carboni, please excuse me. May I take your husband for a moment . . . ?'

'He dances badly,' she tinkled.

The man in property kissed her hand, laughed with her. 'It is the cross of marrying a policeman, always there is someone to take him aside and whisper in his ear. My extreme apologies for the interruption.'

'You have the gratitude of my feet.'

The ghost and the dragoon huddled together in a corner, far from earshot, achieving among the sounds of talk and music a certain privacy.

'Dottore Carboni, first my apologies.'

'For nothing.'

'You are busy at this time with the new plague, the blight over us all. You are involved in enquiries into the kidnappings.'

'It is the principal aspect of our work, though less intense here than in the north.'

'And always the problem is to find the major figures, am I right? They are the hard ones.'

'They protect themselves well, they cover their activities with care.'

'Perhaps it is nothing, perhaps it is not my business . . .' It was how they all began when they wished to pour poison in a policeman's ear . . . 'but something has been brought to my attention. It has

145

come from the legal section of my firm, we have some bright young men there and it was something that aroused their interest, and that involved a competitor.' That was predictable too, thought Carboni, but the man must be heard out if it were not to reach the head of government that a policeman had not reacted to the advice of a friend.

'A year ago I was in competition for a site for chalets on the Golfo di Policastro, near to Sapri, and the man against me was called Mazzotti, Antonio Mazzotti. Around two hundred millions were needed to settle the matter, and Mazzotti outbid me. He took the site, I took my money elsewhere. But then Mazzotti could not fulfil his commitments, it was said he could not raise the capital, that he was over-extended, and I am assured he sold at a loss. It is a difficult game, property, Dottore, many burn their fingers. We thought nothing more of him, another amateur. Then two weeks ago I was in competition for a place to the south of Sapri, at the Marina de Maratea. There was another location where it was possible to build some chalets . . . but my money was insufficient. Then yesterday my boys in the legal section told me that the purchaser was Mazzotti. Well, it is possible in business to make a fast recovery but he paid in bank draft the greater proportion of the sum. From an outside bank, outside Italy. The money has run back sharply to the hands of this Mazzotti. I set my people to find out more and they tell me this afternoon that he is from the village of Cosoleto in Calabria. He is from the bandit land. I ask myself, is there anything wrong with a man from the hills having brains and working hard and advancing himself. Nothing, I tell myself.

Nothing. But it was in foreign draft that he paid, Dottore. That, you will agree, is not usual.'

'It is not usual,' Carboni agreed. He hoped the man had finished, wished only to get back to the music. 'And I would have thought it a matter for the Guardia di Finanze if there have been irregularities of transfer.'

'You do not follow me. I do not care where the fellow salts his money, I am interested in where he acquires it, and how its source springs up so quickly.'

'You are very kind to have taken so much trouble.'

'I have told no-one else of my detective work.' A light laugh.

'In the morning I will make some enquiries, but you understand I have a great preoccupation with the kidnapping of the Englishman.'

'I would not wish my name to be mentioned in this matter.'

'You have my word,' said Carboni, and was gone to the side of his wife. Something or nothing, and time in the morning to run a check on Antonio Mazzotti. Time in the morning to discover whether there were grounds for suspicion or whether a disgruntled businessman was using the influence of the network of privilege to hinder an opponent who had twice outwitted him.

Giuseppe Carboni scooped the pillowslip over his head and downed a cooled glass of Stock brandy, wiped his face, dropped again his disguise and resumed with his wife a circuit of the dance floor.

* * *

When they reached the second-floor room, puffing because they came by the turning staircase as there was no lift in a pensione such as this, Giancarlo stood back, witnessing the drunken effort of Claudio to fit the room key to the door lock. They had taken a room in a small and private place between the Piazza Vittorio Emanuele and the Piazza Dante, with a barren front hall and a chipped reception desk that carried signs demanding prepayment of money and the decree that rooms could not be rented by the hour. The portière asked no questions, explained that the room must be vacated by noon, pocketed the eight thousand lire handed him by Claudio and presumed them to be from the growing homosexual clan.

On the landing, waiting behind the fumbling Claudio, Giancarlo looked down at his sodden jeans, dark and stained below the knees, and his canvas shoes that oozed the wine he had poured away under the table in the pizzeria. He had eaten hugely, drunk next to nothing, was now sobered and alert and ready for the confrontation that he had chosen. The Calabrian needed a full minute, interspersed with oaths, to unfasten the door and reveal the room. It was bare and functional. A wooden table with chair. A wooden single-door wardrobe. A thin-framed print of old Rome. Two single beds separated by a low table on which rested a closed Bible and a small lamp. Claudio pitched forward, as if it were immaterial to him that the door was still open, and began pulling with a ferocious clumsiness at his clothes, dragging them from his back and arms and legs before sinking heavily in his underpants on to the grey bedspread. Giancarlo extracted the

148

key from the outside lock, closed the door behind him and then locked it again before pocketing the key.

Cold and detached, no longer running, no longer in flight, Giancarlo looked down with contempt at the sprawled figure on the bed, ranged his eyes over the hair-encased legs, the stomach of rolled fat and on up to the opened mouth that sucked hard for air. He stood for a long time to be certain in his mind that the building was at peace and the other residents asleep. An animal, he seemed to Giancarlo, an illiterate animal. The pig had called his Franca a whore, the pig would suffer. With a deliberation he had not owned before, as if sudden age and manhood had fallen to him, he reached under his shirt tail and pulled the P38 from his belt. On the balls of his feet and keeping his silence he moved across the linoleum and stopped two metres from the bed. Close enough to Claudio, and beyond the reach of his arms.

'Claudio, can you hear me?' A strained whisper.

In response only the convulsed breathing.

'Claudio, I want to talk to you.'

A belly-deep grunted protest of irritation.

'Claudio, you must wake up. I have questions for you, pig.'

A little louder now. Insufficient to turn the face of Claudio, enough to annoy and to cause him to wriggle his shoulders in anger as if trying to rid himself of the presence of a flea.

'Claudio, wake yourself.'

The eyes opened and were wide and staring and confused because close to them was the outstretched hand that held the pistol, and the message in the boy's gaze was clear even through the mist of station beer and pizzeria wine.

'Claudio, you should know that you are very close to death. I am near to killing you, there as you lie on your back. You save yourself only if you tell me what I want to know. You understand, Claudio?'

The voice droned at the dulled mind of the prostrate man, dripping its message, spoken by a parent who has an ultimatum on behaviour to deliver to a child. The bedsprings whined as the bulk of the man began to shift and stir, moving backwards towards the head rest, creating distance from the pistol. Giancarlo watched him trying for focus and comprehension, substituting the vague dream for the reality of the P38 and the slight figure that held it. The boy pressed on, dominating, sensing the moment was right.

'There is nowhere to go, no-one to save you. I will kill you, Claudio, if you do not tell me what I ask you. Kill you so that the blood runs from you.'

The boy felt detached from his words, separated from the sounds that his ears could hear. No word from the pig.

'It is the P38, Claudio. The weapon of the fighters of the NAP. It is loaded and I have only to draw back the trigger. Only to do that and you are dead, and rotting and fly-infested. Am I clear, Claudio?'

The boy could not recognize himself, could not recognize the strength of his grip upon the gun.

'It is the P38. Many have died by this gun. There would be no hesitation, not in sending a Calabrian pig to his earth hole.'

'What do you want?'

'I want an answer.'

'Don't play with me, boy.'

'If I want to play with you, Claudio, then I will do so. If I want to tease you, then I will. If I want to hurt you, then you cannot protect yourself. You have nothing but the information that I want from you. Give it me and you live. It is that or the P38.'

The boy watched the man strain in the night stillness for a vibration of life from the building, ears cocked for something that might give him hope of rescue, and saw the dumb collapse at the realization that the pensione slept cloaked in night. The big body crumbled back flat on to the bed as if defeated and the coiled springs tolled under the mattress.

'What do you want?'

He is ready, thought Giancarlo, as ready as he will ever be.

'I want to know where the man is hidden that was taken this morning.' The message came in a flurry, as a transitory shower of snow falls on the high places of the Apennines, quick and brisk and blanketing. 'If you want to live, Claudio, you must tell me where to find him.'

Easier now for Claudio. Easier because there was something that he could bite at. Half a smile on his face, because the drink was still with him and he lacked the control to hide the first, frail amusement.

'How would I know that?'

'You will know it. Because if you do not you will die.'

'I am not told such things.'

'Then you are dead, Claudio. Dead because you are stupid, dead because you did not know.'

151

From the toes of his feet, moving with the swaying speed of the snake, Giancarlo rocked forward, never losing the balance that was perfect and symmetrical. His right arm lunged, blurred in its aggression till the foresight of the gun was against the man's ear. Momentarily it rested there, then raked back across the fear-driven, quivering face and the sharp needle of the sight gouged a ribbon welt through the jungle of bristle and hair. Claudio snatched at the gun, and grasped only at the air and was late and defeated while the blood welled and spilled from the road hewn across his cheek.

'Do not die from stupidity and idiocy, Claudio. Do not die because you failed to understand that I am no longer the child who was protected in the Queen of Heaven. Tell me where they took the man. Tell me.' The demand for an answer, harsh and compelling, winning through the exhaustion and the drink, abetted by the blood trickle beneath the man's hand.

'They do not tell me such things.'

'Inadequate, Claudio . . . to save yourself.'

'I don't know. In God's name I don't know.'

Giancarlo saw the struggle for survival, the two extremes of the pendulum. If he spoke now the immediate risk to the pig's life would be removed, to be replaced in the fullness of time by the threat of the retribution that the organization would bring down on his dulled head should betrayal be his temporary salvation. The boy sensed the conflict, the alternating fortunes of the two armies waging war in the man's mind.

'Then in your ignorance you die.'

Noisily because it was not a refined mechanism,

Giancarlo drew back with his thumb the hammer of the pistol. It reverberated around the room, a sound that was sinister, irretrievable. Claudio was half up on the bed, pushed from his elbows, his hand flown from the wound. Eyes, saucer-large and peering into the dimness, perspiration in bright rivers on his forehead. Dismal and pathetic and beaten, his attention committed to the rigid, unmoving barrel aimed at the centre of his ribcage.

'They will have taken him to the Mezzo Giorno,' Claudio whispered his response, the man who is behind the velvet curtain of the confessional and who has much to tell the Father and is afraid lest any other should hear his words.

'The Mezzo Giorno is half the country. Where in the south has he gone?'

Giancarlo pickaxed into the strata of the man. Domineering. Holding in his cage the trapped rat, and offering it as yet no escape.

'They will have gone to the Aspromonte . . .'

'The Aspromonte stretch a hundred kilometres across Calabria. What will you have me do? Walk the length of them and shout and call and search in each farmhouse, each barn, each cave? You do not satisfy me, Claudio.' Spoken with the chill and deep cold of the ice on the hills in winter.

'We are a family in the Aspromonte. There are many of us. Some do one part of it, others take different work in the business. They sent me to Rome to take him. There was a cousin and a nephew of the cousin that were to drive him to the Aspromonte where he would be held. There is another who will guard him . . .'

'Where will they guard him?' The gun, hammer

153

arched, inched closer to Claudio's head.

'God's truth, on the Soul of the Virgin, I do not know where they will hold him.'

The boy saw the despair written boldly, sensed that he was prising open the area of truth. 'Who is the man that will guard him?' The first minimal trace of kindness in the boy's voice.

'He is the brother of my wife. He is Alberto Sammartino.'

'Where does he live?'

'On the Acquaro road and near to Cosoleto.'

'I do not know those names.'

'It is the big road that comes into the mountains from Sinopli and that runs on towards Delianuova. Between Acquaro and Cosoleto is one kilometre. There is an olive orchard on the left side, about four hundred metres from Cosoleto, where the road begins to climb to the village. You will see the house set back from the road, there are many dogs there and some sheep. Once the house was white. His car is yellow, an Alfa. If you go there you will find him.'

'And he will be guarding the Englishman?'

'That was what had been arranged.'

'Perhaps you try only to trick me.'

'On the Virgin, I swear it.'

'You are a pig, Claudio. A snivelling coward pig. You swear on the Virgin and you betray the family of your wife, and you tell all to a boy. In the NAP we would die rather than leave our friends.'

'What will you do with me now?' A whipped dog, one that does not know whether its punishment is completed, whether it is still possible to regain affection. On a lower floor a lavatory flushed.

'I will tie you up and I will leave you here.' The automatic response. 'Turn over to your face on the pillow. Your hands behind your back.'

Giancarlo watched the man curl himself to his stomach. In his vision for a moment was the shamed grin of self-preservation on Claudio's face because he had won through with nothing more than a scratch across his cheek. Gone then, lost in the pillow and its grease coat.

When the man was still, Giancarlo moved quickly forward. Poised himself, stiffened his muscles. He swung down the handle of the pistol with all his resources of strength on to the sun-darkened balding patch at the apex of Claudio's skull. One desperate rearing convulsion that caused the boy to adjust his aim. The breaking of eggs, the shrieking of the bed-springs and the tremor of breathing that has lost its pattern and will fade.

Giancarlo stepped back. An aching silence encircled him as he listened. Not the creak of a floorboard, not the pressure of a foot on a staircase step. All in their beds and tangled with their whores and boys. Blood on the wall behind the bed, spattered as if the molecules had parted on an explosive impact, was running from drops in downward lines across the painted plaster, and above their furthest orbit, untainted, was the smiling and restful face of the Madonna in her plastic frame with the cherubic child. The boy did not look at Claudio again.

He cleared the hip pocket from the strewn trousers on the floor and went on tiptoe to the door. He turned the key, carried outside with him the 'non disturbare' sign, attached it to the outer door handle, locked the door again and slipped away down the stairs. To the portière he said that his friend would sleep late, that he himself was taking an early coach to Milano. The man nodded, scarce aroused from his dozing sleep at the desk.

Far into the night and with little traffic to impede him as he crossed the streets, the wraith, Giancarlo Battestini, headed for the Termini.

Chapter Eight

What in Christ's name am I doing here?

The first thoughts of Archie Carpenter. He was naked under a sheet, illuminated by the light that pierced the plastic blind slats. He flailed his arms at the hanging cloud of cigarette smoke, spat out the reek of brandy from the glasses that littered the dressing-table and window-sill.

Archie Carpenter sat up in bed, putting his memory together, slotting the evidence into place. Half the bloody night he'd spent with the men from ICH. All the way from the airport in the limousine he'd listened and they'd talked, he'd asked and they'd briefed. Convincing the big man from Chemical House of their competence, that's how he saw it. They'd taken care of his bags at the hotel with a finger snap and tramped into his room, rung down for a bottle of cognac and kept up the barrage till past three. He'd slept less than four hours and he had to show for it a headache and the clear knowledge that the intervention of Archie Carpenter had no chance of affecting Geoffrey Harrison's problems. He climbed out of bed and felt the weakness in his legs and the mind-bending pain behind his temples. Half midnight, at the latest, they wound things up in Motspur Park. Had to, didn't they? With babysitters at a pound an hour there wasn't much time after the ice-cream and fruit salad to sit on your arse and chat about the rate of income tax. And the brandy didn't flow, not out there in the suburbs, not at seven pounds a bottle. A quick splash after coffee and the Mums and Dads were on their way. Not that the Carpenters had kids . . . that's another trial, Archie. Not for now, old sunshine.

He'd need a shower to flush it out of him.

Beside his bed, under a filled ashtray, was his diary. He thumbed through for the number the Managing Director had given him. A chap called Charlesworth, from the Embassy and said to be helpful. He dialled, listened to the telephone ringing out, took a time to answer. What you'd expect at this time in the morning.

'Pronto, Charlesworth.'

'My name's Carpenter. Archie Carpenter of ICH. I'm the company's Security Director . . .' Since when had he had a title like that? But it sounded right, just sort of slipped out like a palmed visiting card. 'They've asked me to come out here and see what's going on. With this fellow Harrison, I mean.'

'It's nice of you to ring, but I'm a bit out of touch since yesterday evening.'

'They said in London you'd put yourself out in this business. I was asked to pass on the thanks of the company.'

'That's very kind of you, it was nothing.'

'They thought it was. I have to go out to this EUR place wherever that is, and I have to visit Harrison's

158

missus, so I'd like to meet you before that. First thing.'

Carpenter was aware of a hesitation on the line. A natural request, but it had sparked prevarication.

'I don't think there's very much that I can tell you.'

'I'd like to hear views other than from the company people. They're Italians, every last one of them. I'd like your views.'

'There really isn't much that I can tell you.'

'Not in the line of duty?' Carpenter clipped in, cold, awake, the brandy disgorged.

'I double between political and security. Security doesn't warrant a great deal of time, and the desk is pretty loaded with the political stuff at the moment. My plate's more than full.'

'So is Harrison's.' A flare of anger from Carpenter. What was the bloody fool at? 'He's British isn't he? Entitled to a bit of help from the Embassy.'

'He is,' came the cautious reply. 'But there's debate in the shop about how much help.'

'You've lost me.'

'I'm sorry, then.'

Carpenter closed his eyes, grimaced. Begin again, Archie boy. Start all over again.

'Mr Charlesworth, let's not waste each other's time. I'm not a moron, and I've kidnapping coming out of my ears after last night with the locals. I know it's not straightforward. I understand the threat that exists, that Harrison's on the edge. I know it's not just a matter of sitting in the front parlour and waiting for the shareholders to cough up so Harrison can come back and kiss his sweet wife hello. I know the risks for Harrison. They told me about Ambrosio, shot because a mask slipped and he saw his captors. I

159

heard how they chopped Michelangelo Ambrosio. They told me about de Capua. Now on to the other side of things. I did eight years in Special Branch before I moved to ICH. My rank at Scotland Yard was Chief Inspector. This isn't the time for a "need to know" show.'

A laugh on the line. 'Thanks for the speech, Mr Carpenter.'

'What's the problem, then?'

'I wouldn't want what I say repeated.'

'I've signed the bloody Official Secrets Act, Mr Charlesworth, just like you have.'

'It's a tedious matter of keeping our hands clean. Theoretically it's a criminal offence to pay ransom money, and it would be damaging to us if we could be linked with such a felony. In the Ambassador's view this is a private matter between ICH and a gang of Italian criminals. He doesn't want us to be seen to be condoning the extortion of money, and he feels that any public involvement could give the impression that we're bending the knee to criminal action. If Harrison worked for Whitehall we wouldn't be paying, it's as simple as that.'

'And a chat in your office . . .'

'That's involvement in the Ambassador's eyes.'

'That's bloody ridiculous,' Carpenter barked into the telephone.

'I agree, particularly in a country where ransom payment is the normal way of extrication. If you're that well briefed you'll have heard of a man called Pommarici in Milano. He's a prosecutor and has tried to freeze kidnap victims' assets, to prevent payment. He lost . . . the families said he was endangering the lives of their loved ones. It all went back to the jungle. So what it adds up to is that the Embassy has no role to play. Off the record we can help, but not if it's visible. Do you read me?'

Carpenter slopped back on to his bed. 'I read you, Mr Charlesworth.'

'Give me a ring this afternoon. We'll have an early bite in town.'

'I'd like that,' Carpenter said and rang off. Poor bloody Harrison, but how inconsiderate of him. To get himself kidnapped and embarrass HMG. Not a very good show, my old love.

The wooden shutters, bent and paint-peeled but still capable of restricting light, stayed late across the upper window of the narrow terraced home of Vanni, the driver. The noises made by children and cars in the cobbled street behind the main road through Cosoleto merely lulled the man as he lay in the drowsy pleasure of his bed.

It had been close to midnight when he had returned to his home, and there was the radiance in his worn face to tell his wife that the journey had been profitable. She had not asked what the work had been, what the danger, what the stake, but had busied herself first in the kitchen, then against the muscles of his stomach in the great bed that had been her mother's. And when he had slept she had slid from the sheets and looked with a glowing excitement at the hard roll of banknotes before replacing them in the hip pocket of the trousers thrown with abandon on a chair. A good man he was to her, and a kind man.

While she worked in the kitchen beneath, Vanni was content to idle the early morning hours. Not time yet for him to dress, throw on a freshly ironed shirt, put a sheen on his shoes and drive his car into Palmi for a coffee and a talk with Mario who would make a similar journey if ever he woke – she was an animal, Mario's woman, consumed in the brute passion of the Sicilians. A coffee with Mario if he had satisfied his woman, if he had the sap to leave his bed.

And when Claudio had returned on the morning rapido, then perhaps they all would be summoned to the villa of the capo to take a glass of Campari and talk of the olive trees, the goat herds, and the death of an old man of the village. They would not speak of anything that was immediate and close to them, but they would smile at their mutual knowledge, and each in his own way reflect a peculiar glory.

At least another hour Vanni could keep to his bed.

At Criminalpol, where the Rome police forensic effort is mounted, the first particles of evidence were being gathered in the scientific analysis section. Brought from the central telephone exchange were recordings of all calls received by ICH in EUR and of those directed to the private number of the Harrisons. One of the most far-reaching advances in the hunt for the kidnappers had been the development of a voice bank programmed for the computer to match similarities. The same man, the electronics decided, who had called ICH with the ransom demand had also made the abortive call to Mrs Harrison. Nothing particular in that. The stir of interest among the technicians came when they fed to the brain scores of recordings made from previous interceptions, and sought a similarity with their latest material. On the read-out screens the file on the Marchetti case was flashed. Eight and a half months earlier. A four-year-old boy. Taken from a foreign national nanny in the Aventino district of Rome. No arrests. No clues left on site. A ransom payment of 250 million paid. Marked notes. No sign of ransom money. The Marchetti communication and the calls on the Harrison case had been made by the same man. Vocal interpretation located an accent from the extreme south.

The night work of machines. The recordings were sent by line to the Questura to await the arrival of Giuseppe Carboni.

The Agente di Custodie hurried from the prison officers' mess to the main gate of the Asinara gaol. He had not eaten the breakfast provided for the men coming off night shift after they had supervised the first feeding of the prisoners. The weight of the message that he must telephone to the contact number bore down on him, spiriting up the fear waves of nausea.

His recruitment as a pigeon for the leading members of the NAP held on Asinara when they wished to communicate with the outside world had been a long-drawn-out affair. As a badger will sniff and dig for choice roots, so members of the group at liberty had discovered the turmoil that the Agente and his family lived with as they devoted themselves to the care of their ailing spina bifida baby. Reports had come back of crippling doctors' bills in the town of Sassari on the Sardinian mainland to the south of the prison island. There had been word of the inability of the father to pay for visits to Roma or Milano for consultation with specialists.

The Agente had been ripe for plucking. There was money for his wife, used notes in envelopes. He was no longer in debt and muttered instead and without conviction to the medical men of the help of a distant relative. Not that the child could improve, only that the conscience of the parents might be easier. The numbers that he must telephone changed frequently, and the cryptic messages that he must pass on became a deluge.

On Asinara is the maximum security cage of the Italian forces of justice, escape deemed impossible. It is the resting-place of the most dedicated of the male urban guerilla community, the receptacle for those found guilty of armed insurrection against the State. Originally a prison colony, then a gaol for the liberal few who opposed Mussolini's fascism, the gaol drifted into disrepair before the refurbishment that was necessary for the incarceration of the new enemy. The renovation had been from the drawing-board of the magistrate Riccardo Palma; he had done his work well, and died for it. But through the Agente the words of the Chief of Staff of the NAP could pass beyond the locked cell doors, along the watched corridors with their high closed-circuit cameras, through the puny exercise yards, piercing the lattice of the electrically controlled double gates and their dynamite-proof bars. The message had been given to the Agente as he lined the prisoners in a queue for their food, slipped into his hand, drowned in the sweat sea of his palm.

Beyond the gates and heading for his home, the free house of the prison service where only anxiety and pain awaited him, he had read the message on the scrap of sharply torn paper.

Per La Tantardini. Rappresaglia. Numero quattro.

For Tantardini. Reprisal. Number Four.

The Agente, held in the clutch of compromise, walked in a tortured daze that vanished as the pale broken face of his wife greeted his arrival at the front door. His child was dying, his wife was failing, and who cared, who helped? He kissed her perfunctorily, went to their room to change out of uniform, and then looked in silence through the half-open door at the child asleep in her cot. In his own clothes and without explanation he strode down into the hamlet to telephone to the number he had been given at Porto Torres across the narrow channel on Sardinia. Within one day, perhaps two, he would witness on the little black and white television screen in the corner of the living-room the results of his courier work.

The swollen pressure of his bladder finally awoke Geoffrey Harrison. He stretched himself, jerking at the handcuff, wrenching at his wrist, aware immediately of the inhibitions of his slept-in clothes. Still the suit that he had dressed in for the drive to the office, still with the tie at his neck, and only the top button undone as a concession to the circumstances. The sun had not yet played on the roof of the barn and he was cold, shivering. His socks smelt, pervading the limited space between the rafters and the bales; the nylon ones that he always wore in the summer and that he changed when he came home in the early evening.

Didn't speak the language, did he? Had never

taken a Berlitz. He could only order a meal and greet his office colleagues at the start of the day. So what to shout to the men in the other half of the barn? He wanted to urinate, wanted to squat and relieve himself, and didn't know how to say it. Basic human function, basic human language. He couldn't mess his trousers. That was revulsion, and so from necessity came the shout. Couldn't have an accident.

'Hey. Down there. Come here.' In English as if because of his urgency they would understand him. They'll come, Geoffrey, they'll want to know why the prisoner shouts. 'Come here.'

He heard the sudden movement, and the voices of two men that were closer. A creaking from the swing of the barn door that was hidden from him by the bales, and the ladder-top slid into position and shook from a man's weight. A gun first, black and ugly, held in a firm grip, and following it the contortion of a hood with eye slits. Eerie and awful in the half light before it gave way to the recognizable shape of shoulders and a man's trunk. The gesture of the gun was unmistakable. He obeyed the order of the waved barrel and stumbled back as far as the chain would allow. He pointed down to his zip, then across with his free hand to his buttocks. A grotesque mime. And the hooded head shook and was gone, lost below the lip of the hay.

There were noisy chuckles from below and then a farm bucket arched up, from an unseen hand. Old and rusted and once of galvanized steel. A folded wad of newspaper pages followed. He was left to a slight privacy as he pulled the bucket towards him, turned his back on the ladder and fingered at his belt. Humiliated and hurt, one arm aloft and fastened, he contorted his body over the bucket. He speeded his functions, willing his bladder and bowels to be emptied, before the slitted eyes returned to laugh at his dropped pants and his bared thighs and genitals. How half the world does it, Geoffrey, so get used to it. Don't think I can bloody well take it, not every day, not like this. God, what a bloody stink. The sandwich . . . all stink and wind. Remember the sandwich, back sometime yesterday, that the men in the van gave you, the curse in the guts. He groped down for the paper; damp with the morning dew, must have been outside through the night, and it tore soggily in his hands. He wanted to cry, wanted to weep and be pitied. Harrison cleaned himself as best he could, tears smarting, pulled at his underwear and trousers, zipped himself and fastened the belt.

'I've finished. You can come and take it.'

Movement and repetition. The ladder moved as before and the gun and the hood reappeared. He pointed to the bucket.

'I've used it. You can take it away.'

Just a belly laugh from the covered face and a jumping in merriment of the shoulders, and the hood sinking and going, and the muffled call of fun and entertainment. A bloody great joke, Geoffrey. Do you see it, do you see why he's splitting himself? You asked for the bucket, they've given it to you, given it for keeps. They've given you a little present. It's going to sit there, a couple of yards away. Stinking and rotten and foul. Own pee, own shit, own waste. You've given them a bloody good laugh.

'Come here. Come back.' All the command that he could summon. The tone of an order, unmistakable,

and enough to arrest the disappearance of the hood.
The laugh was cut.

'Come here.'

The head came upwards, revealed again the
shoulders. Geoffrey Harrison leaned back on his
left foot, then swung himself forward as far as the
chain permitted. He drove his right instep against
the bucket, saw it rise and explode, career against
the shoulder of the man, spill its load across his
mask and faded cotton shirt. Stained, dripping, and
spread.

'You can have it back,' Harrison giggled. 'You can
have it again now.'

What in God's name did you do that for?

Don't know. Just sort of happened.

They'll bloody murder you, Geoffrey Harrison,
they'll half tear you apart for that.

It's what they're for, those bastards, to be crapped
and peed on.

Right, dead right. When you've a bloody army at
your back. You're an idiot, Geoffrey Harrison.

I don't know why I did it.

You won't do it again.

They came together for him. The other man leading, the one with the smears on his shirt and hood
a rung on the ladder behind. No words, no consultation, no verbal reproach. Nothing but the beat of
their fists and the drumming of their boots against
his face and chest, and the softness of his lower belly
and his thighs and shins. They worked on him as if
he were a suspended punchbag, hanging from the
beam. They spent their strength against him till they
panted and gasped from their effort, and he was
limp and defenceless and no longer capable of even

minimal self-protection. Vicious, angered creatures, because the act of defiance was unfamiliar and the bully had risen in them, sweet and safe. Harrison crumpled down on to the hay floor, feeling the pain that echoed in his body, yearning for release, wishing for death. The worst was at his ribcage, covered now in slow funnels of agony. When did you ever do anything like that in your life before, Geoffrey? Never before, never stood up, not to be counted. And no bastard here this morning with his calculator. No-one there to see him, to cheer and applaud. Just some mice under his feet, and the stink of his body, and the knowledge that there was a man close by who loathed him and would cut off his life with as little ceremony as picking the muck from his nostrils.

He worked a smile over the pain of his jaw and gazed at the emptied bucket. He'd tell Violet about it, tell her it blow by blow. Not what they did to him afterwards, but up till then, and his foot still ached.

He struggled upright, knees shaking, stomach in torment.

'You're animals,' he shouted. 'Slobbering, miserable swine. Fit to shovel shit, you know that.' The scream wobbled under the low cut of the rafters. 'Get down in your shit and wash yourselves, you pigs. Rub your faces in it, because that's what makes pigs happy. Pig shit, pig thick.'

And then he listened, braced for a new onslaught, and heard the murmur of their voices. They took no notice of him, ignored him. He knew that he could shout till he lifted the roof and that they had no fear of it. He was separated from every civilization that he knew of.

* * *

Without hunger, without thirst, numbed by the annihilation of the big Calabresi, Giancarlo sat on a bench in the Termini, waiting the hours away. Close to exhaustion, near to drifting to fitful sleep, hands masking his face, elbows digging at his legs, he thought of Franca.

There had been girls in Pescara, the daughters of the friends of Father and Mother. Flowing skirts, starched blouses and knee boots, and the clucking approval of Mother as she brought the cream cakes out. The ones that giggled and knew nothing, existed with emptied minds. Crucifixes of gold at their necks and anger in their mouths if he reached for buttons or zips or eye-fasteners.

There had been girls at the University. Brighter and more adult stars who regarded him as an adolescent. There he was someone who could make up the numbers for the cinema or the beach, but who was shunned when it was dark, when the clinching began. The spots, the acne, and the titter behind the hand. It should have been different with the Autonomia, but the girls would not grovel for a novice, for a recruit, and Giancarlo had to prove himself and win the acclamation. Far out in the front of the crowd, running forward with the fire eating into the rag at the hilt of the milk bottle, arcing the Molotov into the air. The battle for approval, and his ankle had turned. Would they even remember him now, the girls of the Autonomia? Giancarlo Battestini had no experience other than in the arms, between the thighs, wrapped warm by Franca. It was the crucible of his knowledge. A long time he thought of her.

Franca with the breasts golden and devoid of the

rim of suntan, Franca with the cherry-pip nipples, with the flattened belly holed by a single crater, Franca with the wild forest that had tangled and caught his fingers. The one who had chosen him. Darling, darling, sweet Franca. In his ears was the sound of her breathing, the beat of her movement on the bed, her cry as she had spent herself.

I am coming, Franca. I am coming to take you from them, he whispered to himself.

I am coming, Franca. Believe it, know it. Thinking of Franca as the station began to live again, to move and function, participate in a new day. Thinking of Franca as he walked to the ticket counter and paid the single fare on the rapido to Reggio. Thinking of Franca as he climbed up to a first-class carriage. Away from the herd of Neapolitans and Sicilians with their bundles and salads and children and hallucinating noises of discussion and counter-discussion. No other passengers in the compartment. Thinking of Franca as the train pulled away from the low platform, and crawled between the sidings and junctions and high flats draped in the day's first washing. The boy slumped back, slid his heels on to the seat in front and felt the pressure power of the P38 against his back.

Out across the flatlands to the south of the city, carving through the grass fields and the close-packed vineyards, skirting the small towns of Cisterna di Latina and Sezze away on the hills, and Terracina at the coast, the train quickened its pace. Blurring the telegraph poles, homing and seeking out the dust-dry mountains and the bright skies of the Aspromonte.

'Believe in me, Franca. Believe in me because I am

Chapter Nine

At the Questura there were barely disguised smiles
from the uniformed men who watched Dottore
Giuseppe Carboni disgorged from his car. The
evidence of the night before was plain and clear-cut.
Bulldog bagged eyes, blotched cheeks, a razor-
nicked chin, a tie not hoisted. He swept uneasily
through the door, searching straight ahead of him as
if wary of impediments, and took the lift instead of
risking the flight of stairs. Carboni had greetings for
none of those who saluted and welcomed him along
the second-floor passage. Ignoring them all, he was
thankful to make the haven of his desk without
public humiliation. They would think he had been
drinking all night, would not know as they
whispered and clucked in disapproval that he had
left the party before two, and back at his flat had
collapsed in a chair with a tumbler of whisky that he
might better search his memory for patterns and
procedures in his latest kidnap burden. Never time
for thought, for analysis, once he was at work with
the telephone ringing and the stream of visitors,
humble and distinguished. And a tumbler had
become two, and merged into half a bottle as he

had picked into the recesses of the problem before him. He had stayed up till his wife, magnificent in her flowing nightdress, had dragged him to her bed, and little enough chance of sleep then.

He sat heavily in his chair and buzzed the connecting speaker for his aide. A moment and the man was there, sleek and oiled and ready with an armful of files, battered brown folders encasing a hillock of typed paperwork. What did the Dottore intend the priority of the day to be?

Carboni winced, the stab of pain ringing in his head. 'The Harrison case. There is nothing else.'

'We have the tapings of the calls to Mrs Harrison and to ICH. The one to Harrison's wife was futile. She couldn't understand what she was being told and rang off.' There was a sneer at the mouth of Carboni's assistant. 'The first tangible steps towards extortion were made in a message to his company. Also from Criminalpol there is voice analysis. They believe there is similarity here with the communication at the Marchetti kidnapping, the child.'

'Just the one message to the company?'

'A single message, the establishment of lines of approach.'

'Leave me with the tapes,' said Carboni, eyes closed, head spinning, wishing deliverance from intelligent and confident young men.

When he was alone he played the cassette many times. Hands over his face, shutting out the noise through the open windows of the traffic below, concentrating his effort on the brief and staccato message. A callow, rasping voice he heard, and the policeman did not need the help of the memorandum that was attached to the package to know that this voice came from the toe of the country, from Calabria, from the land of the Mafiosi chieftains. Where else? A humble, inarticulate voice, reading a message that had been written for him, which was normal. Then there was the tape of the first call to the Marchetti family to be heard. A match; it didn't take a computer to tell him that.

Time now for work on the telephone. He mopped at his neck with his handkerchief. Half an hour in his office and his shirt was soaked. Calls to his subordinates drew a blank. No further eye-witnesses had been produced since he had left for home the previous evening. There was nothing to feed into the machines beyond the very basics of description supplied by the single woman on Collina Fleming: bulk and height and generality of clothing. No faces, no fingerprints, no escape car yet traced. No information had emerged from the tenuous links with the Underworld maintained by the discreeter elements of the anti-kidnap squad. No word and none expected, because to inform in these matters was the sure and fast way to a wooden box. Not for the first time since he had reached his lofty eminence Giuseppe Carboni pondered the value of his work. The servant of a society which stepped back from commitment and involvement. The servant, neither trusted nor appreciated, and struggling for standards that those who lodged even in the higher places renounced. Lockheed, Friuli, Esso Italiana, Belice, even the Quirinale, even the Presidency. Scandals; nasty and deceitful, and the guilty were from the chief echelons of the great Mama Italia. So, who wanted law, who wanted order? The ache was back at his head, the throb of a hungover man, wetted with disillusion. He could take his pension. He could go on his way, and the President would hang a medal round his neck, and his parting would be unseen, unimportant.

Carboni smacked his pudgy hand down on to the desk, felt the shockwaves vibrate back up to his elbow, enjoyed the affliction. There was time for a few more of the great ones to go behind bars, time for a few more handcuffs to be wrapped on the wrists of those who at last would show shame as the doors of the Regina Coeli closed on them. Abruptly he pressed the intercom button, and heard the silken voice of his assistant.

'A man called Antonio Mazzotti, originally from Cosoleto in Calabria.' He had slipped away from the priority of the day because he did not know how to harness the energy he wished to exude for Harrison's freedom. 'He has an office in Rome and deals in property speculation. He has made some development deals in the Golfo di Policastro. I want the telephone number of his office. Just the number and I will call it myself.'

'It will be attended to, Dottore.'

'And not this evening, not this afternoon,' Carboni growled. 'I want it this morning.'

'Of course, Dottore. And the firm of Harrison rang. They would like an Archibald Carpenter to see you. He is the Security Director of ICH head office, from London . . .'

'Around twelve I could see him.'

'I will let the company know.'

'And the number of this man, Mazzotti, no delay.'

'Of course not, Dottore.' The voice dripped. Carboni hated him, would have him shifted. 'Dottore, the news is coming of another kidnapping. From Parioli.'

'I cannot handle it. Someone else will have to.'

'They have taken the nephew of a considerable industrialist . . .'

'I told you, I have enough to concern me.'

'. . . an industrialist who is generous to the Democrazia Cristiana with funds.'

Carboni sighed in annoyance and resignation. 'Get my car to the door, and when I am back I want that number on my desk, and I want this Carpenter here at twelve.'

'Of course, Dottore.'

Vengefully Carboni slapped the intercom button to the 'off' position, locked his desk and headed for the corridor.

Far out on the Nomentana Nuova, set among the high-rise flats that the planners had dubbed 'popular', shadowed by them, was a simple row of garages of precast concrete with swinging, warped doors. The garages were skirted by waste ground, stray dogs and discarded rubbish. Few were in use as the occupants of the flats found them too far from their front doors and out of sight of their windows, and therefore unsafe from the work of thieves and vandals. The garages were generally deserted and distant from the motion and life of the flats. One was a chosen burrow of an NAP cell, rented through an intermediary not to house a car but to provide storage and meeting space. There were guns here. Pistols and automatic weapons from the factories of countries with widely disparate political creeds. Quarry explosives stolen by sympathizers. Boxes full of car number plates. Sleeping-bags and a camping

stove, and the Roneo machine on which the communiqués were run off. None of the possessions
of the cell would have been visible if the doors
had been carelessly opened because time had been
lavished on the garage. If the dirt on the floor were
brushed away the outline of a trap door became
apparent. They had carved through the cement and
underneath had dug out a tomb some two metres
wide, two and a half metres long and a metre and a
half high. A narrow plumbing pipe to the surface
brought air to them. This was the hide-away in times
of great danger, and this was where three young
men sheltered because it was just a day since La
Tantardini had been taken and they had abandoned
their safe house. Though she was a leader, who
could say whether she would talk to her interrogators? Dark and closed, the pit provided a lair for the
men who breathed the damp and must-laden air.
There was the son of a banker, the son of a land-
owner, the son of a Professor of Economics at the
University of Trento.

Above them, and muffled through the thickness
of the cement, came four sharp raps at the closed
wooden doors of the garage. It was a sign they
recognized, the signal that a courier had visited
them. An envelope had been pushed far from sight
under the cover of the doorway, the message it
held despatched four hours earlier from the island of
Asinara.

For Tantardini. Reprisal. Number Four.

In the pit among the cell's papers would be
the code sheet that would identify Number Four, the
target the young men must reach for. They would
wait several minutes in the calm of the darkness

before levering aside the entrance and crawling upwards to find and read the communication.

Through the morning as the sun rose and blazed with its full force on the tin roof above him they left Harrison to himself. No food, no water, and he hadn't the stomach and courage to call for either. Preferring not to risk another beating, he kept his peace, chained in the oven space that they had chosen for him.

There were pains in many parts of his body, slow and creeping and twisting at the bruised muscle layers. And there was the heat, combining with the welts and bruises to empty his mind, leave his imagination as an unused void.

Deep in sweat, heavy in self-pity, slumped on the hay and straw, conscious of his own rising smells, he ebbed away the hours without hope, without anticipation.

Giancarlo was half asleep, meandering in the demistate between dream and consciousness, relaxed and settled, the plan in his mind evaluated and approved. Small and lone and hungry for the action he had decided upon, he was sprawled indifferently between the padded seat back and the hard face of the window's glass. The sights beyond the comfort of the speeding train were ignored.

It would be hot that day in Pescara, hot and shrouded in a sea-top mist, and noisy and dusty from the car wheels and the tramping of the thousands who would have come to roast themselves on the thin sand line between promenade and water. The shop would be open and his father wheedling the lady customers. Perhaps his father would know by now, would know of his boy. Perhaps the polizia would have come, pained and apologetic because this was a respectable citizen. His father would curse him, his mother cry in her handkerchief. Would he shut the shop if the polizia came and announced with due solemnity that little Giancarlo was with the NAP and living in a covo with a feared terrorist, the most dangerous woman in the land and their lad cohabiting? They would hate him. Hate him for what he had done to them. And the base rock of their hatred would be their majestic, colossal absence of understanding of why he had taken his road.

Stupid, pathetic, insignificant, little crawling fleas. Giancarlo rolled the words round his tongue. Grovelling servants, in perpetual obseisance to a system that was rotten and outworn. Cowering behind the façade of phoniness. Savagely he recalled the wedding of his elder brother. Hair oil and incense, an intoning doddering priest, a hotel reception on the sea front that neither the groom's nor the bride's father could afford. New suits and hair trims for the men, new dresses for the ladies and jewellery out from the wall safes. An exhibition of waste and deception, and Giancarlo had left early, walked across the evening town and locked himself in his room and lain in the darkness till his father, much later, hammered at the door and shouted of the offence given to aunts and cousins and friends. The boy had despised his father for it, despised him for the chastity-belt of conformity. Governing them was the necessity of normality; the mayor must come to the flat each year, the bishop to the shop, and after Mass in April the shining new BMW must be blessed by the priest and a fee given. They buckled their knees, ran their hands together damp with nervousness when a town hall official visited to safeguard his votes; a rotten little creep with his hand in the till, and they treated him like Christ Almighty. The relationship was past repair. Past patching and bandaging.

The boy mouthed his insults, sometimes aloud, sometimes without sound, working off, as an athlete sheds weight in roadwork, the relaxed rest that had held him during the early hours of the journey. The society of clientilismo; who his father knew in business, had been to school with, was owed a favour by, the way towards a job for a growing boy. The society of the bustarelle; the little envelopes of old banknotes that smoothed and purred their way around the town hall. The society of evasione; avoidance of commitment to the weak, the ethic of selfishness and personal preservation. That was their society and he had vowed that the break was final, and the adhesive quality of family blood was inadequate to change his determination.

The train rolled on, Napoli left behind.

A boy who had killed and found it no special experience, who sometimes smiled and sometimes laughed and who had no companion, Giancarlo Battestini on the rapido to Reggio.

The screams of the cleaning woman carried far down the column of the staircase well.

The shrieks brought the day porter of the pensione as fast up the steps as his age and infirmity would permit, and when he arrived panting at the upper landing the woman was still bent to the door keyhole, the clean folded sheets on the floor beneath her feet, her bucket in one hand, her sweeping broom in the other. He had fished the pass key from his pocket, opened the door, taken a cursory look, mouthed a prayer and pushed the woman back from the door. He had locked the room again and without explanation scrambled back down the stairs to raise management and authority.

With sirens and gusto the carabinieri arrived, running from the car, leaving the winking blue light revolving, pacing through the hall in a clatter of heavy boots and pounding on the stairs past the opened rooms of those who had been roused and wondered at the intrusion.

The barest glance at the battered head and the accompanying bloodstains was sufficient to convince the maresciallo that hope of life and survival had long expired. One man he sent to the car to radio for the necessary assistance, another he detailed to stand by the door and prevent entry by the gathering crowd on the landing – salesmen, servicemen on leave and waiting for later trains in the day, and the prostitutes who had kept them company during the night. By the time the maresciallo had found the dead man's identity card there were more sirens in the air, warning all those who heard of further misery, the reckoning time for an unfortunate.

Below on the street, another gathering, few of their faces betraying sympathy. The day porter stood among them, a man much in demand at this time, with the story to tell of what he had seen.

A blue Fiat 132 limousine brought Archie Carpenter from International Chemical Holdings through the

old battered dignity of central Rome to the formidable front archway of the Questura. Like a
bloody great museum, he'd thought. More churches
per square yard than any place he knew, cupolas and
domes by the dozen. The history, the markets, the
shops, the women, bloody fantastic the whole place.
Oozing chic steady class, he'd felt; dirty and sophisticated, filthy and smart. Women with a couple of
hundred pounds' worth of summer dress picking
their way between the rubbish bags, dogs crapping
on the pavements of the High Street; never seen
anything like it. And now this place, police headquarters for the city – a great grey stone heap, coated
in pigeon dirt. Flag limp and refusing to stir on the
pole above him.

He gave Carboni's name at the front desk and
showed the official the name written on paper. Had
to do that because they'd looked blank when he
opened his mouth. But the name seemed to mean
something because heels clicked together and there
were bows and ushering arms towards the lift.

Archie Carpenter laughed behind his hand.
Wouldn't be like this if one of their lot came over to
the Yard. Be made to sit down for half an hour while
they sorted out his accreditation, checked through to
his appointment, made him fill out a form with three
carbons. And no chance of getting called 'Dottore',
no bloody chance. All a bit strange, but then it had
been strange all morning – from the Embassy man
who wouldn't talk to the time when he'd gone into
an empty office at ICH and dialled the number
they'd given him for Violet Harrison.

Yes, he could come round if he wanted to. If there
was something that he had to say to her, then he

should come round, otherwise she'd be going out. Carpenter had stuck at it. He had to see her, Head Office was particularly keen that he should personally make sure everything possible was being done for her. Well, in that case, she'd said, he'd better come and she wouldn't go out. She'd stay at home. Like she was doing him a favour, and would about six o'clock be right, and they could have a drink.

Well, not what you'd expect, was it, Archie?

Down the corridors they went, Carpenter a pace behind his escort, bisecting the endless central carpet, worn and faded, hearing all about him the slow crack of typewriters, turning his eyes away when two men came out of an office in front and gave each other a big smacker on the cheeks. Round a corner, down another corridor, like a charity hike.

And then he was there. A young man was shaking his hand and prattling in the local and Carpenter was smiling and nodding, catching on with the manners. The inner door of the office burst open.

The man who came through the door was short, grossly overweight but moving with the speed of a crocodile on the scent of fresh meat. Papers and a cassette recorder were gripped in his left hand, the other remained free for waving as a stage prop to the waterfall of words. Carpenter understood not a phrase, stood rooted to the carpet. Both of them hammering away, and at the body work, arms round the shoulders, heads close enough to recognize the toothpaste. Something had gone well. He was acting as if he'd drawn the favourite in the Irish Sweepstake, the little fellow with the big belly.

A change of gear, an effortless switch to English,

and, the recorder and paperwork passed to his subordinate, Giuseppe Carboni introduced himself.

'I am Carboni. And you are Carpenter? Good. You come from London, from ICH? Excellent. You come at the right moment. Everything is well. Come into my room.'

Can't be bad, thought Carpenter, and followed the disappearing figure into the inner office, where he looked round him, swayed a bit. Massive and tasteful, furnished and carpeted. Prints on the wall of old Rome, velvet drapes on the windows, a framed portrait of the President on a desk half submerged in an Everest of files. He sat himself down opposite the desk.

'Carpenter, this morning I am proud. This morning I am very happy and I will tell you why . . .'

Carpenter inclined his head, had the routine straight, gave him a flash of teeth. Roll on, let the dam break.

'. . . Let me tell you that from yesterday morning when I first heard of what happened to your Mr Harrison, from the time I first telephoned to the Embassy, this has been a case that has worried and disturbed me. To be frank, there are not many of these kidnappings that greatly affect me. Most of the people who are taken are excessively rich and you will have read of how much money they can pay for their release. And after they have been freed many are investigated with enthusiasm by the Guardia di Finanze, our fiscal police. One wonders how it is, in a modern society, that individuals can legally accumulate such funds, hundreds of thousands of dollars are necessary to win freedom. They give us little help, these people, neither the families during the imprisonment, nor the victim after return. They shut us out so that we must work from the side, from the edge. When our record of arrests is decried, then I sweat, Carpenter, because we work with only one hand free.'

'I understand,' said Carpenter. He had heard this, and it stank and ran against all his police training. Intolerable.

'When it is children, or teenage girls, the innocent parties, then it hurts more. But your Mr Harrison, he is an ordinary businessman, I do not seek to denigrate him, but an ordinary fellow. Not important, not rich, not prepared. The shock for him, the ordeal, may be psychologically catastrophic. You know, Carpenter, I was up half the night worrying about this man . . .'

'Why?' Carpenter cut in, partly from impatience at having the news that provoked the ebullience withheld from him, partly because the syrup was too thick. Benedictine, when he wanted Scotch.

'You laugh at me, you laugh at me because you do not believe I am serious. You have not been a policeman for twenty-eight years in Italy. Had you been, then you would know my feelings. Harrison is clean, Harrison is not tainted, Harrison observes legality. He is in our country as a baby, a baby without clothes, without malice, and he deserves our protection, which is why I work to bring him back.'

'Thank you,' Carpenter spoke with simplicity. He believed he understood and warmed all the time to the barely shaven, perspiring man across the desk from him.

'You have come to supervise the payment of an

extraordinary sum for Harrison's release. Why else would you come? . . .'

Carpenter flushed.

'. . . It does not embarrass me, it was my own advice to your Embassy. What I have to tell you is that it may not be necessary. It may not be required.'

The jolt shuddered through Archie Carpenter, straight-backed in his chair, peering forward.

'We try to use modern methods here. We try not to justify the image that you have of us. We do not sleep through the afternoon, we are not lazy and stupid. We have a certain skill, Carpenter. We have the tapes of the telephone calls to Mrs Harrison and to ICH. The computer gobbles them. Then we feed other calls into the machine, from other events. And we have made a match. We have two cases where the contact was from the same man. You understand police work?'

'I did eight years with Special Branch in London, with the Metropolitan Police. What you'd see as the political wing.' Carpenter spoke with a certain pride.

'I know what is Special Branch.'

Carpenter flashed his molars, creased his cheeks.

Carboni acknowledged, then launched himself again. 'So I have a match and that tells me that I am not dealing with a first time out group. I am working against an organization that has been in the field. It tells me a little, it tells me something. Just now I am talking to a man from the office of a business fellow that I have been asked to investigate. You know the situation. Many times when you have my position people come with a whisper for the ear. Look at this man, they say, look at him and think about him. Is everything correct about him? And if he is a

187

Calabrese, if he is from the south and has much cash, then you look closely. I rang the office of a property speculator in Rome this morning, but he is not available, he is away on business. I must speak to his junior.'

Carboni paused, master of theatre, paused and waited while Carpenter willed him on. Seemed to fill his lungs as if the ten minutes of near continuous talk had vacuumed them.

'Carpenter, we need fortune in this business. You know that, we need luck. This morning we have been blessed. You saw me in the office when I hugged that little prig – I detest the man, arrogant and sneering – and I hugged him because to my ear the voice of the man that says his master is in Calabria is the same as that of the man who called the office of Harrison.'

Carpenter bobbed his head in praise. 'Congratulations, sincerely, Mr Carboni, my congratulations. You have a wrap-up.'

'It is not definite, of course. I await the confirmation of the machines.' A coyness across the desk.

'But you have no doubts.'

'In my own mind there are none.'

'I say again, congratulations.'

'But we must move with care and discretion, Carpenter. You understand that we go into surveillance and tapping. Caution is required if we want your Harrison returned . . .'

Sharply, an intrusion on the men's concentration, the telephone rang. Carboni reached for it and even where Carpenter sat he could hear the strident talk. Carboni scribbled on his notepad as the Englishman's excitement dissipated and waned. He had not wanted the spell of success broken and now had to endure interruption of the sweet flow. Carboni had written on and covered two sheets of paper before, without courtesies, he put the telephone down.

'Don't look worried, Carpenter. Complications, yes. But those that thicken the mixture. A man has been found dead in a small hotel close to the railway station. He had been clubbed to death. We have the teleprint of his history. He was held briefly on a kidnapping charge, but the principal witness declined to testify at his trial, the prosecution was lost. He comes from the village of Cosoleto, in the far south, in Calabria. The man that I tried to telephone this morning, he is from that village too. There is a web forming, Carpenter. A web is sticky and difficult to extract from, even for those who have made it.'

'I think you'd prefer that nobody's hopes were raised yet. Not in London, not with the family.'

Carboni shrugged, sending a quiver through his body, and eased his fingers through the rare strands of his forehead hair. 'I have given you much in confidence.'

'I'm grateful to you because you've wasted much of your time. If I could see you tomorrow I'd be more than pleased.' Archie rose out of his chair, would love to have stayed because the atmosphere of investigation was infectious, and for too long he had been away from it.

'Come tomorrow at the same time,' said Carboni and laughed, deep and satisfied. The man who has enjoyed a lively whore, spent his money and regretted nothing. 'Come tomorrow and I will have something to tell you.'

'We should put some champagne on ice.' Carpenter trying to match the mood.

'From this morning I don't drink.' Carboni laughed again and gripped Carpenter's hand with the damp warmth of friendship.

For two and a half years Francesco Vellosi had accepted the escort of a loaded Alfetta, three men of his own squad always in place behind him as he made the four daily journeys to and from the Viminale and his flat. Sun and frost, summer and winter, they dogged his movements. He had people coming for drinks that evening at home, he told Mauro, with his clipped, even voice. But he would be returning to his desk later. Would Mauro fix the movements and co-ordination of the escort? A flicker of the eyes went with the request.

For Vellosi there was now time for a brief rest before his guests arrived. He would not permit them to stay late, not with the papers piling on his desk. When he was inside his front door and passed to the responsibility of the guard who lived with him, the motor escort withdrew. Because he would later return to his office, there were curses from the men who accompanied him, and who would again suffer a broken evening.

Chapter Ten

The shadows had gone now, called away by the sun
that had groped beyond the orange orchard over to
his right. The lines had lengthened, reached their
extremity and disappeared, leaving in their wake the
haze of the first darkness. With their going there was
a cold settling fast among the trees and bushes that
Giancarlo had taken for his watching place. The
building in front of him was no more than a black-
ened outline, indistinct in shape, difficult to focus on.
Around him the noises of the night were mustering,
swelling in their competition. The barking of a far
distant farm dog, the droning of the bees frantic for a
last feed from the wild honeysuckle, the engine drive
of the skeleton mosquitoes, the croak of an owl
unseen in a high tree. The boy did not move, as if
any motion of his body might alert those who he
knew stayed unaware and unsuspicious in the barn
that was less than a hundred metres from him. This
was not the moment to rush forward. Better to let
the darkness cling more tightly to the land, throw
its blanket more finally across the fields and olive
patches and the rock outcrops that were submerging
in the dusk. The ideas of Giancarlo, convoluted and

hesitant when conceived in the rocking pace of the rapido, were now near to fulfilment. Wild and ill-thought at their birth, they now seemed to him to own a pattern and a value. Worth a smile, little fox, worth a grin.

Unchallenged, he had walked out of the small station with its wide platforms on the Reggio esplanade, gulped at a waft of seablown air, and mingled with the stream of descending passengers. If there were watching polizia at the barrier, Giancarlo had not seen them, and there had been no shouted command to halt. He had walked from the station, among the people laden with suitcases and string bags. The snakes of humanity had slithered in their different directions, splintering again and again till he was alone. In a tabacchi he purchased a map of Calabria. The names were clear and well remembered. Sinopli . . . Delianuova . . . Acquaro . . . Cosoleto. He found them where the red ribbons of the roads began to twist into the uplands of the Aspromonte, beyond the green-shaded coastal strip, far into the deeper sand and brown of the rising ground.

In early afternoon with the time of siesta weighty on the empty streets, Giancarlo found his car. Among the white-washed houses, with the light battering back at his unprotected eyes, parked haphazardly as if the owner were late for an important meeting, not just restless for his lunch. The life of the Mezzo Giorno ruled, the land of the half day. Washing hung down, bleached and stiffened, from the balcony of a house under which was abandoned a red Fiat 127. Right outside the front door, keys in the ignition. Shutters fastened to protect the cool in the interior, not a child crying, not a grandmother complaining, not a radio tuned to music. He slipped into the driving seat, eased off the handbrake and coasted slowly down the incline, waiting till he was clear of the corner before firing the engine.

He headed north for the long viaduct, where the Mafiosi had made their fortunes in extortion from those who needed to move in materials and equipment and found it cheaper to concede the dues than to fight. He drove slowly because that was the style of the Calabrian after lunch and his need to avoid drawing attention was as acute as ever. His face was sufficient of a problem, white with the pallor of prison and confinement in the covo; not the complexion of the south, not the burned and dark wood tan of those who owned this country. He drifted past the turn-off signs to Gallico and Carnitello, and climbed high with the road above the sea channel that separated the Sicilian island from the mainland. For a moment he slowed and stared hard away to his left, his gaze held on the sprawl of Messina away across the azure of the water.

Messina, blurred and indistinct, lay white in the sun among the spreading green and rust of parks and waste ground. Messina, where they had built the gaol for the girls. This was where they had taken La Vianale, where Curcio's Nadia had waited for her trial, where if he did not succeed his Franca would decay and crumble. He could not see the prison, not across eight kilometres of reflecting sea, but it was there, a spur and a goad.

The car increased speed. Past the road on the left to Scilla, and on the right to Gambarie. Through the booming length of rock-cut tunnels, and on into the interior. Sinopli and Delianuova were signed to the right and he pulled the little Fiat off the dual carriageway and started the winding negotiation of the hill road. Through Santa Eufemia d'Aspromonte, a barren and meagre community where his coming scattered only the chickens feeding in the road gravel, and his going raised barely an eyebrow of attention from the elderly who sat in black skirts and suits in front of their homes. Through Sinopli where he hooted for the right to pass a bus that struggled in an exhaust cloud on the main street, and where the shops were still padlocked, and it was too hot, too sickly clammy for the ragazzi to have brought out their plastic footballs.

Bitter country now. Laden with rock and precipice, covered with the toughened scrub and trees that grew from little earth. In low gear, rising and descending, Giancarlo drove on, till he was over the old and narrow stone bridge across the Vasi, and into Acquaro. Perhaps some saw him go through the village but he was unaware of them, studying by turns the map laid out on the front passenger seat, and the perils of the curving route. A half-kilometre further, he stopped. There was a lay-by, and a heap of gravel where the workmen would come in the winter when there was ice to make the road safe for motorists. Further back was a turn-in among the trees where perhaps the hunting parties parked their cars on Sundays or the young men took the virgins when they could no longer suffer the claustrophobia of the family in the front room and the watch of the Madonna above the fireplace. Giancarlo grinned to himself. Wrong day for hunters, too early in the evening for virgins. This was a place for him to park hidden from the road. He drove as far between the trees as the track permitted.

From habit, in the quiet of his seat, Giancarlo checked over the P38, stroked its silk barrel length, and wiped on his shirt waist the faint stains on the handle. Eight bullets only, eight to do so much with. He climbed lightly from the car, eased the pistol back into his belt and was lost in the close foliage.

He skirted the road, leaving it what he judged to be a hundred metres on his left, seeking the thickness of the wood, easing on to the toes of his canvas shoes, thankful for the cover. It took him only a few minutes before he found the vantage point for the once-white house from which paint and plaster alike peeled, served by a rutted track. A hovel to Giancarlo, a place for sheep and cows. Medieval, had it not been for the car parked outside the only door. This was the home of a contadino, a peasant; and his wife moved beside the building with a bucket, and his half-clothed children played with a spar of wood. The boy settled himself comfortably on the mould of generations of fallen leaves and watched and waited for the brother of the wife of Claudio.

Not long. Not long enough to try him.

A big man, balding above a flat weatherbeaten forehead. Cheeks that were not shaved, trousers that were held at the waist with string, a shirt that was torn at the armpit. Contadino, Giancarlo spat the word. But of the proletariat, surely? He smiled mirthlessly. A servant of the bosses . . . ? The boy agreed, satisfied in the ideology equation. The man carried a plastic bag and walked down the track from his house to the road, paused there and his eyes traversed a sweep that covered the boy's hide. The man had passed close to where Giancarlo lay before his sounds subsided. Like a stoat, Giancarlo was after him, ears cocked and attuned to the distant noises in front, eyes fastened on the dried twigs and oak leaves that he must not break nor displace.

The tree line covered the rim of a slight hill, beyond it was a roughened field indented from the cattle's wet spring grazing. On the far side of the open ground Giancarlo saw the stone-built barn with its rain-reddened tin roof and two doors facing him. The man he had followed was met by one who had come from the right-hand door and who carried a single-barrelled shotgun, the weapon of the country people. They talked a brief discourse, before the bag was handed over and a gust of laughter carried to the boy. As the man retraced his steps, Giancarlo melted among the trees and undergrowth, unseen, unheard.

When it was safe he came slowly forward to the dry stone wall that skirted the field, and picked his watching place. A boundless pride swept through him. He wanted to stand up and shout defiance and exultation. Giancarlo Battestini, remember the name, because he had found the Englishman of the multi-nationals, and would exploit him, as the foreign companies exploited the proletariat.

Later Giancarlo would begin his advance, edge closer to the building. Later. Now was the time for him to rest, and to relax if that were possible. And to dream . . . and the images of the thighs, warm and muscled in moisture, and of the curling growth and the breasts where his head had lain blasted and echoed through his mind. Alone on the ground, the myriad earth creatures converging on him, he shuddered and knew he would not sleep.

Archie Carpenter had been shown round the flat. He'd made the right noises and stood hesitantly at the bedroom door casting a quick eye over the wide pink coverlet, studied the wall pictures, paced the corridors with his hands joined behind his back in the pose of Royal males factory-visiting, and expressed his opinion as to what a fine place it was. She was a queer one, this Violet Harrison, making it all seem so natural as she marched him over the marble floors, pointing to this and that, offering the limited history of the furniture. She'd poured him a drink. Gin with hardly enough tonic to notice, and splashed some ice cubes in. And he'd seen her hand shaking, rocking like a sick man's and he'd known it was all a damn great sham. All the poise, all the silly chat, just a counterfeit. That's when the sympathy had started to roll, watching the trembling fist and the way the finger talons clutched at the bottle.

Loose and slim in the full flow of her dress, she sat on a sofa, the shape and form projecting without angular emphasis. The sort of woman you could take to your chest, Archie, sort of nuzzle against, and it would be all soft and wouldn't hurt anywhere. He wasn't looking at her eyes when he started to speak, just at the cleavage, where the freckles ran down. His suit was tight and hot and too thick for Roman summer. Bloody strange dress she'd put on for a time like this.

'You have to know, Mrs Harrison, that the company are doing all they can to get Geoffrey back to you. As quickly as humanly possible he'll be home again.'

'That's very kind,' she said, and her words were not easy to follow; it wasn't the first drink she'd had that day. You don't have to stand up like a preacher, Archie, and tell people how to behave and conduct themselves, not when their whole world's falling in.

'Everything possible,' Carpenter hurtled on. 'The Board will rubber-stamp the Managing Director's decision to pay. He wants you to know that the company will pay whatever is required to get your husband back. There's nothing on that count for you to worry about.'

'Thank you,' she said. Raised her eyebrows at him as if trying to show how impressed she was that the Board should make such a commitment.

Bloody marvellous, he thought. What a pair, and not a trace of sweat on her where the neckline cut down and him dripping wet like a horse at the Derby finish. 'There's not a great deal that we can do at the moment, but your husband's colleagues at ICH in Rome are geared to take calls, and make the financial arrangements. It'll probably all be outside the country, which makes it smoother.' He paused, drank it all in, watched the shift of the material as she crossed her legs. 'But you have to soldier on for a bit, Mrs Harrison, for quite a few days. It takes time, this sort of thing, we cannot settle it in a matter of hours.'

'I understand that, Mr Carpenter.'

'You're taking it very well.'

'I'm just trying to go on as I usually would, as if Geoffrey were away on a business trip, something like that.' She leaned forward slightly in her chair.

What to say now, what ground to stumble over?

Carpenter swallowed. 'Was there anything you wanted, anything I could help with?'

'I doubt it, Mr Carpenter.'

'It may take a few days, but we're working on two fronts. We can pay, that's no problem. At the same time the police are co-operating and have a major and discreet recovery effort underway, they have their best men on the case and . . .'

'I don't really need to know that, do I?' she asked quietly.

Carpenter bridled. 'I thought you'd want to hear what was happening.' Cool it, Archie, she's under stress. A brave front and damn-all underneath.

'So what you're offering me is that after a week or two I'll know whether Geoffrey is going to walk through the door, or whether I'm never going to see him again.'

'I think we should look on the bright side of things, Mrs Harrison.' Out of training, Archie. Bloody years since he'd been a beat copper in uniform and knocking on doors with a solemn face to tell the wife that her old man's come off his motor-bike and if she doesn't hurry she'll see him in the hospital chapel.

She seemed to sag, and the tears came, and then the deeper sobs, and the protest in the choked voice. 'You don't know anything. Nothing at all . . . Mister bloody Carpenter. You treat me like a bloody child . . . Let's all have a drink, let's believe it isn't for real . . . What do you know about this place, sweet fuck-all of nothing . . . You don't know where my husband is, you don't know how to get him back. All you talk about is "everything possible", and "major effort", "best men on the case". It's just bloody bromide, Mister bloody Carpenter . . .'

'That's not fair, Mrs Harrison, and don't swear at me . . .'

'And don't you come marching in here oozing your platitudes, telling me everything is going to be marvellous . . .'

'Too bloody right I won't. There's people that don't know when someone's trying to help them.' Carpenter's voice rose, his neck flushed. He pushed himself up from the seat, gulping at the remains of his drink. 'When someone comes and tries to give a hand there's no call for foul language.' He couldn't get smoothly out of his chair, couldn't make a quick and decent exit with dignity. By the time he was on his feet she was between him and the door and the tears were wet on her face, gleaming in the sheen of her make-up.

'I think I'd better go,' he said, mumbling his words, conscious of his failure to complete his task.

She stood very close to him, barring his way, a frail little thing for all the bravura of her language and looked straight into his face. Her head was turned up towards him, with a small, neat mouth, and her arms hung inert down to her hips.

'I think I'd better go . . . don't you? I don't think I can help any more.'

'If you think you ought to.' Brown hazel eyes, deep-set and misted, and around them the morass of freckles that he followed the patterns of, followed where they led.

'Geoffrey's bloody useless, you know.' Her hand came up, wiping hastily across her face, smudged the cosmetic grease, and the smile was there again. Curtained herself from him, just as she had done when she showed him round the flat, taken a public stance. There was a little laugh, bright in his ear. 'I'm not shocking you, am I, Mr Carpenter? Quite bloody useless, to me anyway. I don't mean to shock you, but people ought to understand each other. Don't you think so?'

One hand was sliding under his jacket, fingers rifling at the damp texture of his shirt, the other played at the uppermost buttons of her dress.

'Don't let's mess about, Mr Carpenter. You know the geography of this flat, you know where my room is. Oughtn't you to be taking me there now?' Her nails dug into the small of his back, a small bone button slipped from its hole, the spirals of excitement climbed at his spine. 'Come on, Mr Carpenter. You can't do anything for Geoffrey, I can't do anything for Geoffrey, so let's not pretend. Let's pass the time.' There was pressure on his back ribs, drawing him closer, the mouth and the pink painted lips mesmerizing him. He could smell her breath, could smell that she smoked, but she must have used toothpaste just before he came, peppermint tooth-paste.

'I can't stay,' Carpenter said, a hoarseness at his throat. Out of his depth, wallowing in deep water, and not a life-raft in bloody miles. 'I can't stay, I have to go.'

The hands abandoned his back and the buttons and she stepped aside to leave him space to pass into the hall.

'No hesitations, Mr Carpenter?' she murmured behind him. He was fiddling with the door locks, anxious to be on his way and therefore hurrying and in the process slowing himself; the man who is impatient and cannot unfasten a brassiere strap. 'No second thoughts?'

Teased, bowed by a shame that he could not recognize as coming from either inadequacy or morality, Archie Carpenter, nine-to-fiver, opt-out from the grown-up world, finally opened the door.

'You're a boring bastard, Mr Carpenter,' she called after him. 'A proper little bore. If you're the best they can send to get my husband out, then God help the poor darling.'

The door slammed. He didn't wait for the lift, but took the stairs two at a time.

In pre-war Rome the fascist administration sometimes ordered the lights of the principal government offices to be left burning long after the bureaucracy had gone to their trams and buses; a grateful population would believe that the State was working late and be impressed. The spirit of such deception had long since passed and the prevailing dictates of austerity decreed that unnecessary lights should be extinguished. Giuseppe Carboni was one of only a very few who worked late into that night in the shadowed sepulchre of the Questura. By telephone he had indefinitely postponed his dinner at home as he put off and avoided the anathema of communication with the force that he saw as his principal rival, the paramilitary carabinieri. The polizia and carabinieri existed, at best, as uneasy bedfellows between the communal sheets of law and order. Competition was fierce and jealous; the success of either was trumpeted by its senior officers, and a weak executive power was satisfied that neither should become overpowerful. A recipe for inefficiency, and a safeguard against the all-encompassing police state power that Italy had laboured under for twenty-one years.

Carboni's problem, and it had taken him many hours to resolve it in his mind, was whether or not he should place in the lap of the opposition his information on the speculator Mazzotti. The man was in the far south, apparently at the village of Cosoleto and beyond the striking and administrative range of the polizia at the Calabrian capital of Reggio. Cosoleto would come under the jurisdiction of the carabinieri at the small town of Palmi, his maps showed him that. His option was to allow the man Mazzotti to return from Calabria to the Roman district, where he would again be liable to police investigation. But if the gorilla Claudio were linked to the kidnapping of the Englishman Harrison, then the report of his killing in Rome would serve only to alert those involved. For another few hours, perhaps, the name of the dead man could be suppressed, but not beyond the dawn of the next day. It was immaterial at whose hand the strong man had met his death; sufficient for Carboni that it would be enough to set into play the fall-back plans of the kidnap group. It was not possible for him to delay in his action, but if he acted now, made a request for help that were successful, then what credit would be laid at the door of Giuseppe Carboni? Trivial plaudits, and victim and criminals in the hands of the black-uniformed carabinieri.

Enough to make a man weep.

He broke the pledge of the morning and poured himself a Scotch from his cabinet, the bottle reserved for times of celebration and black depression, then placed the call to Palmi. Just this once he would do the right deed, he promised himself, just this once break the habit of a professional lifetime.

When the call came the static was heavy on the line, and Carboni's voice boomed through the quiet offices and out through the opened doors into the emptied corridors of the second floor of the Questura. Many times he was obliged to repeat himself to the carabinieri capitano, as he was urged to great explanation. He stressed the importance of the Harrison affair, the concern in the matter of high administrative circles in Rome. Twice the capitano had demurred; the action suggested was too delicate for his personal intervention, the Mazzotti family were of local importance, should there not be authorization from the examining magistrate. Carboni had shouted louder, bellowed bull-like into the telephone. The matter could not wait for authorization, the situation was too fluid to be left till the morning appearance of the magistrate in his office. Perhaps the very vehemence impressed the carabinieri officer, perhaps the dream of glory that might be his. He acquiesced. The home of Antonio Mazzotti would be placed under surveillance from three o'clock in the morning. He would be arrested at eight.

'And be careful. I want no suspicions, I want no warnings given to this bastard,' Carboni yelled. 'A little mistake and my head is hanging. You understand? Hanging on my belly. You have the man Mazzotti in the cells at Palmi and I'll be with the magistrate by nine, and have him brought to Rome. You will reap full praise for your initiative and flexibility and co-operation; it won't be forgotten.'

The capitano expressed his gratitude to the Dottore.

'Nothing, my son, nothing. Good luck.'

Carboni put the telephone down. There was a black sheen on the handpiece and with his shirt cuff he smeared the moisture from his forehead. Rome in high summer, an impossible place to work. He locked his desk, switched off his desk light and headed for the corridor. For a man so gross in stomach and thighs there was something of a spring in his step. The scent sharp in the nose of the professional policeman. The old one, the one above pride and expediency. Time to go home to his supper and his bed.

Uncomfortable, irritated by the sharpness of the hay strands, impeded by the wrist manacle, Geoffrey Harrison had been denied the relief of sleep. They left no light for him, and the darkness had come once the slanting sun shafts no longer bored through the old nail holes of the roof. A long darkness, aggravated by the absence of food. A punishment, he thought, a punishment for kicking the bucket over them. As if the beating wasn't enough. His belly ached and groaned out loud in its deprivation.

He lay full length on his back, the chain allowing his right arm to drop loosely on the hay beside his body. Still and inert, occasionally dozing, eking out minutes and hours and not knowing nor caring of their passage.

The voices of his guards were occasional and faint through the thickness of the dividing wall of the barn. Indistinct at best and punctuated by laughter and then loud silence. Little he heard of them, and since one had walked heavily outside the building and urinated with force there had been nothing. His concentration was sharpened by the whisper of the scurrying feet of rats and mice who had made their nests in the gaps between the hay bales under him. Little bastards, eating and crapping and copulating and spewing out their litters, performing their functions of limited life a few feet below his backside. He wondered what they made of the smell and presence close to their heartland, whether they'd summon the courage or curiosity to investigate the intruder. Each movement of the rodents he heard; the vibrations of the small feet, frantic as they went about their business. Perhaps there would be bats tonight; there might have been last night but the sleep had been too great, too thick for him to have noticed. All the phobias, all the hates and fears of bats rushed past him so that he could examine and analyse the folklore – the scratchers, the tanglers, the disease-carriers . . .

And there was a new sound.

Harrison stiffened where he lay. Rigid now on his back. Fingers clenched. Eyes peering upward into the unbroken darkness.

A footfall beyond the side wall away from where his guards rested.

Frightened to move, frightened to breathe, Harrison listened.

A soft-soled shoe eased on to the dirt and mess beyond the wall. A step taken slowly as if the ground were being tested before the weight of a man was committed.

A tree brushing with a laden branch against the coarse granite stone, sweeping across it with the gentle motion of the night wind – that Harrison could identify, that was not what he had heard. An outside man, a stranger was coming silently and in stealth to the barn, without warning, without announcement. A person had come before the sun had set and had called from some way off and there had been greetings and conversation. This was not as then.

Another footstep.

Clearer this time, as if nerve and caution were failing, as if impetuosity and impatience were rising. Harrison willed him forward. Anyone who came with the hush of feet on the tinder grass and the scraping stones, anyone who came with such secrecy had no love nor friendship for the men who waited in the far room of the barn.

Cruel and mocking came the long void of silence unbroken to Harrison's alert ears.

Each noise of the night available to him he rejected because the sounds he searched for were lost. The last footstep had been clear, and perhaps the man had taken fright and would stay still and listen before he came on. The perspiration invaded Harrison's body, floating to the crevices of his body. Who was it who had come? Who would travel to this place?

A shatter of noise, a warning shout, a blasting pistol shot, ripped an echo through the space under Harrison's low ceiling.

In the half light from the storm lamp set low, Giancarlo saw the man nearest him pitch forward, the cry in his throat destroyed. For a moment he caught the reflection of the eyes of a second man, a rabbit's in headlights, and then a stool careered in the air towards him and his ducking weave was enough to take the force of the blow on his shoulder, and to distort his gathering aim. Like a huge shadow the man dived against the wall, but his movements were sluggish and terrorized and without hope. Giancarlo had time before the man reached the shortened shotgun. He held the P38 close with his two fists, cursed as the barrel wavered and the ache sagged in his upper arm. The man stole a last glance at him, without hope of salvation and reached the last inches for the shotgun. Giancarlo fired, two shots for certainty into the target that sank to the earth floor.

Harrison heard the answering whimper, a moan of supplication, perhaps a prayer, before a choked sob sliced it to silence.

He was frozen still, unmoving, uncomprehending.

The leaning door, old and protesting on its hinges, was opened beneath him; the chain was tight between his arm and the roof denying him escape. What in God's name happens now? This was not the noise the police would have made. Not the way it would have been if they were here. There would have been voices all round and shouts and commands and organization. Only the door below him, deep in the darkness, being prised open.

His name was called.

''Arrison, 'Arrison.'

Difficult for him to register it at first. Slow and tentative, almost a request.

'Where are you, 'Arrison?'

A young voice, nervous. A young Italian. They could never get their tongues round his name, not in the office, not at business meetings, not in the shops when he was out with Violet. The fear swelled inside him, the child that lies in the blackness and hears a stranger come. To answer or not, to identify or to remain silent. Pulsing through him, the dangers of the unknown.

'Where are you, 'Arrison? Speak, tell me where you are, 'Arrison.'

His reply was involuntary, blurted out, made not because he had worked out the answers but because there was a plea for response and he had no longer the strength to resist.

'Up here. I am up here.'

'I am coming, 'Arrison.' Heavy in the stumbled English was the tinge of pride. The door scraped across the floor, the caution of the footsteps was abandoned. 'There are more of them, 'Arrison? There were two. Are there more?'

'Just two, there were only two.'

He heard the sound of the ladder thudding into position against the hay wall, and the noise was fierce as the feet came against the rungs.

'Come down quickly, we should not stay here.'

'They have me by a chain, I cannot move.' Would the stranger understand, would his English be competent? 'I am a prisoner here.' Harrison slid into the staccato language of the foreigner, believing that was how his own tongue was best understood.

Two hands clawed at his feet and he could make out the slight silhouette of a man rising towards him. He cringed backwards.

'Don't fear me. Don't be afraid, 'Arrison.' A soft little voice, barely out of school, with the grammar fresh from the reading primers. The fingers, cruising and exploratory, reached along the length of his body. Across Harrison's thigh, scratching at his waist, onwards and upwards to the pit of his arm and then away out past his elbow to the wrist and the steel grip of the handcuff. A cigarette lighter flicked on, wavering and scarcely effective. But from the kernel of light Geoffrey Harrison could distinguish the face and features of the boy beneath the short-thrown shadows. Unshaven, pallid, eyes that were alive and burned bright. A shape to marry to the garlic smell of bread and salad sandwiches.

'Take it.'

An order and the lighter was directed towards Harrison's free hand.

'Turn your face away.'

Harrison saw the shadowed pistol drawn, squat and revolting, a macabre toy. He bucked his head away as the gun was raised and held steady. Squinted his eyes shut, forced them closed. Tearing at his ears was the noise of the gun, wrenching at his wrist the drag of the chain. The pain burned in the muscle socket of his shoulder, but when his arm swung back to his side it was free.

'It is done,' the boy said, and there was the trace of a smile, sparse and cold in the flame of the lighter. He pulled at Harrison's hand, led him towards the ladder. It was a cumbersome descent because Harrison nursed his shoulder, and the boy's hands were occupied with the gun and the flick lighter. The pressed earth of the floor was under Harrison's feet and the grip on his arm constant as he was led towards the opaque moon haze of the doorway. They stopped there and the fingers slipped to his wrist and there was a sharp heave at the bullet-broken handcuff ring. A light clatter on the ground.

'The men, those who were watching me . . . ?'

'I killed them.' The face invisible, the information inconsequential.

'Both of them?'

'I killed the two of them.'

Out in the night air, Harrison shuddered as if the damp loose on his forehead were frozen. The waft of fresh wind caught at his hair and flipped it from his eyes. He stumbled on a rock.

'Who are you?'

'It is not of concern to you.'

The grip on his wrist was tight and decisive. Harrison remembered the fleeting sight of the pistol. He allowed himself to be dragged away across the uneven, thistled grass of the field.

The eye-witnesses to the attack melted and died from the pavement with the wailing approach of the ambulance sirens. Few would stay to offer their account and their names and addresses to the investigating police. Out in the middle of the road, slewed at right angles to the two traffic flows, was the ambushed Alfa of Francesco Vellosi. Mauro, the driver, lay, death pale across his steering-wheel, his head close to the holed and frosted windscreen. Alone in the back, half down on the floor, was Vellosi, both hands clamped on his pistol and unable to stifle the trembling that invaded his body. The door of reinforced armour plate had saved him. Above his scalp the back passenger windows, for all their strengthening, were a kaleidoscope of reflected colours amid the fractured glass splinters. So fast, so vivid, so terrifying, had been the moment of assault.

After eight years in the Squadro Anti-Terrorismo, eight years of standing and looking at cars such as his, at bodies such as Mauro's, yet no real knowledge had accrued of how the moment would find him. Everything he could previously have imagined of the experience was inadequate. Not even in the war, in the sand dunes of Sidi Barrani under the artillery of the English, had there been anything as over-whelming as the trapped rat feeling in the closed car with the sprays of automatic fire beating over his head.

The escort car had locked its bonnet under the rear bumper of Vellosi's vehicle. Here they had all survived and now they were scattered with their machine-pistols. One in cover behind the opened front passenger door. One away in a shop doorway. The third man in Vellosi's guard stood erect in the middle of the street, lit by the high lights, his gun cradled and ready and pointing to the tarmac lest the prone figures should rise and defy the blood trails and the gaping intestinal wounds and offer again a challenge.

Only when the street was busy with police did Vellosi unlock his door and emerge. He seemed old, almost senile, his steps laboured and heavy.

'How many of them do we have?' he called across the street to the man who had been his shadow and guard these three years, whose wife cooked for him, to whose children he was a godfather.

'There were three, capo. All dead. They stayed beyond their time. When they should have run they stayed to make certain of you.'

He walked into the lit centre of the street and his men hurried to close around him, wanting him gone, but reading his mood and unwilling to confront it. He stared down into the faces of the boys, the ragazzi, grotesque in their angles with the killing weapons close to their fists, only the agony left in their eyes, the hate fled and gone. His eyes closed and his cheek muscles hardened as if he summoned strength from a distant force.

'The one there—' he pointed to a shape of denim jeans and a blood-flawed shirt. 'I have met that boy. I have eaten at his father's house. The boy came in before we sat down at dinner. His father is a banker, the Director of the Contrazzioni Finanziarie of one of the banks in the Via del Corso. I know that boy.'

He turned reluctantly from the scene, dawdling, and his voice was raised and carried over the street and the pavement and to the few who had gathered and watched him. 'The bitch Tantardini, spitting her poison over these children. The wicked, contaminating bitch.'

Hemmed in on the back seat of his escort car, Francesco Vellosi left for his desk at the Viminale.

Chapter Eleven

With the headlight beams flashing back from the
roadside pine trees, hurling aside the startled shadows, the little two-door Fiat ground its way into the
inky night leaving behind the cluster of the Cosoleto
lights. Giancarlo forced the motor hard, regardless of
the howling tyres, the crack of the fast-changed gears
and the drift of Harrison's shoulders against his own.
His purpose now was to be rid of the vacuum of
the darkened roads and fields, the silhouetted trees,
and the lonely farmhouses. He was a town boy and
nurtured the urban fear of the wide spaces of the
country where familiarity was no longer governed by
a known street corner, a local shop, or a towering
cement landmark.

He drove on the narrow road to Seminara scarcely
aware of the silent man beside him, contemplating
perhaps the gun that rested on the shelf of the
open glove compartment. The P38, ready and willing
even though its magazine had been rifled in the
barn, still with sufficient cartridges in its bowels to
remain lethal. Through Melicucca where the town
was asleep, where men and women had taken to
their early beds heavy with the wine of the region,

the weight of the food and the condemnation of the priest for late hours. Through Melicucca and beyond before even the lightest sleepers could have turned and wondered at the speed of the car that violated the quiet of their night. He turned sharp left at Santa Anna because that was the route to the coast and the main road.

And the task was only begun. Believe that, Giancarlo. The starting of a journey. The pits, the swamps, all ahead, all gathering, all conglomerating. They are nothing, the boy said soundlessly to himself. Nothing. He slowed as they came to Seminara. A town where people might still be alert, where his caution must be exercised. He'd studied the map in the field near the barn, knew the town had one street; the mayor's office would be there.

A formidable building it was, but decayed and in need of money for repair. Heavy doors tight shut. Sandwiched between lesser constructions and close to the central piazza. Illuminated by the street lights. He braked, and the man beside him lunged forward with his hands to break an impact.

'Get out of the car,' Giancarlo said. 'Get out of the car and put your hands on the roof. And stand still, because the gun watches you.'

Harrison climbed out, his shoulder still paining, did what he was told to do.

Giancarlo watched him straighten, flex himself, and shake his head as if internal dispute had been resolved. He wondered whether Harrison would run, or whether he was too confused to act. He held the gun in his hand, not with aggression but with the warning implicit. He would see the P38 and he would not play the idiot. The movements on the pavement of the Englishman were sluggish, those of a netted carp after a protracted struggle. He would have few problems with this man. From the shelf he took a pencil and a scrap of paper on which had been written on one side the petrol purchases and additions of the car's owner.

'We will not be long, 'Arrison. Stand still because it is not sensible that you move. Afterwards it will all be explained.'

There was no response from the sagging trousers that he could see against the opened door. He began to write with the bold flourished hand that had been taught him by a teacher at the Secondary School of Pescara who prided herself on copperplate neatness. The words came quickly to the paper. There had been time enough on the train to formulate the demand that he would make.

Communiqué I of the Nuclei Armati Proletaria.
We hold prisoner the English multinational criminal, Geoffrey Harrison. All those who work for the multinational conspiracy, whether Italian or foreigners, are exploiters of the proletarian revolution, and are the opponents of the aspirations of the workers. The enemy Harrison is now held in a People's Prison. He will be executed at 09.00 CET, the 27th of this month, the day after tomorrow, unless the prisoner of war held in the regime concentration camp, Franca Tantardini, has been freed and flown out of Italy. There will be no further communiqués, no further warnings. Unless Tantardini is freed from her torture the sentence will be carried out without mercy.
In memory of Panicucci.

Victory to the proletariat. Victory to the workers. Death and defeat to the borghese, the capitalists and the multinationalists. Nuclei Armati Proletaria.

Giancarlo read over his words, screwing his eyes at the paper in the dim light. As Franca would have wanted it. She would be satisfied with him, well satisfied.

' 'Arrison, do you have any paper, something that identifies you? An envelope, a driving licence?' He thrust the gun forward so that the weight of his message would be augmented, and accepted the thin hip wallet in return. Money there, but he ignored it, and drew out the plastic folder of credit cards. Eurocard, American Express, Diners Club. American Express was the one he coveted.

'Perhaps you will get it back at sometime, 'Arrison. With this paper push it under the door. It is important for you that it is found early in the morning. Push it carefully and the card with it, that too is important.'

Giancarlo folded the sheet of paper and wrote on the outside leaf in large capitals the letters of the symbol of the Nappisti. He handed the paper and the credit card to his prisoner and watched him bend to slide the two under the main door to the office of the mayor of Seminara.

'You will drive now, 'Arrison, and you will be careful because I am watching you, and because I have the gun. I have killed three men to come this far, you should know that.'

Giancarlo Battestini slid across into the passenger seat, vacating the driver's place for Geoffrey

Harrison. Their stop in the centre of Seminara had delayed them little more than three minutes.

In the rhythm of driving, the numbing shock wore away, chipped from the mind of Geoffrey Harrison.

Neither attempted conversation, leaving Harrison free to absorb himself in the driving while in the darkness beside him the boy wrestled with the map folds and plotted their route and turnings. As the minutes went by the doldrums cleared from Harrison's thoughts. No explanation yet from the boy, everything left unsaid, unamplified. But he felt that he understood everything, had been given the signs which he now used as the text book of his assessment. The way the hand had gripped his wrist, that told him much, told him he was incarcerated and under guard. The pistol told him more, evidence of lightning attack, of a ferocity of purpose. There was the warning too, the warning in Seminara, spoken as if it were meant kindly. 'I have killed three men to come this far.' Three men dead that Harrison should drive in the warm night past signposts to towns he had not heard of, along the light-constricted visions of a road he had never before travelled on. A prisoner a second time. A hostage with a dropped note setting out terms of release.

Yet he felt no fear of the gun and the youth with the bowed head beside him, because the capacity for terror had been exhausted. Devoid of impatience, he would wait for the promised explanation. Out beyond Laureana, racing alongside the dried-out river bed, Harrison forced the Fiat 127 away from the memories of the barn at Cosoleto and the men with their hoods and kicking boots and fouled shirts.

Hours more till dawn, he reckoned. He had no complaint, only a dulled brain that was exerted by the need to hold the car on the road, the dipped lights on the verge. Only rarely did his attention waver, and when he turned he saw that the boy sat with his arms folded and that the pistol was cupped by an elbow and the barrel faced the space beneath his armpit.

An hour down the road from Seminara, past the sign to Pizzo the silence broke. 'You don't have a cigarette, do you?' Harrison asked.

'I have only a very few.'

Frank enough, thought Harrison, marking the bloody card. 'I haven't had one for a couple of days you know. I'd really like one.'

'I have only a very few,' the boy repeated.

Harrison kept his eyes on the road. 'I don't ask what the hell's going on, I don't throw a fit. I wait to be told all about it in your own good sweet time. All I do is ask for a cigarette . . .'

'You speak too fast for me, I do not understand.'

Hiding, the little bastard, behind the language.

'I just said that perhaps we could share a cigarette.'

'What do you mean?'

'I mean I could smoke it, and you could smoke it, and as we were doing that you could talk to me.'

'We could both smoke the cigarette?'

'I've no known disease.'

The boy reached into the breast pocket of his shirt, reluctant as a bloody Fagan, and from the corner of his eye Harrison saw the red packet emerge. Tight, wasn't he? Not what you'd call the generous type, not like you've hit one of the big spenders of whatever creepy scene this kid owned. Inside the car

219

there was the flash of the igniting lighter, then the slow glow of the cigarette burning, tantalizing and close to him.

'Thank you.' Harrison spoke out clearly.

The boy passed the cigarette. First contact, first humanity. Harrison wrapped his lips on the filter end, pulled hard into his lungs and eased his foot on the accelerator.

'Thank you.' Harrison spoke with feeling and nicotine smoke eddied inside the car's confines. 'Now it's your turn. There'll be nothing funny, I'll keep going, but it's you for the talking. Right?'

Harrison looked quickly away from the road's illuminated markers and the direction lines, gave himself time to absorb the furrow of frown and concentration on the boy's face.

'You should just drive,' and there was the first simmering of hostility.

'Give me the cigarette again, please.' It was passed to him; one desperate intake, like the swill minutes in the pub back in England when the beers are on the counter and the landlord's calling for empty glasses. 'What's your name?'

'Giancarlo.'

'And your other name, what's that, Giancarlo?' Harrison spoke as if the question were pure conversation, as if the answer carried only trivial importance.

'You have no need to know that.'

'Please yourself. I'll call you Giancarlo. I'm Geoffrey . . .'

'I know what your name is. It is 'Arrison. I know your name.'

Brutal going. Like running up a bloody sandhill.

Remember the shooter, if you don't want the ketchup running out of your armpit.

'How far are you going to want me to drive, Giancarlo?'

'You must drive to Rome.' Uncertainty in the boy's voice. Unwilling to be pulled through the wet clothes wringer with his plan.

'How far's Rome?'

'Perhaps eight hundred kilometres.'

'Jesus . . .'

'You will drive all the time. We will only stop when the day comes.'

'It's a hell of a way. Aren't you taking a turn?'

'I watch you, and the gun watches you. Eh, 'Arrison.' The boy mocked him.

'I'm not forgetting the gun, Giancarlo. Believe me, I'm not forgetting it.' Start again, try another route, Geoffrey. 'But you're going to have to talk to me, otherwise I'll be asleep. If that happens it's the ditch for all of us. Harrison, Giancarlo and his pistol, all going to be wrapped round the ditch. We're going to have to find something to talk about.'

'You are tired?' A query. Anxiety. Something not considered.

'Not exactly fresh.' Harrison allowed a flicker of sarcasm. 'We should talk, about yourself for starters.'

The car bounced and veered on the uneven road surface. Even the autostrada, the pride of a motoring society, was in a creeping state of disrepair. The last time the section had been resurfaced the contractor had paid heavily in contributions to the men in smart suits who interested themselves in such projects. For the privilege of moving machines and men into the district he had cut hard into his profit margins. Economies had been made in the depth of the newly laid tarmac which the winter rains had bitten. Harrison clung to the wheel.

'I told you my name is Giancarlo.'

'Right.' Harrison did not turn from the windscreen and the road in front. The smells of the two mingled closely till they were inseparable, unifying them.

'I am nineteen years old.'

'Right.'

'I am not from these parts, nor from Rome.'

No need any more for Harrison to respond. The floodgates were breaking and the atmosphere in the little car ensured it.

'I am a fighter, 'Arrison. I am a fighter for the rights and aspirations of the proletariat revolution. In our group we fight against the corruption and rottenness of our society. You live here and you know what you see with your eyes, you are a part of the scum, 'Arrison. You come from the multinational, you control workers here, but you have no commitment to the Italian workers. You are a leech to them.'

Try and comprehend him, Geoffrey, because it's not the time for argument.

'We have seen the oppression of the gangsters of the Democrazia Cristiana and we fight to destroy them. The communists who should be the voice of the workers are in the DC pockets.' The boy shook as he spoke, as if the very words caused him pain.

'I understand what you say, Giancarlo.'

'On the day that you were taken in Rome by those Calabresi pigs, I was with the leader of our cell. We were ambushed by the polizia. They took our leader, took her away in their chains and with their guns round her. There was another man with us

222

– Panicucci. Not of our ideology at first, but recruited and loyal, loyal as a fighting lion. They shot Panicucci like a dog.'

'Where were you, Giancarlo?'

'Far across the street. She had told me to bring the newspapers. I was too far from her. I could not help . . .'

'I understand.' Harrison spoke softly, tuned to the failure of the boy. He should not humiliate him.

'I could not help, I could do nothing.'

And soon the little bastard will be crying, thought Harrison. If the gun wasn't at his ribcage, Geoffrey Harrison would have been laughing fit to bust. Saga of bloody heroism. Away across the road buying newspapers, what sort of medal do you get for that one? Driving hard past the road to Vibo Valentia, hammering over the bridge and the low reflected waters of the drought-starved Mesima river.

'The one you call the leader, tell me about her.'

'She is Franca. She is a lovely woman, 'Arrison. She is a lady. Franca Tantardini. She is our leader. She hates them and she fights them. They will torture her in the name of their shitty democratic state. They are bastards and they will hurt her.'

'And you love this girl, Giancarlo?'

That deflated the boy, seemed to prick him where the gas was densest.

'I love her,' Giancarlo whispered. 'I love her, and she loves me too. We have been together in the bed.'

'I know how you feel, Giancarlo. I understand you.'

Bloody liar, Geoffrey. When did you last love a woman? How long? Not that recently, not last week.

223

Bloody liar. In the early days with Violet, that was something like love, wasn't it? Something like it . . .

'She is beautiful. She is a real woman. Very beautiful, very strong.'

'I understand, Giancarlo.'

'I will liberate her from them.'

The car swerved on the road, swung out into the fast lane towards the crash barriers. Harrison's hands had tightened on the wheel, his arms had stiffened and were unresponsive, clumsy.

'You are going to liberate her?'

'Together we are going to liberate her, 'Arrison.'

Harrison stared, eyes gimlet clear, out on to the ever diminishing road in his lights. Pinch yourself, kick your arse. Push the bedclothes off and get dressed. Just a bloody nightmare. It has to be.

He knew the answer, but he asked the question.

'How are we going to do it, Giancarlo?'

'You sit with me, 'Arrison. We sit together. They will give me back my Franca and I will give you back to them.'

'It doesn't work like that. Not any more . . . not after Moro . . .'

'You have to hope it is like that.' The cold back in his voice, the ice chill that the boy could summon from the high ground.

'Not after the Moro business. They showed it then . . . they don't bend. No negotiation.'

'Then it is bad for you, 'Arrison.'

'Where were you when Moro was done?'

'At the University of Rome.'

'. . . and weren't there any bloody newspapers there?'

'I know what happened.'

Harrison felt his control sliding, and fought it. His eyes were no longer on the road, his head was swung towards the boy. Noses, faces, unshaven cheeks, mouth breath, all barely separated.

'If that's your plan it's lunatic.'

'That is my plan.'

'They won't give in, a child can see that.'

'They will surrender because they are weak and soft, fattened by their excesses. They cannot win against the might of the proletariat. They cannot resist the revolution of the workers. When we have destroyed the system they will talk of this day.'

God, how do you tell him? Harrison said quietly, chopping his words with emphasis. 'They won't give in . . .'

The boy screamed, 'If they do not return her to me then I kill you.' The wail of the cornered mountain cat, and the spittle flecked Giancarlo's chin.

'Please yourself then.'

Wasn't true, wasn't real, not happening to Geoffrey Harrison. He had to escape from it, had to find a freedom from the snarling hatred.

Harrison swung the car hard to the right, stamped his foot on the brake, whistled to himself in tune with the tyre screech, and wrenched the car to a halt. The pistol was at his neck, nestled against the vein that ran behind his ear lobe.

'Start again,' Giancarlo hissed.

'Drive yourself,' Harrison muttered, sliding back in his seat, folding his arms across his chest.

'Drive or I will shoot you . . .'

'That's your choice.'

'Listen, 'Arrison. Listen to what I say.' The mouth was close to his ear, competing for proximity with the gun barrel, and the breath was hot and gusting in the boy's anger. 'At Seminara, at the town hall, I left a message. It was a communiqué in the name of the Nuclei Armati Proletaria. It will be read with care when it is found, when the first people come in the morning. With the message is your card. They will know that I have you, and later in the morning the barn will be found. It will confirm also that I have taken you when they find the bodies. I have no more need of you, 'Arrison. I have no more need of you while they think that I hold you. Am I clear?'

So why doesn't he do it, Harrison wondered. Not scruple, not compassion. Didn't know and didn't ask. The gun was harder against his skin and the defiance sagged. Not going to call the bluff, are you, Geoffrey? Harrison engaged the gears, flicked the ignition key, and coasted away.

They would talk again later, but not now, not for many minutes. Giancarlo lit another cigarette and did not share it.

Where the carabinieri lay close to the two-storey villa of Antonio Mazzotti they could hear without difficulty the stumbling account of the woman close to hysteria at the front door of the house. She wore a cotton shift dress and a cardigan round her shoulders and rubber boots on her feet as if she had dressed in haste, and the man she spoke with displayed his pyjama trousers beneath his dressing-gown. There had been a brief pause when Mazzotti disappeared inside leaving the woman alone with her face bathed in light, so that the carabinieri who knew the district and its people could recognize her. When Mazzotti came again to the door he was dressed and carried a double-barrelled shotgun.

As they hurried down the road and on to the wood path the woman had clung to Mazzotti's arm and the volume of her tale in his ear had covered the following footsteps of the men in camouflage uniforms. She had heard shots from the barn and knew her husband had work there that night, she knew he stayed at the barn for Signor Mazzotti. Of what she had seen there she could not speak and her wailing roused the village dogs. Mazzotti made no attempt to silence her, as if the enormity of what she described had stunned and shaken him.

When the carabinieri entered the barn the woman was prostrate on the body of her husband, her arms cradling the viciously wounded head, her face pressed to the coin-sized exit wound in his temple. Mazzotti, isolated by the flashlights, had dropped his shotgun to the earth floor. More light poured into the musty room and searched out the second body owning a face contorted by surprise and terror. Men had been left to guard the building till dawn while the capitano hurried with his prisoners to their jeeps.

Within minutes of arriving at the Palmi barracks, the officer had telephoned to Rome, prised the home number of Giuseppe Carboni from an argumentative night clerk, and was speaking to the policeman in his suburban flat.

Twice Carboni asked the same question, twice he received the same deadening answer.

'There was a chain from a roof beam with part of a handcuff attached. That is the place the Englishman could have been held, but he was not there when we came.'

*   *   *

A solitary car, lonely on the road, fast and free on the Auto del Sol. Closing on the ankle of Italy, the heel and toe left in its wake. Coming at speed. Geoffrey Harrison and Giancarlo Battestini headed towards Rome. Geoffrey and Giancarlo and a P38.

Archie Carpenter was at last asleep. His hotel room was cruelly hot but he had lost the spirit to complain to the management about his reverberating air-conditioner. He'd drunk more than he'd intended in the restaurant.

Michael Charlesworth had been purging his guilt at the Embassy's stance by maintaining a high level in Carpenter's glass. Gin first, followed by wine, and after that the acid of the local brandy. The talk had been of strings that could not be tugged, of restrictions on action and initiative. And they had talked late and long on the extraordinary Mrs Harrison. Violet, known to them both, who behaved as no-one else would that they could imagine in those captured circumstances.

'She's impossible, quite impossible. I just couldn't talk to her. All I got for the trouble of going up there was a mouthful of abuse.'

'You didn't do as well as I did,' Carpenter grinned. 'She bloody near raped me.'

'That would have been a diversion. She's off her rocker.'

'I'm not going back there, not till we march old Harrison through the door, shove him at her, and run.'

'I wonder why she didn't fancy me,' Charlesworth had said, and worked again on the brandy bottle.

*　　*　　*

Violet Harrison, too, was deep in sleep. Still and calm in the bed that she shared with her husband, week after week, month after month. She had gone to bed early, stripping her clothes off after the flight of the man from Head Office. Had dressed in a new night-gown, silky and lace-trimmed, that rode high round her thighs. She wanted to sleep, wanted to rest, so that her face might not be lined with tiredness in the morning, so that the crow's feet would not be at her eyes.

Geoffrey would understand, Geoffrey would not condemn her. Geoffrey, wherever he was, would not blame her, would not pick up and cast the stone. She would not be late again at the beach.

Her legs wide and sprawled, she slept on a clear, bright star night.

With a small torch to guide them, their bodies heaving, their feet stumbling, Vanni and Mario charged along the trail in the forest towards the rock face above the tree line.

Word of what had happened at the barn and the villa of the capo raced in a community as small as Cosoleto, travelled by a spider's web of gently tapped doors, calls from upper windows across the streets, by telephone among those houses that possessed the instrument. Vanni had flung his clothes on his back, snapped to his wife where he was going and run from the back door to the home of Mario.

It was a path known to them since their childhood, but the pace of the flight ensured bruised shins, torn arms, and guttural obscenities. Beyond the trees

229

the way narrowed to little more than a goat track, necessitating that they use their hands to pull them higher.

'Who could have been there?'

Vanni struggled on, out of condition, seeing no reason to reply.

'Who knew of the barn?' The persistence of shock and surprise consuming Mario. 'It's certain it's not the carabinieri . . . ?'

Vanni drew the air down into his lungs, paused. 'Certain.'

'Who could have been there?' Mario wrung advantage from the rest, spattered his questions. 'No-one from the villages here would have dared. They would face the vendetta . . .'

'No-one from these parts, no-one who knew the capo . . .'

'Who could it have been?'

'Cretino, how do I know?'

The climb was resumed, slower and subdued, towards a cave beneath an escarpment, the bolt-hole of Vanni.

Past five in the morning the discreet banging at his door woke Francesco Vellosi. In the attics of the Viminale were the angled ceiling closets where men in haste who coveted the clock could sleep. He had worked late after the attack, calming himself with his papers, and neither he nor his guards were happy that he should drive back to his home. And the death of his driver, the killing of Mauro, had rid him of his desire for the comforts of his flat. At the second persistence of the knocking he had called on the man to enter. Sitting on his bed, naked but for a pale blue vest, his hair ragged, his chin alive with the growth of the small hours, he had focused on the messenger who brought blinding light into the room and a buff folder of papers. The man excused himself, was full of apologies for disturbing the Dottore. The file had been given him by the men in Operations, in the basements of the building. He knew nothing of the contents, had simply been dismissed on an errand. Vellosi reached from his bed, took the folder and waved that the messenger should leave. When the door was closed he began to read.

There was a note of explanation, handwritten and stapled to the long telex screed, signed by the night duty officer, a man known to Vellosi, not one who would waste the capo's time. Workmen had come at four in the morning to the offices of the mayor of the town of Seminara in Calabria. The message reproduced on the telex was the text of what they had found, along with an American Express credit card in the name of Geoffrey Harrison.

It was the work of a few seconds for him to absorb the contents of the communiqué. God, how many more of these things? How much longer the agony of these irrelevances in the lifespan of poor, tottering, broken-nosed Italia? After the pain and division of the last one, after the affair of Moro, was all this to be inflicted again? Dressing with one hand, shaving with the battery razor provided thoughtfully beside the washbasin, Vellosi hurried towards the premature day.

The fools must know there could be no concessions. If they had not weakened for the elder statesman of the Republic, how could they crumble now for a businessman, for a foreigner, for a life whose passing would hold no lasting climax? Idiots, fools, lunatics, these people.

Why?

Because they must know there cannot be surrender.

What if they have judged right? What if their analysis of the malaise and sickness of Italia were more perceptive than that of Francesco Vellosi? What if they had discerned that the country could not again endure the strained preoccupation of sitting out ultimatums, deadlines, and photographs of prospective widows?

Was he confident in the sinew of the State?

Over his body they would free Franca Tantardini. Let the bitch out to Fiumicino, bend the constitution for her . . . not as long as he held his job, not as long as he headed the anti-terrorist squad. Badly shaven, temper rising, he headed for the stairs that would lead him to his office. His aides would be at home in their beds. The dawn meetings with the Minister, with the Procurator, with the carabinieri generals, with the men handling the Harrison affair at the Questura, would have to be scheduled by himself.

The route to a coronary, Vellosi told himself, the sure and steady road. He tripped on the narrow steps and cursed aloud in his frustration.

Chapter Twelve

The first spars of light pushed across the inland foothills greying the road in front of Harrison and Giancarlo. A watercolour brush dabbed on the land, softening with pastel the darkness. The grim hour of the day when men who have not slept dread the hours of withering brightness that will follow. They wound down from the hills, running from the mountains as if the sniff of the sea had excited them, towards the beaches of Salerno.

For more than an hour they had not spoken, each wrapped in his committed hostile silence. A fearful quiet lulled only by the throb of the small engine.

Harrison wondered whether the boy slept, but the breathing was never regular, and there were the sudden movements beside him that meant lack of comfort, lack of calm. Perhaps, he thought, it would be simple to disarm him. Perhaps. A soldier, a man of action, would risk all on a sudden swerve, a quick braking and a fast grapple for the P38. But you're neither of those, Geoffrey. The most violent thing he'd ever accomplished in his adult life was to kick that bucket at the guerrillas in the barn. And a smack at Violet once. Just once, not hard. That's all,

Geoffrey, all your offensive experience. Not the stuff of heroes, but it isn't in your chemistry, and for heroes read bloody idiots.

Geoffrey Harrison had never in his life met the dedicated activist, the political attack weapon. It was something new to him, of which he had only limited understanding. Newspaper photographs, yes, plenty of those. Wanted men, captured and chained men, dead men on the pavement. But all inadequate and failing, those images, when it came to this boy.

They're not stupid, not this one anyway. He worked out a plan and he executed it. Found you when half the police in the country were on the same job and late at the post. This isn't a gutter kid from the shanties down on the Tevere banks. A gutter kid wouldn't argue, he'd have killed for the stopping of the car.

'Giancarlo, I'm very tired. We have to talk about something. If I don't talk we'll go off the road.'

There was no sudden start, no stirring at the breaking of the quiet. The boy had not been asleep. The possibility of action had not been there. Harrison felt better for that.

'You are driving very well, we have covered more than half the distance now. Much more than half.' The boy sounded alert, and prepared for conversation.

Harrison blundered in. 'Are you a student, Giancarlo?'

'I was. Some years ago I was a student.' Sufficient as a reply, giving nothing.

'What did you study?' Humour the little pig, humour and amuse him.

'I studied psychology at the University of Rome. I

did not complete my first year. When the students of my class were taking their first-year examinations I was held a political prisoner in the Regina Coeli gaol. I was a part of a struggle group. I was fighting against the borghese administration when the fascist police imprisoned me.'

Can't they speak another language, Harrison thought. Are they reduced only to the compilation of slogans and manifestos? 'Where do you come from, Giancarlo? Where is your home?'

'My home was in the covo with Franca. Before that my home was in the "B" Wing of the Regina Coeli, where my friends were.'

Harrison spoke without thought. He was too tired to pick his words, and his throat was hoarse and sore even from this slight effort. 'Where your parents were, where you spent your childhood, that was what I meant by home.'

'We use different words, 'Arrison. I do not call that my home. I was in chains . . .' Again the warm spittle spread on Harrison's face.

'I'm very tired, Giancarlo. I want to talk so that we don't crash, and I want to understand you. But you don't have to give me that jargon.' Harrison yawned, not for effect, not as a gesture.

Giancarlo laughed out loud, the first time Harrison had heard the rich little treble chime. 'You pretend to be a fool, 'Arrison. I ask you a question. Answer me the truth and I will know you. Answer me, if you were a boy who lived in Italy – if you were from privilege of the DC, if you had seen the children in the "popular" quarter in their rags, if you had seen the hospitals, if you had seen the rich playing at the villas and with their yachts, if you had seen those

235

things, would you not fight? That is my question, 'Arrison, would you not fight?'

The dawn came faster now, the probes of sunlight spearing across the road, and there were other cars on the autostrada, passing or being passed.

'I would not fight, Giancarlo,' Harrison said slowly with the crushing weariness surging again and his eyes cluttered with headlights. 'I would not have the courage to say that I am right, that my word is law. I would need greater authority than a bloody pistol.'

'Drive on, and be careful on the road.' The attack of the angered wasp. As if a stick had penetrated the nest and thrashed about and roused the ferocity of the swarm. 'You will learn my courage, 'Arrison. You will learn it at nine o'clock if the pigs that you slave for have not met—'

'Nine tomorrow morning.' Harrison spoke distantly, his attention on the tail lights in front and the dazzled centre mirror above him. 'You give them little time.'

'Time only for them to express your value.'

Away to the left were the lights daubed on the Bay of Naples. Harrison veered to the right and followed the white arrows on the road to the north and Rome.

Another dawn, another bright fresh morning, and Giuseppe Carboni, alive with the lemon juice in his mouth, arrived at the Viminale by taxi.

It was a long time since he had been to the Ministry. For many months there had been no reason for him to desert the unprepossessing Questura for the eminence of the 'top table', the building that housed the Minister of the Interior and his attendant apparatus. His chin was down on his tie, his eyes on his shoes as he paid off the driver. This was a place where only the idiot felt safe, where the knives were sharp and the criticism cutting. Here the sociologists and the criminologists and the penologists held court and rule was by university diploma and qualification by breeding and connection, because this was close to power, the real power that the Questura did not know.

Carboni was led up the stairs, a debutante introduced at a dance. His humour was poor, his mind only slightly receptive when he reached the door of Francesco Vellosi who had summoned him.

He knew of Vellosi by title and reputation. A well-known name in the Pubblica Sicurezza with a history of clean firmness to embellish it, the one who had made a start at cleaning the drains of crime in Reggio Calabria, ordered significant arrests, and not bowed to intimidation. But the corridor gossip had it that he delighted in public acclamation and sought out the cameras and microphones and the journalists' notebooks. Carboni himself shunned publicity and was suspicious of fast-won plaudits.

But the man across the desk appealed to him.

Vellosi was in his shirt sleeves, glasses down on his nose, cigarette limp between his lips in the gesture of the tired lover, tie loosened, and his jacket away on a chair across the room. No reek of after-shave, no scent of armpit lotion, and already a well-filled ashtray in front of him. Vellosi was studying the papers that piled up on the desk. Carboni waited, then coughed, the obligatory indication of his presence.

Vellosi's eyes fixed on him. 'Dottore Carboni, thank you for coming, and so soon. I had not expected you for another hour.'

'I came immediately I had dressed.'

'As you know, Carboni, from this office I manage the affairs of the anti-terrorist unit.' The rapid patter had begun. 'If one can make such a distinction, I am concerned with affairs political rather than criminal.'

It was to be expected that time would be consumed before they arrived at the reason for the meeting. Carboni was not disturbed. 'Obviously, I know the work that is done from this office.'

'And now it seems that our paths cross, which is rare. Seldom do criminal activities link with those of terrorism.'

'It has happened,' Carboni replied. Non-committal, watchful, the bird high on its perch.

'An Englishman has been kidnapped. It happened two mornings ago. I am correct?' Vellosi's chin was buried in his hands as he gazed hard across the desk. 'An Englishman from one of the big multinational companies that have an operation in Italy. Tell me, please, Carboni, what was your opinion of that case?'

There was something to be wary of. Carboni paused before speaking. 'I have no reason to believe that the kidnapping was not the work of criminals. The style of the attack was similar to that previously used. The limited descriptions of the men who took part indicated an age that is not usually common among the political people; they were in their thirties or more. A ransom demand was made that we have linked with a previous abduction, a further connection has been found with the office of a speculator in Calabria. There is nothing to make me doubt that it was a criminal affair.'

'You have been fortunate, you have come far.'

Carboni loosened. The man opposite him talked like a human being, playing down the superiority of his rank. The man from the Questura felt a freedom to express himself. 'Last night I was able to ask the carabinieri of Palmi near Reggio to keep a watch on this speculator. His name is Mazzotti, from the village of Cosoleto, he has connections in local politics. I acted without a warrant from the magistrate but the time would not allow. If I might digress, a man was found yesterday in a Roman pensione battered to death . . . he had a record for kidnapping, his family is from Cosoleto. I return to the point. The carabinieri behaved faultlessly.' Carboni permitted himself a slow smile, one policeman to another, histories of rivalry with the paramilitary force, mutual understanding on the scale of the compliment. 'The carabinieri followed Mazzotti to a barn, he was taken there by a woman who had heard sounds in the night. The woman's husband was dead there, shot at close range, another man also had been killed. There were signs of a temporary holding place, flattened down hay bales, and there was a chain with a manacle. A pistol, Vellosi, had been used to break the lock of the handcuff. It had been broken by gunshot. We did not find Harrison, nor any trace of him.'

Vellosi nodded his head, the picture unveiled, the drape drawn back. 'What conclusion, Carboni, did you draw from this information?'

'Someone came to the barn and killed the two men that he might have Harrison for himself. It was not a rescue, since there have been no messages from the south of Harrison's arrival at a police station or a carabinieri barracks. I checked before I left my home. I cannot draw an ultimate conclusion.'

The head of the anti-terrorist squad hunched

forward, voice lowered and conspiratorial, as if in a room such as his there were listening places. 'Last night I was attacked. Ambushed as I left my home, and my driver killed.' Vellosi understood from the stunned frowns building and edging across Carboni's forehead that he knew nothing of the evening's horror. 'I survived unhurt. We have identified the swine who killed my driver. They are Nappisti, Carboni. They were young, they were inefficient, and they died for it.'

'I congratulate you on your escape,' Carboni whispered.

'I mourn my driver, he was a friend of many years. I believe I was attacked as a reprisal for the capture of the woman Franca Tantardini, taken by my squad in the Corso Francia. She is an evil bitch, Carboni, a poisoned, evil woman.'

Carboni recovered composure. 'It was a fine effort by your people.'

'I have told you nothing yet. Hear me out before you praise me. There is a town, Seminara, in Calabria. I have no map but we will find, I am sure, that it is close to your Cosoleto. Under the mayor's door an hour ago was found a scribbled statement, not typed, not neat, from the NAP. A credit card of Harrison was with the paper. They will kill him tomorrow morning at nine o'clock if Tantardini has not been freed.'

Carboni whistled, an expiry of wind from his lungs. His pen fumbled between the fingers of his two hands, his notebook was virgin clean.

'I make an assumption, Carboni. The Nappisti reached your man Claudio. They extracted information. They have taken Harrison from the custody of

Mazzotti. The danger now confronting the English-man is infinitely greater.'

With his head bowed, Carboni sat very still in his chair as if a heavy blow had struck him. 'What has been done this morning to prevent an escape . . .'

'Nothing has been done.' A snarl from Vellosi's mouth, and above it the cauterized cheeks, the whitened skin at the temples. 'Nothing has been done because until we sat together there was no dialogue on this issue. I have no army, I have no authority over the polizia and the carabinieri. I do not have the numbers to stifle an escape. I have given you the Nappisti, and you have given me a location, and now we can begin.'

Carboni spoke sadly, unwilling to stamp on the energy of his superior. 'They have five hours' start on us, and they were close to the autostrada and at night the road is free.' His head shook as he multi-plied kilometres and minutes in his mind. 'They could travel hundreds of kilometres in a fast car. The whole of the Mezzo Giorno is open to them . . .' He tailed away, awed by the hopelessness of what he said.

'Bluster the local carabinieri, the polizia, breathe some fire under their backsides. Get back to your office now and hunt the facts.' Shouting now, con-sumed by his mission, Vellosi banged on his desk to emphasize each point.

'It is outside my jurisdiction . . .'

'What do you want? A rule book and Harrison dead in a ditch at five minutes past nine tomorrow? Get yourself on to the fifth floor at the Questura. All the computers, all the Honeywell machines there, get them moving, let them earn their keep.'

Resistance failing, Carboni subsided. 'May I make a telephone call, Dottore?'

'Make it and be on your way. You're not the only one to be busy this morning. The Minister will be here in forty minutes . . .'

Carboni was on his feet, galvanized into activity. With quick, sweaty fingers he flicked in his diary of telephone numbers for that of Michael Charlesworth of the British Embassy.

The early sun was denied entry to the reception lounge of the Villa Wolkonsky by the drawn drapes. The more fancied of the room's collection of rare porcelain had been put away the night before because there had been a small reception and the Ambassador's wife was ever wary of light fingers among her guests. There remained enough to satisfy the curiosity of Charlesworth and Carpenter as they stood close to each other in the gloom. They had come unannounced to the Ambassador's residence, spurred by Giuseppe Carboni's call to Charlesworth sketching the night's developments. The diplomat had collected Carpenter from his hotel. A servant in a white coat, not hiding his disapproval of the hour, had admitted them. If we broadcast we're on our way, Charlesworth had said in the car, then the barricades go up, he'll stall till office hours.

The irritation of the Ambassador was undisguised as he entered the room. A puckered forehead and a jutting chin sandwiched the hawk eyes of annoyance. He wore his familiar dark striped trousers, but no jacket to drape over the braces that held them firm. His collar was unfastened. The opening was abrupt.

'Good morning, Charlesworth. I understand from the message sent upstairs that you wished to see me on a matter of direct and pressing importance. Let's not waste each other's time.'

In the face of this salvo Charlesworth did not falter. 'I've brought with me Archie Carpenter. He's the Security Officer of International Chemical Holdings in London . . .'

His Excellency's eyes glinted, a bare greeting.

'. . . I have just been telephoned by Dottore Carboni of the Questura. There have been disturbing and unpleasant developments in the Harrison case . . .'

Carpenter said quietly, 'We judged that you should know of these – whatever the inconvenience of the hour.'

The Ambassador threw him a glance, then turned back to Charlesworth. 'Let's have it, then.'

'The police have always believed Harrison was kidnapped by a criminal organization. During the night it seems this organization was relieved of Harrison, who is now in the hands of the Nuclei Armati Proletaria.'

'What do you mean – "relieved"?'

'It seems that the NAP have forcibly taken Harrison from his original kidnappers,' said Charlesworth with patience.

'The police are offering this as a theory? We are to believe this?' Spoken with the killer chop of sarcasm.

'Yes, sir,' Carpenter again interjected, 'we believe it because there are three men on their backs in the morgue to convince us. Two have died of gunshot wounds, the third of a dented skull.'

The Ambassador retreated, coughed, wiped his head with a handkerchief and waved his visitors to chairs. 'What's the motive?' he said simply.

Charlesworth took his cue. 'The NAP demand that by nine tomorrow morning, Central European Time, the Italian government shall release the captured terrorist Franca Tantardini . . .'

The Ambassador, sitting far to the front of the intricately carved chair, reeled forward. 'Oh my God . . . Go on, Charlesworth. Don't spare the rod.'

'. . . the Italian government shall release Franca Tantardini or Geoffrey Harrison will be killed. In a few minutes the Minister of the Interior will get his first briefing. I imagine that within twenty you will be called to the Viminale.'

Rock still, his head in his tired, aged hands, the Ambassador contemplated. Neither Charlesworth nor Carpenter interrupted. The buck had been passed. For a full minute the silence burgeoned, causing Charlesworth to feel for the straightness of his tie knot, Carpenter to look at his unpolished shoes and the lace that was loose.

The Ambassador shook himself as if to dislodge the burden. 'It is a decision for the Italian government to make. Any interference, any pressure on our part, would be quite unwarranted. Indeed, any suggestion of action would be quite uncalled for.'

'So you wash your hands of Harrison?' Carpenter was flushed as he spoke, temper surging.

'I don't think that's what the Ambassador meant . . .' Charlesworth cut in unhappily.

'Thank you, Charlesworth, but I can justify my own statements,' the Ambassador said. 'We don't wash our hands of the fate of Mr Harrison, as you put it, Mr Carpenter. We face the reality of local conditions.'

'When this was a criminal matter, when there was only money at issue, then we were prepared to deal . . .'

'Your company was prepared to negotiate, Mr Carpenter. The British Foreign Office remained uninvolved.'

'What's so bloody different between a couple of million dollars and freedom for one woman?' Thanks to all that bloody brandy that Charlesworth had plied him with, he couldn't marshal his sentences, couldn't hit at the smug little sober bastard opposite him. The frustration welled in his mind.

'Don't shout at me, Mr Carpenter.' The Ambassador was cold, aloof on his pedestal. 'The situation is indeed different. Before, as you rightly say, only money was involved. Now we add principle, and with that the sovereign dignity of the Republic of Italy. It is inconceivable that the government here can bow to so crude a threat and release a public enemy of the stature of the Tantardini woman. It is equally inconceivable that the government of Great Britain should urge such a course.'

'I say again, you wash your hands of Geoffrey Harrison. You're prepared to see him sacrificed for the "dignity of Italy", whatever bloody nonsense that is . . .' Carpenter looked across to Charlesworth for an ally, but he had been anticipated and the gaze was averted.

'Well, thank you, gentlemen, thank you for your time. I'm sorry you were disturbed, that the day started badly, and early.'

Carpenter stood up, a little pencil of froth at the sides of his mouth. 'You're putting our man down the bloody bog, and you're pulling the bloody chain on him, and I think it's bloody marvellous.'

There was a passionless mask across the Ambassador's features and he stayed far back in his chair. 'We merely face reality, Mr Carpenter, and reality will dictate that if the losers in this matter are to be either Geoffrey Harrison or the Republic of Italy, then it will be Harrison who loses. If that is the conclusion, then the life of one man is of lesser importance than the lasting damage to the social and political fabric of a great and democratic country. That is how I see it, Mr Carpenter.'

'It's a load of bullshit . . .'

'Your rudeness neither offends me nor helps Harrison.'

'I think we should be on our way, Archie.' Charlesworth too was standing. 'I'll see you later in the office, sir.'

When they were out in the sunshine and walking towards the car, Charlesworth saw that there were tears streaming down Archie Carpenter's face.

For several minutes Harrison had been watching the jumping needle of the fuel dial that bounced against the left corner of the display arc bringing him the knowledge that the tank was drying, emptying. He wondered how the boy would react to the idea that the car would soon be static and useless, considered whether he should alert him to the impending halt of their progress, or whether he should simply drive on till the engine coughed and died, barren of petrol. It depended what he wanted from it, whether it was a fight, or whether it was the easy way and safety, however temporary. Tell him now that they were about to stop on the hard shoulder and perhaps the boy wouldn't panic, would work at his options. Allow it to happen and the boy might crumble under a crisis, and that was dangerous because of the ready presence of the P38.

Same old question, Geoffrey, same old situation. To confront or to bend, and no middle road.

Same old answer, Geoffrey. Don't shake it, don't rock it. Don't kick the bucket of muck in his face because that's the short way to pain, and the gun's close and armed.

'We won't be going much further, Giancarlo.'

Harrison's softly spoken words boomed in the quiet of the car. Beside him the boy straightened from his low-slung sitting posture. The gun barrel dug at Harrison's ribs as if demanding explanation.

'We're almost out of petrol.'

The boy's head in its curled and tangled hair darted across Harrison's chest to study the dial. Harrison eased back in his seat, gave him more room, and heard his breathing speed and rise.

'There's not much more in the old girl, Giancarlo. Perhaps a few more kilometres.'

The boy lifted his head, and the hand that did not hold the gun scraped at his chin as if this were a way to summon inspiration and clarity of decision.

'It's not my fault, Giancarlo.'

'Silence,' the boy snapped back.

Just the breathing to mingle with the steady purr of the little engine, and time too for Harrison to think and consider. Behind their different walls the man and the boy entertained the same thoughts. What would a stoppage mean to the security of the journey? What risk would it offer Giancarlo of identification and subsequent pursuit? What possibility of escape would it present to his prisoner? And it's not only the boy with decisions to make, Geoffrey, it's you as well. He couldn't be as vigilant, could he, if they were stopped on the roadside, pulled into a toll gate, going in search of a petrol station? Opportunities were going to loom, opportunities for flight, for a struggle.

Then he'll shoot.

Sure?

Can't be sure but likely.

Worth a try, whether he'll shoot or not?

Perhaps, if the opportunity's there.

That's the crawling way out, that's the gutless way.

For Christ's sake, it's not a bloody virility contest. It's my bloody life, it's my bloody stomach with the P38 stuck into it. It's my neck with the axe hanging over it. It's not gesture time. I said perhaps, that should bloody be enough.

You won't do it, you won't take him on, you won't fight.

Perhaps, but only if it presents itself.

'We take the Monte Cassino turn-off.' Giancarlo was out of his dream, breaking Harrison's debate.

High above them to the right of the autostrada perched the triumphant monastery. It loomed on the mountain top, a widow's shrine for women of many far countries whose men had staggered and fallen distant years back under the rain of shrapnel and explosive, and bullet swathes. The car plunged past the signs for the turn-off.

Giancarlo raised himself in his seat and pulled from a hip pocket a wad of notes and the autostrada toll ticket taken hundreds of kilometres back from a machine.

'I had not thought of the petrol,' he laughed with a quick nervousness. A drip of weakness before the tap was turned tighter. "Arrison, you will not be silly. You will pay the ticket. The gun will be at you all the time. You are not concerned with what will happen to me, you are concerned with what will happen to yourself. If you are silly then you are dead; whether I am too does not help you. You understand, 'Arrison?'

'Yes, Giancarlo.'

Harrison pulled the wheel hard to the right, felt the tyres bite beneath him, heard their squeal, and the pace of the autostrada diminished from his windscreen mirror. He had slowed the car as they wound on the tight bend towards the toll gate. Giancarlo reached back to the seat behind and grabbed at his light anorak, arranged it over his lower arm and his fist and the gun and again pressured the barrel into the softness at Harrison's waist.

'You don't speak.'

'What if he talks to me?' Harrison stammered, the tension exuding from the boy spread contagiously.

'I will talk to him, if it is necessary . . . If I fire the pistol from here I kill you, 'Arrison.'

'I know, Giancarlo.'

Perhaps, but only if it presents itself. You know the answer, Geoffrey. He pressed the brake as the

249

cabins of the toll gate loomed in front of him. He stopped the car as the bonnet edged against the narrow barrier, carefully wound down the window and without looking passed the ticket and a bank-note out into the cool dawn air.

'*Grazie.*'

The voice startled Harrison. Contact again with the real and the permanent life, contact with the clean and the familiar. His eyes followed his arm but there was no face in his vision, only a hand that was dark and hair-covered with a worn greasy palm that took his money, and was gone before snaking back with a fist full of coins. It had not presented itself. The gun gouged at his flesh, and the man would not even have seen their faces. The voice beside him was shrill.

'*Una stazione de servizio, per benzina?*'

'*Cinquecento metri.*'

'*Grazie.*'

'*Prego.*'

The barrier was raised, Harrison edged the car into gear. Shouldn't he have crashed the gears, stalled the engine, dropped the change in the roadway? Shouldn't he have done something? But the gun was there, round and penetrating at the skin. All right for those who don't know, all right for those without experience. Let them come and sit here, let them find their own answers to cowardice. Within moments the lights of a petrol station shone at them in the half light, diffused with the growing sun.

'You follow my instructions exactly.'

'Yes, Giancarlo.'

'Go to the far pumps.'

Where it was darkest, where the light was masked

by the building, Harrison stopped. Giancarlo waited till the handbrake was applied, the gear in neutral, before his hand snaked out at speed to rip the keys from the ignition. He snapped open his door, thrust it shut behind him and jogged around the back of the car till he was at Harrison's door. He held his anorak across his waist, with an innocence that was above suspicion.

Harrison saw a man in the blue overalls of Agip stroll without urgency towards the car.

'*Venti mila lire di benzina, per favore.*'

'*Si.*'

Would he look into the car, would the curiosity bred from the long night hours cause him to turn from the boy who stood beside the driver's door, and wish to examine the occupant? Why should it? Why should he care who drives a car? This has to be the moment, Geoffrey. Now, right now, not next time, not next week.

How?

Fling the door open, crash it into Giancarlo's body. You'd knock him back with it, he'd fall, he'd slip. For how long? Long enough to run. Sure? Well, not sure . . . but it's a chance. And how far do you run before he's on his feet, five metres . . . ? It's the opportunity. Then he shoots, and he doesn't miss, not this kid, and who else is here other than a half-asleep idiot with his eyes closed, who'll have to play the hero?

Giancarlo passed the man the notes and waited as he walked away, then hissed through the window, 'I am going to walk round the car. If you move I will shoot, it is no problem through the glass. Do not move, 'Arrison.'

Only if it presents itself. Geoffrey Harrison felt the great weakness creeping into his knees and shins, lapping in his stomach. His tongue smeared a dampness across his lips. You'd have been dead, Geoffrey, if you'd tried anything, you know that, don't you? He supposed he did, supposed he had been sensible, behaved in the intelligent, responsible way that came from education and experience. Wouldn't have lasted long on that mountainside in 1944, Geoffrey; wouldn't have lasted five bloody minutes.

Beneath the triumphant monastery on Monte Cassino, Giancarlo ordered Harrison to turn off the autostrada.

He held the pistol hidden between his legs as Harrison paid the sleepy toll attendant at the barrier with the money the boy had given him. They drove sharply through the small town, rebuilt from the ravages of bombardment into a characterless warren of flat blocks and factories, and headed north on a narrow road among the rock defiles, ever watched by the great whitestone eye on the mountain top. They bypassed the sombre war cemetery for the German dead of a battle fought before the birth of Giancarlo and Harrison, and then the road's turns became more vicious, and the high banks more intrusive.

Three kilometres beyond the rugged message of the graveyard cross, Giancarlo indicated an open field gate through which they should turn. The car lurched over the bare grass covering the hardened ground and was lost to sight behind a gorse hedge of brilliant yellow flowers. Shepherds might come here, or the men who watched the goat flocks, but the chance was reasonable in Giancarlo's mind. Among the grass and weed and climbing thistle and the bushes of the hillside they would rest. Rome lay just one hundred and twenty-five kilometres away. They had done well, they had made good time.

With the car stationary, Giancarlo moved briskly. The flex that he had found in the glove compartment in one hand, the pistol in the other, he followed Harrison between the gorse clumps. He ordered him down, pushed him without unkindness on to his stomach, and then, kneeling with the gun between his thighs, bound Harrison's hands across the small of his back. The legs next, working at the ankles, wrapping the flex around them, weaving it tight, binding the knot. He walked a few paces away and urinated noisily in the grass and was watching the rivulets when he realized he had not offered the Englishman the same chance. He shrugged and put it from his mind. He had no feelings for his prisoner; the man was just a vehicle, just a machine for bringing him closer to his Franca.

Harrison's eyes were already closed, the breathing deep and regular as the sleep sped to him. Giancarlo watched the slow rise and fall of his shoulders and the gaping mouth that was not irritated by the nibbling attendance of a fly. He put the gun on the grass and scrabbled with his fingers at the buckle of his belt and at the elastic waist of his underpants.

Franca. Darling, sweet, lovely Franca. I am coming, Franca. And we will be together, always together, Franca, and you will love me for what I have done for you. Love me, too, my beautiful. Love me.

Chapter Thirteen

Giancarlo asleep seemed little more than a child, hurt by exhaustion and dragged nerves, coiled gently. His real age was betrayed by the premature haggardness of his face, the witness to his participation in the affairs of men. His left forearm acted as a shield to the climbing sun, and his right hand was buried in the grass, fingers among the leaves and stalks and across the handle of the P38.

He was dreaming.

The fantasy was of success, the images were of achievement. Tossed and tumbling through his febrile mind were the pictures of the moment of triumph he would win. An indulgent masturbation of excitement. Sharp pictures, and vivid. Men in blue Fiat saloons hurrying with escorts of outriders to the public buildings of the capital, men who pushed their way past avalanches of cameras and microphones with anger at their mouths. Rooms that were heavy in smoke and argument where the talk was of Giancarlo Battestini and Franca Tantardini and the NAP. Crisis in the air. Crisis that was the embryo of chaos. Crisis that was spawned and conceived from the sperm of the little fox. Papers would be set in front of the men and pens made ready by the acolytes at their shoulders. Official stamps, weighty and embossed with eagles, would clamp down on the scrawl of the signatures. The order would be made, Franca would be freed, plucked clear from the enemy by the hand of her boy and her lover. The order would be made, in Giancarlo's dreaming and restless mind there was no doubt. Because he had done so much . . . he had come so far.

He had done so much, and they could not deny him the pleasure of his prize. There was one more element among the images of the boy sleeping in the field. There was a prison gate, dominating the sky-line and shadowing the street beneath, and doors that would swing slowly open, dragged apart against their will by the hands of Giancarlo. There was a column of police cars, sirens and lights bright on a July morning, bringing his Franca free; she sat like a queen among them, contempt in her eyes for the truncheons and Beretta pistols and machine-guns. Franca coming to freedom.

It would be the greatest victory ever achieved by the NAP. Loving himself, loving his dream, Gian-carlo groped downwards with his right hand, urging his thoughts to the diminishing memory of his Franca, conjuring again her body and the sunswept skin.

And the spell was broken. The mirror cracked. The dream was gone with the speed of a disturbed tiger at a waterhole; a blur of light, a memory and a ripple. Lost and wrecked, vanished and destroyed. Trembling in his anger, Giancarlo sat up.

'Giancarlo, Giancarlo,' Geoffrey Harrison had called. 'I want to pee, and I can't the way I'm tied.'

Harrison saw the fury in the boy's face, the neck veins in relief. The intensity of the little swine frightened him, the loathing that was communicated across the few metres of stone and burned field flowers.

He wormed back from confrontation. 'I have to pee, Giancarlo. It's not much to ask.'

The boy stood up, uncertain for a moment on his feet, then collected himself. He scanned all the surroundings as if they were unfamiliar to him and in need of further checks to establish his security. He examined the long depth to the horizon, breaking the fields and low stone walls and distant farm buildings into sectors to vet them more thoroughly. Harrison could see that the boy was rested, that sleep had alerted and revived him. He used a bush of gorse with yellow-petalled flowers to screen himself from the road as he looked around. There was something slow and workmanlike and hugely sinister about his calm. Better to have tied a knot in it or soaked his trousers, Harrison thought, than to have woken him.

Giancarlo walked towards him, feet light on the springy grass, avoiding the stones set deep in the earth, the hand with the gun extended, aimed at Harrison's chest.

'Don't worry, don't point it, I'm not playing heroes, Giancarlo.'

The boy moved behind Harrison, and he heard the scuff of his feet.

'There's a good lad, Giancarlo, you know how it is. I'm fit to bloody burst, you know . . .'

The blow was fierce, agonizing and without warning. The full force of the canvas toe-cap of

Giancarlo's right shoe digging into the flesh that formed the protective wall for the kidneys. The pain was instant, blending with the next stab as the following kick came in fast and sharp. Three in all and Harrison slid on to his side.

'You little pig. Vicious . . . bullying . . . little pig . . .' The words were gasped out, strained and hoarse, and the breath was hard to find. More pain, more hurt, because the wounds of the men in the barn were aroused again and mingled with the new bruising. Harrison looked up into the boy's eyes and they bounced his gaze back with something animal, something primitive. Where do they make them, these bloody creatures? Where's the production line? Where's the factory? Deadened and unresponsive and cruel. Where's the bloody stone they're bred under?

Slowly and with deliberation the boy bent down behind Harrison, the barrel of the pistol indenting the skin where it was smooth and hairless behind the ear. With his free hand Giancarlo untied the flex. It was the work of a few moments and then Harrison felt the freedom come again to his wrists and ankles, the shock surge of the blood running free. He didn't wait to be told but rose unsteadily to his feet. He walked a half-dozen paces with a drunken gait, and flicked at his zip-fastener. The spurting, draining relief. That's what it had come down to; ten minutes of negotiation, a kicking, a gun at the back of his head – all that because he wanted to pee, to spend a penny, as Violet would have said. Being pulled down into the cesspool, being animalized. He looked down into the clear, reflecting pool in front of his feet and in a moment of hesitation between surges saw the traces of his own concerned and wrung-out face.

Geoffrey, we want to go home. We're not fighters, old lad, we're not like those who can just sit in a limbo and be pushed and tugged by the wind. We're just a poor little bloody businessman who doesn't give a stuff about exploitation and revolution and the rights of the proletariat; a poor little bloody businessman who wants to wrestle with output and production and raw materials, the things that pay for summer holidays and the clothes on Violet's back, and a few quid to go on top of a widowed mother's pension. It's not our war, Geoffrey, not our bloody fight. Harrison shook himself, swayed on his feet, pulled up the zip and turned his hips so that he could see behind him. His movements were careful, designed to cause no alarm. The boy was watching him, impassive and with as much emotion as a white-washed wall. The two of them, devoid of relationship, without mutual sympathy, stared at each other. He'd kill you as he'd stamp on a dragonfly, Geoffrey, and it wouldn't move him, wouldn't halt his sleep afterwards. That's why he doesn't communicate, because the bastard doesn't need to.

'What are we going to do now?' Harrison asked in a small voice.

The boy stood out of arm's reach but close. Another gesture from the arm that held the pistol and they walked the few metres towards the car.

'Where are we going?' Harrison said.

Giancarlo laughed, opening his mouth so that Harrison saw the fillings of his teeth and felt the stench of his breath. This is the way the Jews went to the cattle trucks in the railway sidings, without a struggle, making obeisance to their guards, thought Harrison. Understand, Geoffrey, how they forsook resistance? You're gutless, lad. And you know it, that's what hurts.

He opened the door of the car, climbed in and watched Giancarlo walk round the front of the engine. The keys were exchanged, the P38 took up position by his ribcage, the brake was eased off, the gears engaged.

Harrison headed the car back towards the road.

Its headlights shining vainly in the morning brilliance, a white Alfetta swept down the sloping crescent of the driveway outside the Viminale. An identical car with the smoked, half-inch-thick windows and reinforced bodywork had latched itself close behind, the worrying terrier that must not leave its quarry. Alone among the members of the Italian government, the Minister of the Interior had discarded the midnight-blue fleet of Fiat 132s after the kidnapping of the President of his party. For him and his bodyguards bulletproof transport was decreed. The Minister had said in public that he detested the hermetically sealed capsule in which he was ferried in high summer from one quarter of the city to another, but after the chorus of inter-service recrimination that followed the attack on the vulnerable Moro car and the massacre of his five-man escort, the Minister's preferences mattered little.

With siren blaring and driving the motorists on Quattro Fontane languidly aside, the Alfetta plied through the mounting traffic. The driver was hunched in his concentration, left hand steady on the wheel, the right resting loosely on the gear stick.

Beside the driver, the Minister's senior guard cradled a short-barrelled machine-gun on his lap, one magazine attached, two more on the floor between his feet.

For the Minister and his guest, the British Ambassador, conversation was difficult, each clinging to the thong straps above the darkened side windows. The Ambassador was travelling at the Minister's invitation, his presence hurriedly requested. Would he care to be briefed on the situation concerning the businessman Harrison while the Minister was in transit between his offices and those of the Prime Minister? Somewhere lost behind them in the dash and verve of the Roman streets was the Embassy Rolls that would collect the Ambassador from Palazzo Chigi.

Public men both of them, and so they were jacketed. The Italian sported a red silk tie above his blue shirt. The Ambassador favoured the broad colour bands of his wartime cavalry unit. The two men were stifled near to suffocation with the heat in the closed car, and the Minister showed his irritation that he should be the cause of his guest's discomfort. His apologies were waved aside, and there was the little clucking of the tongue that meant the problem was inconsequential.

Unlike many of his colleagues, the Minister spoke English, fluently and with little of the Mediterranean accent. An educated and lucid man, a professor of Law, an author of books, he explained the night's events to the Ambassador.

'And so, sir, we have at our doors another nightmare. We have another journey into the abyss of despair that after the murder of our friend,

Aldo Moro, we hoped never to see again. For all of us then, in the Council of Ministers and in the Directorate of the Democrazia Cristiana, the decision to turn our backs on our friend provoked a bitter and horrible moment. We all prayed hard for guidance, then. All of us, sir. We walked across to church from the deliberations at the Piazza Gesù, and as one we went on our knees and prayed for God's guidance. If He gave it to us He manifested Himself in His own and peculiar way. His message bearer was Berlinguer, it was the Secretary-General of our Communist Party who informed us that the infant understanding between his party and ours could not survive vacillation. The PCI dictated that there could be no concession to the Brigate Rosse. The demand that we release thirteen of their nominees from gaol was rejected. The chance to save one of the great men of our country was lost. Who can apportion victory and defeat between ourselves and the Brigatisti?'

The Minister mopped a smear of sweat from his neck with a handkerchief scented with cologne sufficiently to offend the Ambassador's nostrils. The monologue, the exposition of the day's business, continued.

'Now we must make more decisions, and first we must decide whether we follow the same rules as before or whether we offer a different response. The hostage on this occasion is not an Italian, nor is he a public figure who could by some be held accountable for the society in which we live. The hostage now is a guest, and totally without responsibility for the conditions that unhappily prevail in our country . . . I won't elaborate. I turn to the nature of the ransom demanded. One prisoner, one only. Thirteen we could not countenance, but one we might swallow, though the bone would stick. But swallow it we could if we had to.'

The Ambassador rocked pensively in his seat. They had cut down the curved hill from the Quirinale and surged with noise and power across the Piazza Venezia scattering the locust swarms of jeaned and T-shirted tourists. Not for him to reply at this stage, not till his specific opinion was required.

The Minister sighed, as if he had hoped for the load to be shared, and realized with regret that he must soldier on.

'We would be very loath to lose your Mr Harrison, and very loath to lose the Tantardini woman. We believe we should do everything within our power to save Mr Harrison. The dilemma is whether "everything in our power" constitutes interference in the judicial process against Tantardini.'

The Ambassador peered down at the hands in his lap. 'With respect, Minister, that is a decision the Italian government must take.'

'You would pass it all to us?'

The Ambassador recited, 'Anything else would be the grossest interference in the internal affairs of a long-standing and respected friend.'

The Minister smiled, grimly, without enjoyment. 'We have very little time, Ambassador. So my questions to you will be concise. There should be no misunderstandings.'

'I agree.'

The Minister savoured his question before speaking. The critical one, the reason that he had invited the Ambassador to travel with him. 'Is it likely that Her Majesty's Government will make an appeal to us to barter the woman Tantardini with the intention of saving Harrison's life?'

'Most unlikely.' The Ambassador was sure and decisive.

'We would not wish to take a course of action and afterwards receive a request from Whitehall for a different approach.'

'I repeat, Minister, it is most unlikely that we would ask for the freeing of Tantardini.'

The Minister looked with his jaded blue eyes at the Ambassador, a dab of surprise at his mouth. 'You are a hard people . . . you value principle highly. It does not have much merit in our society.'

'My government does not believe in bowing to the coercion of terrorism.'

'I put another hypothesis to you. If we refuse to negotiate with the Nappisti for the freedom of Tantardini and if as a consequence Harrison dies, would we be much criticized in Britain for the hard line, *la linea dura*, as we would say?'

'Most unlikely.' The Ambassador held the Minister's questioning glance, unswerving and without deviation, the reply clear as a pistol shot.

'We are not a strong country, Ambassador, we prefer to circumvent obstacles that fall across our path. We do not have the mentality of your cavalry, we do not raise our sabres and charge our enemy. We seek to avoid him . . .'

The car came fast to a halt and the driver and bodyguard leaned back to unfasten the locks on the rear doors. Out on the cobbled courtyard of the Palazzo Chigi the Ambassador breathed in the clean, freshened air and dried his hands on his trouser crease.

The Minister had not finished, busily he led the Ambassador into the centre of the yard where the sun was bright and where there was none who could overhear their words.

The Minister held the Ambassador's elbow tightly. 'Without a request from your government, there is no reason for our cabinet even to consider the options over Tantardini. You know what I am saying to you?'

'Of course.'

'You value the point of principle?'

'We value that consideration,' the Ambassador said quietly and with no relish.

The Minister pressed. 'Principle . . . even when the only beneficiary could be the Republic of Italy . . .'

'Still it would be important to us.' The Ambassador pulled at his tie, wanting relief from its grip. 'A man came to see me earlier this morning, he is a representative of Harrison's firm, and I told him what I have told you. He called me Pilate, he said I was washing my hands of his man. Perhaps he is right. I can only give my opinion, but I think it will be ratified by London.'

The Minister, still sombre, still clinging to the Ambassador's arm as if unwilling to break away for his cabinet colleagues waiting upstairs, said, 'If we refuse to release Tantardini, I do not think we will see Harrison again.'

The Ambassador accepted his opinion, nodded gravely.

'I will relay your view to Whitehall.'

The two men stood together, the Ambassador

disproportionately taller. High frescoes in centuries-old paint leered down at them, mocking their transitory plans for history. Both perspired, both were too preoccupied to wash away the moisture beads. 'We understand each other, my friend. I will tell my colleagues that the British ask for no deal, no barter, no negotiation . . . and whatever happens we win the victory of principle . . .'

The Ambassador interrupted his short choked laugh. 'I am sure that Defence would send the Special Air Service, the close-quarter attack squad, as they did for Moro. They could be here this afternoon, if it were helpful.'

The Minister seemed to snort, give his judgement on an irrelevance, and walked away towards the wide staircase of the Palazzo.

Those who came late that morning to their desks in the Viminale on the second floor found that already the corridors and offices were nests of harsh and total activity. Vellosi paced among rooms, querying the necessity of bureaucrats and policemen alike to occupy their premises and their precious telephones, and where he found no satisfaction he commandeered and installed in their place his own subordinates. By ten he had secured an additional five rooms, all within shouting distance of his own. Technicians from the basements were kept busy hoisting the mess of cables and wires, attaching the transmitters and receivers that would secure him instant access to the control centre of the Questura and the office of Carboni. Some of the dispossessed hung about in the corridors, sleek in their suits and clean shirts, and smiled sweetly at the pace and moment of the working men around them and vowed they would have Vellosi's head served up on a charger were he not to deliver Geoffrey Harrison, free and unharmed, by the next morning. It was not the way that things were done in the Viminale. Noise, rising voices, the ringing of telephone bells, the pleas of radio static all mingled and coalesced in the corridor. Vellosi bounced between the sources of the confusion. He had told an examining magistrate that he was a hindrance and an obstruction, a carabinieri general that if he didn't push reinforcements into the Cosoleto area he would face speedy retirement, the persistent editor of the largest Socialist newspaper in the city that his head should be down the lavatory pan and would he clear the line, and sent out for more cigarettes, more coffee, more sandwiches.

At a hectic pace, bewildering to all those who were not central to the knot of the inquiry, the operation and investigation were launched. Those who participated and those who were idle and smirking behind their hands could agree on the one common point. The mood on the second floor of the Viminale was unique. Very few, though, were privy to the telephone conversation between Vellosi and the Minister, who spoke from an anteroom outside the cabinet deliberations at the Palazzo Chigi; only the inner court, the hard men on whom Vellosi leaned for succour and advice.

He had slammed the telephone down, barely a grunt of thanks to the Minister and confided to those in the room near him.

'They're standing firm, our masters. The men of deviation and compromise are holding a line. The bitch stays with us. Tantardini stays in her cell and rots there.'

The four who heard him understood the import-ance of the political decision, and they smiled to each other in a grim satisfaction and dropped their shoulders and raised their eyebrows and returned to their notepads and their internal telephone direc-tories.

The information began to flow as the team hustled, begged and screamed into the telephones; shapes and patterns emerging from the kaleidoscope of mystery and dead alleys with which the day had started. Photographs of the known Nappisti at liberty had been spread out on a table for the portière of the pensione where Claudio's body had been found. He had not wished to be involved, this elderly man whose job required a short tongue and shorter memory. He had turned over many pictures, showing little interest, muttering repeatedly of the failure of his recollection. One flicker of curiosity nullified his reluctance and a detective had seen the betrayal of recognition that the portière had tried to hide. It was the work of a police photographer, and the typed message on the back of the picture gave the name of Giancarlo Battestini.

What name had he used? What identity card had he shown? What had he been wearing? What time had he arrived? What time had he left? The ques-tions battered at the old man in his fading uniform till he had broken the reticence born of the sense of survival and told the story the police wanted to hear. The information breathed a new activity into the squad of men around Vellosi, whipped up their flagging morale and drove them on.

'It's beside the station,' Vellosi stormed down his telephone to a maggiore of the Pubblica Sicurezza. 'Right beside the station, this pensione, so get the photograph of Battestini down to the ticket counters, get it among the platform workers. Check him through all the trains to Reggio yesterday morning. Find the ticket inspectors on those trains, find their names, where they are now, and get that picture under their noses.'

There was so much commitment, so much cajoling and abuse that for a full minute Giuseppe Carboni stood ignored in the doorway of Vellosi's office. He bided his time; he would have his moment. And it would be choice, he thought, choice enough for it to have been worth his while to abandon his desk at the Questura and come unannounced to the Viminale. Vellosi was on his way for another prowl along the corridor to chase and jockey his men when he careered into the solid flesh wall of the policeman.

'Carboni, my apologies.' Vellosi laughed. 'We have been very busy here, we have been going hard . . .'

'Excellent, Vellosi, excellent.' A measured reply, tolerant and calm.

'. . . you will forgive my hurry, but we have discovered an important connection . . .'

'Excellent.'

'The boy of the NAP, Battestini . . . the one we missed when we took Tantardini, this is the kernel of this matter, it was he who killed the gorilla in the hotel. We have established that, and this Claudio was from those who took your Harrison . . . we have not been idle.'

'Excellent.'

Vellosi saw the smile on Carboni's face, as though the man had picked up a book and found it already familiar. His revelation won no recognition of achievement.

'And are you prospering too, Carboni?' Subdued already, Vellosi braced himself. 'Tell me.'

Carboni led the head of the anti-terrorist squad back to his desk. With his heavy rounded fingers he produced from a neat briefcase two facsimile documents. He laid them on the desk, carelessly pushing aside the piles of handwritten notes that had accumulated there through the morning. With his forefinger, Carboni stabbed at the upper sheet.

'This is the statement taken from Battestini by the polizia more than eighteen months ago . . . after his arrest for some student fracas. It carried his handwriting at the bottom.'

'I have seen it,' Vellosi said curtly.

Carboni pulled clear the under sheet. 'This is the statement from the Nappisti found at Seminara along with Harrison's card. Observe the writing, Vellosi, observe it closely.'

Vellosi's nose was a few inches from the papers as he held them to the light.

'It has been checked. At Criminalpol they ran it through the machines for me. The scientists have no doubt that they match.' Carboni savoured the moment. It was perhaps the finest of his professional life. He stood among the gods, the princes of the elite force, the cream of the anti-subversion fighters, and he told them something they had not seen for themselves. 'Giancarlo Battestini, nineteen years old, born in Pescara, university drop-out, probationer of the NAP, he is the one who has taken Geoffrey Harrison. Harrison is in Battestini's hands, and I venture to suggest that is the limit and extent of the conspiracy.'

Vellosi dropped back to his chair. A hush spread across the room and on into the corridor and further offices. Men in shirt sleeves holding cigarettes and plastic coffee beakers crowded to the doorway. 'Is it possible for one man – a mere boy – to have achieved all this?'

'Vellosi, it has happened.' The pleasure shone on Carboni's face. 'I won't detain you, but you should know we are sifting the reports of stolen vehicles from the area of the city of Reggio – there are not many, not at the times that fit. Two cinquecentos, but they would be too small for the purpose. There was a BMW but that is a conspicuous car. Close to the main station at Reggio, a few minutes' walk away, there is reported missing within ninety minutes of the arrival of the rapido from Roma a one-two-seven. It is red, and the registration is going out now. There is the same problem as always with the road blocks because we do not know where to set them, but if it is on the radio and the lunchtime television, then perhaps . . .'

'Shut up, Carboni.' Vellosi spoke quietly. He reached up with both arms, put them round Carboni's neck and pulled the ill-shaven face towards him. Their cheeks met, the kiss of friends and equals. 'You're a genius, Carboni, nothing but a genius.'

Carboni blushed, swung on his heel and left with a little wave of his fingers for farewell. He had stirred

Vellosi's ant hole, changed its direction, shifted the whole basis of the inquiry.

'Well, don't stand about,' Vellosi snapped at his audience. 'We've let an amateur show us what's happening, point to what's been staring at us for hours. We have more in a day than we had in a month with Moro. Use it.'

But for Moro he had had time. For Harrison he had less than twenty-four hours till the expiry of the ultimatum.

Vellosi scuffed among his papers till he found the photograph of Battestini. He searched the mouth and the jaw line and the set of the eyes for information, scrabbling to catch up, scratching to make do with diminishing hours, the tools of a policeman's trade.

'The little bastard could be anywhere.' And Vellosi swore and reached for his coffee that was cold.

He must go back to the basics, back to deep and quiet thought in the midst of the noise surrounding him, back to analysis of the minimal factual evidence available.

Start again, start from the beginning. Return to the face of Battestini, drag from those features the response that should be made.

Giancarlo Battestini, imprisoned in Rome after studying in the capital's university, and a member of an NAP cell in that city. Could the boy have links with the far countryside? Likely or unlikely? Vellosi flexed his fingers. The answer was obvious. The boy would know nothing of Calabria. A city boy, a town boy, a foreigner in the Mezzo Giorno.

He turned and called to a colleague, who stubbed his cigarette, drained his coffee and came to him.

'Battestini would not believe he could survive in the countryside, it is beyond his experience. Correct?'

'Correct.'

'He would try to return to the city?'

'Possible.'

'In the files he is linked only with Rome: would he try to get back here?'

'Perhaps.'

'He is divorced from Pescara. He has nothing there. And if he comes back towards Rome he must come by car because he cannot take a prisoner by train.'

'Probable.'

The momentum carried Vellosi on. 'If he comes by road he must decide for himself whether he will attempt speed on the autostrada, or whether he will go for the safer and slower old roads.'

'I think he would choose the autostrada.'

Vellosi slapped his fist into the palm of his other hand. 'And he must stop . . .'

'For petrol.'

'He has to stop.'

'Certain.'

'Either at a station on the autostrada or he must come off and use a toll gate and a station off the main route.'

'If he is coming to Rome, if he is coming by car, if he is on the autostrada, then that is correct.'

Vellosi thrust his chair behind him, rose to his full height and shouted, 'Work on the petrol stations and the autostrada tolls. Each side of Naples. Call Carboni, tell him that too.'

His colleague was no longer beside him.

Vellosi slumped back into his seat. There was no-one to praise him, no-one to smile and slap his back and offer congratulations. To himself he muttered, over and over again, 'The boy will come back to the city, the boy will return to Rome.'

Chapter Fourteen

While the disparate arms and commands of security forces strove to drag themselves into a state of intervention, the small red Fiat slipped unremarked through the toll gate marking the terminal of the autostrada at Roma Sud and away towards the Raccordo Annulare, the ring road skirting the capital. With the passing of the mass-produced common car through the toll check, the chances of its detection, always remote, were reduced to the minimal.

The two men had exchanged only desultory conversation, preferring to brood to themselves in the confined space. Geoffrey Harrison, the pain gone from his back, drove in a careless and detached way as if concern and anxiety were no longer with him. His mind numbed, his brain deadened, he performed the automatic tasks of keeping the car in the centre lane of traffic, the speed constant. At two places, the petrol station and the toll gate, he told himself there had been the possibility of a break-out from the car. But the will to seek his freedom was reduced. He had sat meekly in the driving seat, neither looking at nor avoiding the man who secured the fuel tank cap and wiped wetly over the windscreen. He had held his silence as the young man at the toll had handed the change through the open window.

Manipulated and broken, too destroyed to weep, too cudgelled to fight, Harrison guided the car around the east side of the city.

For Violet Harrison the mood of the morning alternated between remorse and defiance.

She had lain in bed, curling slowly over, switching the images of a prisoner husband with those of a dark-chested boy with a flat stomach and sinewed hair-covered legs. Both caused her pain.

If she could again find the boy at the beach and forge her liaison, then it would not be the first time, nor the second, nor the third. It was the usual way she found relief when the strain became too much for her. It had nothing to do with loving Geoffrey, whatever that meant, nothing to do with being his wife, sharing his life. All that was irrelevant. But there had to be a valve somewhere when the steam built up, and this was her release: writhing under a stranger, without obligation, without attachment.

There had been an Irish barman from Evesham in Worcestershire, sought out on the day after Geoffrey, the young industrial trainee, had told her there was a discrepancy in the books and that the branch Chief Accountant believed him responsible. He had been cleared of suspicion, but only after Violet had spent an afternoon in an autumn field with a man whose name she had never known.

There had been a West Indian bus driver from Dalston in East London after a Friday night when Geoffrey had come home to report that he had drunk too much that lunchtime and told the head of his department to stuff his job where it would hurt and smell. Geoffrey had apologized on the Monday morning, been accepted back with handshakes and smiles and had never known of Violet's two hours on a Sunday morning in a railway hotel close to King's Cross ridden hard by a muscled lad who called her 'darlin' and bit her shoulders.

Other crises had come, some greater, some lesser. Same palliative, same escape; and Geoffrey had remained unaware of them, of that she was sure and grateful. She remembered once watching on television the wife of the British governor of an island colony, just widowed after her husband had been terribly murdered while taking a late evening stroll in the gardens of the Residence. The woman had worn white and sat on a sofa with her daughters and talked to the cameras with composure and dignity. Had it been Violet, she thought, she would have been in the chauffeur's bed. She knew it, hated it, and told herself she did not have the strength to resist. And if Geoffrey did not know, if Geoffrey were not wounded, then what did it matter? Who else's business was it?

There had been no boy in Rome. God knows there were times when she would have wished for one, hoped for the release from an arched back and a driving thrust. But there had been none. Until she had been to the beach she had not given herself even the opportunity. Isolated and cocooned in a flat where the telephone never rang, the doorbell never sounded, she had been protected from the predators.

She dressed with studied care as if anxious not to crease the bikini and the covering dress, as if forgetful that she would be sitting in her car for the hour-long drive to Ostia or Fregene or Santa Marinella. A peahen jealous of her scant plumage. The bikini was new, and the dress a month old had not been worn. Adornment for the fall. Her hair she combed loosely sitting at her dressing-table mirror and aware of the excitement and the tremble that came with the narcotic, with the contemplation of the unmentionable. It was the only gesture of independence that Violet Harrison was capable of, to climb into her little car, drive away down the road and spend and punish herself of her own volition, in her own time, in her own panting scenario. Would Geoffrey have cared if he had known . . . ? Perhaps. Perhaps not. But it didn't matter because Geoffrey did not know, Geoffrey was away, bound like a chicken with the stubble on his face and a gun at his head. Geoffrey would be thinking of her, hers would be the face in his mind, as clear and sharp as it was in the mirror before her. Geoffrey would be leaning on her, conjuring in his mind only the good times. That was when the remorse always won through from the defiance. That was when it hurt, when the urge was strongest, when she was weakest, least able to struggle.

Smudges of tears were summoned below the neatly careened blond hair.

She was aware of the telephone bell. Long, brilliant calls, summoning her to the kitchen. Perhaps it was Mother from London announcing which flight she was taking, and was her little poppet all right, and did she know that it was all over the papers. Perhaps it was those miserable bastards who had called before and jabbered in an alien language. The ringing would not abandon her, would not leave her, and pulled her off the low chair and dragged her through the doorway towards it. Every step and she prayed that it would cease its siren call. Her entreaties were ignored, the telephone rang on.

'Violet Harrison. Who's that?'

It was Carpenter. Archie Carpenter of ICH.

'Good morning, Mr Carpenter.' A cool voice, the confidence coming fast, because this was the little man who had run from her, the little suburban man.

Had she heard the latest information on her husband?

'I've heard nothing since last night. I don't read the Italian papers. The Embassy haven't called me.'

She should know that her husband was now thought to be in the hands of an extremist political group. She should know that demands had been made to the government for the release of a prisoner before nine the next morning. She should know that if the condition was not met the threat had been made that her husband would be murdered.

Violet rocked on the balls of her feet. Eyes closed, two hands clutching at the telephone. The pain seemed to gather at her temples, then sear through deep behind.

Was she still there?

A faint, small voice. 'I'm here, Mr Carpenter. I'm listening.'

And it was a damned scandal, the whole thing. The Embassy wouldn't lift a finger. Did she know that, could she credit it? Geoffrey had been relegated in importance, dismissed and left to the incompetence of an Italian police investigation.

Fear now, and her voice shriller. 'But it was all

agreed. It was agreed, wasn't it, that the company would pay. It was all out of the Italians' hands.'

Different now. Money was one thing. Easy, plenty of it, no problem. Different now, because it was said to be a point of principle. Said to be giving in to terrorism if the prisoner were to be released.

'Well, what's a fucking principle got to do with Geoffrey? Do they want him dead or what?' She shrieked into the telephone, voice raucous and rising.

They'd say it was the same as in the Schleyer case in Germany, the same as in the Moro case locally. They'd say they couldn't surrender. They'd use words like blackmail, and phrases like 'dignity of the State'. Those were the things they'd say, and the Embassy would support them, every damned inch.

'But it will mean Geoffrey's killed . . .' The hysteria was rampant, and with it the laughter and the breaking of flimsy control. '. . . They can't just sacrifice him. This bloody place hasn't had a principle in years, it's not a word in the bloody language. They couldn't even spell it here.'

Carpenter was going to call Head Office in London. They wouldn't take this lying down. She could rely on that. He'd call back within an hour, she should stay by the telephone.

Her voice had risen to its summit, to its highest pitch, and was now the product of crouched and humiliated shoulders.

'Could you come and see me, Mr Carpenter?'

Did she want him to come to the flat?

'Could you come and tell me what's happening? Yes, to the flat.'

Carpenter was sorry, very sorry indeed. But he

had an appointment, an urgent appointment. She would understand, but he had a fair amount on his plate, didn't he? But Carpenter would telephone her as soon as he had something to say, and that would be, he thought, within an hour.

The cycle of her changing mood swung on. The screaming past, the whimpering gone. Cold again with the veneer of assurance. 'Don't call again, Mr Carpenter, because I won't be here. Perhaps I'll be back this evening. Thank you for telling me what's going on. Thank you for telling me what's going to happen to Geoffrey.'

Before he could speak again she had cut Carpenter off the line.

Violet Harrison strode into her bedroom, swept a swimming towel off a bedside chair, and the underclothes that she had discarded the previous evening to the floor. She dropped them into her Via Condotti shopping-bag and headed for the lift and the basement garage.

Forty minutes after the red Fiat had moved on to the Raccordo with its centre reservation of pink and white oleanders, Giancarlo gestured to Harrison to turn off to his right. It was the Via Cassia junction and within five miles of his home. Strange to Harrison to be in the midst of tried and trusted surroundings. But the disorientation won through and he obeyed the instruction without question. The silence, which for both of them was now safe and losing its awkwardness, remained unbroken.

They had made good time. Giancarlo could reflect that the stamina of the driver had been remarkable.

They had given up the speed of the Raccordo for a

slow, winding road, heavy with lorries and impatient cars, flanked by the speculative flats that over-burdened the facilities. Several times they stopped in the bumper-to-bumper jams. Harrison sat passively, not knowing where he was being led, declining to ask.

Along the length of the Reggio Calabria to Rome autostrada patrol cars of the Polizia Stradale and carabinieri had begun the pin and haystack game of searching for a red Fiat car of the most popular model in use. Scores of motorists found themselves pitched out of 127s, covered by aimed machine-guns as they were searched, ordered to produce identity papers while their faces were examined against the photostated likenesses of Battestini and Harrison. The road blocks were large and impressive, each utilizing a minimum of a dozen armed men, and were comprehensive enough to warrant coverage by the RAI electronic camera teams.

The concentration of effort and manpower was blessed. From the toll gate at Monte Cassino a Fiat of the right size and colour was remembered. A young man had asked for petrol. A small success and one sufficient to whet the appetite as the police concentration built up in the community of Monte Cassino. The garage owner was quizzed in his office.

Yes, he could tell them who had been manning the pumps at that time. Yes, he could tell them the address of that man's home. Yes, and also he could tell them that this man had said the previous evening when he came on duty that after he finished the night shift it was his intention to take his grandchildren into the central mountains. No, he did not know where they would go, and he had waved expansively at the big hazed skyline, and shrugged.

The helicopters were ordered from Rome. The military twin-engined troop carriers were loaded with armed men, sweating in the confined spaces on the baked, makeshift landing-pad outside the town. Four-seater spotter machines were despatched to fly low over the high ranges and valleys, brushing the contours. Lorryloads of polizia were slowly given the co-ordinates on large-scale maps that the whole rugged area might be sealed.

The white walls of the mountain monastery looked down upon the hopeless task, while the shouting and irritation of the flustered staff officers in the commandeered school reflected the feeling that the terrain, rugged and vast, would mock their efforts to find a boy and his captive and his car.

But the element of chance born from the routine moved the chase on, gave it a new impetus, a new urgency. The chance without which the police cannot hope for success in a manhunt and which had forsaken them when the centre of the country was scoured for the ill-fated President of the Democrazia Cristiana.

A young man had gone off duty from his work at a gate on the Roma Sud toll. He had taken the bus home after a six-hour shift, had doused himself under the shower, and dressed and sat down at the kitchen table for cheese and fruit before lying on his bed to rest. His daughter, just a baby, had been crying, and therefore he could not be certain he had heard correctly the description of the two men that had been broadcast on the radio. The detail, rigidly held to, from which he would not deviate, caused the men in uniform and suits to paw at the air in their frustration, but Giuseppe Carboni was master of his own office, was at pains to thank the young man for his gesture in calling his nearest police station. Past eleven in the morning, time hurtling on its way, and Carboni demanded the patience of those around him. The photograph was produced, the picture of Geoffrey Harrison, and the young man nodded and smiled and looked for praise. It was strange, he said to Carboni, that a man who wore an expensive shirt should be unshaven, with grime at his neck and his hair untended.

Carboni's room had disintegrated into movement, leaving the witness to gaze long and hard at the picture.

Telephones, telexes, radios, all into play now to seal the city of Rome. Close it up, was the order, block the routes to L'Aquila to the east, to Firenze in the north. Tighten a net on the autostradas and damn the queues. Pull off the men beginning the search of the Monte Cassino hills, bring them back to the capital. Carboni set it all in motion, then came back to the young man.

'And there was a boy, just a ragazzo, with this man?'

'I think so . . .'

'It is the older man that you are clear on?'

'That was the one that gave me the money. It is difficult to see across the interior of a car from where we sit in the cabins.'

A good witness, would not admit to that which he was not certain of. Carboni replaced the photograph

284

of Harrison with that of Giancarlo Battestini. 'Could it be this boy? Could this be the passenger?'

'I am sorry, Dottore, but really I did not see the passenger's face.'

Carboni persisted. 'Anything at all that you can remember of the passenger?'

'He wore jeans . . . and they were tight, that I remember. And his legs were thin. He would have been young . . .' The toll attendant stopped, head low, frowning in concentration. He was tired and his thoughts came slowly. Unseen to him Carboni held up his hand to prevent any interruption from those who were now filtering back into the room. '. . . He paid, the driver that is, and he paid with a big note and when I gave him the change he passed it to the passenger, but the other's hands were beneath a light coat that was between them, I could see that from my cabin, the driver dropped the change on to the top of the coat. They did not say anything, and then he drove away.'

Pain on Carboni's face. To the general audience he announced, 'That is where the gun was, that is why Harrison drives, because the boy Battestini has the pistol to his body.'

The young man from Roma Sud was sent home.

Fuel for the computer, for the dispersal system of information, and with each piece of typed paper that slipped from his office, Carboni fussed and plotted. 'And tell them to be careful, for God's sake to be careful. Tell them that the boy has killed three times in forty-eight hours and will kill again.'

There was no smirk on the features of Giuseppe Carboni, no expression of euphoria. Geographically they had run their quarry to a ground comprising a trivial number of square kilometres, but the ground, he could consider ruefully, was not favourable. One man and a prisoner to hunt for in a conurbation that housed four million citizens.

Chance had taken the sad, worn-down policeman up a road of promise, and had left him at a great crossroads which boasted no signposts.

He reached for his telephone to ring Francesco Vellosi.

At noon the men held in maximum security on the island of Asinara were unlocked from their cells and permitted under heavy supervision to queue together in the communal canteen for their pasta and meat lunch. Conversation was not forbidden.

The long-term prisoners, those serving from twenty years to the ultimate maximum of ergastolo, the natural end of life, all had radio sets in their cells. Behind the heavy doors and barred windows news had been carried of the kidnapping of Geoffrey Harrison, the ultimatum for the freedom of Franca Tantardini, the failed reprisal against Francesco Vellosi.

Several men sidled close to the leader of the NAP. Who was the boy Battestini, they asked, a name blasted from every news bulletin in the previous hour? How big was the infra-structure organization from which he worked? The capo, the movement's spiritual leader in intellect and violence, had shrugged his shoulders, opened his hands and said quietly that he had never heard of the boy nor sanctioned the action.

A few had felt he was being obsessively secretive, but there were those who waited and shuffled forward with their steel trays who understood the bafflement of the man who claimed absolute domination of the NAP from his island cell.

It was one thing to give orders, another to have them implemented. Many men in the Questura and the Viminale had lent their names and authority to instructions for the sealing of the city. Contingency plans for such measures were to hand, but it was not easy to mount a police and para-military effort of the scale required. Which were the vital routes, which were the areas for the greatest concentration of manpower, where in the streets of the city should the maximum vigilance be observed? They were questions that demanded time for answers, and time was a lost commodity.

The Fiat had turned off the main Cassia road at the village of La Storta, travelled fifteen more kilometres and then turned again, choosing a narrower route that would skirt the hill town of Bracciano and lead towards the deep, blue-tinted volcanic lake beneath the collection of straggling grey stone houses. The car was forty kilometres now from the heart of the capital and here the country was at peace, and the bombs and killings and kidnappings were matters delivered only by the newspapers and television bulletins. This was a place of small farmers, small shopkeepers, small businessmen, people who valued their tranquillity, drank their wine and drew their curtains against the wind of brutality, chaos and graft that blew from across the fields and the main road.

Abruptly Giancarlo pointed to an open field gate

that was set in a wall of stone and blackthorn to the left of the road and some four hundred metres short of the water's edge. The field into which they drove, jerking over the thick grass, was skirted on two sides by a wood of heavy-leafed oaks and sycamores. Tall, shade-bearing trees. Giancarlo had taken a great risk, to travel this far in daylight, but he was sufficiently secure in himself, sufficiently buoyant after coming so far, to believe that he had outstripped the apparati of the nation. Far up the side of the field, where it was shielded from the road, he waved for Harrison to stop, glanced around him and then motioned towards a place close by where the grazing of the field merged with the trees, a place where the cattle would come in winter to escape the ferocity of the rainstorms.

There was a darkness and shadow in the interior of the car as Harrison finally pulled at the brake handle and switched off the ignition. The place was well chosen. Hidden from the air, hidden from the road, perfect in its safety and loneliness. Giancarlo grabbed decisively at the keys, smiled with contempt at his driver, and watching him all the time with the gun cocked, climbed out. He stretched himself, flexed his barely developed chest, enjoyed the sun that filtered and dappled between the leaf ceiling.

'Are you going to kill me here?' Harrison asked.

'Only if by nine o'clock tomorrow morning they have not given me Franca.'

It was the first time that Giancarlo had spoken since they had left the autostrada.

International Chemical Holdings with representation in thirty-two countries of the First and Third

Worlds maintained close links with the Foreign and Commonwealth Office and the Ministry of Overseas Development. Its Board members and principal executives were frequent guests at the black tie dinners given by government to visiting delegations, they figured cautiously in the New Year's and Birthday Honours lists, and to some the workings of the company were regarded as an extension of British foreign policy. An aid package to a newly independent member of the Commonwealth often contained the loan necessary to launch an ICH plant.

Sir David Adams was well known to the Minister both as a businessman aloof from party politics and as a social guest to be valued for his ease and humour in difficult company. On the telephone pad of Sir David's desk in the City tower block was the Foreign Secretary's direct number. He had spent a few brief moments pondering Archie Carpenter's call from Rome before scanning the pad for the number. He had been connected with a private secretary, had requested, and been granted, a few minutes of the Foreign Secretary's time before lunch.

A desolate sort of room, the Minister's working office seemed to Sir David. Not the sort of quarters he'd ever have tolerated for himself. Wretched velvet drapes, the furniture out of a museum, and a desk large enough for snooker. He'd have had one of those young interior decorator chaps in with a bucket of white paint and some new pictures and something on the floor that represented the nineteen-eighties, not the days of dropping tigers at Amritsar. He was not kept waiting sufficiently long for the completion of his refurbishment plans for the office.

They sat opposite each other in lush, high-backed armchairs. There was a Campari soda for the Minister, a gin and French for the Managing Director. No aides, no stenographers.

'Not to beat about the bush, Minister, the message from my chap out there came as a bit of a shock. My chap, and he's no fool, got his feet on the ground, says your Ambassador has just about told the Italians that so far as Whitehall is concerned they should run this new phase in the Harrison business as if our man was any Italian businessman. I find that a bit heavy.' Sir David sipped at his glass, enough to dampen his tongue, little more.

'Bit of an oversimplification, David. Not quite the full story.' The Foreign Secretary smiled over the bulldog lapping folds of his cheeks. 'The actual situation is that a senior member of the Italian cabinet, and this is of course confidential, asked HMG via the Ambassador and at a time when the Italians were having to make early but very important decisions of approach in this matter, whether HMG would be requesting the release of a terrorist to safeguard your fellow. That's not quite the same thing, is it?'

'With respect, it's the germ of the same thing. I'll put it another way and ask you what initiative the British government are taking to secure the release, unharmed, of Geoffrey Harrison?' Another sip, another faint trembling of the liquid line in the glass.

'You should know there can only be one answer. There is no initiative that I can take with regard to the internal politics of Italy . . .'

'You can suggest that it is desirable to get my man back, whether or not that requires unlocking a door for this woman they're holding.'

'David, I have a full programme of meetings.' There was a sternness in the rebuke. 'I should have been at one now but I've relegated it to a junior. When I make that gesture, please do me the courtesy of hearing me out.'

'Accepted. Apologies, and sincerely meant.' An inclined head acknowledged the ministerial rap.

'Italy isn't a business competitor, David. It's not a rival company. If it collapses, if it goes bankrupt, morally or financially, if it's greatly weakened, the Members of the Commons won't stand up and cheer and wave their Order papers as your shareholders would. It's not just a place of funny foreigners, David, of spaghetti and gigolos and bottom-pinchers. It's a major power in the West, it's a NATO ally, it's the seventh industrial power in the world. You know all that better than I do. When things are difficult there we draw no pleasure from it. We do our damnedest to support them, and a friend needs support when she's on her knees. The Moro affair nearly crippled them. The State was held to ransom, the very system of democracy was threatened, but they held firm, and in doing so they lost – they sacrificed – a leader of great standing.'

'It's a fine speech, Minister, and it will do you credit in the House on the day my company buries Geoffrey Harrison. You'll send a wreath, I trust?' The two men eyed each other. The counter-punches had bloodied the noses and the eyes were puffing and there were many rounds to go.

'Not worthy of you, David, and you know better than to taunt me. When the German was missing in Northern Ireland, the one we never found, the Minister of the day didn't have Bonn snapping at him. When Herrema, the Dutchman, was kidnapped in Eire, The Hague was quick to express support for all the measures that Dublin was taking.'

'You're still hiding, Minister.' Sir David Adams was not one to be easily deflected. He pushed his adversary towards the ropes, leading with his chin, a lifetime's habit. 'You're hiding behind a screen of meaningless protocol. I want a young and innocent man back, I want him back with his wife. I don't give a damn for Italian terrorism, nor do I give a damn for Italian democracy. I've done business there and I know the place. I know how much of our payments go to the bank in Milan, how much goes to Zürich. I know about the yachts and the bribes and the villas. I understand why they've an urban guerrilla problem on their doorstep. It's a nasty, clannish society that can't look after itself, and it's not for you to abandon an Englishman in the sewer there in order to start giving those people lessons in principle, or whatever.'

'You haven't been listening to me, David.' Ice cold, the Foreign Secretary, but the temper concealed beneath the frozen smile. 'They sacrificed one of their principal post-war leaders, wrote him off, and on a point of principle.'

'We're going in circles.'

'We are indeed, but I suggest you are leading.'

Sir David gulped at his glass, the impatience winning, half drained it. 'I put it to you, Minister, that there is something you can do that doesn't infringe on the question of "principle" . . .' He rolled over the word, gutting it of all feeling. 'You can find out from your friends in Rome the exact importance of this woman. You can find out her importance to the guerrilla movement. And let's not stand on too high a pedestal. I know my recent history. Northern Ireland, right? . . . We emptied Long Kesh when we were after a political initiative, chucked the Provisionals out on to the streets to get on again with their bombing and maiming. What happened to principle, then? We've given their leaders safe-conduct. We sent the Palestinian girl, Leila Khaled, home from Ealing courtesy of an RAF jet. We're not lily-white. We can bend when it suits us . . .'

'Who's making speeches, David?'

'Don't be flippant, Minister. My fellow has little more than twenty hours to live.' The gimlet eyes of Sir David Adams offered no concessions. 'Italy can live without this woman in a gaol, Italy can survive . . .'

He broke off in response to a light knock on the door behind him. Irritation at the interruption registered on both men's faces. The Foreign Secretary glanced at his watch. A young man, shirt sleeves and club tie, glided across the room with a telex flimsy in his hand. He gave it without explanation to the Minister and withdrew as silently as he had come. There was quiet in the room as the message was read, the Minister's forehead lined, his lips pursed.

'It's the Harrison business, that's why they interrupted.' No emotion in the voice, just an ageing and a sadness. 'He's held by a young psychopath responsible for three killings in two days. The assessment of the Italians is that he will kill your man without hesitation or compassion should the dead-line expire. The woman involved is called Franca Tantardini. She is classified in Rome as a major activist and will face charges of murder, attempted murder, armed insurrection, they're putting the book on her. Our Embassy records the observation that several of the senior and most respected officers of the Italian public security forces would resign should she be released. In addition the Italian Communist Party have endorsed in a statement the government's no deal approach.'

The Foreign Secretary looked across the room to the shadowed face of the industrialist.

'It's not in our hands, David. It is beyond the British government to offer intervention. I am very sorry.'

Sir David Adams rose from his chair. A little over six feet in height, a dominating and handsome man, and one unused to failure.

'You won't forget the wreath, Minister?'

And he was gone, leaving his glass half filled on the small table beside the chair.

Michael Charlesworth from his office and Archie Carpenter from his hotel room had spoken by telephone. These two men of differing backgrounds, drawn from divergent social groups, seemed to want to talk to each other because their feeling of helplessness was overpowering. Both were eunuchs with little to do but listen to the radio, as Charlesworth did, and scan the newspapers and gaze at the staring photographs of Battestini plastered in the afternoon editions, as Carpenter did.

'Shouldn't you be with Violet Harrison?' Charlesworth had asked.

'I called her this morning, said I'd call her back – she said not to bother . . .'

'It's not my job, thank God, holding her hand.'

'Not mine either,' Carpenter had snapped.

'Perhaps.' Charlesworth had let it sink, let the thought drown. He sensed the desperation of the man who had been sent to take decisions, to move mountains, and who was failing. 'You'd better come up to my place tonight and have a bite with us.'

'I'd like that.'

Charlesworth had returned to his radio, moodily flitting between the three RAI services. They portrayed activity and haste and effort, and nothing of substance.

It had taken Giancarlo fully thirty minutes to find the place that satisfied him. He had prodded Geoffrey Harrison through the deeper recesses of the wood, using him as a plough to clear a way between the whippy saplings that sprang back at the eyes and ears and forearms. But the place that pleased him was close to a slight path, where once a giant oak had grown before the wind had pulled it down, tearing open a great gouge in the earth beneath its raised roots. A shallow pit had been left that would only be found if the searcher stumbled to its very rim.

Giancarlo methodically repeated the drill of earlier in the morning. He bound Harrison's ankles with the flex, and then again tied his wrists behind his back. The spare lengths he used to loop around the stronger roots exposed under the earth roof. If Harrison lay still he could rest on his side in some attitude of comfort. If he moved, if he struggled, then the wire would bite at his flesh and cut and slash it. The boy had thought of this, introducing knots that dictated that the reward for movement was pain. There was one refinement from the morning, the handkerchief from Harrison's trouser pocket, twisted like a rope, was inserted between his teeth, knotted behind his ears. Giancarlo was careful in tying the handkerchief, as he had no wish to suffocate his prisoner.

When the work was finished he stepped back and admired it. He was going to get some food. Harrison should not worry, he would not be away long.

Within moments he was lost among the lines of trees and shadows and the slanting columns of light.

Chapter Fifteen

Geoffrey Harrison's field of vision was minimal. It comprised only a slight arc encompassing a score of rising tree-trunks, heavy with lime and flaking bark, that soared above the rim of the small crater in which he lay. Above and around him was the motion of the isolated wood; a pair of woodpeckers in pursuit of a jay, cackling protest at the intrusion of the nest-hunting bird; a tiny pettirosso, its reddened breast thrust forward proudly as it dug and chipped for grubs and insects; a young rabbit that darted in terror among the trees after a brief encounter with a skilful stoat; the wind in the upper branches that collided with one another high up and beyond the limit of his vision. Action and activity. Those that were free and liberated going about the business of their day while he lay helpless and in fear beneath them.

But his brain was no longer stifled. The very solitude of the wood had roused him, made him aware of each miniature footfall, keened and sharpened his senses. The drug effect of the endless miles of autostrada driving was drifting from his system and with the withdrawal from the approaching headlights and the perpetual traffic lanes came the increasing awareness of his situation. That something was stirring in him, some desire once again to affect his future, was clear from the way he tested the skill with which he had been bound. He tried to move his arms apart, seeing how tightly the knots were tied, whether there was stretch in the plastic-coated flex. The sweat crawled again on his chest. Several minutes the effort lasted before the realization came that the binding had been done well, that it was beyond his capabilities to loosen the wires.

So what are you going to do, Geoffrey? Going to sit there like a bloody turkey in its coop, waiting for Christmas Eve and the oven to heat up? Are you going to lie on your side and wait for it, and hope it's quick and doesn't hurt? Should have done something in the car, or at the petrol stations, or at the toll gates, or when the traffic stopped them on the Cassia. When you had the chance, when you were body to body, close in the seats of the car.

And what would he have done about it, precious Giancarlo?

Might have fired, might not, can't be sure.

But it would have been better than this, better than sitting the hours out.

Would it have been that easy in the car? He'd kept the door locked because that way there was one more movement required before it could have been opened, and more delay, more confusion, more chance for him to shoot.

Idiot, Geoffrey Harrison, bloody idiot. It wouldn't have mattered how long it took to get the door open because he'd have been flattened by then, squashed half out of existence, you're damn near double his bloody weight, starved little scarecrow.

But you didn't do it, Geoffrey, and there's no thanks in dreaming, no thanks in playing the bloody hero in the mind. The time was there and you bucked it, preferred to sit in the car and wait and see what happened.

You can see it now, lad, can't you? Half scared to bloody death already, and there's a pain in your balls and an ache in your chest and you want to cry for yourself. Scared out of your mind.

Too bloody right, and who wouldn't be? Because it's curtains, isn't it? Curtains and finish and they'll be getting the bloody box ready for you and cutting the flowers and choosing the plot, and the chaps in Head Office will have sent their black ties to the dry-cleaner's. Through his mind the misery was fuelled. No chance in a hundred bloody light years that Franca would get her marching orders. All in the imagination of the little prig. Couldn't let her out, not a hard line girl that it had taken months to get the manacles on. But that doesn't leave room, Geoffrey. Leaves you on a prayer and a hope ... And what had Geoffrey bloody Harrison done, how come his number was spinning with the lottery balls?

God, he was going to cry again, could feel the tears coming, thirty-six years old and fit to wet himself, and no stake in the place, no commitment.

Wrong again, Geoffrey, you're bleeding the masses, crucifying the workers.

That's lunacy, bloody madness.

Not to this kid, not to little Giancarlo, and he's going to blow the side of your bloody head off just to prove it's real.

Harrison lay with his eyes tight shut, fighting the welling moisture. The foul taste of the cotton handkerchief suppurated around his back teeth. Nausea rising and with it the terror that he would be unable to be sick and choke in his own vomit. What a bloody way to go, choking in your own filth. Eyes so tight closed, lids squeezed so that they hurt, so that they were bruised.

Violet, darling bloody Violet, my bloody wife, I want to be with you darling, I want you to take me away from here. Violet, please, please, don't leave me here to them.

Near to his head a small branch cracked.

Harrison flashed open his eyes, swung his body up and blinked away the tears.

Ten feet from him was a pair of child's knee-high boots, their sheen broken by smears of dried mud and bramble scratches, the miniature replicas of an adult's farm wear, and rising out of them were little baggy trousers with the knees holed and the material faded with usage and washing. He twisted his head slowly higher and gulped in the salvation of a check sports shirt with the buttons haphazardly fastened and the sleeves floppily rolled. There was a sparse and skinny bronzed neck and a young clean face that was of the country and exposed to wind. Harrison sagged back, dropped himself hard against the earth. Thank God. A bloody ministering angel. White sheets, wings and a halo. Thank God. He felt a shiver, the spasm of relief, running hard in him . . . but not to hang about, not with Giancarlo gone only for food. Come on, kid. God, I love you. Come on, but don't hang about. You're a bloody darling, you know that. But there's not all day. He looked up again into the child's face, and wondered why the little one just stood, stationary and still. Like a Pan statue, three paces away, not speaking, demonstrating a graveness at the cheeks, a caution in the eyes. Come on, kid, don't be frightened. He tried to wriggle his body so that the bound wrists would be visible – waste of time, the child could see the gag and the trussed legs. The little feet backed away, as if the movement disconcerted him. What's the bloody matter with the kid? Well, what do you expect, Geoffrey? What did your mother tell you when you were small and went out into the fields and woods to play, and along the street and out of sight of the row of houses that belonged in their road? Don't talk to strangers, there's funny people about, don't take sweets from them.

Harrison stared at the boy, stared and tried to understand. Six, perhaps seven years old, deep and serious eyes, a puzzled and concerned mouth, hands that tugged and pulled the cloth of his trousers. Not an idiot, not a daft one, this child, but hesitant in coming forward as if the man who lay in this contorted posture was a forbidden apple. As best he could through the impediment of the gag Geoffrey Harrison tried to smile at the child and beckon with his head for the boy to come closer, but he won no response. Be a loner, wouldn't he, a self-contained tiny entity? Won't take chewing gum from a man he doesn't know. It can't bloody happen to me. Please, not now, God. Please, God, not a trick like this on me. It was going to take time. But time wasn't available, not with Giancarlo gone only for food. What would the mean bastard do with the child? Think on that, Geoffrey, think on that as you try to win him forward, try to bring him closer. What does Giancarlo do with the kid if he finds him here, all bright eyes and a witness? That's an obscenity, that's foul. But that's truth, Geoffrey . . . Hurry up, kid, come closer quickly. Not just my life, your life is hanging on a cotton thread.

Geoffrey Harrison knew that he had no call on the child, that this was a private matter between himself and the boy Giancarlo. But he beckoned again with his head and above the cloth at his mouth his cheeks creased in what he thought of as a welcome greeting.

The child watched him with neither a smile nor fear, and the small boots stayed rooted, neither slipping forward nor back. It would take a long time and Giancarlo might return before the work was finished.

There were many young campers on the wooded hills and beside the lake at Bracciano and the stubble-cheeked boy in the alimentari on the water-front aroused no comment. High summer holiday season, and for many the cool, shaded slopes and the deep lake in its volcanic crater represented a more welcome resting ground than the scrum pack of the beaches. For those who had abandoned the city, however temporarily, the news bulletins went unheard, the newspapers unread. In the alimentari Giancarlo attracted no attention as he bought a plastic razor, an aerosol of shaving soap, and six rosetti filled with cheese and tomato slices.

From the alimentari he headed for the back lavatory of one of the small trattorie that stretched out on precarious stilts over the grey beach dust. With the cold water and the thickness of his cheek growth and the sharpness of the new blade he had to exercise care that he did not lacerate his face. It would not be a clean shave but sufficient to change his appearance and tidy him in the minds of any who looked at and examined him. He had once read that the art of successful evasion was a dark suit and a tie; he believed it. Who searches for the fanatic among the closely groomed? He grinned to himself, as if enjoying the self-bestowed title. The fanatic. Many labels they would be handing down from the top table of the Directorate of Democrazia Cristiana, and the Central Committee of the PCI, and they had seen nothing yet.

His humour was further improved by the wash, and there were more shops to visit. He bought socks, and a light T-shirt that carried a cheaply stencilled rendering of the fifteenth-century castle of Bracciano that dominated the village. His former clothes he stuffed into a rubbish bin. Further along the pavement he stopped and bought with coins from the newspaper stand the day's edition of *Il Messaggero*. He looked into Geoffrey Harrison's picture, holding the page hard in front of his face. The company portrait, serene and sleek, harmless and smug, beaming success. On an inside page was the information that had led him to need a newspaper, the full story of the hunt with the facts available till two o'clock that morning and the name of the policeman who controlled the search. Dottore Giuseppe Carboni, working from the Questura. Giancarlo's mouth twisted with his innate contempt for his adversary. Among the clatter of loose change in his pocket were four gettoni, enough for his task. He hunted now for a bar or trattoria that had a closed phone booth, not willing to be overheard when he made his telephone call. At a bar he passed there were two coin telephones for the public, but both open and fastened to the wall where there would be no privacy. He walked on till he reached the ristorante attached to the sailing club at the end of the half-kilometre esplanade. There was a closed telephone booth in the hallway leading from the street door to the inner eating sanctum. He had to wait some minutes for two giggling girls to finish. Neither bothered to glance at the frail built boy as they plunged out, loud in their shared noise.

This near to the capital the telephone booths were equipped with Rome directories. He flicked through the first pages of the scruffed edition of the Yellow Pages, running down the addresses and numbers listed under Commissariati PS with his cleaned fingernail. At the bottom of the page he found the answer. Questura Centrale – v. di S Vitale 15 (46 86).

This would stir the bastards.

He would carry the fight to them, as Franca would have wished, carry it right to the doors of the Questura where they sat with their files and their minions and their computers. They would hear of Giancarlo, the hacks and lackeys would hear his name. He was trembling, taut as a whiplash at the moment it cracks on a horse's back. The shaking convulsed his palms and the gettoni rattled dully in his fist.

No nearer, no further from Harrison, the child had sat down. He was cross-legged, his elbows resting on his knees and his hands supporting his chin, the kindergarten pose, listening to a teacher's story.

Like you're a bloody animal, Geoffrey, like he's found a fox half dead in a gin-trap, and he has the patience to wait and see what happens. All the hours in the world the child had to be patient, too young for a watch, for a sense of fleeting time. Harrison's attempts to draw him closer, to engage those small sharp fingers in the binding knots had failed. All the nodding and gesturing with his head had been ignored except for the few times when his most violent contortions had gathered a flash of fear to his face and the child's slim muscles had stiffened and prepared for escape. Don't get excited, Harrison had learned, and for God's sake, even with the eyes, don't threaten him. The child has to be kept there, his confidence has to be conserved, he has to be wooed.

You want to keep him there, Geoffrey, with Giancarlo coming back? Giancarlo and the P38 coming back with the food, and you're trying to keep the child there?

God, I don't know, and the moments were marching, the hands would be sliding on the watch face on his wrist.

There was almost a sadness on the child's face as Harrison peered into its shallow depths. He would be a kid from a farmhouse, self-sufficient, self-reliant in his entertainment, a creature of the woods, and owing loyalty and softness only to his parents. A pleasant child. You'd find one like this on the Yorkshire uplands or the Devon moors, or on the far west shoreline of Ireland's Donegal. God knows how to communicate with the blighter. Can't frighten him, can't please him. If there had been a child of his own, but Violet had said that her figure . . . Can't blame bloody Violet, not her fault you don't know how to talk to a child.

Hope was fleeing from Harrison. His head movements became less frequent, and he noticed that when he subsided into inertia then the start of boredom glazed the child's eyes. That way he would leave, pick himself off the earth and wander on his way. That's what he should do, lie still, bore the kid out, and hope that he was gone before Giancarlo was back; that was saving the kid. That was the proper way, that was diving clothed into an icy pool to pluck a baby out.

God, I don't want him to go. The fear came again, the horror of being abandoned by this child mind, and he nodded again with his head and wore the pantomime face of the clown in his urgency.

Hating himself, with the fever in his eyes as he called mutely for the child to come forward, Harrison strained to hear the footfall of the returning Giancarlo.

'Pronto, Questura.'

Giancarlo stabbed with his finger at the button that would release a gettone to fall into the caverns of the machine.

'Questura . . .'

'Please, the office of Dottore Giuseppe Carboni?'

'A moment . . .'

'Thank you.'

'For nothing, sir . . .'

A hesitation, the sounds of connection. Perspiration dribbled down Giancarlo's chest.

'Yes . . .'

'May I speak to Dottore Giuseppe Carboni.'

'He is very busy at the moment. In what connection . . . ?'

'In connection with the Englishman, 'Arrison.'

'Can I help myself? I work in Dottore Carboni's office.'

'I must speak with him directly. It is important.'

There would be a taping of all incoming calls for Carboni. Giancarlo assumed that, but unless suspicions were aroused the trace procedures would not be automatic. He kept his voice calm, regulated.

'A moment . . . who is it calling?'

Giancarlo flushed. 'It does not matter . . .'

'A moment.'

More delays and he fed another gettone. He smiled mirthlessly. Not the time to lose the call for lack of coins. His last two rested in his hand. More than sufficient . . . He started, clenched at the receiver.

'Carboni speaking. What can I do for you?'

The voice seemed to come from a great distance, a whispering on the line as if there were a great tiredness and the resignation was heavy.

'Listen carefully, Carboni. Do not interrupt. This is the spokesman of the Nuclei Armati Proletaria . . .'

Don't gabble, Giancarlo. Remember that you are kicking them. Remember that you are hurting them as surely as the P38 in Franca's hand.

'. . . We hold the Englishman, 'Arrison. If Franca Tantardini has not been released and flown out of Italy to the territory of a friendly Socialist nation by nine o'clock tomorrow morning, then the multinationalist 'Arrison will be executed for his crimes against the proletariat. There is more, Carboni. We will telephone again this evening, and when your name is asked for then the call must be put through to you immediately, and in your room must be Franca Tantardini. We will speak to her ourselves. If the connection is not made, if Comrade Tantardini is not there to talk to us, then 'Arrison will be killed. The call this evening will come at twenty hours . . .'

Forty seconds on the revolving hand of his watch since he had announced the source of the communication. And the trace system would be in operation. Mad, Giancarlo, mad. It's the behaviour of a fool.

'. . . Is that understood?'

'Thank you, Giancarlo.'

The boy's head jolted forward, fingers white and bloodless on the plastic telephone. A breathy whisper. 'How did you know?'

'We know so much, Giancarlo. Giancarlo Battestini. Born Pescara. Father, a clothes shop there. One metre sixty-eight tall. Weight on release from Regina Coeli, sixty-one kilos. Call again, Giancarlo . . .'

Another twenty seconds departed on his watch, lost. Giancarlo snapped, 'You will have her there. You will have Comrade Tantardini on this telephone?'

'If it pleases you.'

'Do not doubt us. When we say we will kill the man 'Arrison, do not doubt us.'

'I believe you will kill him, Giancarlo. It would not be clever, but I believe that you are capable . . .'

With his forefinger Giancarlo pulled down the hook beside the telephone box, felt the moment of sliding pressure before the sound that told him the call was terminated. Franca had told him they needed two minutes for a trace. He had not exposed himself to their reach. Time in hand. He walked out

of the ristorante and into the lively afternoon
sun, knees weak, breath summoned fast, his mind a
confusion of spattered images. They should have
grovelled and they had not. They should have bent
and they had held the mast erect. Perhaps in the
sinking pit of his stomach there was an alien and
unholy presentiment of the imminence of failure.

But the mood was soon discarded. The chin jutted
and the eyes glowed and he hurried back on the
dust-covered road, retracing his way towards
the wood.

It was more than an hour now since the child had
come, and the crease lines of interest still wrapped
his face.

Harrison no longer moved, no longer attempted
to wheedle the small boy closer. Tried, you poor
bastard, tried all you knew. The ants were at him.
Virile swine, monsters with a swingeing bite, hitting
and retreating and returning, calling for their friends
because the mountain of food was defenceless and
amusing. And the kid hadn't spoken one bloody
word.

Go away, you little blighter, get lost, get back to
your mama and your tea. You're no bloody use
to me. A pretty face the child had, and the frown
lines were worn as if by a martyred infant in the
colours of a church window. Violet would notice a
face like this child's, and she'd enthuse on it and
want to tousle his hair and coo to him. Why didn't
the child respond? God knows, and he's not caring.
He'll be in church, this brat, on Sunday morning,
with his hair combed and his face washed with a red
cassock down to shined sandals and white socks,

probably be singing his bloody heart out in the choir stall, and he won't even remember the strange shape of the man in the woods with the wild gaze and the body twist of fear. He'll be in church . . . if Giancarlo isn't back soon.

The child started up, the rabbit alerted, slid fast to his feet, easily and with the suppleness of youth.

For Harrison there was nothing beyond the lethargic motion of the wood.

The child began to move away and Harrison watched fascinated for there was a silence under the boots that glided over the dry minefield of leaves and sticks. His place, thought Harrison, here among the animals and birds and the familiar; he probably didn't know what the inside of a schoolroom looked like, because this was his playground. He watched the child go, his slight body merging with the pale grey lines of the tree-trunks. When he was at the murky edge of vision, Harrison saw him drop to his knees and ease the fronds of a sapling across his face and shoulders. The child had covered less than twenty yards but when he was settled Harrison had to strain and search with his eyes to find his hiding-place.

Into view, trying to move with caution but failing to find quiet places for his feet, came Giancarlo, source of the disturbance.

He closed quickly, gun in hand, and the brown paper bag held between the crook of his arm and his body. He was alert, hunting between the trees with his eyes, but finding nothing to caution nor alarm him. He dropped to his knee and slipped the pistol into the waist of his trousers. The cleaned face and the bright T-shirt gave him a youth and innocence that Harrison had not seen before.

'Food, and I haven't had mine either. We are both equally starved.' There was a little laugh and Giancarlo leaned forward and put his arms behind Harrison's head and unknotted the handkerchief, pulled it clear and dropped it beside him. 'Better, yes?'

Harrison spat from the side of his mouth, cleared the spittle. Still bent low, Giancarlo bounced on his toes down into the earth crater and worked quickly and expertly at the wrist flex.

'Still better, yes? Even better?'

Harrison looked deep into his face and struggled to comprehend the volatile changes of atmosphere. After hours of silence in the car, after the kicking of the early morning, the new direction of the wind was too complex for him to comprehend. 'What did you get for us to eat?' he asked lamely, rubbing his wrists and restoring the glow of circulation. And what the hell did it matter? What importance did it hold?

'Not much. Some bread, with cheese and salad. It will fill us.'

'Very good.'

'And I spoke to the man who is trying to find you. A fool at the Questura, I called him by telephone. I told him what would happen if Franca were not freed by tomorrow morning.' Giancarlo took a bulging bread roll from the bag, ignored the cheese spillage, and passed it to Harrison. He spoke proudly. 'He tried to keep me talking to give them time for a trace but that's an old trick, you won't hear sirens tonight, 'Arrison. I told him also that I would talk direct to Franca this evening and that they should bring her to his office.'

A chatty, banal conversation. That of two men who have been buried for too long and for whom the quiet has proved oppressive.

'What did you say would happen if Franca were not freed?' Harrison's words were mumbled through the sea of bread and salad.

'I told them you would be executed.'

'That's what you told them?'

'I said that I would kill you.'

'And what did they say?' Harrison ate on, the words of both of them too unreal to be of value.

'Carboni is the name of the man who is hunting for you. He was the only one that I spoke to. He said nothing.'

'Did he say if Franca would be freed?'

'He did not answer that.' Giancarlo smiled. There was a certain warmth, a certain charm in the scrubbed, shaved features. 'He did not answer any of my questions. You know, he knew my name, he knew who it was that he was speaking to. He was pleased with that, the man Carboni. I mean it, I mean it very deeply, 'Arrison, I would be sorry to kill you. It would not be what I want.'

It was too much for Geoffrey Harrison to assimilate. Once in the yard behind his father's house they had watched the chickens prowling beside the fence and decided which one would make their meal and which should survive, and he had tried to communicate to the chosen fowl that there was nothing personal in the choice, no malice.

'It doesn't help you if you shoot me.' Harrison

312

trying to be calm, trying to soften and mollify through dialogue.

'Only that each time you make a threat you must carry it out if you are to be believed. You understand that, 'Arrison. If I say that I will kill you unless I am given something, then I must do it if I am denied. It is credibility. You understand that, 'Arrison?'

'Why do you tell me this?'

'Because you have the right to know.'

Harrison turned his head, a slow, casual movement, traversed across the tree-front and caught like a flash that was there and then gone the blue and white of the check shirt of the idiot child who had sat where Giancarlo now squatted.

'Will they give you back your Franca, Giancarlo?'

'No . . .' he said simply, and his hand dived again in the bag and he passed another roll across to Harrison. An afterthought: 'Well, I do not think so. But I must try, right, 'Arrison? You would agree that I should try?'

With the arrival of Francesco Vellosi from the Viminale, the summit meeting in Carboni's office could begin. Just preceding the head of the anti-terrorist unit had been the Minister of the Interior and before him the examining magistrate who had successfully jockeyed among his profession for the nominal role of heading the investigation.

Tired men, all of them. Harassed and without small talk. At the outset there was argument over priorities around the bowed figure of the Minister, who knew the penalty for failure to arrest terrorist outrage was resignation and could not find in the bearing of the men about him the stimulus for a new initiative.

There were many points for dispute.

Should any new advice be presented to the Council of Ministers regarding the decision to refuse consideration of the freeing of Franca Tantardini?

Should Franca Tantardini be permitted to speak by telephone to the boy Battestini?

At least two gettoni had been used on the telephone communication, the call had come from outside the Rome city limits, and in the countryside the principal enforcers of the law were the carabinieri; should they now control any further search operation, or should the overall direction remain with the polizia?

Was it useful to contact the Vatican Secretariat to explore the possibility of His Holiness issuing a similar appeal to the rejected call of Pope Paul VI for Aldo Moro's life?

Should the President of the Council of Ministers broadcast to the nation?

Why had it not been possible to extract greater information from the location of the telephone message?

Much of it was unnecessary, much of it time-wasting, sapping the concentration of the men in the room. But then, many had to clear themselves if there was a chance of failure to be found in tomorrow's dawn. Reputations could be damaged, perhaps destroyed. Backs must be protected. As one of the most junior men in the hierarchy present, Giuseppe Carboni was finally given what amounted to a free hand. He would be provided with a liaison team to link him with Criminalpol, the carabinieri force, and the armed forces. If he succeeded, then those who had set in motion the search operation would be well to the fore. If he failed, then shoulders would droop, heads turn away, and Carboni would stand alone. When they rose from the meeting the room emptied quickly. It was as if the paint daubs of disaster already swept across the walls. As he stood beside his desk smiling weakly at the Minister's departing back, Carboni reflected that little had been gained, only time frittered and disposed of.

'Look at it another way,' said Vellosi, his arm around Carboni's short shoulder. 'There is little likelihood of us saving Harrison, and perhaps that is not even the first priority. What matters is that we find this scum . . .'

'You talk as if you have reached a state of war,' Carboni murmured.

'What matters is that we find this scum, whether tomorrow, or in a month, or a year, and we kick the shit out of him . . . He never reaches Asinara.'

'They are dragging us down, Vellosi.'

'That is the ground where we meet them, where we fight them, and where we win.'

'If in such times victory is available . . . I am less certain.'

'Concern yourself with the present, Carboni. Find me the boy Battestini.' Vellosi squeezed his arm and walked on out through the door.

In the front parking area of a small trattoria Violet Harrison parked her car. Not tidily, not quietly, but with a splash of movement and rising dust and the protest of an over-extended engine. The parking area was for patrons, but she would take a cup of coffee and perhaps half a carafe of white wine, and that would satisfy the white-shirted waiters of her right to a table. The verandah of the trattoria was at the back, and she walked through the small construction of timber and corrugated iron roofing and past the kitchen where the fires were being stoked for the lamb and the veal. She would sit beneath a screen of interlaced bamboo, and from there she could watch, across some scrub grass and shallow shifting hills of sand, the boys who walked on the beach.

She seemed relaxed, at peace, but the Polaroids on her face hid reddened eyes. She showed a calm pose to the world, obliterated her inner self, sat at the table and waited. Occasionally she swung her head and gazed away down the beach, a searchlight roving, hunting all the time, haunting and punishing.

Chapter Sixteen

Early afternoon in the great slumbering capital.

A wicked heat, clamping on the bodies of the few Romans who moved listlessly on the steaming, paper-strewn streets. Little protection for walkers, even from the high buildings of nineteenth-century finery on the Corso. The pavements, abandoned by their own citizens, were given over to the perspiring, grumbling tourists. The map-clutchers, guide-book-scanners, ice-cream-suckers, groped from ruin to ruin expressing their admiration for what they saw in shrill Japanese, blaring American, dominant German.

Like a stranger in his own community, Giuseppe Carboni threaded an impatient way between the loiterers. He crossed the small square in front of the colonnaded church and hurried up the six shallow steps to the central entrance of the church of San Pietro in Vincoli. The visitors were thick, shoulder to shoulder, huddled close to their guides, serious and solemn-faced as they mopped up the culture and the dampness of their armpits. Here Carboni had been told he would find Francesco Vellosi. The church of Saint Peter in Chains is where the bonds of the saint are reverently kept, shining and coated in dark paint inside a gold and glass-faced cabinet. The central nave was occupied by the groups, soaking up the required information: the age of the construction, the dates of renovation, the history of the tomb of Julius II, the smooth sculpture of the bearded and muscled Moses that was the work of Michelangelo. But in the aisles, in the narrower naves, where the tourists gave ground to the worshippers, Carboni would find his man. Where the shadows were thicker, where the tall candles burned in flickering insecurity, where the women in black came in from the streets to pray.

In the right-hand nave he saw Vellosi, three rows from the front, kneeling hunched on a red hassock. The hard man of the anti-terrorist squad was now bent in prayer because his driver was slain and would be buried in the morning. It was no surprise that Vellosi chose this church. On the same steps that Carboni had climbed the carabinieri had shot to death Antonio La Muscio and captured the girls La Vianale and Salerno. The place acted as a symbol to those who fought the underground of subversion and anarchy, it was their place of triumph and riposte.

Carboni did not intrude. He crossed to the small side altar and waited with hands joined across his stomach. The voices of the guides seemed distant, the brush of scores of feet was near eliminated. A place of tranquil value. A place to shed, for precious moments, the fearsome and desperate load that the two men carried. Watching and waiting, curling his toes, ignoring the passage of time that could not be recouped, Carboni curbed himself. He could be thankful that, if nothing else, he had escaped from his desk, his aides, his telephone and the endless computer print-outs.

Abruptly, Vellosi jack-knifed himself from his knees and back on to his chair. Carboni darted forward and eased himself down beside him. When their eyes met Carboni could see that the man was rested, that the purgative of prayer had refreshed him.

'You forgive me, capo, for coming here to find you?'

'Nothing, Carboni. I came to say some words for my Mauro . . .'

'A good place to come to.' Carboni spoke softly, with approval.

'Here we killed the rat, exterminated La Muscio . . . It is a good place to come to speak with my friend.'

'It is right to remember the success. Catastrophe is burdening, deadening.'

There was a wry smile at Vellosi's lips. 'Catastrophe we are familiar with, success is the star we seek.'

'And too often the cloud obscures the star . . . it is seldom visible.'

The two men spoke in church whispers, Vellosi content to idle till Carboni was ready to unveil the purpose of his visit.

A deep sigh from Carboni. The man who will jump into a winter sea from a breakwater, and must strip off his robe and discard his towel.

'We talked long enough at the meeting,' Carboni plunged. 'Long enough to have settled every matter that was outstanding, but at the end we had decided nothing, nothing beyond the fact that Giuseppe Carboni should take responsibility . . .'

'You had expected something different?'

'Perhaps yes, perhaps no.' Carboni stared in front of him as he spoke, over the shoulder of the wizened sparrow woman with her bones angular under the black blouse who mouthed quiet words to the altar. 'A gathering like that is a farce, a babble of men seeking with one voice to disclaim ultimate responsibility, prepared only to pile it on my shoulders.'

'They are broad enough,' chuckled Vellosi. 'You should work at the Viminale, you would quickly learn then what is normal, what is acceptable.'

'Do we let the woman Tantardini speak to the boy?' Carboni sharper now, play-acting completed.

Vellosi too responded, the smile draining, a savagery in his voice. 'I hate that bitch. Believe me, dear friend, I hate her. I wish to dear Jesus that we had slaughtered her in the street.'

'Understandable and unhelpful.'

Vellosi snatched back at him. 'What do you need most?'

'Now I have nothing. I know only that Battestini was early this morning in the area of Rome. I know that he has travelled on. I have a car number, but that could have been changed. I have no hope of intervention before tomorrow morning.' The ebbing of the bravura.

'So you must have a trace, you must have a location. If the bitch is there and talks to him, then you give your engineers the possibility . . .'

'She has to speak to him?'

'You have to make her.' There was a snarl in Vellosi's voice, as if the discussion had reached obscenity. 'If I were to ask her she would spit in my face.'

Carboni looked around him in response to the protest coughs of those who objected to the interference of raised voices in their worship. He stood up, Vellosi following, and together they walked down the aisle between the colonnade and the chairs. 'What would you tell her?'

'That you have to decide for yourself.'

'I came for help, Vellosi.'

'I cannot aid you. You must read her when you see her. When you meet her you will know why I cannot help you.' The inhibitions of the church quiet were lost on Vellosi. 'She is poison, and you must think of the consequences for yourself if you involve her.'

Carboni stared back at Vellosi as they stopped at the great opened doors. A small and pudgy figure dwarfed by his colleague of the open and strong face. He weighed his words for a moment. 'You are nervous of her. Even from her cell in the Rebibbia she frightens you.'

No denials, no stuttered protests. Vellosi said simply, 'Be careful, Carboni, remember what I say. Be careful of the bitch.'

Through the afternoon little had passed between Geoffrey Harrison and Giancarlo Battestini. Harrison's arms had not been tied again since the food and he lay on his side on the earth of the bunker, his only movements to swat the flies from his face and brush the ants and insects from his body and legs. He might have slept, had certainly dozed in the twilight area. All the while Giancarlo watched him with a casual and intermittent observation and with the gun resting on the leaves close to his hand. The summer sun was high, burning even now through the ceiling of foliage, sufficient to shrivel any wind that might have infiltrated earlier. Sticky, hot and defeated, Harrison slipped into a vegetable sloth, his mind devoid of ideas and expectations. No longer did the presence of the check shirt in the undergrowth a few yards beyond and behind Giancarlo offer any hope of salvation. Just another witness to his helplessness, another voyeur.

The body functions drove Harrison to speak again. 'It's the call of nature, Giancarlo.' Ridiculus that he was embarrassed. Couldn't use the language of the dressing-room, of the men's club. Couldn't say . . . I want to have a crap, Giancarlo . . . I want to have a shit, Giancarlo. Didn't want to say it any other way and feared to foul his trousers. 'It's been a long time.'

Giancarlo looked at him curiously as if experiencing some new buttress of his power. The great man of the multinational must ask Giancarlo's permission again, because otherwise he would smell and lose his dignity, and no more be a person of stature and importance. The cat with the mouse. The boy and the butterfly with the broken wing. Giancarlo teased in mock disbelief. 'Perhaps you are trying to trick me, 'Arrison.'

'Really, Giancarlo, I have to go. I'm not tricking you.'

The boy warmed to the hint of desperation. 'Perhaps you would try to escape from me.'

'I promise there is no trick . . . but quickly.'

'What do you say then, 'Arrison? What were you taught to say when you wanted something?'

'Please, Giancarlo . . .'

The boy grinned, a sneer playing over his lips.

'And you want to go in the trees where you cannot be seen. You think many are watching you?'

'Please, Giancarlo.'

The boy was satisfied. Another victory, another demonstration of strength. Enough, and the pleasure was satiated. He left the P38 on the ground and slowly, taking his time, manoeuvred himself behind Harrison. It was the work of a few seconds to detach the flex that fastened the ankles to the tree roots. 'Four or five metres only, 'Arrison, no more.'

'Aren't you going to loosen my legs?'

Giancarlo was further amused. 'Crawl, 'Arrison, and watch where your hands move, that they do not go close to my knots.'

Once more Harrison gazed away past Giancarlo and towards the hiding-place of the child. Still visible were the flecks of the shirt between leaves and branches. Anger was rising out of the frustration. The little bastard. Like a bloody puppy that's too young to have been trained, that stays and mocks and will not come. On his hands and knees, Harrison crawled, the performing pet, towards a cluster of birch trunks.

'Not too far, 'Arrison.' The mocking call of derision.

His knees scuffed a trail through the leaves and surface earth before he was partially hidden by the trees. He lowered his trousers, squatted using his hands to support himself and felt the constriction and pain gush away. God, the bloody relief of it. Bloody freedom. And the bloody smell too.

'Please, Giancarlo, do you have any paper?'

There was a ripple of laughter from past the trees. 'I have no bidet for you, I have no aerosol for you to spray under your armpits. But paper I have for you.'

Subdued, Harrison thanked him and then repeated himself when the bag that had carried the rolls landed close to his feet, thrown with accuracy. He cleaned himself, retrieved his trousers, scuffed some dirt over the soiled paper and dragged himself back to his captor and his prison. He crawled to the flattened earth in the cavity and lay down, resuming his familiar position, pliant and non-resistant, and curled his arms behind his back.

'Close your eyes.' A command, and with his legs trussed, what chance? Nothing, just pain, nothing. He clenched his eyes shut, and heard only the slight sounds of Giancarlo's feet, and then the hands were cruelly at his wrists and the flex was wound tight and brutally across his flesh, and there was the pressure of a knee on the small of his back.

The weight slid from him and with its going there was again the mocking voice. 'You can open your eyes.'

Above the horizon of the crater rim, Harrison saw Giancarlo standing, observing, hands on hips. Something mindless, something vacuous about the smile and the mouth and the dulled glare of the eyes.

'You're enjoying yourself, Giancarlo. It's sick to be that way. It means that you are ill . . .'

'Now we have a grand speech.' Derision from the boy, the void unbridged by the contact.

'To treat anyone like this, it means you're deranged. You're a bloody lunatic. You know what that means . . . you're mad, Giancarlo, you've flipped your bloody lid.' Why say it? Why bother? What bloody difference does it make?

'I understand what you say.' But the boy was not roused.

'You've become an animal, Giancarlo. A vicious, infected, little—'

Giancarlo with studied care turned his back. 'I do not listen to speeches. I am not obliged to hear you.'

'Why don't you do it now?' The whisper, without fervour, without passion. The words of a second in the boxer's ring when he has seen enough blood, when he is ready to throw in the towel.

'Because it is not time. Because I am not ready.'

'I say it again, Giancarlo, you enjoy it. You must have felt like a kid giving yourself a wrist job when you killed the men back in the barn, jerking yourself. What are you going to do when you kill me, take your bloody trousers down . . . ?'

Giancarlo narrowed his eyes, and on his slight forehead the frown deepened in its ruts. His voice came as a rush of breeze among the trees. 'You know nothing of us. Nothing. You cannot know why a man goes sotto-terra, why a man discards all the trappings so sought after by your stinking breed, why a man fights to destroy a system that is rotten. You were smug and safe and fat, and you were blind. You know nothing of the struggle of the pro-letariat.'

Half into the dirt, Harrison shouted back, 'Bloody clichés. Parrot talk you learned in the drains.'

'You do not make it easier for yourself.'

Attempting an order and a sternness, Harrison called, 'Get it over with.'

'I have said to them that it will be at nine o'clock if I have not my Franca. I will wait till nine. That was my word. Keeping you till then does not threaten me.'

Giancarlo walked away a few paces, discarded the conversation, withdrew to his inner recesses, gone from Harrison's reach.

And he's right, Geoffrey, you know nothing of them, nothing at all of the new and embryo species. Nothing of the hate squashed into that mind. And there's no help, no succour, the cavalry don't come this time. Just a bloody carcase already, that's all, Geoffrey. Harrison looked into the green grey mist of the trellis of sapling branches and leaves, and felt the falling of a greater loneliness. He could not see the child. Perhaps it was his eyes, perhaps he looked in the wrong place, but he could not find the checked shirt though he peered till his eyes ached and hurt him.

A second carafe now stood emptied on the table.

The Bo-Peep act and the boy not to be found. The waiters had served the lunches, waved their patrons away and stripped the cloths from the chipboard tables. Violet Harrison seemed not to notice and with their studied politeness they waited on her pleasure as she toyed and sipped at the last glass of wine. On the big circus wheel she alternated between hope and despair as the young men of the beach sauntered by. Straight-backed, tanned from wind and sun and the flailing blows of the fine grains, cocky assured eyes, combed-down hair. Any would have served her purpose. She saw the boy a long way off on the beach, walking between two companions.

Recognized him instantly.

'Could I have my bill, please.' She rummaged in

her bag for the notes, gestured to the waiter that she required no change, and was on her feet and smiling sweetly.

She walked out from the eating verandah, taking what she hoped was a casual saunter and following a line that would intercept the boy's path. She did not look to her right, the direction from which he was coming, but held her head high and straight and focused on the blue sea's depths and its breaking flecks of spume. She strode on, waiting for the greeting, consumed with a growing, creeping nervousness.

'The English lady, good afternoon.'

She spun round, gouging at the warm sand beneath her sandals. Not that she could claim surprise, but when his voice came, almost behind her, it cut and burned at her consciousness.

'Oh, it's you.' How else did you do it? How to flick up a clever answer when all you were confronting was the stud required for half an hour's brisk anonymous work?

'I did not expect to see you here again.'

'It's a public beach.' Don't frighten him off. Too trite, Violet. God, you'd kick and curse yourself. 'I come here quite a lot.'

She saw the boy's little gesture with his hands, the clipping of his forefinger against his thumb, the message to the other two that the principal wished to be left to his opportunities. Close together but untouching, no bridging contact of fingers, no brushing of thighs, they moved together towards the sea.

'You would like to swim, Signora?'

How he'd speak to a friend of his bloody mother,

thought Violet. 'Not yet. I thought I'd just lie on the beach for a bit.'

'Give me your towel.'

She dived into her bag and produced it for him. He spread it out on the sand, gestured with his hand for her to sit and followed her down. There was little room for both of them if they were to share it. His swimming costume was brief and bulging grotesquely. You understand, Geoffrey. Their hips touched. You won't cast a rock, Geoffrey.

'My name is Marco.'

And Geoffrey wouldn't know. That was the rule. No blows below the belt for Geoffrey. No knowledge and therefore no hurt.

'I am Violet.'

'That is the name of a flower in English, yes? A very beautiful flower, I think.'

I know you are alone, Geoffrey. I too am alone. You cannot move, you cannot help yourself. I too, Geoffrey.

'I said it the last time we met, and I was right. You are a very cheeky boy, Marco.'

He smiled across the inches of towel at her. The toothpaste advertisement, the smile of a child taken to a shop, who knows it is his birthday, knows if he is patient he will receive his present.

'What time is it, Giancarlo?'

'Past five.'

The boy returned to his own chasm of silence.

He had much to think of, much to concern himself with. Less than three hours to the schedule that he had set himself, had insisted on. Less than three hours till he spoke once more with his Franca.

Problems and options bombarded his limited intellect. If they met his demand, if they agreed to the exchange, where should he fly to? Algiers, Libya, Iraq, the People's Republic of South Yemen. Would any of those places take them? And how to choose, a boy who had never been out of Italy. How would he guarantee their safety if an airport rendezvous were permitted? What was the capability of the anti-terrorist pigs? Would they seek a shooting gallery, regardless of the prisoner? It was too much for him to assimilate. Too great the difficulties, too encompassing. A great team the Brigatisti had for the Moro operation, and they now sat in Asinara, locked in their cells, the failed men. As he weighed each trick in the card pack, so too grew the realization of the sheer mountainface he must scale. Start with the haven, start there, because with nowhere to go they were lost. A country to welcome them and harbour them, start there. An Arab country? What else? But even their own people were now shunned and ignored; he had seen the pictures of the lorries blocking the runways in Algiers and Benghazi and Tripoli. If they would do that when an Arab brother was seeking refuge . . . Late for the answers to the questions. The time was ripe for answers before Claudio walked to his room in the pensione, before the rapido sped towards Reggio, before the Calabresi whimpered in their terror.

Perhaps it was all irrelevant.

Did he know in his heart there would be no exchange? And if there were to be no exchange, what then would the leadership want of him? He wrestled in the growing purgatory of the dilemma. Where lay the victory in this skirmish? The body of his 'Arrison

329

in a ditch, the head blasted with the shell of the P38, that or his prisoner released to walk away on a road with a communiqué in his pocket to be printed the next morning in *Paese Sera* and *Il Messaggero*? Where lay the victory for the proletariat's revolution? How had the Brigatisti advanced when they took the life of Aldo Moro on the slime-covered beach at Focene?

He was old enough only for questions, too young for their responses. If he could not conjure the answers then he would not see his Franca again. Not for twenty years and that was for ever. Three days since his hands had travelled her skin, since her golden head had passed across the softness of his belly. To be denied that for a lifetime. The boy felt a gust of pain. There was nothing that was simple, facile, and that was why there was a steel in the comrades who fought, in Franca Tantardini and the men in the island gaol. And what was the sinew of Giancarlo Battestini, in his twentieth year, lover of Tantardini, son of a borghese, member of the NAP? A dozen hours, slow and tardy hours, and he would have the answer.

His hands clutched together, white to the knuckles, Giancarlo waited for the time when he should leave Harrison and make his way again to the lakeside of Bracciano.

In his hotel room Archie Carpenter listened to Michael Charlesworth's clipped and exact résumé.

A voice far away on a bad connection. The situation if anything had deteriorated. Reuters and UPI carried on their wires that a boy, Giancarlo Battestini, categorized as little more than a probationer of the

NAP, had telephoned the Questura to emphasize the terms of his ultimatum.

'I don't know how it is that the Italians allow this sort of information out, but nothing stays secure here. It seems Battestini was full of his threats. There's a fair depression about the way it's going,' Charlesworth had said.

Holding himself, the diver conserving his oxygen, Carpenter had heard him out. Then the explosion.

'So what are you all doing about it?'

'What we were doing about it earlier, Archie. It has not changed.'

'Sweet damn-all.'

'You can put it that way,' Charlesworth placated. 'That way if you want to.'

'What other bloody way is there?'

'Abuse doesn't help, Archie. You've spoken to the Ambassador yourself, he's explained our situation. I've heard since that London have called him. They back him.'

'He's written off my man.'

'Histrionics don't help either. I'm sorry, you're sorry, we're all sorry . . . But you'll come and have that meal tonight.'

'If you want me to.'

'Come on up and help us through a bottle. Did you get in touch with the wife?'

'I rang again, took a bloody effort to, but I tried. There's no answer.'

'It's a filthy business, Archie, but don't think you're alone with the hair shirt. It's shared about a bit, you know.'

Charlesworth rang off.

Archie Carpenter straightened his bed, brushed his

hair, raised his tie knot and drew on his jacket. He took the lift downstairs and walked out through the front foyer of the hotel, stepping irritably over the piled suitcases of an arriving tour. He summoned a taxi and asked for the Questura. Early summer evening, the traffic rushing for home and guaranteeing him an exciting and lively journey among the pedestrians and across the traffic lanes. Carpenter barely noticed. A telephone call from the enquiry desk had promptly led to his being ushered up the stairs to the offices of Giuseppe Carboni, now transformed into a tactical crisis centre.

Shirt sleeves, tobacco smoke, coffee beakers, a three-quarters emptied Scotch bottle, faces lined with weariness, the howl of electric fans, the chatter of teletype machines, and, radiating energy, Carboni in the midst, rotund and active.

Carpenter hesitated by the door, was spied out, waved forward.

'Come in, Carpenter. Come and see our humble efforts,' Carboni shouted at him.

This was the old world, the known scents. An emergency room under pressure. This was something for Carpenter to feel and absorb. He felt an interloper, yet at home, among the men he could find sympathy for. The clock was turned back as he came diffidently past the desks where the paper mountained, past the photographs stuck with tape to the walls that showed shocked and staring faces, past the telephones that demanded response.

'I don't want to be in the way . . .'

'But you cannot sit in the hotel room any longer?'

'Something like that, Mister Carboni.'

'And you come here because everyone you speak

to gives you bad news or no news, and from me you hope for a difference?'

Something lovable about him, Carpenter thought. Overweight, ugly as sin, dirty fingernails, a shirt that should have seen the wash, and a bloody good man.

'It was getting at me, just sitting about . . . you know how it is?'

'I will educate you, Carpenter.' Carboni was sliding on his coat, then turning away to bellow what seemed to Carpenter a score of differing instructions to varied recipients, and simultaneously. 'I will show you our enemy. You will witness what we fight against. I know you policemen from England, detailed and organized men, who have believed that you are the best in the world . . . '

'I'm not a policeman any more.'

'You retain the mentality. It has stayed with you.' Carboni laughed without a smile, a nervous tic. 'The rest of the world are idiots, second-class people. I understand. Well, come with me, my friend. We go across the city to the Rebibbia gaol. That is where we hold the Tantardini woman and I must play the taxi-driver and bring her here, because that is what little Giancarlo wants and we must please him . . . '

Carpenter sensed the swollen anger in the man, wondered where it could find an outlet. The laugh came again, raising and suspending the flesh rolls of the jaw.

'. . . I must please him, because if he does not talk to Tantardini, then your Harrison is dead. I am here to save him, I will do my humble best to save him.'

'I hadn't really doubted that, sir.' Carpenter let the respect run in his voice, because this was a professional man, this was a caring man.

333

'So, come and see her. Know your enemy. That is what you say in England? The better you know him, the better you fight him.' Carboni caught Carpenter's arm and propelled him back towards the door. 'You will see that we risk much at this stage. But don't tell me that it was never like that in London. Don't tell me that always you were supreme.'

'We had the black times.'

'We have experience, we know the black times. Tonight it is that but darker.'

His arm still clamped by Carboni's fist, Carpenter surged down the corridor.

Across the bonnet of the little red Fiat, the child drew with a pliant finger the letters of his name in the dirt covering the paintwork. It had perplexed him at first to find a car edged from the field into the shelter of the trees, and he had skirted it twice before gaining the courage to approach it. He had gazed inside, admired the shiny newness of the seat leather and let his hand flit to the bright chrome door handle and felt it slide down under pressure. But he did not dare to climb into the car and sit in the driver's seat and hold the steering-wheel as he would dearly like to have done. His compensation was the writing of his name in big and bold and shaking letters.

That task completed, his interest moved on and he walked away as the sun slipped, delaying his journey home to the farm only for the time it took to pluck some hedgerow flowers for his mother. He had little sense of the hour but the chill that was rising from the grass, carried by the freshening wind, was enough to dictate his going. He ambled between the chewing cows, holding tightly to the stems of the flowers, admiring their colours. That his mother and father might be cruelly anxious for him was beyond the comprehension of his young mind.

Chapter Seventeen

Together Archie Carpenter and Giuseppe Carboni stood in the courtyard of the gaol, far on the inside from the high swinging gates, ringed by walls and watch-towers and men who patrolled catwalks with the guns ready in their hands. The Rebibbia prison, Carboni said, was the maximum security holding centre for the capital city. A fearsome and odious place it seemed to Carpenter, where even in the open, where the wind could blow, there was the smell of kitchens and lavatories, and a community in confinement.

'She will be here one more day,' Carboni intoned. 'Then we transfer her to Messina to await the courts. God willing, it will be months before they drag her into the light again.'

'This is not your work, these are not the people you are normally with?' A gentle query from Carpenter.

'I am a criminal policeman, I do not have a political background. That is the can of worms for a policeman. But everyone is very willing that I should be the man who takes the weight of this action. There are others better fitted than I, but they did not raise their hands.' There was a tight, resigned sadness on

Carboni's face. 'But that is how we live here, that is our society. We do not fall down and wag our tails and demand to be given the hardest task because there lies the way to honour and promotion, when the risk of failure is greatest. We are survivors, Carpenter. You will learn that.'

He broke off, his attention directed to the side door of a small building that fronted a towering five-storey cell block. Carabinieri with light machine-guns led the way, officers with medal ribbons followed and then the prisoner. It was the sound of the chains, intrusive and strange to Carpenter, that alerted him to the presence of Franca Tantardini, diminutive when surrounded by so many taller men. A flower choked by weeds. Carpenter shrugged. Stop the bloody politicizing, Archie. She's not a bad-looker either. Good pair of hips on her.

There was no fear on the woman's face. A battle-ship under steam, proud and devastating and intimidating. The face that launched Giancarlo, chucked him far out to sea.

'An impressive bit of woman, Mister Carboni.'

'If you find a psychopath impressive, Carpenter, then this one would meet your definition.'

You've overstepped the line, Archie. Taking the guided tour for granted, as of right. You're the work-house boy here, out on a charity ride and taking favours. And remember what they brought you here to see. The bloody enemy, Archie, the enemy of the State. They watched as Franca Tantardini was led into the windowless grey van with her gaolers, and around them there was running and movement and the revving of engines from the escort cars; four of them, back windows lowered, machine-guns protruding.

The rear of the van was held open and Carboni moved rapidly inside, Carpenter following and chastened.

'We are sensitive at this moment . . . about these people.'

'Take my apology, it was the remark of an idiot.'

'Thank you.' A half smile, fast and then obliterated, replaced by the set, hard features of a man about his work. Carboni offered a hand to help Carpenter climb inside. There were two lines of benches in the interior, running against the sides, and the woman rested in a corner far from the door. Illumination came from a single bulb protected by steel mesh. Carboni felt in his waist and produced his short-barrelled pistol and handed it without comment to an escort who would sit at a distance from the prisoner.

'You are armed, Carpenter?'

'No.' A blush, as if he had displayed an inadequacy.

The van drew away, slowly at first, then speeding forward and the echo of the sirens in front and behind bathed the shallow interior.

'Come and join me.'

Carboni, a hand against the ceiling to preserve his balance, had struggled across the heaving floor and subsided on to the bench beside the woman. Carpenter took a place opposite her. Tantardini eyed them indifferently.

'Franca.' The policeman spoke as if it hurt to use her first name, as if afterwards he would soap-rinse his mouth. 'I am Carboni of the Questura. I am in charge of the investigation into the kidnapping of an English businessman, Geoffrey Harrison . . .'

'Am I to be accused of that too?' She laughed clearly. 'Is every crime in Rome to be set against the terrible, the fearsome Tantardini?'

'Listen to me, Franca. Listen and do not interrupt . . .' The talk was fast and in Italian, leaving Carpenter uncomprehending, his attention held only by the calm, bright face of the woman. '. . . Hear me out. He was taken, this Englishman, by a Calabresi group. Now he has been removed from them, and he is in the hands of your boy, your Giancarlo.'

Again the laugh, and the rich, diamond smile. 'Battestini could not deliver a letter . . .'

'He has killed three men, he has moved Harrison half across the country.' Carboni pierced her with his small pig eyes. The heat in the van was intolerable, and he mopped at his face with a stained handkerchief. 'Battestini holds the Englishman in Rome and demands your freedom against his prisoner's life.'

There was a trickle of wonderment and surprise. 'Battestini has done all this?'

'On his own, that is what we believe.'

Almost a chuckle. 'So why do you come to me?'

'You are going now to my office. In little more than an hour, in eighty minutes, Battestini will telephone that office. He has demanded to talk to you. We have agreed . . .'

Carpenter, the eye-witness, watched the tightening of the woman's body, saw the muscles ripple against the cloth of her jeans.

'. . . He is very young, this boy. Too young. I tell you something very honestly, Franca: if any harm should come to Harrison, then Giancarlo will die where we find him.'

'Why tell this to me?'

'You bedded him, Franca.' The words ripped in distaste from Carboni's mouth. 'You poured the paraffin on his calf-love. He does this for you.'

The van had lost its speed, telling the occupants that the built-up sprawl of north-east Rome had been reached, and the sirens bellowed for passage with a greater ferocity. Carpenter watched the woman as she lapsed into silence, as if pondering what she had been told. The blanket of warm air wrapped all of them, and there was a drop of sweat eking from her hairline across the fine chiselled nose.

'What do you offer me?'

'I offer you the chance to save the boy's life. He is not of your sort, Franca. He is not a man of the Nappisti, he is a boy. You will go to gaol for many years, not less than twenty. Help us now and it would be taken into account at your trial, there would be clemency.'

As if from instinct her mouth curled scornfully, before the softness of the woman's lips reappeared. 'You ask me to secure the release of the Englishman?'

'That is what we ask of you.'

'And I will talk with Giancarlo?'

'You will talk with him.'

Carboni looked hard into her, waiting for the response, conscious that he had committed much of his future to the conversation of a few minutes. Whitened skin, pale as the flesh of an underground creature, hair that was not greased and ordered, tired to exhaustion.

'He is very young,' the woman murmured. 'Just a boy, just a pair of clumsy little hands . . .'

'Thank you, Franca. Your action will be rewarded.'

What had been settled Carpenter could not know.

340

Carboni had leaned back against the discomfort of the rolling metal wall, and Tantardini sat very still except that her fingers played on the links of the chains that fastened her wrists. And she wasn't wearing a bra either. Bloody marvellous sight, and the blouse must have shrunk in the last wash. Wrap it, Archie. Carboni seemed happy enough, something would have been sorted.

The van travelled at steady speed towards the inner city.

Only when the last of them had retreated noisily through the low yellow gorse clump beneath the pines did Violet Harrison open her eyes again. It was too dark under the trees for her to see his fleeing back, but there were the sounds for a long time of his blundering feet and his calls for his friends. The pain in her body was intense, bitter and vivid, and there was a chill seeping against her skin. But the cold was nothing, set against the agony of the wounds provided by the boy Marco and his friends. The worst was at the gentle summit of her thighs, on the line where the tan and the whiteness split, where the bruises would be forming. She did not cry out, was beyond tears and remorse, her horizon set only on controlling the violence of the aching. The scratches on her face were alive, where the nails had ripped at her cheeks as she had writhed and sought to escape from them, and the harshness of the ground dug deep into the weak slackness of her buttocks that had been pounded, battered, into the earth surface.

At first it had been right, as she had prepared it, as her fantasies had dictated.

She and the boy Marco had gone together from the heat of the beach to the shade of the pine canopy. A tight path that flicked the gorse against her bared legs below the hem of the loose beach dress had led them to a place that was hidden, where the scrub formed a fortress wall of privacy. Swimming to the ground she had slipped the dress over her head, an absence of words and invitation because everything was implicit and unspoken. First the bikini top, loosened by herself because his hands were jumping with nervousness, and then the cupping of her breasts till the boy was panting, frantic. Fingers leaping over her, and Violet Harrison lying back, willing him on, exposed. Fingers on the smoothness of her belly and reaching down and feeling for her and hunting for her, and she clutching at the dark curled hair of his head. That was when she had heard the giggles of the watchers, and she had started up, arms crossing her chest, and they had come like hyenas to a prey. One on each arm and Marco pulling her knees apart, cutting at her with the sharpness of his nails, and tugging at the slight cotton fabric of the bikini bottom. The sweet smile of respect lost from Marco's face, replaced by the bared teeth of the rampant rat. First Marco, penetrating and deep and hard and hurting her because she was not ready. And when he was spent then the first friend came, and there was a hand across her mouth and her arms were spread for crucifixion. After the first friend, the second, and then again Marco, and nothing said among them. Just the driving of the hips and the gush of their excitement at the forbidden. Too good to miss, Marco's fortune. Right that it should be shared among his friends. The last had not even managed, and when she spat in his face and his friends jeered encouragement he had raked her cheek and she had felt the warm blood sprinkle her skin. He had rolled away leaving only his eyes and those of the other two boys to perpetuate the violation.

The tears would come later, back in the flat, back at their home, when she thought again of Geoffrey.

She stood up on her weakened legs, said aloud: 'God help me that he should ever know.'

What if this were the time that he was preparing to die, what if this was the moment that he clutched at an image of Violet? What if it were now that he looked for her as she was walking on a path in strange woods, her clothes devastated, her modesty wrecked and laughed over and splintered?

'Never let him find out, please God. Never.'

She had not even spoken to him when he left the house that morning. She had lain in the bed, her nightdress tight around her, aware of his movements in the flat, but she had not called him, because she never did, because they had only banalities to speak of.

'Forgive me, Geoffrey. Please, please.'

Only if Geoffrey died would he never know. Only then would she be safe in her secret. And he must live, because she had betrayed him and was not fit for the weeds of the widow, for the hypocrisy of condolence. She must will him to live. A terminal patient of catastrophic internal illness sometimes comes back; always there is hope, always there is chance. And then he will know, if the miracle is enacted he will know.

Violet Harrison ran on the pine needle rug. The

pain of the wounds was subsidiary to the greater hurt of shame and humiliation. She skirted the trattoria, darkened and shuttered, and sprinted for the car park. Her hand plunged in her bag, wrenched at the cosmetics in the search for the car keys. When she sat in the driving seat and the ignition fired, she trembled with the tears that had been stifled.

'Come home, Geoffrey. Even if no-one is there. Come home, my brave darling, come home.'

'Goodbye, 'Arrison.'

Giancarlo could barely see his prisoner against the dirt black of the earth pit.

'Goodbye, Giancarlo.' A faint voice, devoid of hope.

'I will be back soon.' As if Harrison needed to be reassured, as if all his ordeal was a fear of being alone with darkness. A slight stirring of warmth and the nudge of communication. Was the confidence of the boy failing, was the certainty sliding?

Giancarlo slipped away along the path, feeling with his arms outstretched in front of him for the low branches. There was plenty of time.

He had come so far, and yet where was the measure of his achievement? A bramble stem caught with its spikes at the material of his trousers. He tore himself clear. Had he advanced his claim to Franca's freedom? His ankle turned under a protruding root. The P38 dug at the skin of his waist, the acknowledgement that this was his sole power of persuasion, his only right to be heard and known in the great city basking in its summer evening to the south.

*   *   *

The breath of darkness had eddied into the great courtyard of the Questura. The headlights and roof lamps of the convoy from the Rebibbia gleamed out their urgency as they swung through the archway from the outside street into the parking area. More shouting, more running men, more guns as the van was backed towards an opened door that led directly to the cell corridor. Among those who worked late in the city's police headquarters there were many who hurried down the internal staircases and craned from the upper windows that they might catch a brief glimpse of 'La Tantardini'. They were rewarded sparsely, a flash of the colour of her blouse as she was manhandled the few feet from the van steps to the entrance of the building, and disappearance.

Carboni did not follow her, but stood in the centre of the courtyard among the reversing, straightening cars that jockeyed for the last parking places. Archie Carpenter stood a few feet from him, sensing that the policeman preferred his own thoughts for company.

She had been long gone from their sight when Carboni threw off the spell, turned to look for Carpenter. 'You would not have understood what passed between us.'

'Not a word, I'm sorry.'

'I have to be brief . . .' Carboni began to walk towards the principal entrance to the building, ignoring the many who watched him as a related secondary object of interest now that the woman was gone. 'The boy will telephone at eight. I have to trace that call. I must know the location from where he telephones. To trace the call I must have time. Only when he talks to Tantardini will he gabble on. He will talk to her.' Carboni's face was etched with anxiety. 'I have told her also that if Harrison is harmed, then we will kill Battestini wherever we find him, but that if she co-operates then clemency will be shown her in the courts.'

'Which you have no power to guarantee.'

'Right, Carpenter, no power at all. But now they have plenty to talk of, and they will use quickly the time that the engineers need. I have no other option but reliance on the trace procedure.'

Carpenter spoke quietly, 'You have one other option. To free Tantardini for Harrison's life.'

'Don't joke with me, Carpenter, not now. Later when it is finished.'

They stopped at the outer door of Carboni's office. The retort was rising in Carpenter's throat, and he suppressed it and thought for the first time how ludicrous to these people was the proposition that seemed straight and clear and common-sense.

'I wish you luck, Mister Carboni.'

'Only luck . . . you are mean with your favours, Englishman.'

They entered the office, and Carpenter was quick to appraise the mood, sensitive to the atmosphere of downed heads, flattened feet, gloom and frustration. This was Carboni's own team and if they were not believing in success, then who was he to imagine in his mind the incredible. Carpenter watched as Carboni moved among the impromptu desks and tables and the teleprinters in the outer room, speaking softly to his men. He saw the queue of shaken heads, the mournful mutters of the negative. Like he's going round a cancer ward, and nobody's carrying the good news, nobody's lost his pains, nobody thinks he's coming through. Poor bastard, thought Carpenter.

Carboni expended a long, powered sigh, and slumped to the chair behind his desk. With the sense of theatre, of tragedy, he slapped a hand onto the cream telephone receiver in front of him.

'Call Vellosi. Get him to come here. Not the same room as this . . . but ask him to be close.' He rubbed at the weariness in his eyes. 'Bring her up now, bring Tantardini.'

The child fled from the raw, opened hand of his mother.

Neat and nimble on his feet, he dodged the swinging blow, scattered the posy of hedge flowers onto the stone slabs of the kitchen floor, and scampered for the corridor that led to his bedroom.

'All afternoon I've been calling you from the house . . .'

'I was only in the wood, Mama.' He called shrilly in his fright from the sanctuary of his room.

'I even went and bothered your father in the field . . . he called too . . . he wasted his time when he was busy . . .'

She did not follow him, he had achieved safety.

'Mama, in the wood, I saw . . .'

His mother's voice boomed back, surging to him, as in falsetto she mimicked his small voice. 'I saw a fox . . . I saw a rabbit . . . I followed the flight of a hawk. You'll have no supper tonight. Into your night clothes . . . sick with worry you had me.'

He waited, trying to gauge the scale of her anger, the enormity of his fault, then wheedled in justification. 'Mama, in the wood I saw . . .'

She snapped her interruption back at him.

'Silence your chatter, silence it and get yourself to bed. And you'll not sit with your father after his supper. Not another sound from you, or I'll be in and after you.'

'But Mama . . .'

'I'll be in and after you.'

'Good night, Mama, may the Virgin watch over you and Papa tonight.'

The voice was small, the fluency broken by the first tears on the child's smooth-downed cheeks. His mother bit her lower lip. It was not right to shout at a small child, and he had so few to play with, and where else was there for him to go but to the woods or to fields with his father? It would be better when he started school in the autumn. But she had been frightened by his absence, and she consoled herself that her punishment of her only little one was for his own good. She returned to the preparation of her man's supper.

Throughout the city and its suburbs the security net was poised. More than five hundred cars and trucks and riot vans were on the streets. They wore the colours of the Primo Celere, and the Squadra Volante and the Squadra Mobile; others were decorated in the royal blue of the carabinieri. There were the unmarked cars of the undercover men, and of SISDE, the secret service. The agencies of government were poised to spring should the engineers of the Questura basement provide the map reference from which Giancarlo Battestini telephoned. Engines ticking idly, watches and clocks repeatedly examined, machine-guns on the back seats of cars, on the metalled floors of vans. A great army, but one which rested till the arrival of the orders and instructions without which it was a helpless, useless force.

On the fifth floor of the Questura, in the control centre, the technicians had exhausted the lights available on their wall map for marking the position of their interception vehicles. A clock creeping up to twenty hours had silenced conversation and movement, leaving only the mindless hum of an air-conditioning system.

Grim-faced, wearing his years, Francesco Vellosi strode from the central doors of the Viminale to his car that waited at the apex of the half-moon drive. The men who were to escort him to the Questura fidgeted in the seats of the car that would follow. As he settled in the back seat he was aware of the clatter of the arming of weapons. From an upper room the Minister watched him go, then resumed his tiger pacing of the carpet. He would hear by telephone of the night's developments.

Nothing impeded Giancarlo, a fierce moonlight guided his way. There was a stream of cars on the road, but of course there would be cars, for this was a resort of the Roman summer, and no driver would see anything extraordinary in a youth with the long hair of a student, the T-shirt and jeans uniform of the unemployed. On the road he did not flinch from the blinding beams of the headlights. On down the hill he walked till he could see the still reflection of the lights of the trattorie and bars playing on the distance of smooth water. On down the hill, with only occasional stolen glimpses at the slow-moving hands of his watch. The fools with their wives and girls, they would know of Giancarlo Battestini. Those who rushed past him impatiently in their cars would know of him tomorrow. Tomorrow they would know his name and roll it on their tongues and savour it, and try to ask how, and try to ask why.

The pavements beside the lake were filled with those who drifted in aimless procession. They did not glance at the boy. Safe in their own lives, safe in their own business, they ignored him.

At the ristorante the kiosk with the telephone was empty. He darted his eyes again to his watch. Patience, Giancarlo, a few more minutes only. He collected the gettoni from the knot in his handkerchief where they had been segregated. Noise and money-purchased happiness crept from the interior. Where he stood, hemmed in by the glass walls of the cubicle, he could see the mouths that burst with pasta, the hands grasping at the wine bottles, the bellies that rocked over the table-tops. Tomorrow they would not shriek in their gusts of laughter. Tomorrow they would talk of Giancarlo Battestini till it consumed them, till it burned them, the very repetition of the name. His name.

The child's father came to the stone-walled, tin-roofed farmhouse when there was no longer light for him to work his fields. A tired, sleep-ridden man, looking for his food and his chair and his television and his rest.

His wife chided him for the late hour, played the scolder, till she kissed him light and pecking, on a hair-roughened cheek; to her he was a good man, full of work, heavy in responsibility, a loyal man to his family, who depended on the long-drawn-out power of his muscles to make a living from the coarse hillside fields. His food would soon be ready and she would bring it on a tray to their living parlour where the old television set, provider of black and white pictures, sat proudly on a coarse wood table. Perhaps later the boy could sit with him because her anger had evaporated with the passing of her fear at his absence, but only if he had not already drifted to sleep.

He had not replied when she had told her man of the time their child had returned and the punishment imposed, just shrugged and turned to the sink to wash away the day's grime. She held sway over the domestic routine and it was not for him to challenge her authority. Hearing him safely settled, she hurried to her stove, lifted the big grey metal saucepan down and drained the steaming water from the pasta, while through the opened doorway blazoned the music of the opening of the evening's news programme. She did not go to watch beside her husband; all day the radio channels had been obsessed with an event from the city. City people, city troubles. Not relevant to a woman with stone floors to be scrubbed daily, a never-filled purse, and a distant, difficult child to rear. She set the pasta on a plate, doused it in the brilliant red of the tomato sauce, flecked it with the grated cheese, and carried it to her man, flopped in his chair. She could draw satisfaction from the happy and contented smile on her husband's face, and the way that he shook off his weariness, sat himself upright, and the speed with which his fork drove down into the eel lengths of the brilliant butter-coated spaghetti.

On the screen were photographs of a man with

combed hair and a knotted tie and the smile that read responsibility and success, replaced by those of a boy whose face showed confrontation and fight, and the trapped gaze of a prisoner. There was a picture of a car, and a map of the Mezzo Giorno . . . She stayed no longer.

'Animals,' she said, and returned to her kitchen and her work.

At one hundred and forty kilometres an hour, Violet Harrison careered along the dual carriageway of the Raccordo.

Her handbag lay on the seat beside her, but she did not bother to winkle out the square lace handkerchief with which she might have dabbed her puffed, tear-heavy eyes. Only Geoffrey in her thoughts, only the man with whom she lived a rotten, neutered life, and who now, in her fear, she loved more than ever before. Commitment to Geoffrey, the boring little man who had shared her home and her bed for a dozen years. Geoffrey, who polished the heels of his shoes, brought home work from the office, thought marriage was a girl with a gin waiting at the front door for the return of the frontiersman husband. Geoffrey, who didn't know how to laugh. Poor little Geoffrey. In the hands of the pigs as she had warmed and nestled close to a stranger on a crowded beach, and watched the front of his costume and believed that prayers were answered.

Beyond the grass and crash barriers of the central reservation cars rushed past her, swallowed in the night, blazing headlights lost as fast as they had reared in front of her. The lights played on her eyes, flashed and reflected in the moisture of her tears, cavorted in her vision as tumbling cascades and aerosols of lights and stars.

That was why, beyond the Aurelia turn-off from the Raccordo, she did not see the signs beside the road that warned of the approaching end of the dual carriageway, did not read the great painted arrows on the tarmac. That was why she was heedless of the closing headlights of the fruit lorry bound for Naples.

The impact was immense, searing in noise and speed, the agony howl of the ripped bodywork metal of the car. A fractional moment of collision, and then the car was tossed away, as if its weight were trifling. The car rose high in the air before crashing down, destroyed and unrecognizable, in the centre of the road.

The face of Geoffrey Harrison, its lines and contours, was frozen to his wife's mind in the final broken seconds of her life. The sound of herself speaking his name was bolted to her tongue.

There was much traffic returning at that time from the coast. Many sitting behind their wheels would curse the unseen source of the queues that built on either side of the accident, and then shudder and avert their faces as they witnessed in their lights the reason for their delay.

In front of Carboni's desk, Franca Tantardini sat on a hard, unprepossessing chair. She was upright, taking little notice of the men who bustled around her, gazing only at the window with its dark abyss and undrawn curtains. The fingers of her hands were entwined on her lap, the chains removed. More like a waiting bride than a prisoner. She had not replied when she had first come into the room and Carboni had taken her to a corner and spoken in his best bedside hush beyond the ears of his subordinates.

Archie Carpenter's eyes never left her. Not the sort of creature that he had handled when he was with Special Branch in London. His career spanned the years before the Irish watch, before the bombers came in earnest. Not much colour in those days for Carpenter who was concerned with the machinations of the far-out shop stewards, the Marxist militants and that old source of inspiration, the Soviet Trade Delegation from Highgate. His had been the old Branch, the archaeological specimen that withered and died in its ice age before learning the new techniques of the war against urban terrorism. The guerrilla fighter was a new phenomenon for Archie Carpenter, something only experienced through newspapers and television screens. But there seemed to be nothing special about the woman, nothing to put her on the pedestal. Well, what do you expect, Archie? A Che Guevara T-shirt, the hammer and sickle tattooed on her forehead?

The telephone on Carboni's desk rang.

Difficult really to know what to expect. Criminals the world over, all the same. Whether it's political, whether it's material. Big fat bouncy kids when they've the air of freedom to breathe. Miserable little bastards when the door closes behind them, when they've twenty years of sitting on a blanket.

Carboni grabbed at the receiver, snatching it from the cradle.

Thought she'd have more fight in her, from the way they cracked her up. Belt it, Archie, for Christ's sake.

'Carboni.'

'The call that you have been waiting for, Dottore.'

'Connect it.'

The light bulb had been removed from the telephone kiosk. In the half dark Giancarlo watched the second hand of his watch moving slowly on its path. He knew the available time, was aware of the ultimate danger. With one hand he held the telephone pressed hard against his right ear, the noise of the ristorante stifled.

'Pronto, Carboni.' A voice fused in metallic interference.

'Battestini.' He had used his own name, chipped at the pretence.

'Good evening, Giancarlo.'

'I have little time . . .'

'You have as much time as you want, Giancarlo.'

The sweat rivers ran on the boy's face. 'Will you meet the demands of the Nuclei Armati Proletaria . . . ?'

The voice cut back at him, smothering his words. 'The demands of Giancarlo Battestini, not of the Nappisti.'

'We stand together as a movement, we . . .' He broke off, absorbed in the motion of his watch ticking on its way, edging towards fiasco.

'You are there, Giancarlo?'

The boy hesitated. Forty seconds gone, forty seconds of the two minutes that was required for a trace.

'I have demanded the freedom of Franca . . . that is what must happen if 'Arrison is to live . . .'

355

'It is a very complicated matter, Giancarlo. There are many things to be considered.' There was an awful, deadening calmness in the responses. A sponge that he hit at but could not corner and pinion.

Close to a minute gone.

'There is one question only, Carboni. Yes or no?'

The first hint of anxiety broke in the distorted voice, the noise of breathing mingled with the atmospherics. 'We have Franca here for you to talk to, Giancarlo.'

'Yes or no, that was my question.'

More than a minute gone, the hand on its second arc.

'Franca will talk to you.'

All eyes in the room on the face of Franca Tantardini.

Carboni held the telephone mouthpiece against his shirt, looked deep and far into the woman, saw only the blank, proud, composed eyes, and knew that this was the ultimate moment of risk. Nothing to be read from her mouth and from her hands that did not fidget, showed no impatience. Total silence, and an atmosphere lead-laden that even Carpenter without the Italian language could sense and be fearful of.

'I trust you, Franca.' Barely audible the words as Carboni's hand with the telephone stretched out towards the responding arm of La Tantardini.

There was a carelessness now in her smile. Almost human. Long slender fingers exchanged for the fatty, stumpy grip of Carboni's fist. When she spoke it was with a clear and educated voice, no roughened edges, no slang of the gutter. The daughter of a well-set family of Bergamo.

'It is Franca, my little fox . . . do not interrupt me. Hear me to the finish . . . and little fox, do as I instruct you, exactly as I instruct you. They have asked me to tell you to surrender. They have asked me to tell you that you should release the Englishman . . .'

Carboni permitted his eyes, in secrecy, to float to his watch. One minute and twenty seconds since the call was initiated. He saw the image of activity in the Questura basement. The isolation of the communication, the evaluation of the digital dialling process, the routing of the connection back towards its source. He strained forward to hear better her words.

'You have asked for my release, little fox. Listen to me. There will be no freedom. So I say this to you, Giancarlo. This is the last—'

It was the action of a moment. Franca Tantardini on her feet. Right arm high above her head, the fist in clenched salute. A face riven with hatred. Muscles of the neck bulged like sewer pipes.

'—kill him, Giancarlo. Kill the pig. *Forza la proletaria. Forza la rivoluzione. Giancarlo, la lotta continua . . .*'

Even as they were rising to their feet, the men about her, struggling to reach her, she had moved whiplash fast towards the receiver on Carboni's desk. As she wrenched at the telephone, tearing its flex from the wall fitting, they pounded her to the ground. The little men of the room kicked and punched at the unresisting body of the woman while Carboni and Carpenter, separated by the mêlée and on their different sides of the office, sat stock still and assessed the scope of the catastrophe.

'Take her back to the Rebibbia, and I want no

marks on her . . . none that can be seen.' A terrible ice cold in his voice, as if the shock wave of betrayal had broken Giuseppe Carboni.

Another telephone ringing. He picked it up, placed it to his ear and dropped his weight onto an elbow. As he listened he watched Franca Tantardini half carried, half dragged, take her leave of him. Carboni nodded as information was given him, offered no gratitude for the service.

'They say, from the basement, that I had told them they would have a minimum of two minutes to find the trace. They say that I gave them one minute and forty seconds. They say that was not sufficient. I have failed your man, Carpenter. I have failed your man.'

Carpenter spat back at him. 'They gave you nothing?'

'Just that it was from the north of the city . . .'

Carpenter stood up and walked towards the door. He wanted to say something vicious, wanted to let the frustration go, and couldn't find it in himself. You couldn't kick a dog, not one that was already limping, that had the mange at its collar. There was nothing he could say. Grown men, weren't they? Not kids who could bully. All adults, all trying, all confronted by the same cancer that was eating deep and ravenously.

'I'm going round to Charlesworth's place. The Embassy fellow. You can reach me there . . . till late.'

'I will be here.'

Of course he would be. Where else for him? No Embassy duty-free Scotch for Giuseppe Carboni, no shutting out of the problem with seventy per cent proof. Carpenter let himself out, didn't look back at

Carboni, and walked down the corridor to the staircase.

Through the connecting door and into the inner sanctum marched Francesco Vellosi. There was uninhibited hatred on his face, brutal and devastating, informing Carboni that he had heard the words of Tantardini.

'I told you to be careful, Carboni, I told you.'

'You told me . . .'

A strand of sympathy shone. 'Anything?'

'With the time available, nothing of substance, nothing that matters.'

Their arms around each other's waists, in mutual consolation, the two men walked from the room to the wire-caged lift for the fifth floor.

They would saturate an area of slightly more than three thousand five hundred square kilometres, from Viterbo in the north to La Storta in the south, while the western limit would be the coastal town of Civitavecchia and the eastern line would be the Roma-Firenze autostrada. Formality, the task provided by the basement technicians. Too great an area for a manhunt, too great an area to lift the men's bowed shoulders.

As they emerged from the lift Vellosi said softly, 'They will crucify you, they will say she should never have spoken to the boy.'

'It was the best chance to make him talk for longer.'

'Who will say that? You will be torn apart, Carboni, the entertainment of the wild dogs.'

Arms still round each other, faces close, Carboni looking up and Vellosi down, eyes meeting. 'But you will be with me, Vellosi.'

Only a smile, only a tightening of the fist in the material of Carboni's shirt, as they came to the operations centre.

The child's head, wearing a winning smile, drifted around the kitchen door.

'Mama . . .' the plaintive call. 'Can I sit with Papa?'

'You were a bad boy today.'

'I'm sorry, Mama . . .'

She had no stomach for the fight, was pleased the child had come from his room, exorcizing her shame that she had lost her temper and tried to strike him. God knows they both worshipped their lone son.

'Papa is tired.' She heard the distant steady snore from her man's throat, the warm food cosseted in him, the burned energy of the day seeking replacement. 'You can sit with him, but don't you bother him, don't you wake him . . .'

The child waited for no more hesitation from his mother. He raced in his light bare feet, his loose pyjamas flowing, through the kitchen and into the living-room.

His mother listened.

'Papa, are you asleep? Papa, can I tell you what I saw in the wood? Please, Papa . . .'

She slapped the towel across her hands, summoned herself across the room in a cloak of annoyance and hissed through the doorway at the sofa where the child snuggled against his sleeping father.

'What did I say to you? That you were not to wake him. Another word from you and you go to your bed. Leave Papa alone. You talk to Papa in the morning.'

'Yes, Mama, can I watch the programme?'

A concert flickered on the aged screen, the harmony of the notes suffering from the distortion of the set. She nodded her head. That was permitted, and it was good for the boy to sit with his father.

'But don't you wake Papa . . . and don't you argue when I call you for bed.'

Chapter Eighteen

The sounds of the returning Giancarlo carried from far away to Geoffrey Harrison. The arrival was blundering and clumsy as if silence and stealth were no longer of importance. The noise spread through the quiet of the wood, where there was nothing to compete with the snapping of branches, the crushing of fallen leaves. He would not be able to see the boy's face when he came, would not be able to recognize the mood and the danger. A blessing or an additional wound? Better to know when the boy was still far from him, better his news while the creature was still distant.

They say some men die well, and others die badly. Harrison remembered when he was a kid and he'd read in a magazine stories of executions by law in a gaol. They said some had screamed and some walked with a high head, and some were carried, and some went unaided and thanked the men around them for their courtesy. What bloody difference did it make? Who looks at a skinned pig hanging from a butcher's hook and says, 'That pig would have died well, you can see it on his face, brave bugger, well done'; who looks at the carcase and thinks of its going?

You'll crawl, Geoffrey, grovel on your knees, because that's the way you are. The bender and the compromiser. Have to be, don't you? Because that's the way you do business, and you're good at business, Geoffrey. That's why International Chemical Holdings sent you here, sent you to lie on your side with the hair growing on your face and the smell from your socks and pants, and the hunger in your belly, and the pain at your wrists, and a kid coming to kill you. Crawl, Geoffrey, play the lizard on his stomach, scuffing through the deadwood. That's the way of commerce. Know when you can fight and when you can lose, and if it's defeat, then turn the cheek and summon the sweet words and save something for the shareholders. Bloody shareholders. Fat women in Hampstead, poodles and jewels, apartments with lifts, and deceased husbands. For you, you bitches, for you I'm lying here, listening to him coming.

There were the escape moments, Geoffrey. In the car, plenty of them, each time you stopped . . . God, do we go through all that again? It's a big grown-up world, Geoffrey. Nanny isn't here any more. No-one to save you but yourself. Why isn't little Giancarlo messing his knickers, why isn't he frightened that his time is coming? Because he believes in something, idiot. It's a faith, it has a meaning to him.

And Geoffrey Harrison has no creed.

Who does Geoffrey Harrison fight for? What principle?

Where is his army of companions who will weep if one of their number falls?

Another bloody casualty, Geoffrey, and there will

be a public sadness in Head Office, and a few will scratch their heads and try and remember the chap who went abroad because it paid more. But don't expect there's going to be any wet on the blotting-paper, any stains on the ledgers, any flags pulled down.

Remember the bar at the Olgiata Golf Club. Red faces and long gins. Men who were always right, always knew. Certainty of opinion. Remember the bar of the Golf Club when Aldo Moro was cringing for the world to see and urging in letters to his friends for government weakness to preserve his life from the Red Brigades.

Despicable behaviour. The man's no dignity.

What you'd expect from these people.

Only have to go back to the war, in North Africa, show 'em a bayonet and you've more prisoners on your hands than you can feed.

What a wonderful wallowing security, membership of the Golf Club. They'll make hay of you, Geoffrey. The man who came back for nine holes after he'd been on his knees with the tears on his cheeks and the sobbing in his throat, and pleaded and held the legs of a boy half his age.

Got to fight 'em, show 'em there's going to be no nonsense. That's the way to beat the scum.

Giancarlo was very close, and his voice pierced the darkness.

'They want you dead, 'Arrison.'

Harrison wriggled and dragged at the wires, tried to turn to face the boy. Managed a few inches.

'What do you mean?'

'They do nothing to save you.'

'What did they say?'

'They tried only to use up time so that they could trace the call.'

'What did Franca say?' The questions from Harrison blurted at the centre of the shadow above him.

'Franca told me to kill you. She said they would not release her. She told me to kill you . . .'

A whisper from Harrison. The breached corn sack, from which the essence is lost. 'Franca said that?'

It's a bloody dream, Geoffrey. There's no reality here. It's fantasy.

'I'm not your enemy, Giancarlo. I've done nothing to hurt you.' And where was the bastard's face, moulded in the blackness? How could you creep before a boy with no face, how did you win him with your fear and your misery? 'I've never tried to harm you . . .'

'Franca said I was to kill you.'

'For Christ's sake, Giancarlo. I'm no enemy of the Italian proletariat, I'm not in the way of your revolution.'

'You are a symbol of oppression and exploitation.'

'It's like you're reading out of the telephone book, they don't mean anything, those words. You can't take a life for a slogan.'

The same dripping voice, the same cruelty in the unseen eyes. 'There can be no revolution without blood. Not just your blood, 'Arrison. We die in the streets for what we believe is a just struggle. We face the living death in the concentration camps of the regime. Twenty years she will exist in Messina . . .'

'Don't talk to me about other people.' The dream clearing, the nightmare fading. 'It helps you not at all if you kill me. You must see that, Giancarlo, please say you can see that . . .'

'You are pathetic, 'Arrison. You are of the middle class, you are of the multinational, you have a flat on a hill . . . should you not defend that way? Should you not defend that exploitation? I despise you.'

The silence fell fast because the killing words of the boy struck far. Harrison abandoned his efforts, lay still and heard the sounds of Giancarlo dropping to sit on the ground a dozen feet from the bunker. Man and boy they drifted to their own thoughts.

Crawl to him, Geoffrey. It's not the Golf Club's life, forget the humiliation, screw the dignity lapse. That he couldn't grovel, what a thing for a man to die over.

Shrill little words and a voice he did not recognize as his own. 'What do I have to do, Giancarlo? What do I have to do for you not to kill me?'

The Judas moment, Geoffrey. The betrayal of his society. The boy had read him, that he belonged nowhere, was a part of nothing. 'Answer me, please.'

Endlessly the boy waited. The wave rolled back from the beach, then gathered itself in white-crested accumulation, burst again, shattering with force on the sand. The reply of Giancarlo.

'You cannot do anything.'

'Afterwards I will say what you have told me to say.'

'Franca has ordered it, you cannot do anything.'

'I will go to the newspapers and the radio and the television, I will say what you want me to . . .'

The boy seemed bored, as if wishing the conversation terminated. Could the man not understand what he was told? 'You chose a way for your life, I have chosen mine. I will fight against what is rotten, you will prop it. I do not recognize the white flag, that is not the way of our combat.'

Harrison was crying, convulsing, the great tears welling in his eyes, dribbling on his cheeks, wetting his mouth. 'You take a pleasure in it . . . ?'

There was a sternness in the boy. 'We are at war, and you should behave like a soldier. Because you do not I despise you. It will be at nine o'clock in the morning. You have till then to become a soldier.'

'You horrid, repulsive little bastard . . . they'll give you no mercy . . . you'll die in the fucking gutter.'

'We ask for no mercy, 'Arrison. We offer none.'

Quiet again in the forest. Giancarlo spread himself on the leaves. He pushed with his hands to make the surface more even, wriggled on to his side so that his back was turned on Geoffrey Harrison and beneath a ceiling of moonlight flecked by the high branches, settled himself. For a few minutes he would hear the foreign sounds of his prisoner's choking sobs. Then he found sleep and they were lost to him.

The sun of the day and the food of the evening ensured the farmer's sleep, and the comatose rest was escape from the worries that burdened his life. The price of fodder, the price of fertilizer, the price of diesel oil for the tractor could be shut out only when his mind was at peace. His child stayed silent, close to the rise and fall of his father's chest, and waited with a concentrated patience, fighting off his own tiredness. Beyond the doorway the child heard the sounds of his mother's movements, and they encouraged his stillness as he lay fearful that any stirring on the damaged springs of the sofa would alert and remind her that he was not yet in his small narrow bed.

Mingled with the music were the mind pictures that the child drew for himself. Pictures that were alien and hostile.

'Come on in, Archie.'

'Thank you, Michael.' Didn't slip off the tongue that easily, not the Christian name bit, not after the hard words. Charlesworth stood in the doorway with a loose shirt on him, no tie, and slacks and sandals. Carpenter fidgeted at the door in his suit.

'Come on into the den.'

Carpenter was led through the hall. Delicate furniture, a case of hardback books, oil paintings on the wall, a vase of tall irises. Do all right, these people . . . Stop the bitching, Archie, drop the chip off your shoulder. You can't blame people for not living in Motspur Park, not if they've the choice.

'Darling, this is Archie Carpenter, from Harrison's head office. My wife Caroline.'

Carpenter shook hands with the tall, tanned girl presented to him. The sort they bred down in Cheltenham, along with fox-hunters and barley fields. She wore a straight dress held at the shoulders by vague straps. The wife back in the semi would have had a fit, blushed like an August rose, no bra and entertaining.

'I'm sorry I'm late, Mrs Charlesworth. I've been at the Questura.'

'You poor thing, you'd like a wash.'

Well, he wouldn't have asked for it himself, but he'd worn a jacket all day and the same socks, and he stank like a hung duck.

'I'll take him, darling.'

An older man was rising heavily from a sofa. Washing could wait, introductions first. Charlesworth resumed the formalities. 'This is Colonel Henderson, our military attaché.'

'Pleased to meet you, Colonel.'

'They call me "Buster", Archie. I've heard about you. I hear you've a straight tongue in your head, and a damned good thing too.'

Carpenter was led to the peace of an outer bathroom. Time for him as he stood in front of the pan to examine the sentry row of deodorant sprays on the window-sill, enough to keep the Embassy smelling sweet for a month. And books too. Who was going to read classical Greek history and contemporary American politics while having a quick squat? Extraordinary people. The reek of public school and private means. He washed his hands, let the day's grime dribble away, pushed a flannel round the back of his neck. Long live the creature comforts. Soap and water and a waiting gin.

They sat around in the lounge, the four of them, separated by rugs and marble flooring and sprouting coffee tables. Carpenter didn't resist the demand that he shed his jacket, loosen his tie.

'Well, tell us, Archie, what's the scene at the Questura?' Charlesworth setting the ball rolling.

'I think they've screwed it . . .'

'For that poor Mr Harrison . . . ?'

Carpenter ignored Caroline Charlesworth. What did they want, a coffee-morning chat with the neighbours, or something from the bloody horse's mouth?

'Tantardini got her hands on the telephone too early in the game for the trace people. Told her boy

369

to chop Harrison, then pulled the connection. The call was still at switchboard but the boy had the message. He rang off, and that's about it.'

Charlesworth was leaning forward in his seat, glass held between his hands. The honest, earnest young man, he seemed to Carpenter. 'She gave a specific instruction for the boy to kill Harrison?'

'That's the way Carboni put it. "I have failed your man", those were his words. Biggest bloody under-statement of the day.'

'He's a good man, Giuseppe Carboni.' Charles-worth spoke with enough compassion for Carpenter momentarily to squirm. 'It's not easy, not in a country like this. Right, Buster?'

The Colonel swirled his whisky round the glass. 'We had full powers in many places, what you'd call nowadays totalitarian powers, in Palestine and Malaya and Kenya and Cyprus. Here the legacy of pre-war fascism is that the security forces are kept weak. But for all we had, it didn't do us a great deal of good.'

'But that was far from the great Mother Britain,' Carpenter interjected impatiently. 'This is different, it's on their own doorstep that they're being whipped. Carboni excepted, they're ambling about like bloody zombies . . .'

'They're trying, Archie,' Charlesworth intervened gently.

'I wouldn't care to make a judgement on their efficiency if I'd been here just a few hours.' The Colonel cut at the air, the swinging of the old cavalry sabre.

Carpenter put his hands above his head, grinned for a moment, dissolved the temper. 'I'm outnumbered, outflanked, whatever . . . So what I want to know is this: when they say they'll chop him, when Battestini says it, do we take that at face, is it gospel?'

Caroline Charlesworth started from her chair. The plea to be excused from the blunt assessments. 'The dinner won't be more than a few minutes.'

'You answer that, Buster,' Charlesworth said. 'It's the pertinent question of the evening.'

The hard, clean eyes of the veteran fixed on Carpenter. 'The answer is affirmative. When they say they'll kill, they're as good as their word.'

'Black tie job?'

'I repeat, Mr Carpenter, they're as good as their word.'

Caroline Charlesworth appeared from the kitchen doorway. The food was ready. She led, the men followed. In the dining-room Carpenter saw the wine on the table, the port and brandy on the sideboard. There was solace to be found here, escape from a hideous and crippling mess.

Late into the evening, the child's mother came at last for him. With a sweep of her hand she hushed his protest, and swept him up so that he sat on her hip as she took him from the side of his father. It was done quickly and expertly and the farmer seemed as unaware of the child's going as he had been of his presence. She nuzzled her nose against her son's neck, saw the fight that he made to keep his eyes open and chided herself that she had left him for so long. She carried him to his room.

'Mama.'

'Yes, my sweet.' She lowered him into the bed.

'Mama, if Papa wakes soon, will he come to see me?'

'You will be asleep, in the morning you will see him.' She pulled the coarse sheet to his chin.

'I have to tell him what I saw . . .'

'What was it, a wild pig, the big dog fox . . . ?' She watched the yawn break on the child's face.

'Mama, I saw . . .'

Her kiss stifled his words, and she tip-toed from the room.

It was the work of the Agente to check finally the cell doors after the prisoners held in maximum security had finished communal recreation and were consigned for the night to their individual cells. His practice was to take a quick glance through the spy-hole and then slide the greased bolt. Others would come after him when the lights were dimmed to make the last muster call of the night.

The Agente had found the paper, folded once, on the mat at the front door of his house. A small piece, ragged at an edge where it had been torn from a notepad. There was a pencil-written number on the outside flap that was immediately relevant to the Agente. Three digits, the number of the cell of the Chief of Staff of the Nappisti.

When he reached that door, the Agente pushed it a few inches, tossed the paper inside, crashed the bolt home, and was on his way. Any colleague who might have seen him would not have been aware of the passing of the message.

The capo abandoned his weekly letter to his mother in the hill city of Siena, saw the paper and slipped from his chair to gather it.

L'amministrazione dice non per Tantardini.

No freedom for Tantardini. It was as he had said. What he had anticipated, because the Englishman was of insufficient importance. Inevitable, but better that way, better if the ultimatum were to expire, the gun were to be fired. The strategy of tension they called it in the Roman newspapers, the creation of intolerable fear. The death of the enemy created fear, something not achieved by negotiation and the making of deals. Better if the Englishman were killed.

But who was the boy, Battestini? Why had he not heard of a youth who could implement so much? The radio in his cell had told him the police held the opinion that the boy worked alone . . . remarkable, outstanding . . . and the commentator called him the lover of Franca Tantardini and expounded that this was the reason for the boy's action. Who in the movement had not been the lover of Franca Tantardini? How many of the Nappisti in this same cell block had not taken comfort from hours spent strangled by the arms and legs of Tantardini, taken pleasure from the flesh and fingers of the woman? His table lamp lit a mirthless smile. Perhaps it was the boy's first time, and he believed he had made a conquest. If it was the first time the boy would climb a mountain for that woman, perhaps he'd die for Tantardini. Certainly he would kill for her. When the ultimatum was met he would issue a communiqué in his own name from inside the walls of Asinara. Courage, my child. We love you, we are with you. But why had he not been told of this boy?

* * *

Like sharks homing for offal, the mosquitoes slipped through the opened window of the farmhouse parlour and turned their incisive attention to the arms and neck of the resting man. Instinctively he slapped the side of his face in irritation, and in his growing consciousness there was the drone of their wings, the rising surge of their attacks. He started up, blinked in the flickering light of the television and heard the sounds of the kitchen through the closed door, water running, the quiet clatter of dishes and tins. He scratched savagely at the bitten skin where the bite mark had grown enough for him to gouge a sharp trickle of blood, he rubbed the back of his hand into his eyes, then headed for the kitchen. Time for him to be going to his bed, time for him to encourage her to follow.

His wife put her finger across her mouth, the call for quiet, and pointed to the half-open door that led to their son's room. A tall, broad-shouldered woman, red-faced, dark hair pulled back in an elastic band, thick bare arms and a faded apron. She had been his woman since he was seventeen and had shyly courted her with the encouragement of her parents, who knew of the farm he would inherit.

'The little one is sleeping?'

She worked at the final flurry of the day's sink work. 'It's taken him long enough, but he's nearly there.'

'Did he tell you where he'd been?'

She slopped warm water from a kettle into the bright plastic sink bowl. 'In the woods, where else?'

'What kept him there?' He was tired, yearning for his bed, and there was much hay to be moved by trailer in the morning. Perfunctory conversation, made only because she was not ready to follow him to their cumbersome, heavy oak wedding bed.

'He saw something, he said.'

'What did he see?'

'I don't know – something. He wanted to tell you about it. I said it would keep till morning. Perhaps it was a pig?'

'Not this far down the hillside,' he said softly.

She sluiced the pan in which she had made the sauce for the pasta.

'You have much more to do?' he asked.

'I have to wash some socks through, then it is finished.' She smiled at him, kind and dark-eyed.

'I'll say good night to the boy.'

The frown crossed her face. 'Don't wake him, not now. He's dead to the world, don't wake him now.'

'I'll see his bedclothes aren't on the floor.'

When he had gone, she could muse as she doused the socks in water that her man loved his child as the most precious thing in his life. God be thanked, she thought, that if we were to have but one child it should have been a boy. Someone for him to work for, someone for him to dream would one day take over the running of the farm. She worked quickly, the soap lathering in a sea of bubbles among the wool, some whole and some darned. Shirts she would do in the morning, after the chickens had been fed.

'Mama.'

She turned abruptly in response to the strained voice of her man. He stood at the kitchen door, his face dazed and in shock, his hand resting loosely on the shoulder of his son.

'You've woken him.' The petulance rose in her voice.

'You never asked him what he had seen?' The farmer spoke hoarsely.

'A fox, a rabbit, perhaps a heron, what difference does it make, what difference at his age?' She bridled, before her senses responded to the mood her man set. 'What did he see?'

'He found a red car hidden in the bushes beside the small field and the wood. He has a toy, a toy car that your mother gave him last Easter, the one he plays in his bed with. He said to me that the toy was the same as the car that he had found. His toy is a red Fiat Uno Venti Sette. They showed a car on the television, the car for the foreigner who was kidnapped. Fiat Uno Venti Sette, and red . . .'

'A red 127, there would be half a million . . .' Her hands were drawn from the water, wiped nervously at her apron. There should be no involvement, not with something hostile.

'He found a man who was tied.'

'The boy dreams. It is a world of his own.'

'He saw a youth come, with a gun.'

She stammered, 'It's not our business.'

'Dress him.'

Her eyes wide, her lips moving in fear, she attacked in defence of her child. 'You cannot take him there, not in the darkness, not if you believe that he has seen these things.'

'Get his clothes and dress him.' It was an instruction, a command. She did not resist and scurried to the child's room for his day clothes.

From the hallway the farmer took a thick sweater and the small-bore shotgun that he used for pigeon and rabbit when he went with his neighbours to shoot on a Sunday morning. From a nail high in the back door to the yard he unhooked a rubber-coated torch.

Together they dressed their son.

'You remember, Mama, what Father Alberti said at the Mass after Moro. He said these people were the antiChrist. Even Paolo Sesto they rejected, even the appeal by him that Moro should be spared. They are the enemies of the Church, these people, they are the enemies of all of us. You remember what Father Alberti said? On the television it was said they would kill the foreigner tomorrow morning. We have to go, Mama, we have to know what the boy has seen.'

They slipped the child's shirt and coat and trousers over his pyjamas, drew on his boots over his bare feet. The mother's hands fumbled and were slower than her man's.

'Be careful, Papa, be careful with him.'

The father and his son walked out of the door and into the night. She followed the passage of the torch before the bend in the lane obscured its light, and then she sat at the kitchen table, very still, very quiet.

The wine had gone and the port after it and Caroline Charlesworth had fled the scene for her bed. The three men sat around the table and the ash and cigarette ends made their molehills in the coffee saucers. They'd been over all the ground, all the old and trampled paths. The issues of principle and pragmatism were digested and spat back. The debate on negotiation had been fought with anger and spite. And then the brandy had taken its toll and soaked and destroyed the attack of Carpenter and the

377

defence of Charlesworth and the attaché. They were resting now and the talk was sporadic. Geoffrey Harrison was no longer the principal subject, replaced by the rate of income tax, Church aid to the Patriotic Front of Rhodesia, decadence on the streets of London. The familiar fodder for Britons abroad.

Michael Charlesworth stood up from the table, murmured something about checking with the Embassy, and moved unhappily away from the safety of the chairs.

'He's a damn good man.' Carpenter had problems with the words.

'Damn good,' growled Buster Henderson. 'You're right, you know, a damned good man.'

'I've given him some stick since I've been here.'

'Wouldn't give a hoot. Knows you've a job to be getting on with. A damn good man.'

'I've never felt so bloody useless, not in anything before.'

'I once did a stint at G2 Ops. Shut up in a bloody office, out in Aden. We had a couple of Brigades in the Radfan, tribesman-bashing. Damn good shots they were, gave our chaps a hell of a run for their money. I couldn't get clear of my desk, and m'brother-in-law was up there with a battalion. Used to rub it in with his signals, wicked devil. Used to get me damned cross, just talking and not doing. I know how you feel, Carpenter.' The weathered hand reached again for the bottleneck.

Neither man looked up as Michael Charlesworth came back into the room. He paused, and watched Henderson refilling the glasses, slopping brandy on the polished wood surface.

'You'll be needing that, Buster, I've just heard something awful . . .'

His voice attracted, mothlike, the eyes of his guests.

'. . . it's Harrison's wife. Violet Harrison, she's just hit a lorry on the Raccordo. She's dead. Ran slap into a lorry. Killed outright, head-on collision.'

The bottle base crashed down onto the table and trembled there together with the hand that held it. Carpenter's fist shot out for his glass and dashed a saucer sideways, spewing ash on the white crocheted mats.

'Not bloody fair.' The Colonel spoke into the hand that masked his face.

'I made them repeat it twice, I couldn't believe it.' Charlesworth was still standing.

Carpenter swayed to his feet. 'Could you get me a taxi, Michael? I'll wait for it downstairs.' He didn't look back, headed for the front door. No farewells, no thanks for hospitality. Going, getting out, and running.

He didn't call the lift, kept to the stairs, hand on the support rail, the fresh air freezing the alcohol.

God, Archie, you've screwed it now. Throwing the shit at everyone else but not yourself. Laying down the law on how everyone else should behave. Ran out on the poor bitch, Archie, hid behind the prim chintz curtain and clucked your tongue and disapproved. Bloody little pharisee with as much charity as a weasel up a rabbit burrow. Preaching all day about getting Geoffrey Harrison back to his family, but he hadn't shut the door and seen there was a family for the bastard to come home to. What had Carboni said? 'I've failed your man.'

Join the club, Giuseppe, meet the other founder member.

He fell into the back of the taxi. Gave the name of his hotel and blew his nose noisily.

The dog fox crept close to the two sleeping men. With a front paw it scratched the P38 a little further from Giancarlo and its nose worked with interest at the barrel and the handle before fascination was lost.

Four times the fox went over the ground between Giancarlo and the pit as if unwilling to believe there was no food remnant to be rifled. Disappointed, the animal moved on its way, along the path that led to the fields and hedgerows where mice and rabbits and chickens and cats could be found. Abruptly the fox stopped. Ears straight, nostrils dilating. The noise that it heard was faint and distant, would not be felt by the men who slept, but for a creature of stealth and secrecy it was adequate warning.

A dark shadow, flitting comfortably on the path, the fox retraced its steps.

The farmer had laid the shotgun on the ground and knelt at the front of the car. The torch was in the boy's hands, and the farmer cupped his hands around it to minimize the flare of the light as he studied and memorized the number plate. Not that it was necessary after he had seen the prefix letters before the five numbers. RC, and the television had said that the car had been stolen from Reggio Calabria. Cunningly hidden too, a good place, well shielded by the bank and the bushes and the trees. He rose to his feet, trying to control his breathing, feeling his heart battering at his chest. He switched off the torch in the boy's hand and retrieved his gun. Better with that in his hands as the wood threw out its death hush. The farmer reached for his son's hand, gripping it tightly, as if to provide protection from a great and imminent evil.

'Two men were in the wood?'

He sensed the nodded response.

'Where was the path to their place?'

The boy pointed across the car's bonnet into the black void of the trees. By touch the farmer collected with his fingers three short fallen branches, and made an arrow of them that followed his son's arm. He put his hand on the boy's shoulder and they hurried together from the place, back across the fields, back to the safety of their home.

Chapter Nineteen

Giuseppe Carboni was dozing at his desk, head pillowed lopsided on his folded arms.

'Dottore . . .' The shout of excitement and pounding feet boomed in the outer corridor.

Carboni flicked his head up, the attention of the owl, his eyes large in expectation. The subordinate surged through the open door, and there was a gleam and an excitement on his face.

'We have the car, Dottore . . .' Stuttered out, because the thrill was great.

Chairs were heaved back, files discarded, telephones dropped, men hurrying in the wake of the messenger gathered at Carboni's desk.

'Where?' Carboni snapped, the sleep shed fast.

'On the hill below Bracciano, between the town and the lake.'

'Excellent,' Carboni sighed, as if the burden of Atlas were shifted.

'Better than excellent, Dottore. A farmer found the car . . . his son, a small boy, took him to the place, and he thinks the boy watched Battestini and Harrison in the wood in the day . . .'

'Excellent, excellent . . .' Carboni gulped at the

foetid air of the room which had taken on a new
freshness, a new quality. He felt a weakness in his
hands, a trembling at his fingers. 'Where is Vellosi?'

'At the communications centre. He said he would
not return to the Viminale tonight.'

'Get him.'

The room had been darkened, and now Carboni
moved to the door and rammed down the wall
switch. The response was blinding light in the room,
all bulbs on the chandelier illuminated, sweeping
away the shadows and depressions.

'The liaison officers of carabinieri and SISDE, get
them here too . . . within ten minutes.'

Back at his desk, moving with uncommon speed,
he pulled from a drawer a large-scale map of the
Lazio region. His aide's pencil raked to the green plot
of woodland dividing the built-up grey shades of the
town of Bracciano from the blue tint of the Lago di
Bracciano. Carboni without ceremony relieved him
of the pencil and scratched the crosses on the yellow
road ribbons for the perimeter that he would throw
around the boy and his prisoner. Seal the road to
Trevignano, the road to Anguillara, the road to La
Storta, the road to Castel Giuliano, to Cerveteri, to
Sasso, to Manziano. Seal them tight, block all movement.

'Has the farmer alerted them at all . . . is there that
risk?'

'He was asked that, Dottore. He says not. He
went with his son to the car, identified it, and then
returned home. He left the child there and then
he walked to the home of a neighbour who has a
telephone. He was careful to walk because he feared
the noise of a car would startle the people in the

wood, though his farm is at least a kilometre away. From the house of his neighbour he telephoned the carabinieri in Bracciano . . .'

'The carabinieri . . . they will not blunder . . .' Carboni exploded, as if success was so fragile, could be snatched from him.

'Be calm, Dottore. The carabinieri have not moved.' The aide was anxious to pacify.

'You have them, Carboni?'

The direct shout, Vellosi striding into the office, hands clapping together in anticipation. More followed. A carabinieri colonel in pressed biscuit-brown uniform, the man from the secret service in grey suit with sweat stains at the armpit, another in shirt sleeves who was the representative of the examining magistrate.

'Is it confirmed, the sighting . . . ?'

'What has already been done . . . ?'

'Where do you have them . . . ?'

The voices droned around his desk, a gabble of contradiction and request.

'Shut up!' Carboni shouted. His voice carried over them and silenced the press around his desk. He had only to say it once, and had never been known to raise his voice before to equals and superiors. He sketched in his knowledge and in a hushed and hasty tone outlined the locations he required for the block forces, the positioning of the inner cordon, and his demand that there should be no advance into the trees without his personal sanction.

'The men best trained to comb the woods are mine . . .' Vellosi said decisively.

'A boast, but not backed by fact. The carabinieri are

the men for an assault.' A defiant response from the carabinieri officer.

'My men have the skills for close quarters.'

'We can get five times as many into the area in half the time . . .'

Carboni looked around him, disbelieving, as if he had not seen it all before, heard it many times in his years of police work. His head shook in anger.

'It is, of course, for you to decide, Giuseppe.' Vellosi smiled, confident. 'But my men—'

'Do not have the qualities of the carabinieri,' the colonel chipped in his retort.

'Gentlemen, you shame us all, we discredit ourselves.' There was that in Carboni's voice that withered them, and the men in the room looked away, did not meet his gaze. 'I want the help of all of you. I am not administering prizes but seeking to save the life of Geoffrey Harrison.'

And then the work began. The division of labour. The planning and tactics of approach. There should be no helicopters, no sirens, a minimum of open radio traffic. There should be concentrations before the men moved off on foot across the fields for the inner line. Advance from three directions; one force congregating at Trevignano and approaching from the north-east, a second taking the southern lakeside road from Anguillara, a third from the town of Bracciano to the west to sweep down the hillside.

'It is as if you thought an army were bivouacked in the trees,' Vellosi said quietly as the meeting broke.

'It is a war I know little of,' Carboni replied as he hitched his coat from the chair onto his wide shoulders. They walked together to the door, abandoning the room to confusion and shouted orders and ringing telephones. Activity again and welcome after the long night hours of idleness. Carboni hesitated and leaned back through the doorway. 'The Englishman who was here in the day. I will take him with me, call him at his hotel.' He hurried to catch Vellosi. He should have felt that at last the tide had turned, the wind had slackened, yet the doubt still gnawed at him. How to approach by stealth, through trees, through undergrowth, and the danger if they did not achieve surprise. The thing could be plucked from him yet, even at the last, even at the closest time.

'We can still lose everything,' Carboni said to Vellosi.

'Not everything, we will have the boy.'

'And that is important?'

'It is the trophy for my wall.'

They destroy us, these bastards. They make the calluses in our minds, they coarsen our sensitivities, until a good man, a man of the quality of Francesco Vellosi believes only in vengeance and is blinded to the value of the life of an innocent.

'When you were in church, Francesco, last night . . .'

'I prayed that I myself, with my own hand, might have the chance to shoot the boy.'

Carboni held his arm. They emerged together into the warm night air. The convoy stood ready, car doors open, engines pulsing.

The damp of the earth, rising through the leaf mattress, crawled and nagged at the bones of Giancarlo, till he writhed in irritation and the refuge of sleep fell from him. The hunger bit and the chill was deep at his body. He groped across the ground for his pistol and his hand brushed against the metal of the barrel. P38, I love you, my P38, present to the little fox from Franca. Sometimes when he awoke in a strange place, and suddenly, he needed moments to assimilate the atmosphere around him. Not at this awakening. His mind was sharp in an instant.

He glanced at the luminous face of his watch. Close to three. Six hours to the time that Franca ordered for the retribution on Geoffrey Harrison. Six hours more and then the sun would be high, and the scorch patterns of the heat would have flung back the cold of darkness, and the wood would be dying and thirsting for moisture. There would have been two or three of them with Aldo Moro on this night. Two or three of them to share the desperate isolation of the executioner as he made ready his equipment. Two or three of them to pump home the bullets, so that the blame was spread . . . Blame, Giancarlo? Blame is for the middle classes, blame is for the guilty. There is no blame for the work of the revolution, for the struggle of the proletariat. Two or three of them to take him to the beach by the airport fence of Fiumicino. And they had had their escape route.

What escape route for Giancarlo?

No planning, no preparation, no safe house, no car switch, no accomplice.

Did Franca think of that?

It is not important to the movement. Attack is the factor of importance, not retreat.

They will hunt you, Giancarlo, hunt you for your life. The minds of their ablest men, hunting you to eternity, hunting you till you cannot run further. The enemy has the machines that are invulnerable

387

and perpetual, that invoke a memory that cannot weary.

It was an order. Orders can never be bent to accommodate circumstance. In the movement there has been great sacrifice.

And there is advantage in the killing of 'Arrison . . . ?

Not for your mind to evaluate. A soldier does not question his order. He acts, he obeys.

The insects played at his face, nipping and needling at his cheeks, finding the cavities of his nostrils, the softness of his ear lobes. He swatted them away.

Why should the bastard 'Arrison sleep? When he was about to die, how could he? A man with no belief beyond his own selfish survival, how could he find sleep?

For the first time in many hours Giancarlo summoned the image of his room in the flat at seaside Pescara. Bright on the walls of Alitalia posters, the hanging figure of the wooden Christ, the thin-framed portrait from a colour magazine of Paul VI, the desk for his schoolbooks where he had worked in the afternoons after classes, the wardrobe for his clothes where the white shirts for Sundays hung ironed. Insidious and compelling, a world that was lit and conventional and normal. Giancarlo, one-time stereotype, who sat beside his mother at meals, and wanted in the evenings to be allowed to help his father at the shop. A long time ago, an age ago, when Giancarlo was on the production line, held in the same precision mould as the other boys of the street. 'Arrison had been like that.

The ways had parted, different signposts, different

destinations. God . . . and it was a lonely way . . . terrifying and hostile. Your choice, Giancarlo.

He slapped his face again to rid himself of the insects and the dream collapsed. Gone were the savours of home, replaced by a boy whose photograph was stuck with adhesive tape to the dashboards of a thousand police cars, whose features would appear in a million newspapers, whose name grew fear, whose hand held a gun. He would never see Franca again. He knew that and the thought ripped and wrenched at him. Never in his life again. Never again would he touch her hair, and hold her fingers. Just a memory, a recollection to be set beside the room in Pescara.

Giancarlo lay again on the ground and closed his eyes.

Up the Cassia northwards from the city headed the convoys.

The riot wagons of the Primo Celere, the Fiat lorries of the carabinieri, the blue and white and prettily painted cars of the polizia, the unmarked vehicles of the special squads. There were many who came in nightclothes to the balconies of the high-rise flats and watched the stream of the participants and felt the thrill of the circus cavalcade. More than a thousand men on the move. All armed, all tensed, all drugged in the belief that at last they could assuage their frustration and beat and kick the irritant that plagued them. At the village of La Storta, where the road narrowed and was choked, the drivers hooted and blasphemed at the traffic police, and demanded clearance of the chaos, because all were anxious to be in Bracciano when dawn came.

Past La Storta, on the narrower Via Claudia with

its sharp bends between the tree lines, Giuseppe Carboni's car was locked into a column of lorries. It was a quieter, more sedate progress because now the sirens were forbidden, the rotating lights were doused, the horns unused. Archie Carpenter shared the front seat with the driver. Vellosi and Carboni were behind among the bullet-proof waistcoats and the submachine-guns, taken as if by a careful virgin from the boot before the departure from the Questura.

Water dripped from Carpenter's hair onto the collar of his shirt and down the back of his jacket, the remnant of his shower after the telephone had broken the total, drink-induced sleep that he had stumbled to. Now that he was awake, the pain between his temples was huge.

A boring bastard, she'd called him. A proper little bore. Violet Harrison on Archie Carpenter.

Well, what was he supposed to do? Get her onto the mattress in the interests of ICH, take her on the living-room carpet . . . ?

Not what it was about, Archie. Not cut and dried like that. Just needed someone to talk to.

Someone to talk to? Wearing a dress like that, hanging out like it was going out of fashion?

Wrong, Archie. A girl broken up and falling down, who needed someone to share it with. And you were out of your depth, Archie, lost your lifebelt and splashing like an idiot. You ran away, you ran out on her, and had a joke with Charlesworth, had your giggle. You ran because they don't teach you about people under high stress in safe old Motspur Park. All cosy and neat there in the mortgaged semis, where nobody shouts because the neighbours will hear, nobody has a bit on the side because the neighbours will know, where nobody does anything but sit on their arses and wait for the day when they're pushing up daisies and it's too late and they've gone, silent fools and unremembered. She needed help, Archie. You galloped out of that flat as fast as your bloody legs would take you.

A proper little bore, and no-one had ever called him that before, not to his face.

'Did you hear about Harrison's wife, Mr Carboni?' Spoken offhand, as if he wasn't concerned, wasn't involved.

'What about her?'

'She was killed in a car crash, late last night.'

'Where was she?' Puzzlement rang through Carboni's preoccupation with the procedures of the coming hours.

'Out on what's called the Raccordo.'

'It is many kilometres from where she lives.'

'She was driving home, she was alone.' Carpenter spewing it out.

'No-one with her, no friends with her . . . ?'

'So, if we get the man out, that is what we have to confront him with.' A light, chilled laugh from Vellosi. 'Incredible, Carboni; when a man's cup is overfilled . . .'

'It is criminal that at this time a woman should be alone.' A distaste hung in Carboni's words.

'I suppose no-one thought about it,' said Carpenter dully.

At the junction to the lake road they saw the stationary rows of lorries and vans parked on the grass verge. They passed queues of walking men in uniform, the headlights glinted on the metal of firearms, and there were glimpses of cordons forming in the fields. The car winged on down the steep hillside before turning hard to the right along a weeded driveway with a military barrier and a concentration of elderly brick buildings awaiting them. Carpenter tried to loose the load of self-pity and stared about him as the car stopped.

The doors snapped open, Carboni was out quickly, and mopped himself and turned to Carpenter. 'It used to be a flying-boat station, long before the war, with its lake frontage. It is a place now just for dumping the conscripts. They maintain a museum, but nothing flies. But we are close to the wood here and we have communications.' He took Carpenter's arm. 'Stay near to me, now is the time for you to wish me well.'

They were swept through the ill-lit door of the administration block, Carpenter elbowing to keep contact with the bustling Carboni, and on into a briefing room. Hands out to greet Carboni, hugging and rubbed cheeks, a clutch of bodies around him, and Carpenter relegated to a chair at the back while the policeman found sufficient yet reluctant silence to make a short address on his plan. Another surge of the men in suits and uniforms and battle-dress, and Carboni, the emperor of the moment, was speeding for the doorway. They won't stop for you, Archie. They won't hang about for that bloody Englishman. Carpenter shoved and pushed, winced as a Beretta holster dug at his stomach and won his way to Carboni's side. In the wedge at the door Carboni smiled at him, looking up, perspiring.

'I have made a great decision. The anti-terrorist unit demanded the right to lead, so did the carabinieri. Both thought they were best fitted. I have satisfied everybody. The carabinieri will come from the north, Vellosi's men from the south. I am an Italian Solomon. I have sliced Battestini in two.'

Carpenter stared coldly at him.

'Allow me one levity, I have nothing else to laugh at. At any moment Battestini may kill your man, he may already have done so. We are going forward in the dark, we are going to stumble in the dark through the wood.'

'You're not waiting for daylight?'

'To wait is to take too great a risk. If you pray, Carpenter, now is the moment.'

They were out of the building.

Muffled, subdued orders. Men in the grey half light hitching over their heads the heavy, protective clothing that would halt all rounds other than high velocity. The cocking and arming of weapons. Ripples of laughter. Tramping feet away into the last remnants of the night. Should have a bloody stirrup cup, Archie, and a red coat, and a man to shout 'Tally Ho'.

The group with Carboni at its heart set off towards the road, and walking beside him was a short, firm-bodied man who wore torn trousers and boots and a thick sweater and carried an old shotgun broken and crooked, farmer's style, across his inner elbow.

From the hard bare mattress of her cell bed, Franca Tantardini heard the soft-soled footsteps in the outside corridor. A bolt was drawn back, a key inserted and turned, and the man who had been her interrogator let himself in.

He smiled at the woman as she lay with her head

propped on her clasped hands, with the golden hair spilling on the one pillow.

'I have some news for you, Franca. Something that you would wish to know.'

Her eyes lit at first, then dulled, as if her interest betrayed her before the discipline triumphed.

'I should not be telling you, Franca, but I thought that you would wish to hear of our success.'

Involuntarily she half rose on the bed, her hands forsaking her neck, propping her up now.

'We know where he is. Your little fox, Franca. We know where he hides, in what wood, close to which village. They are surrounding the place now. At first light they will move in on your little fox.'

The light from the single bulb behind its casing of close-mesh wire bit down at the age lines of her face. The muscles at her mouth flickered.

'He'll kill the pig first.'

The interrogator laughed softly. 'If he has the courage, when the guns are around him.'

'He'll kill him.'

'Because Franca told him to. Because Franca from the safety of her cell ordered it. His pants will be wetted, his hand shaking, guns round him, aimed on him, and he is dead if he does what his Franca has told him.'

'He will do as he was ordered.'

'You are certain you can make a soldier from a bedwetter, that was what you called him, Franca.'

'Get out.' She spat her hatred.

The interrogator smiled again. 'Let the dream be of the failure, Franca. Good night, and when you are alone think of the boy, and think of how you have destroyed him . . .'

She reached down beside her bed for the canvas shoes, snatched at one and hurled it at the man in the open doorway. Wide and high, and bouncing back from the wall. He chuckled to her and grinned.

She heard the key in place, the bolt thrust across.

The noise of Giancarlo twisting from his side to his back was the agent that roused Geoffrey Harrison from sleep. As soon as he woke the bite of the wire at his wrists and ankles was sharp. The first, instinctive stretch of his limbs tautened the flex, dug the knots into the underflesh of his wrists and ankles. A man who awakens in hell, who has purchased a great vengeance. Nothing but the bloody pain, first sensation, first thought, first recollection.

God, the morning that I die.

The mental process that became a physical happening, and his body cowed to a foetal position of fear. No protection, nothing to hide behind, nothing to squirm to. The morning that I die. He felt the tremble and the shudder take him, and the awareness was overwhelming. God, the morning that I die.

The first precious beginnings of the day were seeping into the wood. Not the sunlight, but its outriders in the grey pastel that permitted him to detect the lines of the nearest tree-trunks. This morning, with the birds singing, at nine o'clock. Another shape, suffused and vague and hard to alert himself to, as Giancarlo rose and stood above him and looked down. Giancarlo, called by Harrison's movements and inspecting the fatted goose of the feast.

'What time is it, Giancarlo?' He could hear the watch ticking on his wrist, could not see it.

'A little past four . . .'

The little bastard had learned the role of gaoler, thought Harrison, had taken on the courtesy of the death cell attendant. The hushed tone, and 'Don't you worry, lad, it doesn't hurt and it's quick'. The warm eyes of sympathy. Well, that never helped a poor lad who was going to swing at nine. What do you know about that, Geoffrey? I read it. That was other people, Geoffrey, and half the fucking population saying 'And a damn good thing too'. That's for a criminal. 'No sympathy' and 'Deserves all he's getting'. That's for men who've shot policemen and raped kids. That's not for bloody Geoffrey Harrison.

'Did you sleep?'

'Only a little.' Giancarlo spoke simply. 'It was very cold on the ground.'

'I slept very well. I didn't dream.'

Giancarlo peered down at him, the definition of his face growing with the slow coming light.

'That is good.'

'Are you going to get some food?' He could have kicked himself when he'd said it, could have spat on himself.

'I am not going for any food . . . not now . . . later, later I will eat.'

Cheaper to feed one. More economic to sustain the single-person family. Silly man, Geoffrey. Should have your calculator there, the one beside the desk in the office, the one you use for all the arithmetic of ICH, then you'd know the boy would be only shopping for one, and how many lire he would save that way. Only for one, because there will only be one mouth. Not on the bloody bread list, Geoffrey, because you'll be past food, past caring about the ache in your guts.

Geoffrey Harrison's voice rose in crescendo, down the paths of the wood, high with the branches, fluttered the thrushes and blackbirds.

'Don't hurt me, Giancarlo. Please, please, don't hurt me . . .'

He was answered far back, from the shadows among the trees, distant and beyond sight, by the rampage of a dog's bark.

And in the wake of the bark was the drumming of running feet and the crash of branches swept aside.

An avalanche, circling and nearing.

Giancarlo had crouched, bent double, at the sound of the dog. At the noise of the approach of men he surged towards Harrison, pulled him to the limit of the wire and flung himself into the gap between his prisoner and the earth roof where the roots had taken the ground high out of the pit. He panted for breath, wriggled to get lower, held the gun at the lower hairs of Harrison's head.

'If you shout now you are dead.'

The gun squirming against his neck, Harrison played his part, the one he was familiar with. 'Run, you little fool. Run now.'

He could sense the boy's shock of terror imparted through their clothes, body to body, flesh warmth, through the quivering and pulsing of the blood veins. He didn't know why he called, only that this is what he would have done. This was his way. Avoid contact, avoid impact, stall the moment, the lifestyle of Geoffrey Harrison.

'If you go now you have a chance.'

He felt the boy drive deeper into the pit, and then the voice, small and reeded.

'I need you, 'Arrison.'

'Now, you have to go now.' Father and mother, didn't the little bugger understand? Time for running, time for ducking, time for weaving.

'If I go now, they will kill me.'

What was he supposed to do? Feel sorry for the little pig? Wipe his bottom for him, clean his pants out?

'We stay together, 'Arrison. That is what Franca would have done.'

The man and the boy, ears up, lying in the shallow hole and listening.

Around them, unseen, among the trees an army advanced, clumsy and intimidating in its approach, breaking aside the wood that impeded its progress. Closing on them, sealing them, the net tightening. Fractured and splintered branches in front and behind them, stamped leaves and curses of discomfort to right and left. And the baying of dogs.

Harrison turned his body from his side, a ponderous movement, then twisted his neck further until he could see the face of the boy. 'It is too late, Giancarlo.' He spoke with a kind of wonderment, astonished because the table was turned and the fear exchanged. 'You had to go when I said.'

'Shut up,' the boy spat back at him, but there was a shiver in his voice. And then more slowly as if the control were won with great effort, 'That is not our way.'

Carboni with his pistol drawn, Vellosi trailing in one hand a submachine-gun, Carpenter keeping with them, all were running in their own fashion down the narrow path, spurred on by the shouts of the advance, and the roars, fierce and aggressive, full and deep-throated, of the police attack dogs. They sprinted on the shadowed surface, buried in the surrealism of the dawn mist that ebbed between the tree towers.

Carpenter saw the shape of the polizia vice brigadiere materialize from the foliage at the pathside, rising to block Carboni and Vellosi. The stampede stopped, men crouched about them and struggled to control the heaving of their lungs that they might be quieter. The trees were infested, the undergrowth alive. Static from the portable radios, whispered voices, distorted replies. A council of war. Grown and elderly men on their knees, huddled to hear, the weapons in their hands.

'Carpenter, come close,' Carboni called, his voice blanket-shrouded. 'The dogs heard voices and barked. They are about a hundred metres from us. We are all around them but I do not wish to move further till there is light. We wait here for the sun.'

'Battestini, will he pack it in, will he give himself up?'

The big sad eyes rolled at Carpenter, the shoulders heaved their gesture. 'We have to try. If the spell of Tantardini is still on him . . .'

Left unsaid because Carpenter mouthed his obscenity and understood.

'But he can kill him now, while we are here.'

'We wait for the sun.' Carboni turned away, resumed the hush of conference.

This was where it all ended. In a damp wood with mud on your shoes and dirt on the knees of your trousers. Right, Archie. Where the family picnickers might have been, or boys with tents, or a kid with his condom and his girl. Only the method and the style to be decided. To be determined only whether it was champagne or a mahogany box. You're within rock-throwing distance of him, Archie. You could stand up and shout and he'd hear you. A few seconds running, you're that close. God, the bastard can't shoot him now. Not now, not after all this. Not after Violet.

The dawn came steadily, imperceptibly, winnowing behind the trees and across the leaves, cloaking the men who peered forward and fingered the mechanisms of their firearms. Drawn-out, lethargic, mocking their impatience, the light filtered into the wood.

Chapter Twenty

Horizontal and thrusting with its brilliance, the dart of a lance, the first sunray pierced the wall of trees. The shaft picked at the ground in front of the fallen trunk, faded in the eddy of the branches, then returned. The sharpness held sway over the grey shadowed light.

It was the moment of ultimate decision for Giancarlo Battestini. Move now or be damned and finished, vulnerable to the sniper's aim, naked to the gas and nausea cartridges, open to the bone-splintering bullets of the marksmen. His hands furtive, he reached for the flex at Geoffrey Harrison's ankles, swore at the skill of his own knot, and with difficulty loosened it. By the collar of the shirt he pulled his prisoner close to him and back down into the pit, so that the wire tied to the wrists and the roots would have more play. That was easier to unfasten, the work of a few seconds.

'What are we doing, Giancarlo?'

A grim, set smile. 'We go on another journey, 'Arrison.'

'Where are we going?'

Busy with his work, scraping together the strands

of wire, Giancarlo muttered, 'You will know.'

The boy bound together the length of wire that he had used on Harrison's legs to the piece now trailing from his wrists.

'Kneel upright.'

Harrison stretched himself to the extent of the pit, wriggled and turned his ankles to restore the circulation and slowly raised his head above the rim. He lifted his shoulders, tautened his spine, and grimaced at the stiffness carried by his trapped night's sleep. Giancarlo looped the wire around the front of his chest, then snuggled it behind his own back, drew it beneath his armpits and then again to Harrison's wrists. Pressed hard against his man, the boy entwined the knot that closed them together, linked them as one. With a hand he pulled Harrison's shirt from the waist of his trousers and the metal pistol barrel was formidable against the skin in the small of Harrison's back. The front gun-sight carved a scratch line in the flesh as Giancarlo armed the weapon.

'It is a light trigger, 'Arrison. When we start you should not talk, you should not slip. My finger will barely have to move, you understand?'

Harrison nodded, the questions stifled in his throat, choked on his tongue. No more compulsion to ask questions. Just a new horror, and what use explanation? Just a new abyss, and he was plunging.

'We stand up, and carefully.'

They straightened as one, the vibrations mingled, and Giancarlo pressed his head against Harrison's collar-bone.

But your legs don't work, Geoffrey, been tied too long. You'll slip, you'll bloody stumble . . . and then the bloody trigger goes. How far does the finger move, how far . . . quarter of an inch, eighth of an inch? Concentrate, you bloody fool. One leg forward, put it down slowly, ease the weight on to it, stop, put the other foot forward, test the balance, stop again, put the next foot forward . . .

Harrison looked around him, blinked in the air, drank in its freshness, felt the erosion of Giancarlo's stale breath. It was a certain sort of freedom, a certain sort of release. Breathing something other than the odour of the earth. Nothing moved at the front, but there would be an army there, concealed, close and waiting. The voice bellowed behind his ear.

'Is Carboni there?'

Ahead of them was the path that they had walked down the previous morning, long ago, separated by infinite time. The route that Giancarlo had used to get his food and to drift away down when he went to the telephone in the darkness, and it was the way the child had come.

The stream of the sun caught the three men square as they came forward on the path. They wore their badges of nationality, their flags for recognition. A short, rolling man at the front, balding, sallow. One behind him who held a submachine-gun diagonally across his waist, hair combed, the trace of a clipped moustache at his upper lip, his tie sombre and silk. The last was a stranger, clothes of a different cut, hair of a different trim, rounded shoulders and a pallor denied the Mediterranean. Two Italians and an Englishman. Harrison felt the weakness at his knees, the shake at his thighs and shins that was irresistible. The bastards had come. Long enough about it.

Harrison and Giancarlo were fused as one, responsive to each other's tremors, pliant to each other's movements. Three men facing them.

'I am Carboni.'

The words echoed in the trees, bounced from the moss-coated trunks.

Harrison felt the boy stiffen, readying himself. The last great battle, striving for strength and steel stamina.

'Listen, Carboni. This is your 'Arrison, this is your foreign dirt. I have tied him to me, and against his back, behind his heart, I have the P38. It is a hair-trigger, Carboni, tell your criminals, tell your gunmen that. If they shoot, my finger will move on the trigger . . . you are listening, Carboni? If you hit me, 'Arrison is dead. I am going to walk down the path, I am going to walk to my car. If you want 'Arrison alive, you do not impede me.'

Harrison was aware that the pressure of the circled barrel grew in his back, the impetus growing for movement.

'I am going to move forward. If you want 'Arrison, stay back.'

'What does he say?'

Carboni did not turn towards Carpenter and his sharp anxiety. He gazed on down the path at Harrison and Giancarlo. 'The boy has the gun at Harrison's back. He says it is hair-triggered. He wants to drive away from here . . .'

Vellosi, in English, because that was the language of the moment.

'Giuseppe, he doesn't walk out of here.'

'Then Harrison dies.'

404

'The boy cannot leave here.' The spitting whisper of the cobra.

'I am here to save Harrison.' Confusion, catastrophe ravaging at Carboni.

'If Battestini walks out of here, if he leaves the wood, he has ridiculed us. One boy and he has beaten us . . .'

'I have to save Harrison.' Carboni wavering, torn and pulled and tossed.

'We have to save Italy . . . Think, Carboni, of the implications if the boy walks clear. One against so many, and he wins because we have no courage.'

Violet Harrison dead and mangled on her back in a plastic sack on the morgue slab, incised for autopsy, viewed by pathologists. And Geoffrey Harrison to lie beside her with a pencil hole in his back and a cavity large enough to fit a lemon into at his chest. Get off your arse, Archie Carpenter. Get into the big boys' league. It's your man out there, Archie, so get off your bloody arse and get walking.

A short jab of his elbow and Archie Carpenter was past Carboni and Vellosi. Three quick strides and he was clear of them . . . and who was going to run forward to pull him back?

'Watch the boy, Carboni, watch the boy and be ready.'

Giancarlo watched him come. Saw the purposeful clean steps eat into the dividing distance. Nothing to be read from the face of the man, nothing that spoke of danger and risk, nothing from which to recognize his emotions. The command to halt, the shout, was beyond the boy. Fascinated, spellbound. And the light caught at the man's face as he passed between

405

two trees and there was no shop window of fear. A man with a job to do, and getting it over with, and wearing a crumpled suit.

Giancarlo felt his hand on the pistol butt cavort with the weapon. He could not hold it still and motionless.

Francesco Vellosi spun on his heel, raking the trees and bushes behind him till he saw the carabinieri sergeant with the rifle, kneeling and in cover. His fingers snapped for the man's attention and he tossed the submachine-gun towards him, gestured for the rifle and caught it as it was thrown to him. The rifle slipped to his shoulder. Rock steady, unwavering, and the needle of the front sight rested centrally in the V of the rear attachment by his right eye. The line was on the small part of Giancarlo Battestini's head that was visible to him.

The void cut, the gap halved, Archie Carpenter spoke. Almost surprised to hear his own voice. Brisk and full of business.

'Geoffrey Harrison. I'm Archie Carpenter . . . does this Battestini speak English?'

No preamble, dominate from the start, the way they taught them far back, the Metropolitan Police drill on approaching an armed man.

He saw the half head on Harrison's shoulder, an unfinished ventriloquist's dummy, dumped on a perch, lacking a body. Harrison's lips moved and then his tongue brushed against them, the moisture glistening. Poor blighter's at the limit.

'He does.'

Still moving, still hacking and cutting at the

intervening space, Carpenter called, 'Giancarlo . . . your name, right? . . . I've come for the gun.'

Edging his way forward, slower steps as the distance telescoped, and the spots and the beard growth on Giancarlo's face were sharp and visible, and the colour at his eyes was dark and haunted. Ten yards short and the scream from the boy.

'Stop, no closer.'

'Just the gun, Giancarlo, just give it to me.' But Carpenter obeyed and now stood his ground, fair and square across the path. Saw the sweat on the boy's forehead and the tangled skeins of his hair and the yellowed teeth.

'You move aside, you give us room . . .'

'I'm not moving. I'm here and I want the gun from you.'

Where did you get it from, Archie, which silk hat? Out of the hallway of a flat, out of the staircase of a high building, out of a woman past her break-point. Ran once, not again. Once was enough to turn the shoulder, not ever again.

'If you do not move, I shoot . . .'

'Empty threat. I don't move, you don't shoot.'

Who'd know you, Archie? The girls in the office, in the typists' pool? The men in the pub off the evening train from the City? The neighbour who borrowed the push-mower alternate Saturday mornings? Who'd know Archie Carpenter in a wood at Bracciano?

'I have the gun at his back . . .'

'I don't care where you've put the bloody thing. I don't move, you don't shoot. It's easy, a ten-year-old knows that.'

Stretching the boy. Out into the risk area, out into

the storm. Watch the eyes, Archie, watch the blinking and the uncertainty and the fidget. Traversing and hesitant, and the fear's building. The bully when he's outnumbered, when the other kids come back to the playground. Careful, Archie . . . Gone past that place, off Mum's knee, playing it the grown-up way.

'You do not believe that I will shoot . . .'

'Right, Giancarlo. I don't believe it. I tell you why. You're thinking what happens if you do. I'll help you, I'll tell you. I strangle you, boy. With my hands I strangle you. There's a hundred men out there behind me that want to do it. They won't get near you. You'll be done by the time they reach you.'

Carpenter held him unswervingly. Never left the eyes of the boy. Always there when he turned back, always present. Lowering over him, heavy as a snowcloud, absorbing the hatred.

'I've no gun, but if you fire on Harrison, I'm on you. You've trussed yourself, silly boy, that's why I'll get you. I used to be a policeman, I've seen people that have been strangled. Their eyes come half out of their head, they shit themselves, they wet their legs. That's for you, so give me the gun.'

You never saw anyone strangled in your bloody life, not ever. Steady it, Archie. Turn it over, could be possible that the physical isn't the soft belly of the boy. Don't make him play the martyr, don't put coal on that fire. What else gets to a psychopath?

'I'm going to start walking, you cannot take him from me . . .' Giancarlo holding his defensive line. The rout not accomplished. 'Get out of our way.'

Harrison gazing at Carpenter, like he doesn't know what's happening, like he's out on his feet. Best bloody way. Who's going to tell Geoffrey

Harrison? Who's that one down to? Archie Carpenter going to do it? Well done, Geoffrey, we're very pleased you've come out of this safely . . . excellent show . . . but there's been a bit of bother while you've been away . . . well, the missis actually . . . but you understand that, Geoffrey, good lad, thought you would . . .

Throw in the big one, Archie. Go for broke. All the chips on the green cloth, into the centre of the table.

'I saw your woman last night, Giancarlo. Raddled old bitch. Bit old for a boy, wasn't she?'

He saw the short-worn composure break on the boy's face, saw the anger lines form and then knit on his forehead.

'I wouldn't have thought a boy would be interested in a work-horse like that.'

The blood was running fast to the boy's cheeks, the flush dispersing under his skin, the eyes slitted in loathing.

'Do you know what she called you when they interrogated her? You want to know? A little bedwetter. Franca Tantardini's opinion on lover boy . . .'

'Get out of my way.' The words came fast and weighted by the boy's fury.

Carpenter could see the nausea rising in Geoffrey Harrison's face, the eroded self-control. Wouldn't last much longer, wouldn't sustain the supreme effort. Batter on, Archie, belt the little bastard.

The sound of the voices carried easily among the trees. Carboni had eased his pistol from the jacket pocket and it hung from his fingers as a token of participation. Beside him Francesco Vellosi still stood, eye at the gun-sight, tight in anticipation, ignoring the fly that played at his nose.

'Why does he say these things?'

Vellosi never wavered from his aim. 'Quiet, Giuseppe, quiet.'

'How many others have there been, boy, do you know? I mean, you weren't the first, were you?'

'Get out of my way . . .'

Not much longer, Archie. Hold your ground and it's disintegration time, spitting collapse. Forgetting where he is, and what he's here for, like we want him to be. Don't run now, Archie, just round the corner is Shangri-La that you came for. Almost at the fingertips, almost there to touch.

'They'd all been there, boy, every grubby finger, every sweaty armpit in the movement, did you know that . . . ?'

He's rising, Archie. The slimed creature forced out of the deep water. Coming for you, Archie. Hold the line, sunshine. Come on, Archie bloody Carpenter from Motspur bloody Park, don't let old Harrison down now, not when he's flaking, not when Violet's on her back and cold. Watch him, watch the struggle in the shirt. The gun comes next. You'll see the barrel, you'll see the fist on it, and the finger that's lost behind the trigger guard. Hold the bloody line, Archie.

'I wouldn't have done what you've done, not for a cow like that. You know, Giancarlo, you might even have got the scabs from her . . .'

Carpenter laughed out loud, shaking in his merriment, confronting his fear. Was laughing as he saw the pistol emerge from behind Harrison and be raised at him as fast as a snake strikes. He looked into the torture of Giancarlo's face, sucked at the agony. Well done, Archie, you made it, sunshine. First time in your bloody life, across the finish line and in front. Ludicrous, the look on the kid's face.

The gun was coming, something bright with menace from beneath a winter sea. The pistol showing, sharp and tooled, and aiming.

The one shot, the whiplash crack.

Carpenter was on the ground, thrown backwards, the involuntary reflex. Cemented and imprinted high on his face was a splitting smile.

Harrison staggered, legs weak and resisting his efforts to withstand the weight of the smitten Giancarlo dragging down the wire that wrapped their wrists. Blood on Harrison's face, loose and dripping, and a mess of brain matter and no hands free to clear the sheen of destruction from his eyes.

Carboni recoiled from the explosion beside his ear. He pivoted towards Vellosi, gazed at him and saw the grim pleasure spreading like an opening flower on his companion's face.

And then the running.

Men rising from their hidden places, careering over fallen branches, bullocking through undergrowth. Carboni joined the herd as if time now were at last special. Francesco Vellosi dropped the rifle barrel with deliberation, bent down and picked up the single brass cartridge case and pocketed it. He turned and with an easy movement tossed the gun back to its owner, the carabinieri sergeant.

Revenge exacted. He walked, tall and erect, towards the huddle that was gathering around Geoffrey Harrison.

With a knife a policeman sliced through the flex that held Harrison to Giancarlo Battestini. The body of the boy, shorn of its support, slumped to the ground. One half of his face was intact, unblemished and waxen; the other was obliterated, removed as if in tribute to the marksmanship and the brutal power of the high velocity bullet. Freed, rubbing hard at his wrists, Harrison dived away from his helpers, turned his back on them and vomited into the dried grass at the edge of the clearing. They gave him room, respected him.

Archie Carpenter pulled himself to his knees, rose unsteadily to his feet, and clamped his fingers together to hide the tumult and the shaking that gripped them. He stood aside, a stranger at a party.

When Harrison came back to the group, he spoke simply, without idiocy. 'What happened . . . I don't know what happened?'

Vellosi pointed across the clearing to Carpenter. 'This man was prepared to offer his life for yours.' He spoke gruffly, and then his hand slipped in support to Harrison's armpit. 'He gave himself to Battestini that you should be saved.'

Their eyes met in a fleeting moment, then Carpenter turned his head from the deep puzzlement of Harrison's gaze, and seemed to those who watched him to shrug his shoulders as if an episode had ended, a man had done his work and needed no praise nor thanks. Studiously Carpenter began to wipe the clinging leaves and sticks from his back and his trousers.

They moved from the clearing. Vellosi and Harrison setting the slow pace at the front, Carboni busy and bustling behind them, Carpenter trailing. Harrison did not look round for a final glimpse of Giancarlo's body, stumbled away, reliant on the help of the hand that helped him. They moved at cortège speed and the route along the path was lined with the unsmiling faces of men in uniform who held rifles and submachine-guns and did not flinch from the hurt daubed on Harrison's face. They masked their feelings, those who stared, because death was recent among the trees and the devastating speed of the violence had stripped from them the elation of victory.

'I didn't understand what he was doing, this man Carpenter.'

From behind Harrison's shoulder, Carboni spoke. 'He had to get the pistol from your back, he had to produce the pistol against himself if your danger were to be taken. That was why he taunted the boy. He gave the opportunity to Francesco. Francesco had a half face to shoot for. That there was the chance was because of Carpenter.'

Carboni, still walking, swung his head towards Carpenter, saw only a shaded half smile, a tint of sadness.

'My God . . . God help us.' Harrison walked with his eyes closed, led as a blind man on a street pavement. He struggled for his words, confronting the shock and exhaustion. 'Why was another life . . . why was another man's life, less important than mine?'

'I don't know,' said Carboni.

'Get me home, please, get me to my wife.'

The quick light of warning flashed between the

policeman and the head of the anti-terrorist squad. Carboni stopped and grabbed surely for Carpenter's sleeve and drew him forward. The procession had stopped. The four men were in a group, a huddle of shoulders, and those in uniform faded back, abandoning them.

'You have something to tell your man, Archie,' Carboni spoke in a whisper.

'Charlesworth can . . .'

'No, Archie, for you, it is your work.'

'Not here . . .'

Archie wriggling, sliding in the mud stream, seeking to extricate himself, and Harrison peering into him, unshaven face close, bad breath reeking. Come on, Archie, this is what you saved him for, this is the moment you preserved him for. Can't slip the buck to Charlesworth, can't push it further away. It's now it has to be said, and it's you who have to say it.

'It's about Violet, Geoffrey . . .' Carboni and Vellosi watched the shame driving up on Carpenter's face, realized the bewilderment creeping again into the man whose arms they held.

'What about her?'

'Violet . . . I'm sorry.'

'Where is she?' The shriek coming from Harrison, the embarrassment flowing into Vellosi and Carboni.

A sudden coldness from Carpenter, as if from this came his protection, as if his face could be hidden by chilled words. 'She's dead, Harrison. She piled into a lorry last night. She was alone.'

Vellosi and Carboni hurried forward, half carrying, half dragging the weight of Harrison between them. Carpenter detached himself and hung back. Nothing more to be said, nothing more to be done.

The speed of the group quickened, past the man who stood with the broken shotgun and the small boy, past the field hedgerows, on down to the road. They slid Harrison into the back of Carboni's car, Carboni followed him, clapped his hands and the driver accelerated away.

His arm hanging from Carpenter's shoulder, Vellosi watched the car spin round the first curve.

'You did well, my friend.'

'Thank you,' said Carpenter.

THE END

A SELECTED LIST OF FINE WRITING
AVAILABLE FROM CORGI BOOKS

14496	7	**SILENCER**	*Campbell Armstrong*	£5.99
14497	5	**BLACKOUT**	*Campbell Armstrong*	£5.99
14645	5	**KINGDOM OF THE BLIND**	*Alan Blackwood*	£5.99
14646	3	**PLAGUE OF ANGELS**	*Alan Blackwood*	£5.99
09156	1	**THE EXORCIST**	*William Peter Blatty*	£5.99
14586	6	**SHADOW DANCER**	*Tom Bradby*	£5.99
14578	5	**THE MIRACLE STRAIN**	*Michael Cordy*	£5.99
14654	4	**THE HORSE WHISPERER**	*Nicholas Evans*	£5.99
14495	9	**THE LOOP**	*Nicholas Evans*	£5.99
13990	4	**THE FIST OF GOD**	*Frederick Forsyth*	£5.99
13991	2	**ICON**	*Frederick Forsyth*	£5.99
13678	6	**THE EVENING NEWS**	*Arthur Hailey*	£5.99
14376	6	**DETECTIVE**	*Arthur Hailey*	£5.99
14591	2	**REMOTE CONTROL**	*Andy McNab*	£5.99
54535	X	**KILLING GROUND**	*Gerald Seymour*	£5.99
14605	6	**THE WAITING TIME**	*Gerald Seymour*	£5.99
14682	X	**A LINE IN THE SAND**	*Gerald Seymour*	£5.99
14723	0	**FIELD OF BLOOD**	*Gerald Seymour*	£5.99
14722	2	**HARRY'S GAME**	*Gerald Seymour*	£5.99
14724	9	**THE JOURNEYMAN TAILOR**	*Gerald Seymour*	£5.99
14731	1	**A SONG IN THE MORNING**	*Gerald Seymour*	£5.99
14733	8	**HOME RUN**	*Gerald Seymour*	£5.99
14729	X	**ARCHANGEL**	*Gerald Seymour*	£5.99
14732	X	**AT CLOSE QUARTERS**	*Gerald Seymour*	£5.99
14730	3	**IN HONOUR BOUND**	*Gerald Seymour*	£5.99
14726	5	**KINGFISHER**	*Gerald Seymour*	£5.99
14725	7	**THE GLORY BOYS**	*Gerald Seymour*	£5.99
14728	1	**THE CONTRACT**	*Gerald Seymour*	£5.99
14391	X	**A SIMPLE PLAN**	*Scott Smith*	£4.99
10565	1	**TRINITY**	*Leon Uris*	£6.99